LOVE
BLACKOUT

Cover Design By: Dark Midnight Design Co.

Line & Copy Editing By: Fervor & Ink Editorial

LOVE
BLACKOUT

DEDICATION

For the eldest daughters.

Remember to put yourself first
every now and then.

AUTHOR'S NOTE ON AI

No generative Artificial Intelligence (AI) was used at any stage
of creating this book nor any of the author created art and
digital assets associated with this book. Not when researching,
not when writing, not when debating whether cheese curds can
be readily found in Pennsylvania. (SPOILER ALERT: APPARENTLY
THAT'S FIRMLY A MIDWEST TREAT.)

Each and every em dash within these pages was carefully, and
agonizingly, chosen by the author, and probably argued over
with her editor, just for good measure.

I want to be firm on my stance that AI sucks
and you will never find it in any form of my work.

CONTENT WARNINGS

This book contains adult content, including:
references to childhood trauma
the death of a parent (off-page, in the past)
the death of a sibling (off-page, in the past)
endangerment of a sibling
sexual harassment
frequent alcohol consumption
explicit sexual content
explicit language

Adultery, manipulation, and emotional abuse are
also present in the story, but are not elements
of the main characters' relationship.

LOVE BLACKOUT
LOVE BLACKOUT
PLAYLIST
SCAN THE QR TO CHECK IT OUT

TOUR SCHEDULE

Glendale, Arizona
Arlington, Texas
Houston, Texas
New Orleans, Louisiana
Tampa, Florida
Atlanta, Georgia
Nashville, Tennessee
Pittsburgh, Pennsylvania
Philadelphia, Pennsylvania
East Rutherford, New Jersey
Foxborough, Massachusetts
Cincinnati, Ohio
Detroit, Michigan
Indianapolis, Indiana
Chicago, Illinois
Minneapolis, Minnesota
Kansas City, Missouri
Denver, Colorado
Las Vegas, Nevada
Inglewood, California
Santa Clara, California
Seattle, Washington

FEBRUARY

important
Soho RSVP!!

○ air tags for luggage
○ call Antoni about dress
○

SUN MON TUES WED THUR FRI SAT

1

2 3 4 5 6 7 8
9a Coffee 9a Team 8a Security Mtg 5 Weeks!
w/ Mel Weekly 12p Promo Shoot

9 10 11 12 13 14 15
12p Strat 9a Team 8a Jamie 4 Weeks!
Team Mtg Weekly 1:1

16 17 18 19 20 21
9a Team 3 Weeks!
Weekly

23 24 25 26 27 28
Sibling 9a Team 8a Jamie 2 Wee
Dinner! Weekly 1:1

call hotel concei

before we leave:
schedule press packet delivery: New Orleans
Glendale Tampa
Arlington Atlanta
Houston

glendale & arlington: meet and gree
finalize influencer event confirm time
call stadium about media debrief

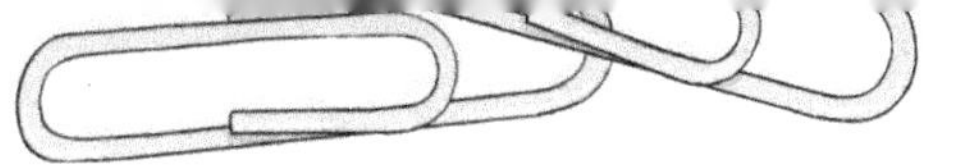

ONE

NATALIE

Nothing More Than A Stranger

"Is that a crown on fire?" I point at the photo on my sister's phone, the metal of the jewelry just barely decipherable beneath the flames on the small screen.

Melanie smirks at me over her shoulder as she flips to the next image. We tip our heads together, looking at the grainy details while she talks animatedly about the costumes and choreography she finalized with her team this week.

I have to hand it to them; the details for this production are good. This concert series is going to be unlike anything I have ever seen, and the excitement is starting to outweigh the anxiety I'm feeling over all the work left to be done before we leave.

My sister and I are at The Brew, our favorite café in downtown Nashville. At the moment, we're tucked behind a decorative partition installed by the owners that gives us a semblance of privacy. You almost can't see Knox, Melanie's bodyguard, hovering behind it, guarding the space between us and the rear entrance. It's a cute little setup that makes us feel like we're normal, everyday people.

On my own, I could easily pass as an average customer, but there's nothing normal about my sister. Melanie Bennett is currently one of the hottest names in the music industry, her name and image are everywhere.

I, however, am just her publicist. The limelight is not for me, but helping my sister navigate that territory is something I thrive at.

Right now, the entire company is all hands on deck preparing for her cross-country tour: a twenty-three-week trip that will have us in a brand new city every weekend. We have just a handful of weeks left until we hit the road and about a million little details that still need to be ironed out.

Despite the pile of work on my desk, this morning's priority was sisterly duties, including this recap of the newest choreography and special effects that Mel's team has been working on.

I sip my coffee, smiling to myself as I listen to my sister, still flipping through colorful sample photos and stage mockups. Costumes, props, and dancers in painful-looking poses flash across the screen as she talks about the different songs and sets that are part of the final lineup for the show.

I love seeing her like this; she's so full of joy and in her element. Ever since her latest album release last fall, my poor sister has been going through more than a single person should have to deal with. Releasing an album and planning a tour are enough to keep anyone busy, but on top of all that, she's in the middle of a highly contested divorce from her husband and label manager, Gunner Greene. The light in her eyes has only recently returned and this tour is the thing that's bringing her back to life.

Mel and I, and our younger brother Dex, are about as close as three siblings can be. The three of us lost our parents when I was just eighteen. It was hard for several years after that, suddenly trying to get my sixteen-year-old sister and twelve-year-old brother through school. When they're all you have though, you form a unique bond.

We always knew Mel was going to make it big. Call it blind faith or some form of intuition, but I never once doubted this was what she was meant to do with her life. It was a simple decision for both Dex and I to coordinate our own education, knowing we wanted to go into this business together. I went to school for public relations, spending the last twelve years working my way through various internships and corporate publicist positions before coming to work full-time for Mel and her team. Dex majored in entertainment management and now he holds the reins as her tour manager. Not everyone can work this closely with their family. I'm constantly with one or both of my siblings, but it's what I love most about this job.

Dropping my cup onto the table, an airy echo bounces off the surface. "So, do you think you're ready? To kick this tour off? That was the last of the big decisions for the performances, right?"

Mel's lips tip up into a soft smile.

"As ready as I'll ever be, I think." Her dark brown eyes, a twin pair to my own, look up at me from under her perfectly mascaraed lashes. "I'm ready to get back out there, you know? Do something fun. Forget Gunner exists."

Her voice drips with disdain, and I nod in agreement, knowing full well what she means. Awful exes are just one of the many things my sister and I have in common. Fortunately, I never married my long-term boyfriend, so my escape from relationship hell was easier than hers has been. I got to walk away, leave the asshole in the dust without looking back, but she still has to claw her way out of her own nightmare before she can truly move on.

I lean close, dropping my head on her shoulder and wrapping an arm around her waist as I squeeze tight. My red hair drapes over her dark brown hair, a stark contrast between our two shades. Both Melanie and Dex have gorgeous brunette hair, in a chocolate brown color that's so deep it's almost black. Mine is a coppery auburn, significantly brighter than their dark hue.

"We're going to get you through this, I promise, Mel. I've got every member of my team keeping tabs on him. We won't let him ruin this tour. And with any luck, by the time we get home, you'll be a single woman—free and clear."

It's a long shot, but Mel's lawyer is fighting hard for Gunner to wrap up these divorce negotiations. He's being a real fucking pain about it; contesting every point in the mediations, sending forms back to Mel's lawyer to be rewritten or redone entirely. It's childish, to be quite frank. But that's Gunner. He's always loved making Mel's life difficult.

"Thanks, Nat." She shifts in her chair, busying herself with collecting the crumbs that have separated from her muffin and placing them into the wrapper on the table.

"That's what I'm here for. Actually, speaking of the tour plans... I finished the project I was working on." I reach down, pulling out a giant three-ring binder from my tote bag.

I keep a copy of every important tour detail in this binder. There's a second copy of every file on my computer, but I prefer to work off paper. It never fails to annoy my brother, which is a silent perk of the process.

I can hear his voice in my head as I crack the binder open. *"Why keep everything in two places? You're doing double the work."* Maybe I am, but it makes my analytical brain very happy.

So sue me, Dex. Catch me forgetting something important... never.

Sliding my fingers between the crisp, white pages, I flip to the color-coded tour schedule I've been working on. Melanie leans in, her eyes going wide as I go through the details with her.

"This is all twenty-three weeks of the tour," I gesture to the grid. "The travel days are in pink, concert days in red, PR days in yellow... and your days off in green."

"What are the tiny stars on the green days?" She flips forward a page as she continues, "You have them on almost every one."

A thought comes to me as my eyes scan the calendar. Grabbing a pen, I jot a quick note in the margin for the first week of the trip. "Oh, those are for me. I have a secondary list of things I need to accomplish on those days. When I said, 'Your days off are in green,' I meant you, the band, and the dancers."

"And your days off are... where?" She flips back to the first page of the calendar again.

"I'll fit them in as needed, but I want to make good use of the time on the road." I quickly thumb to a green tab in the back, labeled with a matching star. The pages contain lists of smaller tasks I aligned with the tour schedule to keep ahead of everything that I need to accomplish.

"We're going to come back to that." She gives me a pointed look before she shifts her attention back to the paperwork on the table. "You've got a whole traffic light aesthetic going on here."

"Yeah, that's kind of what I was going for." I flip to a new section, showing a fresh page with a list of cities and PR events.

She runs her hand over the paper and offers me an affectionate smile. "This looks absolutely amazing. Do you think you can send me a copy of this?"

I know my sister better than I know myself some days, so expecting what she needs, or will want, is second nature to me. "It's already in your assistant's inbox. I'm also going to run full packets for the security team and Dex's team so everyone knows the game plan. Our crews are all operating on the same schedule, so this should help with our planning and prep."

"You're a machine, you know that? Seriously, Natalie, what would I do without you? You keep my life together—" She's cut off as the alarm on her phone blares, the sound shrill in the space between us.

"That's my cue, I guess," Melanie says, reaching to silence the noise. "Time for rehearsal. Are you sure you don't want to come today?"

The chair grinds against the tile floor as she pushes back to stand, sliding her sunglasses over her eyes as she does. "It's always more fun when you're around."

"I'd love to, but I think I'll stay and get some work done. I'll be there later this week, though. I want to see those new songs in person."

We share a quick hug before she slips around the divider. She pauses as Knox nods to me, turning and moving out the door just before her.

I watch the two of them disappear, the cold gust of February air sneaking in behind them as they go. Shivering, I trade my tour binder for my laptop in the bag at my feet. I'm about to dive into my email when my eyes land on my empty coffee cup and the collection of wrappers surrounding it. Deciding that fresh motivation is a better place to start, I snap the lid closed again and gather up all of my trash.

Heading to the counter, the click of my heels echoes in the quiet café. There are only a few other people mulling around, most at tables working. I toss my empties into the trash, heading around to the service counter to reorder another of both the coffee and lemon bread.

Juggling a fresh pastry bag and my to-go cup, I reach for the tiny packets of cream and sugar, before turning to head back to my table. Before I can take a full step, I slam straight into a hard body.

The lid snaps off my cup with a sharp pop, and the contents erupt all over the clean white shirt of the person standing before me. The plastic cap hits the tiles as I jump back reflexively, holding my elbow out at an awkward angle to keep the coffee that is now running down my arm from landing on my outfit.

Heat creeps into my cheeks as I stand immobilized, the coffee pooling at my feet.

A low "fuck" hissed in a deep, heady voice has my head snapping up. I instantly regret existing when I meet dark brown eyes belonging to the victim of my coffee explosion.

God, he is attractive.

And completely covered in my coffee.

His dark hair is trimmed close to his head on the sides, with a slightly longer length on top. He's got thick, dark stubble on his face, nearly disguising his sharp jawline. Over his now-ruined white tee, he wears a black leather jacket, which looks to have escaped any damage. I watch as he shakes his t-shirt, trying to pull it away from his chest. The soaked fabric clings to his body, the defined cut of his abs just barely visible through the coffee stain. My eyes trail the hint of a "v" that disappears into his pants before I realize I'm about to be caught checking him out.

I quickly cut my eyes back to his face, stammering awkwardly as I balance all the items in my hands, "Wow. I'm so sorry."

He stares down at me, eyebrows pinched together, shoulders rigid. Even the tiny indents forming between his eyes are attractive.

I drop everything on the counter beside me, my brain completely misfiring in my state of panic, and scoop up some napkins, spinning back to face the man across from me.

Grabbing roughly for his coffee from his outstretched hand, I force the pile of napkins at him.

"I just… I really… I am so, so sorry," I clear my throat to stop myself from adding anything else to that sentence.

His fist clenches before he moves, separating the napkin wad as he attempts to mop up some of the excess liquid. The scent of his cologne has me leaning closer, trying to take it in. The amber and cedar combination mixes with the coffee in the air, and it's heavenly.

His eyes lift to mine, lips drawn in a tight line.

I've just been caught… sniffing him. Clearing my throat, I take a step back.

Holy shit, this is mortifying. Is there a hole I can crawl in?

"I can pay for that, you know, buy you a new shirt. My purse is over there. In my chair." I cringe as my brain and mouth remain entirely disconnected, common sense nowhere to be found.

"I'll be right back." I turn to walk away when a warm hand closes around my wrist, tugging gently to keep me from leaving. I spin back, just inches from him as he leans forward.

"You know, I think we're good here..." he trails off, his eyes narrowed on me.

"Natalie." I blurt, much too loud for the quiet space. I can feel the eyes of nearby customers watching us.

Clearing my throat, I try again. "I'm Natalie."

He remains stoic, dropping my arm and pivoting to toss the soaked napkins into the bin. His jacket stretches across his broad shoulders as he reaches across his body, talking to me over his shoulder. "I think we're good, Natalie. I'm not worried about the shirt."

His gaze lands on me again as he turns to face me and I shrink back, overwhelmed by his presence, his scent, just... him. "Please? It's the least I can do since I ruined the one you have on."

"It's really ok. My shirt, and my wallet, will both be just fine." He gestures beside us. "It looks like you're going to need another coffee, anyway."

We both look at the sad cup next to us, droplets of coffee pooling beneath it on the butcher block countertop.

"Unless you're planning on keeping mine," his eyes shift to the coffee I stole from him. The one I'm still holding in my hand.

I smile sheepishly. "Sorry. Um, here. I hope this didn't ruin your day. I'm really sorry about the mess."

"It's fine." He grabs the zipper on the leather jacket, fastening it together and zipping it up nearly to his neck.

He takes the cup from my outstretched hand, his face passive, eyebrows still pinched.

"Well, I'm just going to... see myself out now." I laugh nervously. "It was really nice to meet you..." I trail off, mimicking him as I search for his name.

"Jake." His eyes flash with amusement, but it's gone as quickly as it appears.

"Right, Jake. It was... really nice to meet you." Smiling, I scoop my empty coffee cup, and the rest of my mess, off the counter. I hustle across the room and slip back into my hidden spot in the corner, my face on fire and my pulse racing.

I slouch down into my seat, dropping the items onto the table before pulling my laptop open in front of me. Turning, I peer through the decorative divider to see Jake glancing back over his shoulder. His eyes scan the room one last time before he pulls the door open and exits the building.

The lead weight on my chest shifts, the relief of his leaving palpable. I watch the cursor on the screen blink back at me as I let out a long breath, thankful Jake is nothing more than a stranger.

We're All Professionals

Running late on the first day of a new job is definitely not a good look. Glancing quickly both ways before hurrying across the street, I use my free hand to drag the zipper on my leather jacket down. The chilly winter air bites at me through the liquid covering most of my chest. Here's hoping the wind will help dry out my wet t-shirt on the two-block walk before I show up to work looking like I just lost a fight in a coffee shop.

I carefully slurp the coffee overflowing from the lip of the cup in my hand, thinking back through the interaction at the café, wondering if Natalie thinks I'm a total asshole for the way I reacted.

Grumpy bastard is not my usual personality, but the shock of being covered in her drink short-circuited my brain. When I looked up and caught the sheer panic painted on her gorgeous features, common courtesy went right out the door.

I shake my head. I can't entertain thoughts of random, redheaded women, no matter how pretty, when I need to be focused on this new assignment.

Approaching a brown brick building with the Shield Security logo painted on the front windows, I step under the awning and let myself in. The chime sounds loudly as I push the door open. I've only been here once before today, but the building already feels familiar. The gray concrete floors spill through the entryway and down two long hallways leading further back into the building on either side of the front desk. Dark ceilings and wooden walls enclose the space, with greenery peppered throughout the room.

Re-zipping my jacket to hide the mess, I approach the front desk. A short, blonde woman, probably in her mid-to-late forties, looks up from the computer and pastes a smile on her face.

"Good morning, Jake!" The receptionist greets me far too loudly. I remember the unbridled enthusiasm from the day I was here for my interview. It's just as overwhelming this morning as it was two weeks ago. She stands quickly and comes around the front of the desk. "We're so glad you're here!"

She sticks out her right hand, and I accept the handshake, offering her mine in return. "Good to be here."

"Everyone else is already in the conference room if you want to go on back." She beams as she gestures down the hallway on her right, which ends in a pair of double doors—a mass of bodies behind the clear glass. "You got here just in time. I don't think they've started the meeting yet."

"Great," I exhale in relief. "I'll just..." I gesture in the general direction of the conference room, then thank her and stride off. The office is quiet as I make my way down the narrow corridor.

The heavy door closes slowly behind me as I let myself in. This room is just as clean and modern as the rest of the office. The table has three leather chairs on each side and a large, white screen covering the exposed brick wall behind it. I slide into the room and hover near the back wall.

Taking a cautious sip of my coffee, I scan the area. People bow together in several small groups, chatting animatedly with one another. A small group of four men, including myself, are tucked away in the back of the room. We all stand awkwardly, plenty of space acting as a buffer from one another.

Working for a company like this will be an interesting change. It's been a long time since I've worked for someone else. Typically, I take contract jobs that are one, sometimes two guards, operating independently for the clients that hire us. Large-scale security operations have never been in my wheelhouse, but when a buddy of mine mentioned Shield was looking for experienced guards, it was conveniently at a time I was looking to line up my next job. Though I still don't know what this contract entails, I liked the management when I interviewed, so I decided to try something different.

"Gentlemen, if you would please…" A deep timber cuts through the loud hum of the men in the overcrowded conference room. Heads snap in his direction and bodies shuffle as we redirect our attention to the front of the room. Those close enough to chairs drop into one, but since the number of people here outnumbers the chairs 2:1, the rest of us move to stand against the walls.

"I appreciate your time." Connor Culver, my new boss, clears his throat and looks around expectantly. "I know we're really packing it in this morning, but I promise to keep this brief. A group of this size is unusual for one of our contracts, but this contract itself is unusual. The twelve of you will spend the next six months providing services for the summer concert tour for Melanie Bennett."

The sip of coffee I've just taken spills into my airway. My eyes immediately water as I lock my jaw, refusing to let the coughs currently clawing their way out call attention to me.

I clear my throat as discreetly as possible, but getting the air flowing correctly again takes several long moments. When I rejoin the meeting, the sound of murmurs has broken out in the room as the men turn to one another, eyes wide and excitement obvious on their faces.

Apparently, no one here was aware of what they had signed up for. It's not unusual for me to take a job and find out the client later. Hell, I've taken jobs when I didn't know where I would work, or how long the contract was. The details you're afforded vary depending on the situation. Higher profile clients tend to keep details under wraps for as long as possible.

Case in point.

Honestly, guarding a pop star and her entourage should be nothing new for bodyguards of this caliber. This isn't your run-of-the-mill security firm. They're supposed to specialize in high-profile clients.

I keep my face clear of any emotion as I cross my arms, pressing my tacky t-shirt into my chest. Uncomfortable, I quickly change my mind, instead sliding my free hand into my pocket and leaning on the wall as I wait for my boss to continue.

"Simmer down. We're all professionals in this room." He pauses and waits for the guys to silence themselves. "Now, tours are not new to us at Shield Security, but the scope of this gig is much larger than we normally take on. Melanie is a longtime client of ours, working only with Knox until we signed for this tour."

He gestures to a guy with long dark hair sitting in front of him. Connor shifts his hand up, moving the attention from Knox to the back of the room where I stand. "Obviously, you can see we've brought in several fresh faces for this contract. Finding available guards with six months open in their schedule isn't easy, but the new men joining us come here with years of experience, so I expect they'll fit in just fine."

He pauses again, scanning the faces of the new hires, all of us congregated together. "Back of the room there, you will see Jordan Michaels - wave if you would please, Jordan. Great, thank you. Caleb Talbot... Patrick Miller... and Jacob Alder."

I stick my arm up briefly as my name is called last, dropping it quickly as everyone's attention returns to the front of the room.

"I expect you all to welcome them to the team starting today. I want to run through the timeline of this job, and then I can break out assignments and schedules." He taps a pile of manila folders sitting on the table in front of him. "We've got a hefty info packet for each of you here to take before you leave."

The screen behind him lights up, and he runs through prepared slides on the key highlights of this assignment. I listen closely as I lift my coffee cup to my lips and take a deep drink.

Though concert tours are something I haven't had experience with, I feel comfortable that this is something I'm more than capable of handling. I have a resume a mile long, working for celebrities and clients in high-profile situations where additional protection was necessary. Honestly, it might be kind of nice to be on a team instead of the one in charge.

As his spiel wraps about twenty minutes later, Connor hands out packets, and everyone exits the room, one at a time. When I move to accept my own packet, Connor motions for me to grab the now open seats. I oblige, noting the table now has just three veteran Shield Security employees and myself seated at it.

"You boys have the lead roles on this assignment." Connor says. Addressing me directly, he adds, "Jake, I wouldn't normally pass this on to a new hire, but given the circumstances, I think your experience here will be an asset to the team."

I nod as I take the folder in his outstretched hand. Placing the documents on the table, I flip through the top few pages as Connor continues addressing me.

"I'm putting you on Melanie's detail with Knox. The two of you can work out how you handle the shifts, but she's expected to have one of you with her at all times and both when traveling out in public."

I open my mouth to argue the assignment before I think better of it, snapping my jaw shut again. I'm sure he's had a look at all our resumes. The rest of these guys work for him. If this is the decision he's made, he obviously thinks it's the right one.

Connor continues, not noticing my reaction. "Asher, you will work with Melanie's publicist and tour manager. As they're also Melanie's siblings, it's unlikely they'll both need you at once. They'll always be in the same hotel, so I think you can manage what they need without issue. Our primary concern is public coverage. You can flex as needed to make that work. Melanie is the only one who needs the extra protection."

His gaze shifts back to his own papers as he continues. "Chase, I want you to take the lead with the rest of the security team for this assignment. You can divide them up as needed between the band and dancers - again, we're mainly concerned about when they leave the premises. I already set up a meeting with the four of you and Melanie's team so you can meet the clients and get the finer details sorted out. Knox can lead that one. You don't need me micromanaging everything here.

"We have the full security team starting in about six weeks, so they have time to wrap up any personal affairs. As previously discussed with each of you, the four of you start now, so you have time to get plans in action and acclimate to the tour team. This is an extensive tour with full-time coverage for twenty-three straight weeks, so there will not be the availability for many vacation days. We've set a rotation for the wider crew for a day off each week, but the four of you will need to work out any time off amongst yourselves. I want all absences between the four of you covered by another member of this core team. Chase, pull from your team when needed to cover any other gaps."

He combs through the details of the assignment for several more minutes before asking if we have questions. I'll hand it to Shield Security, the details in this file are good, much better than some other assignments I've been on. Seems like they have their shit together.

"I'll leave the coordination at each venue up to you four as well. In each folder, there's a list of some of the security details and contacts on the tour. You'll have to work with Melanie's team to get what you need for each venue. For the most part, I don't think there will be much overlap between the event security and your own jobs, but you'll want to check in with their teams before you arrive and make plans to hit the ground running at each stop. Tour logistics are a little more hands-on than our usual contracts, but I think the four of you will handle this fine." He gathers the papers that have spilled around the table while he spoke and shovels them back into his own folder. Knocking his knuckles against the wooden top of the table, he wraps up. "Let's square up a couple more times before the tour kicks off. We can go through the logistics outlined in these folders after you've had a chance to review them, but I think for today that will do it."

We murmur our assent, following his lead, stacking papers and closing folders. I push back from the table, moving around it as I head for the door.

"Jake!" I hear my name called from behind me, pulling up short as I step off to the side.

The man Connor addressed earlier reaches out a hand to me. "I'm Knox Montgomery. I work with Melanie Bennett full-time. For the next few weeks, you'll be with me until the tour kicks off so we can get you acclimated to Mel's team and the tour needs."

I return his handshake, nodding in acknowledgment. "Great. It's nice to meet you."

"If you want to follow me, I can show you the office, and then we can take off in a bit to grab Melanie from rehearsal. We're throwing you right into the deep end." His laugh is loud, but friendly.

"Sounds good. Might as well get this rolling."

We both start down the hall, passing a second, smaller conference room and a lunchroom before hanging a left and entering a bullpen area.

"We don't have much around here, since most of us are primarily in the field, but we all have a locker in the back and a communal workspace situation." Knox gestures around the area, where about a dozen desks sit. Each workspace has a computer and some filing racks, along with the usual office paraphernalia. "We'll get you set up with a laptop, but your login to the central database will also work on any of these desktops. I have an office over in Melanie's building that you're welcome to use, too."

"Have you been with Shield Security long?" I ask.

"About eight years. I've been working with Melanie for the last five. It's a nice gig. Shield pretty much lets you do your thing as long as the reports are filed on time and the client's happy."

Knox hands me a pile of paperwork requested by HR with a promise to return as soon as he hunts down one of the other guys.

I grab a seat, flipping through the stack, as I look over the forms. It's all pretty basic information, so I dive in, filling out the employment forms, tax ID information, and other paperwork. When I get to the emergency contact form, I pause with a sigh.

I never know what I should include on these damn things. I have no contact with my parents, and my brothers are all living out of state. There hasn't been a significant other in… well, ever. That's not an idea I allow myself to entertain. I distance myself from people for a reason, and it's not usually an issue… until someone is asking me who to contact in case of an emergency.

Deciding on my oldest brother, I pull up his contact information in my phone. We're not close by any means, but he's the best option I've got. In a worst-case scenario, I know he'd be there, and I suppose that's really all the qualifications an emergency contact needs.

I'm penning my name on the last form when Knox returns, another man in tow. I stand to join them as they approach.

"Jake, you've met Asher. He's gonna join us today." He gestures to the stack of papers in my hand. "Let's get those turned in, and we can be on our way."

The three of us head up front, leaving the paperwork on the front desk.

"Anyone need to refresh their coffee?"

I shake my empty cup. "I could use some. I feel like I'm gonna need it today."

"Perfect." Knox claps me on the back. "There's a coffee shop on our way."

THREE

JAKE

Ticking Time Bomb

"You do this how many times a week?" I say to Knox as we stand off to the side of the stage. It's Wednesday afternoon, three days into this new job, and we're currently on site with Melanie, watching her and fourteen of her backup dancers work with the choreographer to practice the routines for the show.

"Six lately." Knox adjusts his stance. He pulls a pack of gum out of his pocket, offering me a stick before taking one for himself. "We just transitioned to the stadium rehearsals this week, though. We've been holed up in a dance studio downtown for the last several months. This is a nice change of pace, to be honest."

I chew on the gum, softening it before popping a bubble, as I absentmindedly focus on the routine the dancers are working through.

Being a bodyguard sounds a lot more glamorous than it is in reality. This is what we spend most of our time doing: waiting around for other people. It's nice though, in a venue like this, because we don't have to be as focused as we would in a public setting. We're still monitoring, paying attention, but it's more relaxed. More enjoyable.

"Honestly, I'll be glad when this tour starts. Melanie's running herself into the ground with all the rehearsals, costume fittings, planning meetings, and other prep they have her doing. She's got her hands in all of it and, fuck, at this point, we're both just tired. Getting out on the road will feel like a vacation."

"Well, she wears it a lot better than you do." We're both watching her dance at the front of the group, microphone in hand. She's smiling and laughing as they move around the stage.

"Sure as shit does," he mumbles. "I feel like I'm watching her work twenty hours a day. The woman barely sleeps."

I hum in acknowledgment. I didn't know Melanie personally before this week, but I've been around industry people long enough to have heard about her, both good and not-so-good. So far though, she's been nothing but kind and welcoming. "Well, you have to admire it. You don't get where she is by half-assing things. And if her team works as hard as she does, I can see why she's got the leverage she does in the industry right now."

We watch them from our spot for a few more minutes before I glance at my watch. "I think I'll take a spin through the stadium. I feel like getting a behind-the-scenes look."

"Sounds good, man. I'll be here." He adjusts his sunglasses on his face and crosses his arms as I step away.

The nice thing about shadowing for a bit, not being the one in charge, is the freedom to do things like this. Once we're out on tour, it will be hectic. A couple weeks in the stadium, with the full stage setup, will be convenient to familiarize ourselves with everything.

I move through the space, weaving behind the lighting technician in the main lighting panel. The number of lights blinking up at him is dizzying, but he's focused. I pass a few small clusters of stagehands standing around, awaiting further direction. We all pause, turning and watching the performance for a bit, seeing the dancers, backup vocalists, and the band working in tandem with Melanie.

A flash of red across the way catches my eye, a shorter woman in high heels standing alongside Knox, her back to me. She's dressed in a pencil skirt and blouse, reminding me distinctly of the redhead that collided with me at the coffee shop the other day.

I spend several long moments back in that coffee shop, reliving Monday morning. Grimacing, I force myself back to the task at hand and continue my path along the stage.

This is the third or fourth time in as many days that she's crossed my mind. I ran into her one time, met her for all of two minutes, and it's like her presence latched on with iron claws, forcing its way into my brain and refusing to loosen its grip. I don't even know this woman, so I can't figure out why she keeps cropping up. There's no reason I shouldn't be able to shake her.

I wind backstage, scoping out the area. There are even more people back here, moving around like a well-orchestrated army. Some are hauling equipment, others point to the scaffolding as they talk, no doubt ensuring everything is exactly how Melanie and her team need it.

I've never worked on a tour before, and seeing this side of a production is fascinating. I'm looking forward to this contract—six months behind the scenes and on the road with what's being heralded as one of the most anticipated tours of the year.

Shit, I might even be a little *excited* about this, and I can't say the last time work was exciting. Typically, I prefer it's not.

When I finally make my way back to Knox, Melanie and the team are wrapping up for the day. She leads us around the stage, a large gym bag slung over her shoulder. We're just entering the main hallway when Knox's phone chimes. He lets out a groan before saying, "Hang a left, Mel. We're gonna take off out of the parking garage exit. The driver just messaged. We have paparazzi camped out at the main parking lot."

"For fuck's sake," I hear her mumble, taking a sharp left toward the rear of the complex.

"How big of a problem is this for her? Paparazzi avoidance?" I pose the question carefully, not sure how sensitive a topic it might be for them right now.

Knox falls into step beside me as he answers, his voice echoing in the empty hallway. "It's not usually this chaotic, but the closer the tour gets, the more the fans really seem to want to know what she's up to. Melanie prefers to keep her off-stage life very private. She doesn't do much publicity outside of strategic tour-related events, and the press doesn't like that. Especially with all the coverage the divorce has been getting. The photographers are getting harder to avoid. I almost feel like they have to be getting her schedule from someone, but I can't figure out who it would be."

Melanie has slowed down, waiting for him to catch up before heading outside. Knox sidesteps her, opening the door and checking both directions before waving us through with him. I stay behind Melanie as Knox marches in front of her. A few short strides later, and we're piling into a sleek black SUV. I'm still buckling my seatbelt when the driver puts the vehicle in gear and takes off again.

"So, you really think someone is tipping off the paparazzi about her whereabouts?" I ask Knox as I look over at Melanie across the car from us, curled up into a ball in her seat, dark shades covering her eyes as she stares out the window watching the city flash by.

"I mean, it seems the most likely answer to the increase in volume we're dealing with lately. But maybe it's not that complicated. It could just be the demand right now with everything going on. The press wants answers, and Melanie isn't playing their games."

I lean back in my seat, mulling that over as I get comfortable. She certainly has a lot on her plate right now. I can see why the press would be hungry for news, sightings, and photo ops. It's sick, the kinds of things photographers will do to make a buck.

It's hard to keep secrets when everyone in the world wants to know what you're up to. But, from what I can tell, that's one thing Melanie Bennett seems to do well. Her personal life was never really talked about until she and Gunner released a joint statement announcing their separation and later, their divorce. It's given her what she wanted: that privacy. Separation of personal and stage presence. But it's also created a wildfire of interest now that both sides of her life are playing out publicly. Shit like this is almost always a ticking time bomb. It has me wondering just how long until it all implodes.

An hour later, after leaving Knox and Melanie at her house, I pull my truck into the garage attached to my house in the suburbs, just twenty minutes outside Nashville. I cut the engine as I wait for the garage door to close behind me, the fading sunlight bouncing off the shiny black motorcycle in the space next to my truck.

I stare at it longingly, trying to decide how long it's been since I've ridden it, but I can't come up with an answer. With all the contract jobs I take, I'm rarely home for more than a handful of days at a time. It's by design, this way of living, but sometimes, I wonder why I have nice things if I never get to use them.

Sighing at that depressing thought, I hop out, slamming the truck door behind me. Letting myself into the quiet house, I toss my keys on the kitchen counter, dropping my leather jacket over the chair.

I bought this house a few years ago but haven't done much of anything with the place. The furniture is modern, clean, with lots of natural wood tones and dark colors. It's nearly dark inside right now, the light of the fading sun the only light reflecting through the main floor. I like it this way. It's peaceful. I know that soon, peace and quiet will be a rare commodity, so I soak it in, leaving the lights off as I trail through the house, winding past the kitchen island as I make my way toward the staircase.

I take the stairs two at a time as I make my way toward my bedroom. Heading up the stairs, the framed photos on the walls move past me as I go. They're the only memories I keep in this house, the only photos I have anywhere at all. Hanging them in the stairwell was strategic—a spot where I can see them each day, a way to keep them front and center so I'm not tempted to forget everything I've lost.

My eyes scan over a family photo, my parents and my three siblings with me. The next one is just the four of us kids, our arms wrapped tightly around one another. The third and fourth photos are of me with varying combinations of my siblings. In the middle of the woods, up in a tree, is my youngest brother in the last photo, taken the week before he died.

He's seven in that photo, and I can say without a second thought exactly where we were, who was with us, and how the air smelled that day. My mom left that photo in a pile on the counter when she was scanning images for the funeral, and I snagged it as soon as she was done with it. It's moved around with me ever since, graduating from a box under my bed during my teen years, to the framed place it holds now in my house in my late twenties.

With me on my one and only tour of duty overseas, it's well-worn from having traveled thousands of miles. It felt important somehow to have my brother with me during that period, though I'm not sure I could say why. Although he had been gone for a decade at that point, I couldn't leave him behind. His prominent position on the wall keeps him a fixture in my life, even now.

I shove the memories down—both of my brother and my time in the military. I like to keep the memories fresh enough that they're not forgotten, so I don't drift from the path I've set myself on since the day my brother died, but I also have to be careful not to let my mind go too far down that road. I keep that period of my life locked up tight, and every time I linger on the memories for too long, the lock falters, the box reopening. It gets a little harder to close every time I have to relatch it.

It's a fine line I walk, always one step away from pushing it too far, but I worry that without the memories in front of me, I'd be tempted to become too complacent, too comfortable again. And I never want to find myself in a position to hurt someone I love ever again.

I can't. I won't survive it.

After quickly showering, I make my way back into the kitchen, keeping the lighting low as I shuffle through the cupboards, pulling out ingredients to make dinner.

Once that's prepped, I pop the top on a beer from the fridge and settle in on the couch. Before I can get too comfortable, my phone vibrates on the coffee table in front of me, and I grab it, checking the caller ID.

Debating for a moment, my thumb hovers over the green button. "Hey man. Haven't talked to you in a minute."

A deep voice comes over the line, loud in the quiet of the living room. "Jake. It's been too long. How ya doing?"

"Uh, fine. Good." I run my thumb through the condensation on the bottle, debating what prompted this phone call. "How are you, Gunner?"

"I'm good, man. Better now, actually. I heard you got a new gig."

The beer bottle clinks as it meets the coffee table. "I... might have. You know I can't talk about my contracts."

"I do know that, but no worries. I don't need details. I know what I need to know."

"How'd you hear about that?" My tone is unintentionally sharp, the unease sliding into my voice.

"I hear lots of things, Jake."

His evasiveness is a little off-putting. "I'm sure that's true, as connected as you are these days."

"You're not wrong." He laughs at that. "So anyway, since you have this new gig—"

A sigh slips out. "No. I know what you're about to say, and it's not gonna happen."

"Really, Jake? You're in the perfect position to help a guy out. I'm never gonna put this behind me if I don't have something to give me an edge."

"Listen, man. I appreciate that you've been a constant in my life. We have a history, and you've done a lot for me, but you know I can't be handing out information under a contract."

"I'm not asking for you to hand me anything. I'm just saying, you'd be in the perfect position to help a guy out. I got you into the industry. I'm sure there's a way you can use your leverage, within the parameters of your contract, to get me one or two things I might need."

I run my free hand through my hair, unsure. Despite the strange nature of our relationship, it's nice to have a connection to someone, considering it's the only tether I've kept in my life. Holding on to an acquaintance has always been easier for me than holding onto family, especially when the guilt was all-consuming.

The line is quiet as I contemplate the request. "I can't make you any promises. I'll see what I can do."

"You're a good friend, Jake. I appreciate you. Listen, I don't want to keep you. We can talk in a few weeks, when you're settled in."

"Sounds good."

"Take care of my ex-wife for me."

The call disconnects, and I'm left in the silence of my living room, wondering if maybe this contract is more than I bargained for.

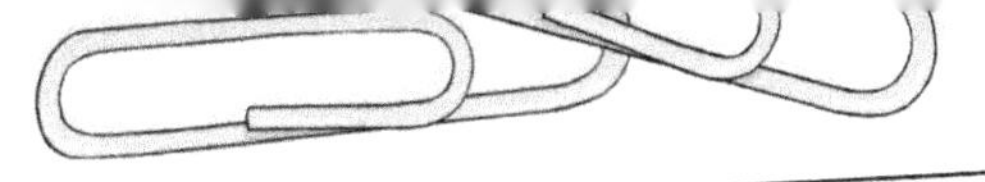

FOUR

NATALIE

Thursday morning, I'm making my way through the hallway at the offices, heading for our main conference room. I have my coffee in one hand and my tour binder in the other. This morning's project completed, my focus is on my mental checklist for this afternoon when I round the corner and collide with a hard body.

Again.

My stomach drops as a tingling sensation races up my neck and across my face, flames spreading over my skin as I crash into someone for the second time in under a week.

What the actual fuck is wrong with me?

Thankfully, everything remains in my hands and cup this time. The metal tumbler I have today is sturdier than the cardboard to-go cup from the coffee shop. That familiar amber and cedar cologne haunts me, and I look up, once again meeting the intense glare of brooding dark brown eyes.

The same pair I met on Monday morning.

"You have got to be kidding me." Jake's low growl meets my ears.

I curse silently under my breath, feeling a profound sense of déjà vu. Of course it would be him again. It's not enough that he caught me off balance the first time. No, he has to see me looking incompetent multiple times.

I watch as he examines his shirt, clearly recalling our last meeting just as well as I do. He skipped the leather jacket today, instead pairing a black t-shirt with black jeans and a pair of black work boots. It would appear his wardrobe is a direct reflection of his personality. *Cute.*

"We've got to stop meeting like this," I say, laughing nervously as I try to break the tension between us. I take a step back, forcing myself to remain calm. I will not look like a fool twice.

His eyes slowly scan over my body, making their way to my face, hands settling on his hips. I meet his gaze, hard and unforgiving, my chest tightening at the look on his face.

"Trust me, Natalie. This was never my plan," he replies shortly, hostility coming off him in waves. I try not to react as my name rolls off his tongue, though I am surprised he remembered it.

"I'm not usually this clumsy," I offer, as if a simple explanation will wash away the mortification settling in again.

"I'm sure." I keep my face neutral, internally flinching at his tone.

The pieces suddenly click together as I remember what I'm doing, where I am and... why is he here?

"Is there... something I can help you with? Are you looking for me?" I glance around, trying to figure out how he ended up in my office building.

"What? No, I'm not looking for you." His brows furrow in confusion as he checks the watch on his wrist, growing more agitated. "I'm here for a meeting with my security team."

"A security meeting? With Melanie Bennett's team?" I hedge, the implications of what he's saying sinking in.

"Yes?" His tone tells me he's over this conversation.

"You work for Shield Security?" Apparently, all I have left is endless questions.

"Yes, I just said I'm here for the security meeting. Is there more than one?" He runs his hand through his hair, staring me down with those intense brown eyes.

Fuck. Me.

"No, no, there's only one." Clearing my throat, I stand up straighter, deciding to sort my feelings out later. I can just pretend this man isn't the same one I dumped my coffee all over. I can also just pretend he doesn't think I'm fucking incompetent after running him to him... twice.

I'm great at pretending.

"You can follow me. The conference room is down the hallway you just passed."

I march past him, my high heels clicking loudly on the tiles of the hallway floor. The sound echoes as the stomp of his boots accompanies us.

"You work here then?" Jake interrupts my thoughts as we make our way down the long hall.

"I do," I say over my shoulder, refusing to slow down or turn around to have a conversation. "I'm Melanie's publicist."

He doesn't reply as I come to a stop in front of two large glass doors, the Melanie Bennett Music logo printed in large letters on each one.

"The publicist. Also, the sister." Jake's voice comes from over my shoulder. It's a statement, not a question.

I let out a long breath as I reach for the door on the left, pulling it open and finally turning back to Jake.

"Correct. It's a family affair around here." I plaster my fake PR smile on, the false cheer in my voice an octave too high. He scans my face again before taking the door from me, and we both enter the room, the bright space gleaming in the morning sun shining through the windows. The ambience is much too light and airy for my mood right now.

I look around the room, spotting Melanie already seated near the end of the large table. I'm about to head straight for her when Knox's voice stops me.

"Morning, Natalie, Jake. I see you two have already met." He nods to each of us.

Before I can stop myself, I snort out loud at that comment. He raises an eyebrow in my direction, and I shift my stance, pivoting to face him and cutting Jake out of my peripheral vision. "Yes, we have. I found him in the hall on my way here."

Knox looks over my shoulder at Jake, addressing him. "Glad you found the place ok. Asher is already here. He's over by the coffee bar, if you want to grab a cup. We'll get started in just a few."

I mutter a quick acknowledgment to Knox and turn on my heel, marching straight past Jake and making my way to the opposite end of the room. Sliding into the chair next to Melanie, I drop the binder on the table a little more carelessly than I intended.

The slap of plastic on wood makes her jump. "Everything ok? That was an aggressive entrance."

She looks over at me as I get situated, moving my coffee to the side and sliding my tote bag beneath the table at my feet.

"Define OK," I mutter, flipping the top on the cup and taking a long pull of the warm coffee.

"Uh oh." She waits for me to finish drinking, her full attention on me as she sits in her chair.

"You know Monday, when you left me at The Brew?" She nods, the ponytail on top of her head bobbing animatedly, a look of concern painted on her face.

"I ordered a fresh coffee and as soon as I turned around, slammed right into the most gorgeous man. Literally ran face first into a rock-hard set of abs, my entire cup of coffee emptying onto his shirt."

She snickers, quickly covering her mouth with her hands as she watches me. I can feel the flush on my face deepening as I continue, recalling the entire conversation with Jake for her.

"So you just dumped your coffee all over this guy and then offered him money to make it go away?" She laughs out loud this time, the glee in her tone almost offensive.

"Yeah, well. It's about to get better."

Her eyes widen. "Oh god, there's more?"

"I ran into him again this morning." She buries her face in her hands. The mortification I feel is mirrored in her movements. "Yes, literally. Again."

"No. Stop it. Where?"

"Yep." I pop the p loudly, using the sound like it's a punchline in my story. "In the hallway just now. He's the dark-haired one in the black tee across the room talking to Dex and Knox."

Her head shoots up as she scans the room, stopping when she lands on the group of guys across the space, deep in conversation. Dex and Knox have their backs to us, but Jake and a guy who I assume to be Asher are both facing our direction. Dex shifts to the left just as Jake looks up, his eyes meeting mine as he catches both Melanie and me staring right at him.

The white-hot embarrassment comes rushing back. I can feel the heat emanating from my cheeks as his eyes hold mine.

"JAKE? Mystery man is Jake?" She whispers to me, but it comes out more like a soft shout.

I groan, turning away quickly, my focus coming back to Melanie. "You've met him?"

"Of course, I've met him. He's working with Knox."

A long, dramatic sigh leaves me. "Seriously, I was really hoping never to see the guy again. The whole thing is so fucking embarrassing."

She snickers quietly, clearly getting a kick out of my situation. "I'm sorry. I don't mean to keep laughing. It's not funny."

"No, no, go on. Have a good laugh at my expense." She tries to keep the grin off her face but fails miserably.

We're interrupted when Dex slides into the seat on Melanie's other side. He looks between us before he leans in. "What are you up to over here?"

Melanie shifts her eyes between the two of us, as if she's waiting to see whether I'm going to loop him in.

Before I can decide if I really want to share with our brother, the chairs across the table from us roll back and three hulking forms drop into the seats, one right after another.

Jake takes the seat immediately across from me, with Asher and a third man I've never met on his right. I slide my eyes from Jake to Asher, who is similar in build. Broad shoulders, gorgeous face. I'd guess around the same height too, but it's hard to tell when we're all sitting down. Where Jake has dark hair with equally dark eyes, Asher is his complete opposite with blond hair and ocean blue eyes.

The third man is also ridiculously attractive, with a deep brown skin tone and short black hair. Like the two men beside him, he has impossibly broad shoulders and an imposing presence.

The presence makes sense for a group of bodyguards, but does everyone have to be good-looking to work for Shield Security?

A throat clears beside me, and I look over, Dex staring at me with one eyebrow cocked and his head tilted.

"Sorry, what was that?" I ask, trying to play off the fact that I was clearly checking out the three men across the table.

"I asked if you've met Chase, Asher, and Jake?" He gestures at them as he talks. "They are working with Knox as the leads on the security contract."

Feigning indifference, I turn on my PR grin, standing slightly as I reach across the table and shake each of their hands. "I haven't had the pleasure, no. It's so nice to meet you. I'm Natalie, Melanie's publicist."

Knox takes that moment to interject, sparing me from having to further the conversation. He launches into a quick speech about the security contract and some details for the tour. We listen to him talk, with input from Dex on the tour details, for the next thirty minutes. The entire time, I am painfully aware of Jake's presence across the table from me. Logically, he's not sitting there critiquing every move I make, but I think the multiple collisions have fried my brain because there's no convincing it otherwise.

I distract myself by running my thumb over the pressed penny in the back of the notebook in my lap as I listen to them talking about venue coordination, going over details Dex and I covered in a meeting earlier this week. It's a silly thing to carry around, but I have a million of them that I used to collect as a kid. One day, I found this penny lying around and instead of putting it back in the closet, I slipped it into my notebook. Now, I purposefully keep one in the tiny pocket that lines the back of my portfolio, right where the pen attaches. It's a nervous habit, but it's weirdly relaxing.

When my phone vibrates on the table beside me, I snatch it up, a quick glance at the screen telling me it's the printer. I excuse myself, hurrying out into the hall to take the call, a sudden lightness coursing through me as the door falls shut behind me.

Sorting out a formatting issue with the printer takes close to forty-five minutes by the time I make it back to the conference room. I can see Melanie standing there, talking to Knox and Jake, my tote and binder in her hands.

I let myself back into the room, the shutter of the glass door closing causing all three of them to turn and look at me.

"Sorry about that." I say, a fake smile plastered on my face once again.

"Everything ok?" Mel asks me, cause for my concern apparently the theme for the day.

"All good. The printer had an issue with the PR packets I sent over this morning. I wanted to make sure it was cleared up. Sorry I missed the end of the meeting." I direct the last sentence toward Knox.

"No worries, we just wrapped a few minutes ago. We haven't been waiting long."

"Waiting?" I ask, looking from Knox to Melanie.

"Mmhmm." She's smirking at me as I try to figure out what's going on. "We have that photoshoot with the social media team across town, remember?"

"I remember..." I trail off, trying to decide how to ask why the hell Jake is still here, staring at me, without giving myself away.

It turns out I don't need to when Melanie continues on. "Jake is shadowing Knox for the next couple of weeks, you know, getting a feel for everything, meeting the whole team, learning how we work. That kind of thing."

My stomach sinks, realizing I might have missed something important when I took that phone call. "Oh, right. Because he's..."

"...my second bodyguard." Melanie finishes. "He will be with Knox and I from now on."

I meet her eye, and there's a glint in her expression that looks an awful lot like mischief.

It suddenly feels like this is going to be a very long tour.

Her publicist. And her sister.

The redhead that's haunted me for the last week is not only working for, but also related to, my client.

Fucking fantastic.

I'm distracted as we exit the vehicle immediately in front of the main doors to the event center. Ignoring the "closed for a private event" sign on the front entrance, I pull on the heavy glass door and scoff. Knox cuts by me, Melanie and Natalie following before I make my way inside behind them. We cross the large, open entry space, turning into a hallway to the left.

Stalking down the hall, I keep my distance as I watch Natalie's perfectly constructed bun bob with each step she takes. She and Melanie are deep in conversation, going on about something I can't hear from behind them.

Apparently, the universe has seen fit to test me with this contract. I thought it would be enough of a challenge working for Gunner's ex-wife, but also having to deal with her sister for the next six months is going to keep me on my toes.

I stop short, not realizing I've caught up with the three of them, waiting outside a door labeled "Main Office." As if on cue, it swings wide to reveal a tall blonde woman.

"Melanie! We're so glad you made it!" she coos animatedly, rushing forward to greet Mel. She places both hands on either shoulder and makes a show of air kissing her cheeks. Melanie's face remains warm, a broad smile across it.

The woman shifts, welcoming Natalie in the same fashion. "Hi, it's so good to see you again. Thanks for hosting us today for this shoot."

"Of course, you're always welcome here. Your room is all set. If you need anything, you know where to find me. Several of my staff are already on the second floor waiting for you."

"Quick question," I interject, as the noise in the hall comes to a screeching halt. I wasn't after the entire group's attention, but I'll take it. "Can we address the front door?"

"I'm sorry, what?" The blonde asks, with a look of confusion crossing her face.

"The front door," I clarify. "It was unlocked when we entered. Are you planning on locking it?"

"No, I don't... we rarely lock our doors during business hours, Mr..."

"Alder, Jake." I fill in. "You have an A-list celebrity paying to rent this entire building. She just entered through a very visible front door. Anyone could have seen her. A sign on the door will not keep out an unruly fan."

"I'll see what I can do." She replies cooly, clearly put out by my request.

"I can wait downstairs while you take care of that. We just want to make sure Melanie is as safe as possible. I'm sure you understand." Forgetting I'm not the one in charge, I flick my eyes over to Knox, who just nods in agreement with me.

The blonde throws me a glare, turning on her heel as she reenters her office. I watch as the group takes off down the hall, rounding the corner, seeing Natalie's head turn my way before she disappears completely from sight.

It takes several minutes before the woman returns with her keys in hand. She jingles them in my direction as she silently stalks by.

I follow her back out into the main lobby and watch as she secures the front doors.

"There, that should be adequate. Anything else, Mr. Alder?"

"No, but thank you. I appreciate your help." She purses her lips before turning on her heel and making her way back to her office. I follow her, continuing past the office door as it closes beside me, and head for the elevator. On the second floor, I follow the sound of voices, finding everyone in a large ballroom with various backdrops and scenery situated around the area.

I make my way over to Knox, who has found a chair off to the side, out of the way of the commotion, but with a full view of the room. Dropping into the seat next to him, my eyes scan the space, noting the activity in front of us.

As I sit there, I comb back through the last few days with Melanie. It's still early in our relationship, but I'm having trouble seeing what Gunner has spent years complaining about. Toward the end of their marriage, it felt like every call was just a vent session about his wife. He made her sound like a true nightmare. So far, she doesn't seem to be any of the nasty things Gunner described, but I suppose thirty-six hours with someone isn't going to tell you what three years of marriage will.

I'm quickly distracted from my thoughts as I watch Natalie fussing with her sister's sparkly bodysuit. She's wearing a pencil skirt and blouse, a stark contrast to Melanie's costume. There's nothing glamorous or overtly sexy about her outfit, but the curve of her hips in that black skirt, the way the light colored blouse hints at the bra she has on beneath it... shifting in the chair, my cock twitches in my pants as I take her in.

My head snaps to the left as the door opens to the ballroom and four men walk in, each one wearing a similar combination of dark clothing. I recognize the guitarist from a brief meeting the other day, with his long brown hair tied up into a knot on the top of his head. I can't see the other three clearly from where I sit, but it's safe to assume they're the rest of the band members.

They make their way over to the photographers, who immediately push them through to the makeup team, before dragging them to the set where Melanie waits.

The entourage of people move around the space for several hours while Melanie rotates through a series of costumes, her band members remaining in their original outfits. Each series of shots presents a clear dichotomy: the shiny, sparkly pop star with four burly band members in the backdrop of every photo. They shift through poses, scenery, and lighting as the photographers click away, capturing damn near every minute on camera. Melanie's smile never fades or falters.

Natalie remains there the entire time as well, on the front lines fixing and fluffing each costume. I'm pretty sure they have a wardrobe person here, but Natalie doesn't seem to notice, or care, as she flits around Melanie, making sure everything is flawless for each shot.

When the shoot finally wraps up, the light is fading from the Nashville skyline. The orange streaks in the sky are spilling in through the large windows of the ballroom, tinting everything in warm hues.

Knox and I make our way over to Melanie just as she exits the changing room one last time. Natalie is hot on her heels, and the four of us make a quick and quiet exit, retracing our steps through the building, this time leaving out the back exit and into the waiting SUV. It's silent as we make our way back toward the office. The girls are both curled up in their seats, heads lolled against the windows, clearly exhausted from the busy day.

When we pull up at the front of the MBM offices, Natalie gathers her things, quickly wrapping her arms around Melanie as she says, "Good work today. You killed it, as always."

Melanie smiles back at her. "Are you sure you don't want to come back to my house for dinner? You just worked for like twelve hours. Turn it off and take a break."

A look of concern crosses Melanie's face, but Natalie brushes it away. "Not tonight. I left a few projects on my desk, and I want to get them finished before I head home. I'll order something for delivery here."

She shimmies her way toward the door of the vehicle.

Shifting toward the exit, I lean forward, opening the door. "I'll see you up. I have to grab some paperwork from Knox's office before I take off, anyway."

I can hear the long exhale that escapes her as the two of us climb out of the back seat. Sweeping my hand out in front of me, I let Natalie lead the way into the building, both of us silent as we make our way to the elevator and step inside. I'm careful to keep as far away as the small box will allow while we wait impatiently for the car to arrive on our floor.

"So, your sister's publicist? How long have you been doing that?" I mean the question genuinely, but it comes out sounding more judgmental than I intended.

"Four years with Mel. I'm sure you think it's nepotism, but I'm more than qualified for this job." She shoots me a look, leaning away from me.

"I was just asking. I never said that—"

"Your face said it for you." She crosses her arms, her hip popping as she does.

A short laugh slips out of me. I may not have said it, but I did think it, she's right. Everything Gunner has shared about Melanie would lead me to believe that's exactly the case. But then again, so far what I see and what he's shared don't mesh, so I'm unsure what to believe.

One thing that is abundantly clear though is that this woman has no qualms about saying exactly what's on her mind. "Honest to a fault, too, aren't you?"

Natalie stares at me, her nose wrinkling. "I've spent almost a decade in corporate PR positions. I started as an intern in college and have painstakingly worked my way through this industry, carved out a place for myself on my own, before I started working directly for Melanie. I wasn't about to come here until I brought something to the table she needed; certainly not just because she's my sister."

I've clearly hit a nerve, but I'm not going to lie; seeing her fired up like this is entertaining. It's a different kind of attitude than I've gotten from her, and I like the fire behind her eyes. I don't reply to that, the venom in her voice making it clear this is not up for debate.

"Are you sure you're qualified to be working for Melanie? You seem a little…" She trails off, her eyes roaming over me, not at all shy as she takes me in. I might have offended her, but she's not put off by it.

"Oh, this ought to be good." I lean forward, closing the gap between us. "A little what, Natalie?"

She cuts her eyes back to mine, straightening her back before she says, "Inexperienced."

It takes everything in me to keep a straight face, the urge to laugh out loud strong, but I keep my features neutral. I don't answer her, instead scoffing at her assumption.

Undeterred, she presses on. "You're Knox's shadow? That's cute. Just how long have you been doing this?"

I slide my hands into my pockets, leaning back against the side of the elevator. "Making a lot of assumptions tonight, aren't you? If you had stayed for the whole meeting this morning, you would have gotten my detailed resume."

She looks immediately offended. "Excuse me for having actual work to do. I, unlike you, am in charge here. I don't get the luxury of playing second fiddle."

I roll my eyes at that, unable to keep from reacting to her verbal sparring. "Hardly second fiddle here, honey."

Her jaw ticks as she glares at me, fingers tightening on her still-crossed arms. "Keep telling yourself that because from where I'm standing, you're not the one calling the shots, are you?"

"Nope. But maybe I took this job because I don't want to be."

This time she scoffs. "Or I'm right, and you're just inexperienced."

I take a step in her direction, closing the space between us. She has to tip her head back to maintain eye contact. Even in her heels, there's still a noticeable height difference. "I've been working some form of personal security for over a decade. My roster of clients is longer than your little black book. My credentials are the last thing you need to concern yourself with. I took this job because it presented itself at the right time, not because I'm unqualified for anything else."

I watch as she swallows, her face remaining a perfect mask of indifference.

I quirk a brow. "Aren't publicists supposed to be friendly? Maintain a positive public image and all that?"

"You're confused." She uncrosses her arms, taking a step toward me, the space between us mere inches now. "My job is protecting Melanie's image. I couldn't care less what you think of me, *honey*."

Before I can reply, the elevator dings as it reaches our floor. Without another word, she steps around me and through the open doors. I follow her out, watching as she turns away from me, our respective destinations on opposite sides of the floor.

"Have a good night, Jake." She says sharply, ever the professional, her back to me as she heads down the hall.

"Yeah, you too." I reply, more to myself than to her. I watch as she disappears around the corner before I move toward Knox's office.

I've known this woman in a professional capacity for a day, but it's already obvious she doesn't miss a detail. Her title might be publicist, but as far as I can tell, she's a one-woman show keeping everyone hyper-focused on Melanie and the tour. She seems like the kind of woman who has to know everything, whether or not it involves her, which means I need to be careful. No one on this team knows my connection to Gunner, and, as far as I'm concerned, that's not information anyone needs to find out.

SIX

NATALIE

Whatever You Need

"Oh my god, stop. Or that trip to the Mall of America where they had those penny machines everywhere and Natalie made us stop at every. Single. One?" Melanie is laughing, her entire body shaking as one hand holds her glass, the red wine sloshing against the sides, the other coming up to cover her mouth.

Melanie and I met Dex at a cute little farm-to-table restaurant just outside of downtown Nashville for dinner. It's one of our favorite places to eat because they are known for catering to high-profile celebrities, making it another on the short list of places we feel comfortable coming to eat publicly.

The three of us are seated on a private balcony overlooking the interior courtyard of the restaurant. It's peaceful and just what I needed after a hectic week of work. We used to have these dinners more often, but ever since Melanie announced the tour, our sole focus has been on preparing for that, and prioritizing family dinners fell by the wayside.

At the moment, the two of them are having a great trip down memory lane at my expense, recounting the annual family vacations my parents used to plan, back before they passed away. Knox and Jake are both here, standing inconspicuously off to the side. Knox is never willing to take us up on the offer to join the table when he's on the clock. Jake seems to have followed his lead, and while the physical distance is great, I can still feel his eyes on me as he watches me from across the small space.

It's been almost two weeks since our official meeting at the MBM offices. Two weeks of seeing him damn near everywhere I go. He's become impossible to avoid, always right there anytime I'm with Melanie and Knox. He's curt and grumpy most of the time, so in return, I'm tense and snappy. It's clear we're not going to get along, but the constant over-analyzing of every move I make is starting to exhaust me. I've convinced myself I've moved on from our first couple of meetings, put the embarrassment behind me, but I'm still cautious around him, afraid to give him any other reasons to think I'm incompetent. It's clear he thinks Mel hired me because I'm her sister, and I've made it my mission to prove him otherwise.

"Ok, but listen. I still have those pennies, so it was an investment, really." I sip my wine as the two of them trade looks across the table from me.

Dex cuts off a piece of his steak, shoveling it in his mouth with a scoop of potatoes. "Yeah, those pennies and about 1,500 more from every trip we've ever been on."

"So sue me. Those are good memories. I love my pressed penny collection. I found those cute little books they all go in."

"Sorted and organized by date, right?" Melanie is snickering again, full-blown hysteria one more joke away.

"I mean, it's a logical solution." It's embarrassing how easy I am to read, even if they are the two people who know me better than anyone else. "Besides, I stopped that when the family trips stopped. It's been years since I've added a new penny to the books."

"We're just picking on you. That's our job, isn't it?" Dex smirks at me, a boyish grin painted on his face.

"You two are menaces." They busy themselves with eating as I sip on my wine, debating a second glass.

"Honestly though, it's a cool collection." Dex wipes his mouth, dropping his napkin back into his lap as he leans forward, resting his forearms on the edge of the table. "You shouldn't have stopped."

"It lost some of its appeal when the vacations stopped. No one wants a pressed penny from a random tourist attraction in Nashville." I set my wine back down, stabbing at a couple of pieces of chicken on top of my salad.

"We're about to go on tour." Melanie says excitedly. "It would be the perfect time to start again! You could grab a new penny from each city."

"I'm thirty-four years old now; I think I've outgrown it at this point."

"Not if you love them," she argues.

"It really doesn't matter either way. I don't have time to hunt down tourist traps for the sake of childhood memories. I'll be working." I push the salad around my plate as she stares at me.

I make the mistake of looking up, catching Jake's eyes trained on me as I do. He smirks as he mouths the word, "pennies?" at me.

I set my fork down, picking up my napkin. Pretending to wipe my mouth, I use the movement as an excuse to flip my middle finger in Jake's direction. His sudden cough sounds an awful lot like a laugh as I turn my attention back to my meal.

"I'm just saying…" Mel forges on. "Think about it. Your collection is cool. I don't have anything like that."

"You don't collect anything?" Dex asks. "I think your collection of awards would beg to differ."

Melanie laughs. "Fair enough, but those aren't *really* the same thing. There's no childhood nostalgia when I look at them."

"Yeah, I can see how looking at a shiny Grammy doesn't feel sentimental at all." Melanie throws her napkin at Dex for that comment. He snatches it out of the air, dropping it next to him on the table.

I continue eating my salad, ignoring their antics, far too familiar with the back and forth of the two of them. Part of me loves the playfulness of their relationship. Part of me is envious. I seem to have missed that personality trait.

"Listen, I'm good, ok?" I take another sip of my wine. "I don't need to dredge up old memories."

"Ok, fine. But no one here thinks it's dumb or pointless. It's ok to have something for yourself, just because you want to." Mel returns to her own plate, the conversation dropped.

The two change the topic, animatedly talking about a TV show that follows the crew on a cruise ship somewhere down by New Zealand. Dex immediately jumps in to talk over Melanie as they go back and forth arguing about the newest deckhand. I have no idea what they're talking about, and I'm struggling to even follow along as they gossip about the drama at the black tie dinner on board, so I sit back, enjoying my wine as the two of them rile each other up.

When Dex begins vehemently defending something the captain said last episode, I decide I'm too sober for this conversation and flag down our server.

"Excuse me. Sorry. Can you bring another bottle when you have a chance?" I pluck the bottle of red wine off the table, wiggling it between my thumb and forefinger.

Maybe enough glasses will drown out this uncomfortable feeling of loneliness in a room full of people.

We say goodbye to Dex an hour and a half later. Since I polished off the better part of the second bottle by myself, Mel is driving us home. The two of us are upfront in Mel's car. Knox and Jake are sitting quietly in the back, eyes focused on the passing scenery outside the car's window. It isn't often we drive ourselves anymore these days, and while the two imposing presences in the backseat don't really allow us to feel like we're alone, we can pretend.

I connect my phone to her radio, streaming our favorite local show, The Tracks. We've worked with Austin and Indy, the show's hosts, a few times in the past on press and promotion for Mel's album releases, and we always loved hanging out with them. Over the years, we've become regular fans of their show.

Mel taps her fingers on the steering wheel, both of us quiet as we listen to Austin and Indy debate the best song on the newest Billboard Top Ten List for a while. I'm about to turn on a playlist, so we can have our own debate over the best songs, when they suddenly shift topics, diving into breaking news on "one of Nashville's hottest couples."

Somehow, I know this segment is about Melanie before they even get into it. My stomach sinks as I turn the volume up.

"Straight out of The Grapevine, America's top print tabloid, we're being told a new story is dropping tomorrow morning—an exclusive interview with the CEO of River Pearl Records, Gunner Greene. Greene opened up to The Grapevine about his separation from his wife of three years, pop star Melanie Bennett. We've got a verified caller on the line right now, who works for The Grapevine, dropping in to give us the scoop on what to expect tomorrow morning."

The voices on the radio fade to white noise as I focus on the road, breathing in deeply through my nose and out through my mouth. A high pitch ringing starts in my ears, and when I glance over at my sister, her face has lost all color. Her knuckles are white as she grips the steering wheel. Suddenly, the car slows, and Mel eases the vehicle off the expressway, pulling onto the narrow shoulder and flipping the hazards on.

My hands ache from digging my nails into my fists, tiny crescents peppering my palms. I rub the painful indentations as I force myself to tune back into the hosts and their caller.

"Thanks so much for having me, Austin! You know I love getting to hang out with you and Indy."

"Thanks so much for calling in. We're excited to have you here to share this breaking story. So tell us, what are we going to see tomorrow in the new Grapevine article?" Austin's deep voice should sound soothing, but right now it's a cheese grater on my nerves.

"I can't give you all the details, of course, but I can tell you one thing Austin, it's gonna be a doozy. Greene has made some pretty serious allegations against his wife and boy, he did not hold back on any of the details. You may be hearing it through The Grapevine, but this hot gossip is gonna be juicy."

I immediately turn the radio off, slamming my finger into the power button. That fucking tagline is so stupid. That fucking tabloid is...

I'm too angry to finish my thought. Mel throws me a dirty glare for turning the radio off. I take a deep steadying breath, knowing it's my job right now to pull myself together. Sometimes it gets hard when your client is your sister, but this is what she pays me to do.

So I'll do it.

I'll pretend.

"He's not about to reveal what the article says. It's just a teaser. There's no point in listening to the whole thing and getting even more worked up than we already are. Let's just—"

My phone pings in my lap, a Google Alert flashing across the screen. Snatching my phone up, I swipe to unlock it. I click through apps quickly, loading the alert.

As the screen flips over, I see the breaking news.

Gunner Greene tells all!

Gunner Greene: coming clean.

Within moments, my phone starts blowing up. Messages ping through in the notification bar in quick succession, my assistant and my brother both filling the screen:

JAMIE

Natalie, you need to call me IMMEDIATELY.

I need to know what you want to do.

DEX

What is this? [image attached]

What the fuck is going on?

JAMIE

This is everywhere, Natalie.

I'm internally berating myself for not knowing this was coming, for not having a heads up on this article dropping. How did The Tracks get this information before anyone else? I have an entire team working for me to keep an eye out for *anything.* I've spent years building relationships and close contacts so that surprises like this don't happen.

A knock on the window has me jumping, the seatbelt locking as it digs into my shoulder with the speed of the moment. I look over toward the driver's side to see Knox, his knuckle brushing the glass as he pulls his hand back and opens the door.

When did he get out of the car?

His face is sympathetic as he says, "Come on, Mel, let me drive us back. You and Natalie can take the backseat and do whatever you need to do."

She nods, climbing out of the vehicle. My nerve endings are still firing on all cylinders as I unbuckle my seatbelt and step out into the cool night air, goosebumps immediately pebbling my skin. I turn to face Jake, who has stepped out as well. He holds a hand out to me, helping me around the open door on the steep shoulder of the road. I feel his fingers graze my lower back as I pass in front of him. Flinching away from his touch, I drop into the backseat. As soon as I'm settled, he gently closes the door, his eyes meeting mine from the other side of the glass, a softness in them I haven't seen before. I turn my head, ignoring him as he slides into the passenger seat in front of me.

Annoyance rolls through me, adding to the utter frustration I feel. The last thing I want right now is his sympathy.

We're quiet for a while as I thumb through my phone, reading the messages, opening up a link from my assistant with more information on the article. No one knows exactly what the article says. There are just endless promises that it's going to be "shocking" and "reveal all."

... just what the fuck is it going to be revealing?

I'm flipping through my mental file cabinet, trying to decide what would be such a dirty secret it would immediately start a fire like this. As far as I know, Melanie doesn't have any skeletons in her closet. She just has one shitty ex who treated her like she was worth less than those stupid pennies she and Dex were teasing me about.

I look over at Melanie, but she shakes her head, her eyes brimming with tears. I know if there was something truly scandalous that Gunner could use as ammo against her, I would already know about it.

I send off texts to my team, immediately working to gather as much information as possible, as quickly as I can. I need to fix this, but I'm so blindsided, I'm scrambling.

Fucking Gunner. *Of course, he would create a huge publicity stunt. I should have expected this move from him.* He's been a giant pain in the ass throughout this entire divorce. It was foolish to think that his bad attitude was going to be the extent of it. That's not his style. He has always taken every opportunity to gain clout, spin stories, and get his name in the headlines. I should have expected something like this.

"Knox, can you take me to the office?" I glance up to see Melanie staring listlessly out the window, her eyes glazed over, deep in thought. I won't be sleeping tonight, so I might as well try to get a head start on fixing this.

"And then take Mel home?" I add.

She shoots me a dirty look, but I hold up my hand.

"We don't know what's happening. We don't know the scale of this. It's better if you go home, where we all know you're safe, while we wait. I don't want you at the office; that's the first place the paparazzi will show up."

"Fine," she concedes, though clearly unhappy with the idea.

"As soon as we have any information at all, I'll call. You know I won't leave you out of the loop."

"I know." She sighs heavily before shifting her attention to the front seat. "Jake? Will you go with her?"

I freeze in my seat, my entire body going rigid. "That's... probably unnecessary. I'm just going to be working in the office."

"I know, but I'd feel better if you weren't alone in the middle of the night with shit hitting the fan. Please, Nat? For me?"

The puppy-dog eyes win me over, as they do every time, and I nod quietly.

"Of course, Melanie, whatever you need." Jake's voice is firm, but quiet. He doesn't turn around, his eyes remaining on the road in front of us.

This time it's me sighing heavily, but I shelve my personal feelings so I can focus on my sister. Quickly, I move over to the middle seat, replacing my seatbelt, before I pull on Mel's arm, tugging her close enough to me so that I can wrap my arms around her. I don't know what to say to her right now, so I say nothing. We ride in silence, her head on my shoulder.

It takes a small eternity for Knox to get us back to town, even though I'm sure he was doing well over the speed limit the entire way back. When Knox pulls up in front of the building, I grab Melanie's hand, squeezing tightly as I silently reassure her I will fix this.

No matter what it takes, I will fix this.

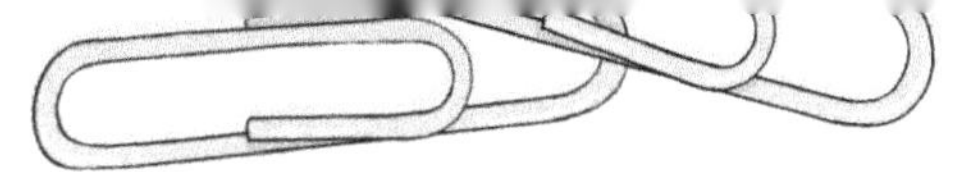

SEVEN
NATALIE

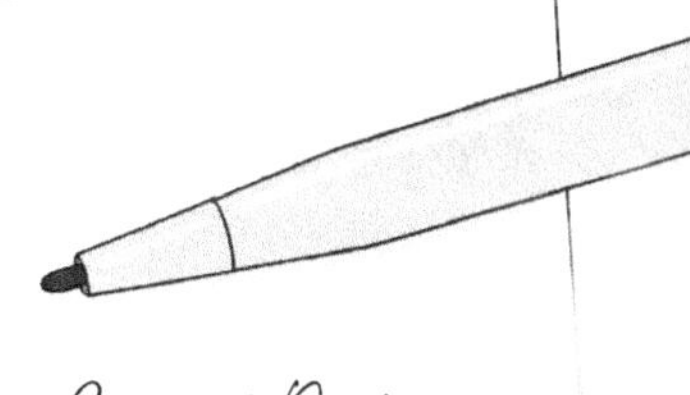

It's nearly 4am and Jake and I are still at the office. I called in reinforcements, so my brother and both our assistants are here too.

Does Dex have the PR experience to be dealing with this?

No, not at all.

But since it's our sister who is about to be all over the news, and since I'm in dire need of an immediate solution, I called him in. And Grayson, his assistant, showed up shortly after with coffee, donuts, and one fiery attitude that is single-handedly keeping me going at this early hour.

I've reached out to everyone I know, and I mean literally *everyone I know,* looking for someone who could get me an early copy of the article that Gunner is publishing. The fact that it's the middle of the night is making it hard to reach people, but that's not stopping me from trying.

It was Dex who finally had success, reaching a contact of his from The Grapevine's sister company who was willing to call in a favor and snatch a copy of the magazine from the printing room for us. Apparently, the digital files are all encrypted until publication, but the print version is easier to get a few hours in advance.

It irks me to no end that Dex is the one who had the solution to this piece of the problem. I wasn't even able to get the information we need, much less combat it. I feel like I'm at least eight steps behind in this mess, and the pressure of failure is weighing heavily on my shoulders. I have one job.

One job.

Protect my sister.

And I'm failing over and over again tonight.

I groan as I lean back in my chair, stretching my legs under my desk, the stiffness in my body reaching the point of pain from damn near twenty-four hours in these heels.

We're currently waiting for Dex's friend to show up with the magazine. Dex is scrolling on his phone on the couch in my office. Jamie, my assistant, and Grayson are out in the conference room next to us, fielding the overnight phone calls and emails from the press for us. It's true what they say; *gossip never sleeps.*

An energy drink appears on the desk in front of me, Jake's low voice cutting through the silence in the room. "Felt like you could use a pick-me-up."

I wearily lift my eyes to meet his. His face remains emotionless, that usual mask of indifference firmly in place, but his eyes sparkle in the office lighting, like maybe there's more to him than his harsh exterior.

"Oh, thank you." I reach for the can, cracking the tab open as he retreats, making his way back to the chair in the opposite corner of the room. The one he's been occupying since Knox dropped us off.

My mind is a mess. I can't deal with this PR disaster, my sister's personal nightmare, and deal with Jake. We've spent two weeks at each other's throats, and on the drive here, he flips a switch. If he thinks I need him to be nice to me now, he's mistaken.

My emotions are as frustrating as this fucking article, and I'm tired. A stray piece of hair falls into my eyes, and I rip the ponytail holder out of my hair, combing through the tangled mess before quickly tying it back up out of my face.

The whole situation is impossible. We know that whatever Gunner is up to is not going to be good. We know he's going to drag Melanie through the mud, but the man is a loose cannon. He could say or reveal anything in this article, and with shit like this, it's almost always one person's word against the other's. You have a leg up when the first word is yours, whether or not it's the truth.

My phone chimes with an incoming feed from the building's intercom system. I hit the connect button and see Dex's friend standing out front, a large manila packet in her hands.

I'm out of my chair and down the hall before Dex and Jake can even clear the doorframe to my office. I jam the elevator button just as they both catch up to me.

Reaching the lobby, I take off in a run across the brightly lit space; the light bouncing off the shiny tiled floor, the smell of recently applied cleaning chemicals burning the insides of my sinuses. I reach the front door first, throwing it open to greet my savior.

"You are an absolute godsend, you know that?" I'm panting as I grab the manila envelope from her hands, ushering her into the lobby at the same time. Too anxious to wait until I'm back upstairs in my office, I leave her with Dex as I situate myself on the nearest lobby bench, unfolding the clasps on the envelope. Jake follows me, keeping his distance as he stands a few feet over.

She's stuffed several copies of the magazine in the envelope, so I pull at the top one and slide it out. I set the package aside and fan through the magazine, stopping abruptly when I come across Gunner's photo, taking up three quarters of the page midway through. He's wearing headphones, posed to look like he's working on something. His t-shirt reads, "cannot destroy."

You have got to be kidding me.

I scoff none too quietly before I start reading, my eyes flying across the page, my breath growing tighter with each new paragraph.

Six months ago, Gunner Greene and his soon-to-be ex-wife, Melanie Bennett, made a joint press release announcing their intent to separate. "We have made the tough decision to split," the couple said in the statement, which was later reported by The Grapevine in August. In the official release, the couple shared that they simply grew apart.

The Grapevine has come to learn the couple's split was less than amicable. River Pearl Records CEO, Gunner Greene recently sat down in our studio with columnist, Ryan Wilson, to set the record straight.

"You know, unfortunately for Mel and me, an amicable split just isn't on the table anymore." Gunner sits across from me in the lounge, his head hung low as he fiddles with the papers rolled up

in his hands. I can tell this is hard for him to share, but he bravely pushes on. "I tried, I really did. I wanted to make it work with Mel. In an industry like this one, it's so hard to find that one person who wants the real you, as you are. I thought I had that with Melanie, but it turns out she didn't feel the same."

I give Gunner some time to collect his thoughts, but the next thing he reveals is the last thing I expected. "Things had been difficult at home, you know how it can get sometimes, with all the travel. Releasing a new album and planning a tour would stress anyone out, but once Melanie's behavior turned manipulative and verbally abusive, I knew our marriage would not last."

His eyes shine as Gunner goes on to reveal intimate details about the end of his marriage. Obviously overcome with emotion, he briefly summarized the crux of the issue: Melanie, fresh off the release of her sixth studio album, Far From Alone, became aggressive and emotionally unstable.

The revelation of Melanie's toxic behavior came as a complete shock to everyone at The Grapevine Studio. Nashville's sweetheart, it turns out, isn't so sweet. "It's hard," Gunner concludes in our interview, "when you think you know someone, but it turns out, you never really knew them at all. I think the pressure to perform just ate at her. And now the woman I'm married to is someone I don't know at all..."

I slam the paper down in my lap. My chest constricts as my breaths come short and fast. Of all the things my mind had conjured up in the last ten hours, this was not one of them. Gunner is a tool, for sure, but I didn't think he was an outright liar.

Sitting there, mouth agape, Dex comes over and settles beside me. He gently removes the packet of magazines from my lap, pulling out a copy for himself, and diving into the article.

I continue to sit there, staring aimlessly at the stark white walls across the room from me, turning the information over in my head.

Once.

Twice.

Three times I mentally comb back through the article, trying to understand how someone could do this.

It's *cruel.*

If his goal is to ruin the tour, I think he's on the right track. This is going to be a disaster to clean up.

From a personal standpoint though, I'm devastated. Who does this to someone they claim to love? Or used to love?

I have had my own issues in the past. Failed relationships that have made me more than a little wary about love as a concept. But watching the way my sister, the kindest human who wants nothing but the best for everyone, has been dragged through the mud, used as fodder in Gunner's sick game... it cuts deep. Leaves a scar that reminds me love is fickle.

Convenient when it works in your favor.

Devastating when it's wielded against you.

I'm pulled from my internal spiral when Dex's head snaps up, finally finished reading. His eyes are wide with worry, and I know he's thinking the same thing I am.

What is this going to do to our sister?

And how the hell do we fix this before the tour starts?

EIGHT
JAKE

What Am I Missing?

Melanie's house later that morning is absolute pandemonium. Every seat in the oversized kitchen and most of the living room are filled with people. Melanie and Dex are sitting at the kitchen table, heads bent over a computer screen. Several members of each of their teams, and the entire social media team, are also filling out the giant table.

Out on the back deck, I can see Melanie's manager, Jason, with Natalie, the two of them having a heated conversation if the arm gestures and finger pointing are anything to go by. I watch as she speaks animatedly, her red hair shining in the morning sun. The woman is a fucking magnet for my attention, and I can't figure out how to stop the pull.

Last night was a long one. Spending hours in the office with Natalie, and later Dex and their assistants, was enlightening, to say the least. Natalie is every bit the powerhouse I made her out to be at the photoshoot. She was a one-woman show, busting ass to get her hands on a copy of that magazine. She claims she called Dex in because she needed extra hands, but if we're being honest, he didn't do much. He made a few phone calls, and yeah, it was him in the end with the contact at the printer, but it was Natalie putting in the time. The effort. Dex got lucky.

The woman is high-strung, and that's putting it nicely. The anxiety she's dealing with over this situation is palpable. I've enjoyed our back and forth for the last couple of weeks, but adding to her stress last night felt... *wrong*.

I had little to do overnight besides watch them work, and it was clear Natalie's entire focus is her family. It goes completely against how I've lived my life, barely speaking to my siblings, never reaching out to my parents, despite all four of my remaining family members being alive and well. I don't try to connect. I never have.

With Natalie, things are *very* different. I've worked with a lot of high-profile clients over the years, but the relationship the three of them have is unique. Unique and likely to make my job here harder.

But that's a worry for another time.

I watch Natalie pace the deck as she continues to talk *at* Melanie's manager. I'm no longer convinced he's actively taking part in the conversation based on their body language. Her tall heels move across the boards, the motion fluid and elegant. Despite the late night and early morning, Natalie still showed up here completely put together, looking gorgeous, even with no sleep. She stopped at home on her way over from the office, swapping one uniform for another. Her usual pencil skirt is visible underneath a black coat, the bright blue color of her skirt a stark contrast to the creamy color of her skin and the dark tones of the jacket.

A loud noise from the opposite side of the counter grabs my attention. I shake my head, realizing I've been standing here for far too long, watching Natalie as she works. I scan the room quickly, everyone deep in their own conversations, oblivious to my behavior.

Pivoting around, I make my way toward the other side of the island. Gleaming stainless appliances wink back at me in the stream of light coming through the windows. Knox is rifling through the fridge, so I move across the space, opting to wait for him as I lean against the granite countertop, crossing one leg over the other. It's several long seconds before he notices my presence, but I can see the look of relief on his face when he turns, his arms full of eggs, veggies, and two bags of shredded cheese. I reach out, grabbing several of the items off his pile and shuffle them over to the counter, setting them down as Knox does the same with his ingredients beside me.

"I can't stand here and watch them lose their shit anymore, so I'm making omelets." He shrugs before bending down to rifle through the cupboard beneath us.

Arranging the items on the counter, I ask, "Doesn't Melanie have a chef for this?"

"She does, but she gave the staff the morning off so we could work here privately, at least until they have some sort of plan in place. I don't mind cooking. Honestly, I need something to do or I'm gonna lose my mind too."

He finds what he's looking for, pulling two stainless steel pans out from the cupboard and setting them on the stovetop. He turns the burners on, leaving the pans to warm before adding a set of mixing bowls to the countertop beside me.

"Do we think this is the best idea, having everyone here at Melanie's house?" I scan my eyes over the people filling the kitchen.

"It's safer for Melanie. I don't want her going downtown with this article breaking. The paparazzi are going to be bloodthirsty. They'll be dying for a shot of her after this. You saw the gate. It's gonna be ten times worse in the city if they get wind she's out and about."

I nod in acknowledgment, having driven through the hoard of paparazzi on my way up her driveway this morning. If Knox thought they were a problem before today, they're about to become vultures.

Gunner and I are not particularly close, but the fact that he would drop an article like this is surprising to me. We've talked enough over the years that I definitely got the impression his relationship with Melanie wasn't great, but I didn't think it was quite *this* bad. I've spent the last couple of weeks trying to mesh the Melanie that Gunner has portrayed with the Melanie I'm now working for, and the two are not lining up.

I'm lost in my head as I help Knox, both of us busying ourselves moving around the kitchen. About thirty minutes later, Asher strolls into the house to join us. He lets out a low whistle when he sees us and shakes his head, meandering over to where Knox and I are now plating the finished omelets for everyone.

"What's up, *Martha*?" Asher eyes the omelets. He reaches out to snatch a cherry tomato from the basket next to the plates. "These look good."

Knox smacks his hand, pointing at him. "Not yours. Get out of here."

He laughs, stealing a tomato anyway, then plops his ass on a bar stool at the island.

I like Asher. We haven't spent a ton of time together since I've been on the job, but aside from Knox, he's the Shield employee I've had the most contact with. He's younger than me by several years, but his outgoing personality and sense of humor are tolerable, unlike most guys in their early twenties. In the close quarters of a tour like this, it's nice to know he's someone I can get along with easily.

We distribute omelets around to the group, leaving extra on the island for Natalie and Melanie's manager, who are still outside on the back porch.

Asher and I grab the remaining plates, but before I can sit down, Knox quietly ushers us into the formal dining room through a door on the opposite side of the kitchen. He drops into the seat at the head of the table, while I settle in at his right and Asher takes his left.

"So, what happens now?" Asher breaks the silence before he takes a big bite of his omelet.

Knox shakes his head and swallows his own bite of food. "Honestly, I don't know, man. The press situation has been ramping up slowly as the tour gets closer, but this? It's going to push them right over the edge. I want to see what Melanie's PR team comes up with before I go see Connor. Knowing their plans will help."

We eat quietly for a few minutes, each of us mulling over his own thoughts. I'm the first to dive back into the conversation, curiosity getting the better of me.

"What's the angle here?" I ask, wiping my mouth before balling the napkin up and dropping it next to my place. I've been trying to answer this question on my own all morning. "What does he gain from releasing an article like this?"

Knox looks up, fork frozen in mid-air. He sets it down slowly as he contemplates my question.

"I don't know the motives, but honestly, a stunt like this is very on-brand for him. I've worked for Mel since before the two of them were married and, genuinely..." He looks around carefully before he continues, "I cannot fathom why she ever married him. The dude is an asshole. I never liked the guy."

I find Knox's disdain for Gunner surprising, but I'm careful to keep my face neutral as I process what he just said. "Not a fan?"

"No, not at all. The guy's a snake. He's hungry for money, and he'll push until he gets what he wants." He takes a sip of his orange juice, setting it back down with a loud echo as the glass meets the wooden tabletop. "About a year into their marriage, he dropped the nice guy façade and the real Gunner showed up. I always got a weird vibe from the guy, but it's not really the bodyguard's place to question the client's choices, you know?"

I nod, leaning back in my chair, crossing my arms over my chest as he continues.

"If you want my opinion, he was never in it for the right reasons. I think he just saw her potential. And he pushed her to reach it, but not for her. For himself. She released three albums during the four years of their relationship. That pace is unheard of in the industry. I don't think it was solely her ambition pushing her to work that hard."

I take in what Knox is saying, aligning it with the things I know about Gunner personally. I have always known him to be an industry powerhouse. He was pretty popular on his own several years back, but when he started signing other artists to his label, that's when he really grew in notoriety. I've known him to have an attitude, but it's always seemed to me more like a man in power, familiar with people working under him. I've never considered it from another angle before.

"Doesn't the industry hold Gunner in pretty high regard?" I word my question carefully, wanting Knox's answers without wanting to push too hard or reveal too much. This is the first time I've seen someone with such a dislike of the man. I just can't discern whether it's because Knox is close to Melanie or if I've missed something along the way.

"They worship the ground he walks on. His public face and his real face are two very different masks. And Mel's too polite to show the world what an ass he is. She thinks the drama belongs behind the scenes."

"Interesting," I mumble to myself.

"Didn't he get sketchy toward the end there?" Asher directs his question at Knox. "I feel like I remember you saying something along those lines a while back."

"Yeah, he started cutting me out. The press was milder back then, and I didn't have to be everywhere Mel went, but even with my more lax schedule, he started cutting hours, switching my shifts. He'd dismiss me in the middle of the day unexpectedly, or right before events, at times when it didn't make sense."

"For what purpose?" Something isn't adding up, but I can't put my finger on it.

"Can't say. There didn't seem to be any rhyme or reason. I tried to stay out of it because Melanie insisted everything was fine. I did my job in public and left them to it when they went home."

"Bold move to print blatant lies, though. He must have something to back up his claims. Otherwise, why would he go to the press with false accusations?"

"No one ever accused Gunner of being smart. He's conniving and clever, sure, but not particularly intelligent. He has nothing." Knox sounds confident, and as the person spending all of his time with Melanie, I'm inclined to believe he's telling the truth.

"So how long have you been doing around the clock coverage for her?" I shift gears, feeling uncomfortable prodding any further.

"Since she left Gunner. The public took an immediate interest, and she wasn't comfortable going anywhere alone. I started the new contract within days of their separation."

I take that in for a minute before I excuse myself. Standing, I collect my dishes and trash, bringing everything with me back into the kitchen.

As I rinse my plate in the sink, I contemplate Gunner's side of this situation. There has to be more to this story. The question is... what am I missing?

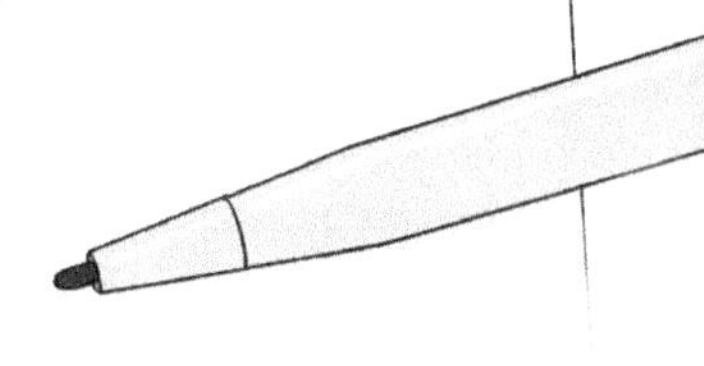

NINE
NATALIE

Dex pushes a plate of food in front of me as I drop into an open spot at the table. My mouth waters at the scent of eggs and fried vegetables. I eye the omelet, smothered in cheese, as I mindlessly grab my fork and immediately shove a large bite into my mouth.

Looking up, I meet my brother's eyes as he places a cup of coffee in front of me as well. He gives me a weak smile before turning away. Returning moments later, he takes the seat next to Melanie, pushing a matching cup of coffee in her direction. She wraps her hands around the mug, dropping her head onto his shoulder. She looks exhausted, with deep purple circles blooming under her eyes, her dark hair piled on top of her head in a haphazard bun. It's been a long fucking night for us, but I can only imagine how much worse Melanie is feeling right now.

I inhale my cup of coffee, sucking down large gulps between bites of the omelet. I've been too worked up and distracted to realize how hungry I was, but now that there's piping hot food in front of me, my stomach has taken notice.

As soon as I'm done, I clear my dishes from the table. I turn, intent on making for the coffeepot when I see Jake coming from the opposite side of the kitchen, already doing the same. Spinning quickly on my heel, I decide to skip the coffee, opting instead to continue my current record of avoidance, not having said a word to him yet this morning.

Childish? Maybe, but I've got work to do, and sparring with Jake is an unnecessary distraction.

I make my way back to the table before taking another seat, this time at the opposite end, right in the middle of our team.

The table is covered in papers, printouts of articles and commentary on The Grapevine's release this morning. Jamie has been working with the rest of our team here to gauge the level of damage we are working with. It's not been good. For every one article that gives Mel the benefit of the doubt, we find three more that are siding with Gunner.

She needs legal action; to sue him for damaging her reputation. But unfortunately, the damage is done. Going after him legally won't fix her reputation fast enough. Once gossip is out there, it's hard, if not impossible, to pull it back.

A bombshell like this could ruin the tour.

It could ruin Melanie.

A man in the industry with these kinds of accusations against him? *Oh, he's misunderstood. I'm sure there's an explanation. Well, that's just how men are.* His image isn't going to suffer in a world built for his success.

But a woman being accused of being manipulative and abusive? She will not get the same grace or even the *opportunity* to be heard. She's expected to be perfect, expected to be kind, beautiful, talented... the fact that Melanie *is* all those things doesn't matter when she's been painted to look like the villain. The second a woman falls outside the parameters of the industry expectations of her image, of her behavior, she has to fight twice as hard to clear her name.

There's no room for error when you're a woman.

And it doesn't matter whether or not the fault is hers.

For all I know, this was his intention. He's such a miserable fucker. I wouldn't put it past him to try to tank her tour before it's even officially started. Though, as an owning member of the label, he should know that's a stupid-ass move.

Whatever the reason for it, it's still my job to fix this, and I'm sitting here without a single goddamn idea of how we're supposed to repair my sister's reputation before this tour takes off. We're down to the wire with just over two weeks before we leave, and I need a solution. Now.

Every option has been considered. We've talked about the options we've used in the past to control press damage: releasing statements, an article of our own, a TV interview... every approach that we would normally take to refute a news article, but this time, it's not enough.

A rebuttal statement is going to look exactly like that: Melanie saying what she needs to say to take the heat off her.

With the entire country watching her, she needs more. She needs something that will prove beyond a shadow of a doubt that she is a good person.

I pull out my laptop, running my hands through my hair as I get comfortable in the chair. I catch the reflection of Jake and Knox on my blank screen, the two of them talking with Asher, who is barely visible behind their hulking forms.

I can see Jake's side profile immediately behind me, his focus straight ahead on Knox as he talks. His hair is styled as usual, swept back out of his face, looking significantly more put together than I feel this morning. He has several days' worth of stubble on his face, the sharp cut of his jaw hidden behind the hair, but somehow making him even more attractive.

Grumbling quietly to myself, I jam the power button on the computer, annoyed that the man has a way of capturing my attention every time we're in the same room. I have an awareness of his presence that I don't recognize with anyone else, and the fact that it's *there*, distracting me, is grating on my nerves.

Busying myself, I click through documents and articles, loading links from my team as I go through them all again. I scan the information we've already covered this morning, hoping that one of these items will spark something I can work with.

Several minutes pass, but nothing worth pursuing comes to mind. My conversation with Jason this morning was fruitless, although we spent hours hashing it out. His immediate position was wanting to punch back at Gunner, and I firmly believe that's not the best response here.

I click over to The Tracks website, opting to pull up the video version of their show from last night, listening to the teaser they dropped for today's article. I don't know what I'm expecting it to do for me, but my brain is so frazzled, starting back at the beginning to walk through the press won't hurt anything.

I slip my headphones in, listening to The Tracks hosts, Austin and Indy, chatter about the article. Gazing up over the top of my laptop, I stare out at Melanie's backyard, watching the trees sway slightly in the breeze. Austin's deep voice plays in my ear, talking about what to expect in the article.

I'm annoyed all over again, relistening to the conversation from last night. What a stupid way to start this segment when they never actually told you what was in the article. All they ever said was expect it to be big.

Expect a bombshell.

Expect big drama.

This industry is built on prefabricated expectations.

A light bulb goes off. My pulse quickens as my brain clicks the pieces into place, a plan suddenly coming together from the jumble of information floating around inside my head.

Jumping up from my seat, the chair screeches, sliding across the ceramic tiles as it pushes out behind me. The noise has every head turning in my direction.

"I know what to do!" I shriek. Realizing I still have the podcast playing in my ears, I yank my headphones out and place them down on the table.

Looking up, I meet the eyes of each person settled around the table, the adrenaline rush making me feel more awake than I have in days.

This is *it.* I know it is.

I dive straight in, forgetting no one else has my train of thought. "We need to hire The Tracks."

I'm met with silence. Confused faces and furrowed brows look back at me.

"We need to hire The Tracks to come with us on the tour," I try again. "We need to bring them along, let them film behind the scenes of everything that goes on: watching Mel prep for tour, being on the road, the shows, backstage… the whole thing!"

"I'm... not sure I see how that fixes things, Nat." Dex is flipping his pen through his fingers. Our assistants exchange looks. Melanie meets me with a blank stare, her mouth hanging open.

Realizing I need to walk them through this, I take a deep breath.

"People are reading this article, being *told* who Melanie is by Gunner and his team. Gunner is painting this picture, however inaccurately, of who Melanie is as a person. He's created expectations. When people look at her now, it's going to be through that filter. They're going to have preconceived notions about her character because they were told what to think already." I'm flying, the words tumbling from my lips at a rapid pace. I'm desperate to get this out before someone interrupts me. "We have to *show* people who Melanie is. We have to repaint the picture, reset those expectations. Sure, we could issue a statement or write our own article, but that's only going to add fuel to the fire. It's going to *look* like we're trying to fight Gunner..."

"... we are though?" Melanie cuts in.

"We are." I agree quickly. "But we don't want it to scream, 'Believe us and not Gunner!' That will not buy us allegiance. It's just going to make us look desperate to clear your name. We need to be more clever than that."

I lean forward, dropping my hands to the tabletop with a soft slap. "We need to give fans unshakable proof of who you are as a person."

I pause, looking around the room, watching the team contemplate what I'm saying.

"Think about it." I push back up, continuing. "The Tracks love behind-the-scenes features. They do it all the time. This is just something bigger, better for them. We can hire them to come on tour with us. They're around 24/7, filming their show on location. We're seeing Melanie in her element, learning who she is, effectively slamming everything that Gunner has claimed, but without ever saying a word directly to him or about the accusations."

Melanie chews on her nails, her eyes meeting mine. "I... don't know Natalie. I've always tried so hard to keep my personal life... personal. I don't love the idea of every moment being splashed across the internet."

"I know," I reassure her, meeting her eye. I need her to know I'm on her side, but I also need her to recognize the importance of doing this. "There are boundaries we can set to keep it from being overwhelming. But I don't think we have the option of leaving the door completely shut anymore. People believe Gunner because they have nothing else to go on. They don't *know* you. They have no idea how generous you are to your crew, that you make donations to the women's shelters in every city we visit, that you're constantly investing in small businesses. They only know what they've seen in the media, what they've been told. It's time we opened the door, *showed* them who you are. Actions speak louder than words and all that."

My gaze shifts as Dex chimes in. "What's the incentive for The Tracks, though? We're asking these two people, and probably part of their team, to give us months of their time? To travel the country? Why would they be on board at the drop of a hat? There's no way."

I chew my bottom lip as I think it through. He's right; I don't know if we have *enough* to offer to make this enticing for them.

"Well, obviously Melanie is a huge name in the music industry, so they would be attached to that. It would catapult their show, their brand. We would effectively be asking them to pick a side in this PR nightmare..." I trail off, trying to decide if that's going to be a problem. We have a casual relationship with them already, Mel having done a handful of shows with them in the past. I don't know if that's going to be enough, though. I don't know if they've already chosen a side, since they were the ones to break the news about the article.

"Well, the obvious perk is comping the travel." My assistant says from their end of the table. "We put them on our bus, put them up in a hotel, give them the space for recording their podcast on the road. We can even give them a meal stipend."

I can see Dex's wheels turning. It won't be cheap to bring on an extra team, especially so last minute, but in the grand scheme of the tour, it's really not *that* much. I scan around the table, looking at Mel's manager, who I can see is contemplating the idea.

"I think it's worth a shot," Dex taps his pen on the table. "It could work out really well for both parties if we can pull it off. But that's only if Melanie is open to the idea. It's her entire life she'd be putting on display. It's one thing when you're on stage in front of cameras; it's another when they follow you home later too. There will be no privacy. There will be no hiding."

He looks over at Mel, who meets his gaze. Something silent passes between them, and she nods, turning her head in my direction.

"I don't think I have a choice at this point. It's this or risk all the negative press burning this tour to the ground."

"No one is going to force this on you." I reassure her, hesitating before I continue. I decide quickly to just go with the truth. "I do think this is going to be the quickest, most effective way to turn the story around. It's immediate, and it's ongoing. We can grab people's attention now because they'll want to see inside Melanie's world—figure you out. If we can get them to stay, keep tuning in, we get the chance to show them the real you."

Melanie meets my eyes. She's always trusted me implicitly, even when I'm not sure I deserve that trust. I smile back at her, hoping she can feel my determination.

This is right. I know it is.

"And what about the immediate response right now?" Mel's manager interjects.

I mull that over again. *The question* we've been trying to flesh out all morning. I realize the answer is right in front of me.

"We don't give them one." I answer confidently. "We already know part of the reason Gunner did this was for attention. What we're doing right now, what we've been doing all night long, is exactly what he expected from us. He wanted the scramble, the panic... We need to go the other way. Give him absolutely nothing."

I'd laugh if I weren't so tired. It seems like the most obvious answer in the world. I was just too tunnel-visioned to see it.

"So, we're not going to even acknowledge the heinous article circulating all over the country right now?" he asks, leaning forward to rest his elbows on the table as he clasps his hands together in front of his face. He clearly doesn't like this approach.

"Melanie isn't, no. She's going to give them nothing." I reiterate firmly. "If you want to issue a statement, I think that's fair. Mel's management team could issue something short, rebuking the article, validating the team's experience working with her. We can give them that much.

"But Melanie should stay out of it right now. We continue on with the tour prep as if this never happened. I mean, obviously, we're going to be dealing with more paparazzi, more attention, a lot more eyes everywhere we go, but I think we can handle that. Not addressing the allegations will keep the interest up, and when the shows drop, people will want to listen and watch. They'll be looking for answers because we haven't given them any."

"If we're not tamping down the media interest, I assume we'll have a plan in place for increased security?" Dex jumps in, shifting topics, his eyes moving to Knox, sitting at the island behind me.

"Yeah." Knox leans forward, resting his elbows on his knees, running his hand through his hair. "I was waiting for your plan of action before I started thinking about changing the security protocols, but if this is what you're set on, we can start adjusting things on our side, too."

"What are your thoughts?"

"I think we'll pull up the schedule; start the twelve-person team full-time immediately. We'll have an increased presence at all the rehearsals and public outings. We'll make sure everything is coordinated to have several bodyguards when you have the crew together. The plan was always for Melanie to have two guards. Jake's already around most of the time. Asher can jump in full-time with Dex and Natalie."

Melanie drops her head, both hands scrubbing over her face before she looks back up, this time across the room at Knox. "I want someone with Natalie all the time too. Asher can't be split between them."

I snap my head back in her direction as she shoots me a look; her face etched with discomfort. I've never had full-time security of my own. The odd bodyguard at events, sure. But I've never needed or wanted someone with me *all the time.*

"That feels… unnecessary." I hedge.

Melanie ignores me, her gaze cutting back to Knox. "I want someone with her, Knox. She's my *publicist.* The only person who will be hounded more than me about all of this is going to be her," Melanie retorts firmly. "Put Asher with Natalie, even if it's just for a few weeks. She's going to need the added protection right now, too. The media are going to have a field day, and I don't want her in the line of fire."

Knox considers her request, mulling it over quietly as we wait. His eyes scan across the table and then back to Jake and Asher beside him. "Let's do this then. I want Jake with her. Asher, you can be my second."

I flick my eyes at Jake, sitting on the bar stool, his face empty of any reaction.

Why is this just my luck? My sister would want me to have a bodyguard, and it would be the one person who is on my last nerve.

"We don't have to upset the balance. There's no need to hash out all the security details right now, honestly. We can pick this up later." I offer, desperate to keep as much space from Jake as I can. I don't know what it is about him that sets me off like it does, but I *really* do not want to find out.

As if hearing my internal commentary, Knox rebukes it. "No, this is good. We're all here. I have clearance to do whatever needs to be done. I'll just file the changes later."

His eyes cut away from me, back to Melanie. "Jake has more experience. He's used to these situations. If we're splitting up, he's better solo. Asher would be a better fit with you and me than alone with Natalie."

"And Dex? We were supposed to be sharing someone?" I pipe up again. A last-minute attempt to derail this plan that is coming together a little too seamlessly.

"Honestly, I argued that from the beginning." Dex shifts in his chair. "That feels unnecessary to me. I'm hardly in the public eye. You and Melanie are the ones doing the public engagements, the ones out and about. I'd rather know you're taken care of. Give Natalie Jake. Let Mel take Asher. If I need someone, I'll let you know."

He glances toward Asher and Jake. Asher nods immediately.

Jake's eyes flick over to mine. Without looking away, he asks, "Are you sure that's the arrangement you want, Knox? Connor seemed firm about having me with Melanie."

I feel hot; my skin flushed from the intensity of his gaze. He clearly doesn't like this idea either. My eyes narrow as I meet his stare. I know why this is a miserable idea, but fuck him if he thinks working with me is going to be a pain in his ass.

His eyes stay locked on mine until Knox answers.

"If this is what Melanie wants, then yes. It makes the most sense. Asher is plenty qualified; you just have more experience. It makes more sense to split the two of us," his hands gesture between himself and Jake as he continues, "the two with the most familiarity in these situations. And this way, Mel gets what she asked for, and her coverage won't be compromised to do it."

Jake nods this time, and my stomach sinks as he replies, "Then that's what I'll do."

"Alright then." Knox slaps his knee as if to punctuate the end of the discussion. "I'll call Connor when we're done here and get the paperwork started."

Fan-freaking-tastic.

Now not only do I have to convince one of the hottest shows on air to readjust their plans for the next six months and join us on the road at the drop of a hat, but I also have to figure out how to survive six months with absolutely no separation from a man who is trying real hard to become my enemy.

I'm good at managing chaos, but this might be too much for even me to handle.

TEN
NATALIE

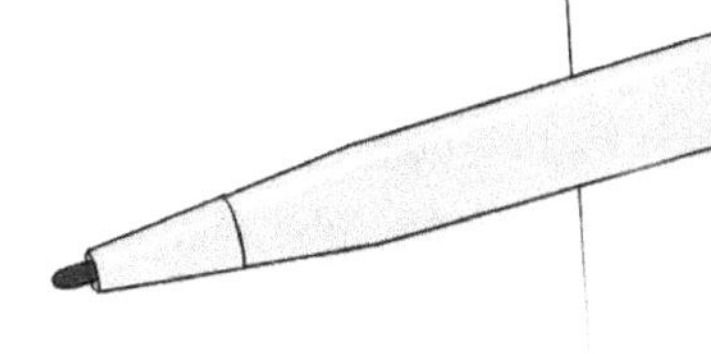

Frankly, Good Riddence

In the aftermath of the article's release, the fallout ended up being both what the team had expected and, somehow, also a total slap in the face.

As expected, the presence and interest in Melanie grew astronomically. Temporarily, the security team has had to put a full stop on any outside activities not directly related to the tour, hoping interest will die down quickly. Melanie's hounded anytime she sets foot outside her house. Her daily practice at the stadium now starts with a waiting crowd at the venue entrance. It's so overwhelming; an outsider would probably think she was having daily concerts with that many people showing up. The venue security and Shield have had to find a more discreet way for her to enter the premises.

Knox and Asher have their hands full with Mel's new security protocols. Chase, the fourth Shield lead, and his secondary crew are now all working full-time at the stadium as well, trying to keep things going as the tour draws closer, but still keeping everyone as safe as possible.

Unexpectedly, a 'Gunner Fan Club' has emerged from this whole thing. He's a well-known label executive, who has a past life as a musician himself, but it's been so long since he released anything under his own name. Seeing fan groups pop back up for him was shocking, to say the least. He's been out of the direct spotlight since before Melanie married him. Nonetheless, fans have resurfaced, showing up in the crowds waiting outside the stadium, with signs reading "Gunner deserved better" and "Loyal to Gunner."

The general sense of chaos has just amplified this week. As a result, I haven't gone anywhere except home or the office in days. I've spent the last few days completely immersed in this presentation, until eleven or twelve at night, back at it by seven the next day. Hardly taking any breaks during the day; I'm so hyper-focused on getting every detail just right. I have one chance to talk The Tracks into this. I can't afford to fuck it up.

Before the paperwork was even pushed through, Knox had Jake on my security detail. It's been interesting having him here in the office with me *every single day.* Jake's less than thrilled with this work schedule, but I can't see why he's complaining when he gets to spend all day couch-rotting, watching me work.

I'm still doing my best to avoid him, but in an office this small, it's impossible. He keeps doing nice shit, like refilling my coffee or grabbing an energy drink for me, and it's making it hard to continue to loathe him. Especially when every time he's near me, the scent of his cologne is all I can smell. I should hate it, but it smells so good. Several days in, and I can't escape it anymore; it's now just part of the air in my office.

Honestly, if anyone should be annoyed here, it's me. The one person I was keenest to avoid is now my full-time babysitter.

Sighing as I hit the icon on my browser, I run copies of the documents I've been working on for Indy and Austin. I hear the printer whirring to life across the room just as my phone rings.

Picking it up without a second glance at who is calling, I answer. "Natalie Bennett."

"Natalie, Dex Bennett here. How's it going?"

"You moron," I chide my brother. "What do you want?"

"You were way more friendly when you were being Publicist Natalie. Can I have her back?"

"I'm knee-deep in a project. I didn't even look at my phone before I answered. I might have hit ignore if I'd known it was you."

"Ouch, Nat. You wound me." I can practically see him clapping his hand over his heart. Dex is overly dramatic, all the time. He's always the life of the party, people gravitating toward his outgoing and energetic personality. It's so far removed from my personality that I have a hard time relating to it, but it fits him. He's always been the levity for the three of us siblings, and sometimes I wonder where we'd be without him. He carried us through our roughest patches with his easygoing nature and pure optimism. His humor is usually a personality trait I love about him, but it's more entertaining when I'm not trying to remain focused on something.

"I love you, and you know it. What's up?"

"I'm looking for that guide you did for me—the one with the bus driver's schedules and route maps. Thought I had them in my email, but I'm not finding them. I need to send the newest updates over to Grayson so he can double-check our accommodations. I thought he'd like your handiwork better than the original documents."

"You mean that 95-page directive with no table of contents or diagrams? Who wouldn't?" I smirk. "I'll forward them to Gray and cc you on the email. Do you want me to print you a copy for your binder as well?"

I make my way across the office, coming to a stop in front of the printer as I wait for the presentation to finish. I can feel Jake watching me from behind his phone screen, but I don't acknowledge him.

"You and I both know I don't use the tour binder. I love it. It's great, but I can't keep track of physical papers."

"Well, you can't keep track of emails either, apparently."

"You're brutal today."

"I'm honest." Collecting my papers, I shuffle the stack into a neat pile before heading back to my desk. "Is that all you needed? Not to be *brutal* or anything, but I have things to do if you've got what you needed."

"Yeah, that was all. You know, you're a fucking rock star at what you do." I laugh at his choice of compliment, given that our sister is a literal rock star.

"Well, thanks. I do what I can… you know me."

"I think you're minimizing what you do. You keep everyone around you in line, and we both know this tour wouldn't be happening without you." He pauses. The soft hum of the phone call is the only noise on the line. It's quiet for so long, I double-check that he didn't hang up on me.

"You're taking care of yourself too though, right? After everything with the article last week…" he hedges. "You have a habit of taking care of everyone else. I just want to make sure you're taking time for *you* too, you know? Not just throwing yourself into problem solving this."

I can hear the hesitation in his voice. We have conversations like this often enough, Dex constantly concerned that I'm not taking care of myself. He's well aware that it drives me nuts when he offers his input in my life.

"I think you've told me that once or twice, yeah." Setting the papers on my desk, I drop into my chair, pinching the bridge of my nose between two fingers. I don't really have the energy to do this right now.

"I tell you that because it's true. You have a pattern of this. Last fall, when you dove headfirst into work after Sean? Honestly, I don't think you've ever come up for air after that. I appreciate you and all you do, but I worry about you, too."

"There's no need to bring up Sean, Jesus." I don't mean to snap quite as harshly as I do, but I hate when he brings up my ex.

"I didn't mean this to be about Sean. I was making a point. This is about you. How you handle shit when it hits the fan."

I pick at the cuticles on my thumb, trying to break loose a hangnail as Dex talks in my ear. He's not wrong. When everything went down with my ex, I moved on from Sean by immediately entering a full-time relationship with my job.

I work more hours now than I ever have, but I'm also the best I've ever been at my job, so, if you ask me, it's justified. I realized quickly the harder I work, the more value I add to Mel's entire company. There's always something that needs my attention, and at some point, I stopped turning my attention away from the job. I put on blinders, and anything that wasn't immediately related to Mel and her music became less important, including the remnants of my life.

I never really rebuilt a personal life after I caught Sean in bed with a mutual acquaintance. We broke up; he took half our things and all our friends.

Frankly, good riddance.

But I stayed right where I was. Focusing on my career and never looked back. It was what I needed to heal, to put it all behind me. I don't know how to change who I am now. If I slow down, if I work less, I won't be as productive. Truthfully, I won't be valuable to Melanie anymore. She can afford to hire anyone, but she hired me. I have to prove I'm worth it.

Right now, this problem *is* my job. I don't have an alternative. But I won't sit here and argue any of this with my brother.

"If you don't need anything else for work, Dex, I have to run. I have a lot to get done today." Though I expect him to, he doesn't fight me on the excuse. A quiet sigh comes over the line, and I can tell he's going to let it drop.

"Right." He pauses, like there is more he wants to add but thinks better of it. He eventually settles on, "Thanks, Nat."

"Of course, you're welcome." I try to placate him. "Love ya, Dex."

"Love you, too."

Tossing the phone down on the table lightly, I lean forward as I rest my palms flat on the smooth surface.

"There's an awful lot of sighing happening over there..." I lift my head as Jake's voice cuts across the quiet office space.

"Not your concern, but thanks for the observation." I clear my throat as I shift, turning away from him.

"Did you want to take a lunch break?" He checks the time on his phone. "It's well past lunchtime, and you never ate break—"

"Can you not?" I cut him off, irritation rolling through me at everyone's fucking need to check in on me. "I don't need a babysitter."

"I was just asking."

"Well, that's not your job. Bodyguard, remember?" I slam my hand down on the hole punch with more aggression than necessary. "Not a personal assistant. I already have one of those."

"Feels like you might need to eat..." His voice is so low it barely carries to me at my desk.

"I heard that." I can't quite tell, but I swear he's laughing to himself. Gritting my teeth to stop myself from saying anything more, I organize the pages behind dividers, adding tabs for the different sections. It's quiet for several long minutes before Jake interrupts again.

"So, who's Sean?"

I meet his gaze with a cutting look of my own. "None of your business."

If looks could kill, he'd be six feet under and I'd have silence again.

"Just curious, that's all."

"Find something else to be *curious* about. My ex is off limits."

"You don't want to get to know each other?"

I scoff at that, crossing my arms over my chest. "What happened between you and your ex?"

"Alright, fair. I went there first. Bold of you to assume I'm not currently seeing anyone though."

A smirk crosses my lips. "Am I wrong?"

"You're not. And there isn't one."

"There's no ex? None? At all?" I find that hard to believe. The guy is annoying as hell, but no one can argue he's not attractive. Men like him always have a situationship, or ten, in the past.

"Nope. That ok with you?"

I throw my hands up. "Hey, not me you have to impress here. I thought we were just getting to know each other."

It's quiet for only a moment before I decide I want to know more. Shifting my full attention to him, I ask, "So, do you just... not date? Are you celibate or something?"

He scoffs. "Hardly."

"See, a conversation only works if it goes both ways. If you wanted to get to know each other, you have to actually, you know, *talk.*"

"There's no history because I don't do relationships. But lack of relationship does not mean lack of sex." He smirks this time.

"Fair enough." I feel my cheeks burning at the thought. I probably should have seen that coming.

"Now, who's Sean?"

I take a deep breath. "An ex with a wandering eye and a fear of commitment. Spent too long trying too hard for someone who was looking elsewhere."

That familiar feeling of failure settles into my gut. I hate it. I hate that I can't think about him and our time together without feeling like it's *my fucking fault* because I couldn't hold his attention.

I clear my throat, shifting my attention back to my desk. "Happy now? You've got your answer."

"Shit. Natalie—"

I cut him off, not wanting to be placated. "It's fine. Honestly."

He doesn't reply, and I don't acknowledge that. Busy with finishing my presentation, I don't look in his direction again until it's time for us to leave the office, several hours later.

ELEVEN

JAKE

I'm Not Your PI

We park in a lot near The Tracks offices at 2:15, respectfully early for Natalie's 2:30 meeting. She hops out as I shut my door, marching up the block to the main entrance of the building with the local radio station offices, where The Tracks rent their office space as well.

"Hey, speed racer. How about you wait for me?"

She scoffs, but keeps going.

My large strides eat up her smaller ones, and in a few quick steps, I'm reaching out, my hand closing around her wrist as I pull her to a stop in front of me.

"Listen, there are rules now, Natalie. I need you to chill for a minute and at least wait for me. It's a little hard to *keep you safe* if you're marching two blocks ahead of me."

Her eyes narrow as she shakes off my hold. "I... Sorry. I'm a little on edge over this."

"You don't say," I deadpan.

She drops her eyes, her booted foot scuffing at the pavement. "Sorry, I don't actually mean to be a bitch."

That makes me snicker, the silent laugh vibrating through my chest. The honesty is a nice change of pace.

"Stop apologizing. You're not." I reassure her. "I get it. Maybe just follow my lead, yeah?"

She dips her head as her cheeks darken. I can't help the smirk that crosses my face; the idea of being *in charge* of this fiercely independent woman is a little *too* enticing.

A movement in my peripheral vision catches my attention. I snap my head up, scanning the immediate area. I don't see anything, but now I'm on edge too. Something feels... off.

Moving closer to Natalie, I place my hand on her lower back as we head up the block again. She looks up at me, a question in her eyes, but I just shake my head. Before long, we're entering the front door. I scan the sidewalk in front of the building one more time before we're fully inside, seeing nothing out of place as I do.

"Sorry, I thought I saw something." I offer in explanation. She nods in acknowledgment before turning on her heel and making her way further into the building. We pass through the dated lobby and head up the back stairwell.

Two flights later, we enter the hallway, walking down the long, poorly lit space. Natalie stops in front of a glass door with The Tracks logo on it. A bell jingles softly as she swings it open. A young girl wearing a Tracks hoodie sits behind a desk to the right as we enter, her dark hair up in a ponytail. She has her headphones in as she bops along to the music in her ears, oblivious to our presence. Natalie clears her throat, knocking loudly on the countertop in front of us, startling the girl. She jumps clear off her seat, hastily pulling the earbuds from her ears and swinging the chair around.

"Oh my god, I am so sorry!"

Natalie smiles politely, her grip tightening on her tote bag.

"No worries!" She says, far more chipper than I have ever seen her. "We have a 2:30 meeting with Austin and Indy. I'm Natalie Bennett."

"For sure! Let me just pop in and let them know you're here. I'll be right back." She hops up, hurrying through a door behind her. I hear her moving down the hall as I look back over at Natalie, who is shifting impatiently from foot to foot.

"You good?" I whisper to her, the space quiet and empty, my words echoing around us.

"I'm fine," she hisses at me, clearly not wanting to admit she's nervous. I don't think she realizes it, but Natalie is easy to read; the woman wears her emotions on her sleeve.

The brunette reappears in the doorway, with a man following behind her. He's about my height, maybe an inch or two shorter, with golden brown skin and jet black hair. He's clean-shaven, looking casual in his white button-down and khaki pants, his sleeves rolled to his elbows.

He extends his arm out to Natalie, smiling warmly at her as he takes her hand in his. "Natalie! It's been a while!"

"Hey Austin." She hits him with a megawatt smile I've never seen from her before, and I feel a tug from somewhere inside my ribcage. I rub my hand over my chest as I clear my throat, feeling uncomfortable. Gesturing to me, she adds, "This is Jake Alder. He works for Melanie's security team."

"Hey, Jake. I'm Austin. It's good to meet you." He drops her hand and offers a handshake to me, which I accept, returning the gesture with a little more force than is strictly necessary.

He clears his throat, and I let go, stuffing my hands into my pockets. *What am I doing right now?*

"Well, come on back. Indy's in the conference room waiting for us."

We follow him through the hallway; the dated aesthetic of the main building nowhere to be found. The Tracks have clearly updated their offices; the dark tiled floors shining in the small space. The clean gray walls make the room feel warm and welcoming.

It's quiet as we approach the outside of the conference room. Austin gestures for Natalie and me to enter, so I follow behind her, grabbing a seat immediately to her right when she sits down. Across the table from us, a woman waits, dark curls pulled up on top of her head, her brown skin shown off by the strapless white dress she's wearing. I watch as she stands to round the table, enveloping Natalie in a hug as the two talk animatedly. It's clear they've worked together before from the way they're immediately comfortable with one another.

"I was so excited when you called," Indy is saying to Natalie, "it's been so long since we've seen you and Melanie! And with everything going on lately..." she trails off, as if she's uncertain she wants to broach the topic.

"Anyway, I've been thinking about you two!" She shifts her attention to me. "I'm sorry, how rude of me, I'm Indy."

I take her hand, offering her a weak smile. "Jake. Alder. It's nice to meet you."

"Mel assigned me a full-time bodyguard," Natalie explains as she slides her coat off, folding it over the seat behind her, "so Jake has the pleasure of my company around the clock."

She smiles in my direction, but it's forced, not the open warmth she offered to both Austin and Indy when she greeted them.

I grit my teeth, shifting my attention across the table. Austin slides a bottle of water to each of us as he says, "To what do we owe the pleasure, Nat?"

He's so casual in the way he addresses her. I wonder just how much they've worked together in the past. If there's more than a working relationship there…

That uncomfortable pinch is back at the thought that these two might be more than just acquaintances.

"Well, I have an opportunity for you guys, and I thought offering it in person was the best way to share it with you." She launches into the prepared presentation I've heard her working on for the last several days. She's so wildly different in a professional setting than she has been with me. The snappy, anxious girl is nowhere to be seen. Natalie's poised and confident, talking through the gist of the request, framing it as an enticing offer for The Tracks. She runs through all the things they would stand to gain from going with Melanie on tour, a true professional as she spins the favor she desperately needs so that it almost sounds like it's a favor she's doing for *them*.

From time to time, Austin and Indy interject, throwing some questions at her, the logistics of the arrangement, specifics on the timeline, details about the compensation and travel. Natalie has an answer for every question, eventually producing printouts and a packet, bound and titled, for each of them to flip through.

"This is… wow." Austin is flipping through the pages of the packet as he speaks to her. "You really have thought of everything."

I can see charts and graphs as the pages turn, a timeline, a map, and several pages with bullet-pointed information. He flips the packet closed, pushing it out in front of him as he reclines in his chair. "This is definitely a unique opportunity. I think Indy and I have a lot to discuss.

We'll have to go through it with our producer and the managers as well. There's more than just the two of us to consider for this commitment."

"Six months is a little… overwhelming." Indy hedges, trying to be polite even those she's clearly hesitant. "And on a couple weeks' notice… I'm really not sure this is something we could take on. But like Austin said, you know we love Mel. It's definitely something we're interested in. We'll talk about it and let you know ASAP."

Natalie grins another genuine smile at them, looking hopeful and excited.

"And you know, that episode last week was nothing more than business." Austin looks sheepish as he addresses Natalie. "They called looking for an outlet, and we cleared the contents of the interview before we agreed. We knew beforehand they were not revealing the accusations live on air."

"There are no hard feelings, Austin." I watch as his shoulders drop with her reassurance. "We understand the business. Ratings are ratings. We're just hoping that from now on, we can have you on our side to get them for you."

"Of course." He smiles at her as we stand, putting our coats back on. Austin leads Natalie and me out into the lobby, Indy following along behind us.

There's another round of handshakes, and hugs for the girls, before we venture back down the hall and out the front entrance once again. We're quiet as we make our way back out front, heading down the block back to Natalie's car.

The shrill sound of my phone ringing cuts through the air, and I check the name that flashes across the screen. I hide the phone as I silence Gunner's call, double-checking that Natalie can't make out the name from where she stands as the call rings through to voicemail.

I know he's looking for information, but I don't know that I want to provide it. Initially, I agreed because I felt like I should help him, with all he's done for me, but after a few weeks with Melanie, I'm thinking it's pretty obvious who is in the wrong here, and it's not her. I have no desire to give him any information that might further his case in court against her, if this is who he actually is as a person.

I shelve the uncomfortable feeling in the pit of my stomach. That has to be a problem for another time.

Sliding the phone back into my pocket, I look up, spotting a photographer down the block, partially hidden behind a large planter outside a flower shop a few doors down. He's watching Natalie through the lens of his camera.

I speed up, stepping around her and moving to place myself between Natalie and the paparazzi. I pick up the pace as I gesture behind me, silently urging her to follow suit. We make our way into the parking lot, weaving between the vehicles as we approach Natalie's car.

"Get your keys out." I tell her as I pull her in front of me, ushering her down the row as we pass several more vehicles, Natalie's white car entering my line of sight.

"Why?" She turns her head to look at me, still moving along quickly.

"Please, Natalie. Your keys." I guide her around to the passenger side, holding my hand out for the keys as we both come to a stop. She hits the unlock button, looking at me in confusion. I pull her door open as I simultaneously take the keys from her.

"Hey! You're not driving—"

I cut her off, moving her body between me and the open door. I pin her upper back against the frame of the car as I step into her. Leaning in, my mouth just inches from her ear, I say, "There is a man with a camera trailing us through this parking lot."

She jerks, her head tilting. I reach out, stopping her, her jaw held between my thumb and pointer finger, and I lean in even further. "No, don't look. He wants your attention, and you're not going to give it to him. I want you to sit down and lock this door behind you. Please."

She listens without argument, lowering herself into the seat in front of me as I take a step back. When her feet are tucked in on the floorboard, I shut the door, using the remote to start the vehicle as I round the hood.

I slide into the driver's side, shifting the car into gear as the door closes, and pulling out of the parking space. I glance quickly in front of me, seeing no other pedestrians as I drive toward the exit to the lot.

We're held up at the gate, needing to scan both the parking ticket and a credit card to get out of the lot, but I navigate the machine as quickly as possible, before turning on to the main road.

We're half a block down when Natalie speaks out from the seat beside me. "What in the world was that?"

"Paparazzi." I say shortly, the answer obvious.

"Yeah, thanks. Got that. What would they want *my* photo for?"

I raise my eyebrow as I glance in her direction. "You're Melanie's sister. That's enough of a reason right there."

"I'm literally doing nothing."

"That doesn't matter to them. Right now, anything related to Melanie or Gunner is worth money. You're related."

"Yeah, but—"

She's cut off sharply when I slam on the brakes a moment later, my right hand flying out as I do, coming down on her chest, just below her neck. Her eyes go wide with shock as we watch a black car cutting in front of us to make a right from the left-turn lane. A series of rapid flashes go off out of the rear passenger window as it passes in front of us.

"Jesus fuck," she breathes, her heart racing under the palm of my hand. Her own hand snaps up, gripping mine tightly. Without making a conscious decision to, I rub my thumb up and down slowly, as if I can lessen her anxiety for her.

I scan the road in front of us, checking both the side and rearview mirrors before continuing through the intersection.

"Oh, shit. Sorry." Natalie suddenly jerks away, dropping my hand like she's been bitten. The sting of the cold air hurts more than it should as I place both hands on the wheel in front of me. Tightening my grip, I watch in the mirror for any sign of the black car. I head down a couple of blocks before taking a series of turns, doubling back the long way around to the expressway.

We don't talk again until we're back at the MBM offices.

Climbing into my truck later that night, my phone rings again, Gunner's name flashing across my screen for the third time today. I frown, deciding it's best to just get this over with.

"Gunner." I answer with a curt greeting as I slide into the driver's seat, shutting my door behind me.

"About time, man. I feel like you've been avoiding my calls."

There's no point in denying it. "I have."

"What the hell?"

"Listen, I don't think I can help you with the whole Melanie thing. If you're looking for a leg up in the divorce, you're gonna have to find your own evidence."

"Really, Jake?" He sounds put out, like I'm the problem here.

"Really, Gunner. I can't help you. I *won't* help you."

"I asked you to find one little thing that could help me. I'm really not asking that much."

"It's not the effort that's the issue. It's the *ask* to begin with. I'm not your private investigator, man. I'm under a contract. I'm not about to abuse my position to get you some information that, frankly, I don't think will even help you accomplish whatever it is you're trying to do in court with these divorce proceedings."

"You know, I don't really feel you appreciate what I've done for you, Jake. Who kept in contact with you when you were overseas?! Who let you crash on his couch when you came home and had nowhere to stay? Who got you your job in this industry in the first place?"

I can hear his heavy breathing through the phone. Clearly, I've pushed the wrong button. Before I can respond, he continues on.

"I ask for *one* favor in all our years of friendship, and this is what I get?"

"Gunner, I—"

"I'd think real hard before cutting ties here, Jake. I'm on your team. I've always been on your team. I don't think you can say that about many other people in your life, can you?"

The truth of the statement cuts straight through me. He's right. He is the only person who has been a constant presence in my life for years.

"That's what I thought. I'd prefer a little more *help* the next time I call. And stop ignoring me."

I roll my eyes as I say, "Sure thing, Gunner."

"You're just lucky I don't need your ammunition this week. I think Mel's probably got enough on her plate with this article and that sudden spike in attention that always seems to find her."

I don't like the change in tone as he finishes his sentence; the snide remark not sitting right.

"What does that mean, Gunner?"

"It doesn't have to mean anything..."

A conversation with Knox from a few weeks ago comes back to me.

"Wait, are you tipping off the paparazzi about where Melanie is?"

A low snicker is all the response I get.

"How the fuck are you getting that information? I thought you needed me for dirt on Melanie? Why ask if you're already getting it elsewhere?" I should pose my questions more carefully, a little more thoughtfully, but the anger rushing through me is clouding my judgment. Melanie has been having one hell of a time dealing with the press, and somehow, it's Gunner behind it?

"I don't *always* need people doing the dirty work for me, Jake. Talk to you soon."

The call ends, and I'm left staring straight across the parking garage. What the hell does he mean *he doesn't always need people doing the dirty work?*

Fishing my keys out of my pocket, I turn the ignition over, listening to my truck roar to life. As the dashboard lights up, my phone in my lap vibrates, the display reading, "twenty-three minutes to home" as the GPS connects to my CarPlay.

For fuck's sake—You've got to be fucking kidding me.

I swipe my phone off my lap, dialing Knox immediately. It rings once, twice... on the third ring he answers.

"Hey Jake, what's up?"

Dropping any semblance of calm or collected, I skip the niceties and dive right in. "Have you checked the team's phones for tracking apps?"

"What?" He sounds confused, but I can't blame him. This is essentially coming out of nowhere. Unfortunately, he can't know where it *is* coming from.

"Have you scanned the team's phones for any suspicious software? Dex? Natalie? Melanie? Any of the assistants?" I feel guilty as fuck having this information, almost certain I'm right with this conclusion, and not being able to address it head on.

"No, why do you ask?"

"I think it might be a good idea to check. You mentioned all the paparazzi issues. We're seeing them get worse with this article release. It can't all be bad luck on Melanie's part. It wouldn't hurt just to make sure there's not something out there we've missed." I pause, wanting to elaborate but knowing that revealing the truth right now is not a great idea. "We don't know who the team hangs out with on their off time; it doesn't take a lot to add a background app. It just seems like it's at least worth a look."

Knox is quiet for a minute before he replies. "Good call, man. I'll call the IT team right now, let them know to do it ASAP."

"Sounds good. Let me know if you need anything."

"Will do. Thanks, Jake."

With that, he hangs up. I should feel lighter, having possibly solved one issue for Melanie. Instead, I just feel more guilty.

I'm going to have to come clean about knowing Gunner. About knowing what he's up to.

I just don't know *when* the right time to do that is.

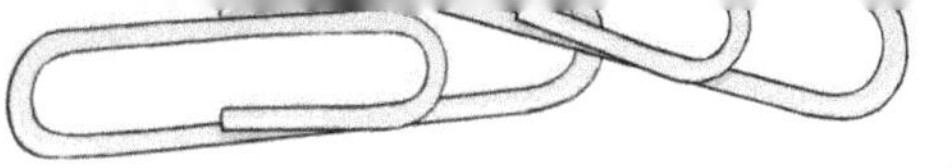

TWELVE

NATALIE

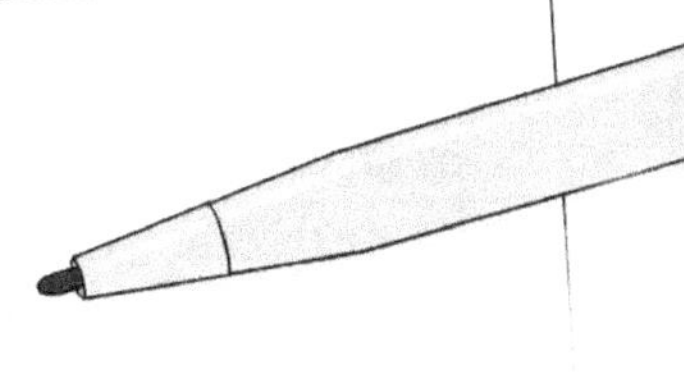

I'm pacing in my office, watching the snow fall outside the window. Jake is across the room, sitting on my loveseat, scrolling mindlessly on the phone in his hand.

It's been three days since the meeting with The Tracks and the almost run-in with the paparazzi, and I've been too chickenshit to go anywhere or do anything since then.

I didn't actually believe Melanie when she suggested I would be a target for the paparazzi. I went along with her bodyguard idea just to make her happy, but now I'm glad I did. I hadn't even noticed the man following us until Jake brought it to my attention.

The photos must not have been worth anything because I haven't seen them pop up anywhere. Although it's only been a few days, so maybe it's still to come. I can't stop worrying the photographer might have gotten a photo of Jake leaning over me, my chin in his hand, when we were against my car, and the thought of an image like that circulating makes me uneasy. The last thing Melanie needs right now is another scandal attached to her name.

I blush at the thought of his actions, recalling the few moments Jake had me pinned in that parking lot. I should be furious at being manhandled that way, but I… am not. At all.

I'm furious about these conflicting emotions, though, because his behavior should not turn me on. It *should* piss me off. And the fact that he's this far under my skin is adding to the stress I'm feeling right now.

Jake and I haven't spoken much in the last few days, not that we were really talking much the week prior to The Tracks meeting either. We've really mastered the ability to ignore each other, if avoiding one another includes overlooking the fact that I can feel him watching me work far too often.

I've tried to keep myself from thinking too much about that situation by focusing on tour prep, but even that hasn't been distracting enough. Three days of trying, and failing, to keep myself busy inside this office, so I don't focus on the fact that Indy and Austin haven't called.

Or emailed.

Or sent a text message.

I'd take a fucking carrier pigeon at this point. So much is riding on this decision, and I just need them to make it.

I should put together a Plan B if The Tracks say no, or assemble press packets, or do literally anything productive, but I'm not. Since the meeting, I've been staring at my computer screen, constantly refreshing my email window. I feel stuck, unable to move forward until I solve this problem.

I stop pacing, standing still as I watch the world move by below me. We rarely get snow in Nashville, especially in early March, but instead of admiring the beauty outside the window right now, I'm focused on the tiny dots scurrying along the sidewalk, rushing to their next stop. I don't know who they are or where they're going, but I feel a stab of unease; they clearly know their next destination. I'm sitting here just twiddling my thumbs, waiting to find mine.

I don't do this, and I think that makes me the most uncomfortable. I don't just sit around and wait for shit. I don't wait for answers, and I certainly don't wait for other people to do things.

Yet, here I am.

I jump when the phone on my desk rings, hustling over to pick it up, Austin's name flashing across the screen.

Fucking finally.

I heave a huge sigh of relief, pushing the green answer button as I bring the phone to my ear.

"Austin! How are you?" The nerves have my voice coming out an octave too high, but hopefully, he doesn't notice. I see Jake's head pop up from across the room, his attention now also on this call.

"Hey, Natalie. I'm doing well, thanks for asking. Look, I'm calling to let you know we've decided on the offer you brought to us last week."

"Of course! What did you and Indy decide?" I hold my breath, waiting for him to continue.

"It's really a phenomenal opportunity, Nat, but I just don't think it's something we can pull off right now. Not on such short notice. It would require a lot of finagling to get coverage here in the office, and I don't think that's something we can take on right now. The team is too small to support a remote show for a long period."

He continues on, providing very logical reasons this won't work for him and Indy, but I don't hear anything he's saying to me. I chime in when expected, an "of course" here and an "I totally understand" there, but I *feel* nothing.

I feel empty.

Actually, I feel sick, if I'm being honest.

God, this entire article situation has been a shitshow from the moment the news broke. There hasn't been a single second where I felt like I was handling it well, and the longer this goes on, the more out of control it makes me feel.

"I appreciate you approaching us with this. We both do. In different circumstances, we would love to make this happen, but right now, we just can't commit."

"I get it, Austin. It's not a problem at all." The false cheer in my voice sounds forced. "If anything changes, just let me know. You're welcome at any time. We'd love to have you."

"Sounds good, Natalie. Thanks again."

With that, he's gone, the click of the call ending reverberating in my ear. I stand there, motionless, as I hold the phone for another few seconds. Eventually, I set the device on my desk, still standing, staring aimlessly toward the windows across the room.

I'm trying to figure out what to do now when I hear shuffling behind me. Jake has pulled out his backpack and is digging for something. When he comes up with a packet of chips, he drops the bag and shifts his attention to the plastic packaging in his hands, trying, and failing, to tear it open.

The sound claws at my skin, my irritation and frustration at this entire fucking situation reaching a breaking point.

"Can you not?" I whirl around, snapping at him as his head tilts to look up. He raises an eyebrow, not moving another muscle as he stares across the room at me.

"The noise. Can you not? It's so fucking loud I can't think." He remains silent, continuing to stare.

"And can you stop just *staring*? What the fuck, Jake? Do something besides just sitting there. You're irritating the hell out of me."

"I'm irritating *you*?" He clarifies, a look of confusion crossing his face.

"That's what I just said, isn't it?"

"My sitting here doing *nothing* is what's irritating you?"

"Yes!" I throw my hands up in the air, letting them fall back to my sides dramatically. "You sitting there, making the most irritating noises, *repeating yourself,* is driving me mad. Just... go somewhere. Do something. For fuck's sake, get out of my hair."

I can feel myself unraveling, the insatiable energy from the stress of all of this becoming too much for me to contain. He sets the snack on the coffee table in front of him. Instead of leaving, as requested, he throws his left arm out, using the back of the loveseat to prop it up, assuming the world's most casual and relaxed position, like I'm not having a complete meltdown while he just sits there and watches me.

"You know what, fine. You stay. I'll go." I spin around, digging in my desk for my purse and keys. When I find them both, I slam the drawer shut with more force than is strictly necessary.

I stomp over to the door and rip it open. Before I can take a step through it, a large hand reaches beside me and forces the door closed in front of me. I'm cornered between the door and Jake's body.

And I. Am. Furious.

"Are you fucking kidding me right now?" I pivot, coming face to face with his chest. God, he's so tall, and now *that* is pissing me off too. Using my free hand, I push him, trying to force my way around him, but the man is a brick wall. He stands there, completely unaffected by me.

"Move, Jake. I don't want to be here right now, and you're not going to stop me." I don't even have the energy to cringe at myself for the snotty tone I'm taking. I sound like I'm six, but I don't care.

"I'm not?" He asks, looking down at me. "Because it looks like I am."

"Why are you like this?!" I yell at him, the inability to escape the situation, to escape him, snapping the last tether left on my self-control. "Why are you always here, in my face, witnessing every time I fuck up?! Why can't I get away from you?"

I gesture angrily around myself. He stands there, one hand pinning the door closed, his body still boxing me in between him and the door, the entryway table closing off the space opposite his extended arm.

"It's not me you're mad at, Natalie." He whispers it, like he's not sure he should be speaking right now.

He's right. He shouldn't be.

"Oh, what do you know? You have no fucking idea. You've been around me for a handful of weeks and you think you have opinions? We're not friends. We're not even acquaintances. Fuck off, Jake."

"Why don't you take a deep breath and then we can try this again?" His tone is gentle, his eyes sympathetic.

"Stop patronizing me. I don't need to breathe, Jake. I need you to *move.*" I push at him again, this time using both hands. Instead of me gaining the space I need to move away, his arm snaps down from the door, both hands coming out close around my wrists, holding them between us. He steps into me, forcing my body back into the door. The entire time, his eyes never leave mine.

"Just... take a breath, Natalie. Listen to me." He says, his eyes searching mine. "You didn't fuck up. This isn't on you."

Heat races through me as his gaze meets mine. The temperature in this office is suddenly too hot. I can feel my body reacting to his proximity, with barely any space between the two of us, and it's fueling the rage coursing through me.

I don't want to feel like I'm lighting up when he's near me.

I don't want to be aware of his every move.

I don't want to feel *anything.*

I grit my teeth, tipping my head back. "Sure, it's not. It was my mess to clean up, and what did I do? Nothing. So, yeah, it is on me. This is my fucking job. You don't have to placate me, Jake. I can own when I fuck up. I just need you to stop being here *every single time* it happens."

"What are you talking about?" He asks as I wiggle my hands in his grip. He loosens his hold, letting me free myself from his grasp, but his feet stay planted, his body still entirely too close to mine.

"What do I mean?! Every time I'm around you, I do something stupid and make myself look incompetent. Every mistake I make, you're there. *It's always you.*" I poke his chest with my finger to punctuate my sentence.

"When have you ever fucked up in front of me?" He finally backs up one step, crossing his arms over his chest.

I laugh, both in response to his question and the sudden relief of another few inches of space between us, a psychotic cackle breaking from the confines of my chest. "Where do you want me to start? The coffee shop? The hall before the security meeting? The paparazzi taking photos of us? The Tracks? Pick one, Jake. The list is long."

He tilts his head to the side, studying me. "None of those were you fucking up, Natalie. Being clumsy? Sure. The paparazzi had *literally* nothing to do with you. And The Tracks? Your presentation was flawless. Them not wanting to work for Melanie has nothing to do with you."

"It's my job, Jake! It's my job to anticipate problems and fix them. It's my job to take care of my sister and I can't fucking do it." The last sentence comes out as a whisper, my throat suddenly too tight, my eyes growing watery.

"Look at me." Jake's face softens as he tips my chin toward him with one finger. "Mel's image might be your job, but you're also a human, Natalie. You don't need to know all the answers, and nobody expects you to solve every single problem. Shit happens. You can't win every battle you fight. Put the weapons down, ok? Take a second for yourself."

I pause, letting his words sink in. I'm well aware my stress and anxiety have made me unreasonable, but hearing someone contradict the voice inside my head is surprisingly sobering.

"Really?" I ask, my voice cracking on that single word.

"Yeah, really." He rubs my cheek with his thumb before dropping his hand. The loss of contact unexpectedly stings.

It's quiet for a moment, our eyes still locked on one another before he says, "Still want to leave?"

I consider his offer, knowing I won't be productive if I stay here. So I nod.

"Then give me the keys. I'll get you out of here."

For the first time since Austin hung up, I take a full breath.

"No way. You're not driving my car." It's mumbled, but I see a smirk cross his face at the response. Now that the anxiety and rage have dissipated, I feel better. More like a reasonable person.

"Fine, then put your keys away. We'll take my truck." He reaches around me to open the door, holding out his arm to gesture for me to leave first. I throw him a look, passing through the threshold, but I don't ask questions.

All of this tour prep and Gunner stress has obviously fried every nerve I have. I'm done thinking for today. I'm turning it off.

Despite my inclination to fix everything myself, I decided today, I'm just… not.

I'm going to let Jake take the lead this time.

Change Of Scenery

As I watch Natalie climb into the passenger seat of my truck, I realize I have no fucking idea what I'm doing. I watched her spiraling, and for some unknown reason, I had to get her out of there.

I couldn't spend another goddamn minute in that office, so I can only imagine how much worse it is for Natalie right now. We've been holed up in there for over a week, and I think we might both be losing our minds.

Pretending I have a plan, I put the truck in reverse to make my way out of the parking garage. I turn the radio on to break the silence; a local country station streaming quietly in the background.

I make my way through downtown, stopping at a drive thru coffee shop to buy myself some time. Turning to Natalie, I pull up to the window.

"What do you drink?"

"Vanilla latte is good, thanks." She answers, her voice little more than a whisper.

I place our order, drumming my fingers on the steering wheel as I wait for our drinks. What do you do with someone so far inside their own head, she doesn't know which way is up anymore? I don't know her story, but something tells me that hyper-independence, that innate overprotective nature, is so ingrained in Natalie that she's lost the ability to accept help in any form.

Mentally racking my brain for a destination, it occurs to me where I could take her. It's winter, which isn't the *best* time to be there, but despite the flurries, the cold is bearable today, and fresh air is always a good idea.

A few minutes later, the barista returns to the window with our drinks. Before sliding my own into the cup holder in the center console,

I pass Natalie's over to her. With a destination in mind, I pull out onto the main road and make my way toward the expressway.

Checking behind me as I merge onto the interstate, I say, "I thought you'd have a fussier order."

She huffs a laugh. "Nope. I like pretty much all coffee. It doesn't have to be fancy."

"How do you feel about a drive? I thought I'd take you somewhere I used to go when I needed to get away from life."

"Um, how far of a drive? I don't know that I should be—"

Knowing where this is going, I cut her off. "With all due respect, Natalie, I think a day out of the office might be good for you."

She throws me a look, but I don't respond, pretending to be focused on the road as I watch her out of the corner of my eye.

"I guess you're probably right." She looks over at me, her eyes scanning my features as I continue to feign indifference. "Let's go for a drive."

The lack of fight tells me how exhausted she is; there's not an ounce of her usual fire in her. She settles into the passenger seat, staring ahead once again as she takes a sip of her coffee. We're quiet for the rest of the drive, but the silence is comfortable, not as hostile as it felt in her office. It takes about forty-five minutes to get there, a pretty winding drive through the mountains on the expressway out of downtown. I ease off the interstate at our exit, maneuvering the back country roads for a bit before I pull down a gravel road, taking it until it ends abruptly at a bridge out sign.

I shift the truck into park, cutting the engine.

"Where are we?" she asks.

I let the silence linger around us for a moment before turning toward her. "I used to live on this road when I was a kid. There's a small clearing in the woods along the riverbank that I come to when I need to clear my head."

I don't give her a chance to reply before I'm hopping out. I grab a blanket from beneath the back seat before rounding the hood of the truck, just as she opens her own door.

My eyes fall to her feet, to the high heels she insists on wearing on a daily basis. "Hold on. Those will not cut it."

Her eyes drop to where I'm looking before she looks back up. "I don't have anything else with me."

"You're in luck." I shift to the left, opening the back door beside us, reaching for a spare pair of boots under the seat. "Put these on. They'll be too big, but they'll be warm."

She scoffs, refusing to move as I wiggle the boots in her direction.

"C'mon, Princess. You can't wear heels on uneven ground. The hospital is too far away."

That pulls a smirk from her. "Absolutely not. I'm not going anywhere with you if you're giving me nicknames."

"Not a fan?"

Pursed lips are her only response, but she reluctantly reaches out, grabbing the boots. Making a quick switch, she tosses her heels onto the floorboards and tromps away from the truck in my oversized boots.

I shut the doors behind us before leading her around the bridge out sign, walking a few yards up to the bridge itself. I don't move to cross it, instead cutting to the side, following a short, overgrown path along the riverbank. The best path, with my favorite spot to sit, is on the other side of the bridge, but I'm smart enough not to try that trail in the winter. Even though it's not icy, the path is still steep, the ground hard from a winter of cold weather.

I lead us into the woods, periodically offering Natalie an arm to stabilize herself as she stumbles across the uneven terrain in my shoes. We come to a stop in a clearing where the trees open up along the riverbank. There's a large trunk from a fallen tree sitting back several feet, and I lay the blanket out across it, plopping down on top of the makeshift seat. I pat the log next to me, inviting Natalie to join me.

She does, sitting down gingerly as she takes in the view in front of us. Tucking her hands into the pockets of her coat, she buries her chin in her purple scarf. The river babbles as it flows by, the rustle of the trees in the light breeze the only other noise in the area.

After several long minutes, Natalie's voice breaks the silence. "You lived out here?"

"I did, yeah. My parents owned the white house just down the way from where we parked, across from the bridge. My brothers and I would spend most of our summer down here, fucking around on the out-of-order bridge. Not the smartest thing we've ever done, but I don't regret it now. Those were some damn good memories."

"How long ago did they move?" She asks innocently, not knowing the can of worms she's threatening to open.

"About sixteen years ago. We moved away the summer I turned twelve." I pause, not sure how much of my life story I really want to be sharing. "It's just one of those places I've come to think over the years. A place to clear my head, find some perspective. I think because I only have good memories here, and I can't say that for any other place I've been in my life. I thought maybe it might help you."

She's quiet, staring ahead as I ramble on.

"Sorry, this is—"

"No, don't apologize." She cuts me off, her eyes softening as she looks in my direction. "This is really thoughtful, thank you."

I meet her gaze for a few more seconds before nodding and turning away.

"Seemed like you might need a change of scenery."

"Yeah, I guess I do." She hesitates before she continues, a long sigh breaking the silence. "I just... so much was riding on that phone call. I hadn't really stopped to consider what would happen if it fell through. With everything that needs to be done before we leave, I haven't had the time. And I feel like this week was just wasted... and now I'm back to square one. I have nothing.

"I needed this for Melanie. I needed the opportunity this presented for her—a chance to rewrite the story Gunner is smearing everywhere. She's such a good person, but he's twisting her image. I feel like it's my job, not just in title, but as her sister, to stop that. To fix it. And I'm not. I can't." Her voice breaks on that last word, the sharp edges of her pain causing an inexplicable ache in my chest.

I don't offer her placating words or attempt to band-aid her problems for her. Instead, I just let the silence stretch between us as we rest there quietly, watching the river in front of us, letting her have this time to just sit with whatever she needs to.

"I'm supposed to take care of her, you know? Our parents died when I was eighteen, and ever since then, it's been on me to look out for her, for both of them. I feel like I'm not just failing Mel right now, but our parents too."

"Shit, I'm sorry you had to do that alone. That's a lot to ask of someone who's barely an adult themselves."

She offers me a watery smile, shifting her eyes away from mine as quickly as they meet. "It is what it is. It was hard then, but we all survived. Feels like a lifetime ago now."

"Well, for what it's worth, you're not failing anyone now, Natalie. In the few weeks I've been working with your team, I've seen you in action. I don't think there's any problem you can't solve. Hell, half the problems you solve aren't even yours to begin with."

She smirks at that. "What are you saying, Jake?"

I lift my hands up in a defensive gesture. "I'm not saying anything. My point was just that I'm sure you'll find a solution."

She's quiet for a while before I hear, "I feel like I owe you an apology."

"Me? No, you don't."

I already know she wants to apologize for being short, for her attitude earlier, and maybe I should let her. But it's become clear to me that she has too much on her plate and she has no idea how to put herself first. I think she might just need someone who can be there for her.

"No, seriously, I've been—"

"Dealing with a lot, stressed the fuck out, and handling everything thrown at you on your own. You don't owe me an apology for anything."

She smiles, looking over at me. "Thank you."

"Anytime."

We sit there for another thirty minutes before we're both too cold to stay outside any longer. Making our way back to the truck, I toss the blanket in the bed before climbing in, cranking the heat.

As we head back to the city, a quiet, companionable silence settles around us. After weeks of tension and animosity, an afternoon of quiet conversation feels... nice. I don't know what to do with this warm feeling that is bubbling up in her presence. I can't put a label on it, but whatever it is, it's now wrapped in another layer; the feeling that maybe things have shifted between Natalie and I.

I just can't tell if that's a good thing or not.

MARCH

- [ ] Mel's talking points for Grammys
- [ ] Dex's directive - print extra copies
- [ ] call forwarding for office phone

SUN	MON	TUES	WED	THUR	FRI	S
						1
2	3	4 9a Team Weekly	5	6 2p Final Fittings	7 1 Week!	8
9 Grammy Night!	10	11 9a Team Weekly	12	13	14 Leave For Glendale!	
16	17	18 9a Kick Off Mtg	19 Glendale Station Interviews Influencer Event	20 Cast & Crew Party	21	Glend
23	24	25 9a Team Weekly	26 Meet & Greet Event	27	28	A

Arlington Drive

glendale & arlington:
confirm cast & crew venue
(24 hours before)
~~florals for influencer event~~
cleaning crew for 3/19

confirm set up co
for meet & g
remind Jamie

houston & nola:
schedule press packet delivery!
media passes - confirm qty
call 1052 about interview

prep for To
MBM bo

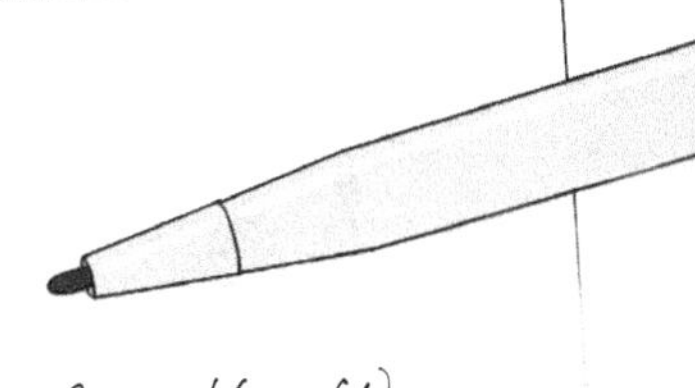

FOURTEEN
NATALIE

Anything You Want

"Natalie, are you ready to go?" My sister hollers at me from down the hallway. I finish applying my lipstick and smack my lips together, capping the tube before tossing it into my purse. Running my fingers through my red hair, I shake it out quickly, then retie it into my usual bun.

The door to my office flies open, and Melanie appears in the doorway. "The hair looks perfect, as always. Can we go now?"

I check the mirror one more time before calling the situation good enough and turn on my heel to face her.

"Alright, alright. You're like an eager puppy. You know we don't have to be there for another hour, right?" I slide the strap of my crossbody over my head as I snatch my keys off the table next to me.

Not much has changed in the last couple of days. The public interest in Mel is still at an all-time high, and the situation with The Tracks still has me feeling like a failure. I haven't come up with an alternative yet, and the team is getting antsy.

The lack of immediate response, ironically, seems to have worked out well. All the media has to go on is speculation, so the subsequent stories are losing credibility quickly. Long-term plans would be much more ideal because even if this fizzles out, I know Gunner will be back for more, and we have to do something before that happens.

For today, though, that problem isn't on the table for consideration. For the first time since everything with Gunner happened, I'm actually looking forward to getting out. We're heading out of town to visit Mel's wardrobe designer, who is also a good friend of ours. She's due for one last fitting before they pack the outfits up and send them to Glendale for the first show. Since we're going out of town, the likelihood of there being any press to follow us is slim to none, which makes today's outing a relatively safe one.

"I know, I know. I'm just… a little excited." Mel says as we step into the hallway. "I love fittings."

"I know you do." I laugh, matching Mel's pace as we make our way down the hall, the sound of our steps on the tile floor loud in the otherwise quiet office. Most of the staff has been working from home as much as possible, and it's like a ghost town around here.

"So, how's it going?" She looks over at me.

"How's what going?"

"Working with Jake. Are you still tripping all over yourself, or have things smoothed out?" The wide grin on her face tells me she's getting a kick out of my circumstances.

"Oh, hilarious. Yes, my clumsiness is comical. Appreciate your concern."

She snickers to herself. "No seriously, is it getting better? Less awkward? I know it's weird when you spend 24/7 with someone. I didn't know how to behave around Knox for the longest time."

I think back to the trip to the woods, the coffee, the conversation. I can confidently say things have changed. What I haven't decided is what that means for us.

"It's definitely getting better. We've learned to tolerate one another, I think."

She laughs. "Well, that sounds like a good start."

Her phone chimes in her purse, and she pulls it out, checking the display.

"Is that a new phone?!" I note the shiny white phone, covered in a clear case. I'm pretty sure that last week her phone was black.

"Oh, yeah. Knox had the IT team replace my phone because he was worried about tracking software." She taps the screen a few times before dropping the phone back into her bag.

"Interesting." This is the first I'm hearing of this. "What prompted that?"

"Jake, actually. Knox said it was his idea. They are going to scan everyone's devices, but I've had that phone for like three or four years, so I told them to toss it and I just got a new one."

"Do they really think someone's tracking our phones?"

"Knox said it seemed like it could be the case with all the issues we've been having with the paparazzi. I told him I think it's just the uptick in media attention, but he wants to run the scans anyway."

I don't have time to continue the conversation as we pass by the elevators, making our way around the corner to find both Jake and Knox sitting in Knox's office waiting for us. I tuck this new information away for later when I can ask Jake what prompted the idea.

"We're ready to go," Melanie announces as she enters the room. It doesn't appear that they've heard us enter, though, the two of them deep in conversation.

"That's a bullshit argument. He deserved MVP last year, and you fucking know it." Knox is heated, his pointer finger aiming right at Jake as he punctuates his sentence.

Jake snorts, crossing his arms as he leans against the desk. "The hell he did. It shouldn't be a popularity contest. The MVP shouldn't be someone who played mediocre ball but happened to be on a good team that went to the World Series."

Knox scoffs. "I'm sorry, but if a talented player scoring the winning run in game seven to bring it home shouldn't be MVP, who the fuck should?"

"It's not about one game! Consider what the team's record would have been *without* him! And their record would have been the exact fucking same."

"Bullshit! Did you even watch a game last season?" Knox's face reddens as he glares at Jake.

"Ahem. Boys?" Melanie clears her throat as I choke back a laugh. "We're ready to go when you two are done here."

She points her finger at Knox, wiggling it between him and Jake as the two of them turn to look at us. Knox looks appropriately chastised, his ears turning red.

"Right," he clears his throat. "Costumes."

He rounds the desk, grabbing his coat off a hook by the door before continuing, "We're good here. Jake's fighting a losing battle, anyway."

"Oh, fuck off. I am not." Jake tosses back at him, pushing off the desk he was leaning against.

"Whatever you say," Knox snickers as he waltzes over to us. He holds a hand out in front of him. "After you, Mel."

I follow Melanie out of the room, Jake closing the door behind us as he trails after Knox. We ride the elevator silently to the first floor, the four of us standing awkwardly in the small lift. Jake shifts beside me, sliding his hand into his pocket, his arm pressed against mine. He doesn't break our contact, and despite the layers between us, I would swear I can feel the heat from his body leaching into mine. I close my eyes, trying to ignore the pounding in my ears at his proximity.

The newfound lack of animosity between us has left an opening for a new feeling to fill that gap, and so far, I've been careful not to examine that too closely. But as we stand here, his body pressed against mine, even as innocent as it is, I'm aware this is a development I'm going to have to address sooner rather than later.

Twenty minutes later, we pull up outside a seemingly abandoned warehouse. The driver drops us at the front door, the four of us piling out.

Antoni, Mel's lead costume designer, and owner of this warehouse, likes to keep people on their toes, and this building is the prime example. It looks so outdated and forlorn. You wouldn't suspect anything actually happened in here if it weren't for the coming and going of vehicles outside.

But inside, it's a work of art. Sprawling dark hardwood covers the entire main floor. Industrial stairs on the left lead up to the loft, opening up to rows and rows of colorful clothing. In the back is a row of workspaces with platforms surrounded by mirrors.

I'm taking in the building, listening to the soft murmur of voices, the sound of ambient jazz music filling the air, when I hear a loud squeal. "She's HEREEEEEE!"

We're suddenly accosted by a young, twenty-something man with perfect olive skin, stunning six-inch heels I could never pull off, and the biggest grin on his face.

"Antoni! It's so good to see you." Mel offers him a hug before I do the same. Not everyone is best friends with their costume designer, but Antoni has been with Mel from the start of her career, doing the wardrobe for almost every important event for her: her first tour, all of her album covers, and countless awards shows.

"Come in! Come in! I've got some of your dancers in the back already. My assistants are doing the final fittings on their costumes, but I wanted to save yours for myself!" His gaze cuts behind us to Jake, who's standing awkwardly with his hands in his pockets. Antoni immediately pauses, his attention shifting.

"Who's the handsome new shadow?" He squeezes between the two of us, making his way to Jake, who holds out a hand in greeting. Swatting it away, Antoni envelops Jake in a hug. He looks so taken aback at being hugged, I almost can't contain the laughter bubbling up inside me.

"Jake. Alder." I hear him choke out from inside Antoni's bear hug.

"Jake is my bodyguard." I fill in as Melanie and Knox both laugh beside us.

"Wellllll, Jake!" Antoni pulls back, holding Jake by his shoulders as he scans his face. "It's so good to meet you!"

He pats Jake on the cheek and spins quickly on his heels, hugging Knox before turning back to us. "Good to see you too, Knoxy. Come on, ladies, I have costumes to show you!"

He takes Mel's hand and pulls her across the space. I race along behind them, hustling to keep up.

When I reach the back of the room, Antoni already has Mel stationed in front of a rack of gorgeous costumes. The colors are vibrant and rich; the fabrics look so soft, I almost want to pet them. I grab Mel's purse from her hand and then settle myself and both of our bags onto the couch next to where she stands. Jake and Knox shuffle over to the wall behind us, leaning carefully against the surface. I can hear Mel and Antoni murmuring quietly about where to start.

"Start from the beginning." I chime in. "Let's see them in order of the performances."

Antoni grins, "As you wish!" He sweeps a dress off the rack and ushers my sister behind the curtain.

She steps out a few minutes later, swathed in sparkly black tulle, dripping with silver sequins that reflect like stars in the fabric. The spaghetti straps on the top drop to a sweetheart neckline on the bodice. A belt cinches the dress at the waist, where the fabric splits into two, revealing a pair of black satin shorts underneath. The dress itself hits just above Mel's ankles, with sparkly black boots on her feet to complete the look.

"Oh my god, that is stunning! You look like a bottle of starlight in that." My jaw drops as she spins, the light refracting off each of the sequins sewn into the dress.

"I know, right?" Mel comments. She spins once more for good measure before stepping onto the podium so Antoni can assess the outfit for any final alterations. She runs her hands over the material gently, admiring the details. "We wanted it to look like the night sky since the opening song is 'Stars Intertwined.'"

"I love that song," I sigh. "It always makes me teary-eyed."

"Ah, being a romantic at heart will do that to you, love," Antoni chimes in, pulling and pinching the tulle at Mel's hips.

I snort as one of Antoni's assistants appears behind me, champagne arranged on a tray balancing on her fingertips, and hands a glass out to me.

"Thank you so much," I whisper as I take the glass and turn back to the fitting. "Wrong sister, Antoni. Melanie is the romantic at heart. I'm the realist in the family."

"I beg to differ. It's there inside you, Natalie. We're all romantics at heart. You just have to find the one who brings it out of you." He says it with such conviction I almost want to believe it. But lived experience tells me otherwise.

Antoni knows all about Sean and the mess he left me with last year. Some people have hair dressers, Mel and I have a costume designer who's our unpaid therapist, as eager for the gossip as we are for someone to unload it on. He got all the gritty details, so he should know as well as I do there's no romantic living in this heart.

"I still stand by what I said last time I was here: I don't have time for that shit." Taking another sip of the champagne, I can hear Jake behind me, a suspicious cough suddenly coming out of him. I throw him a glare over my shoulder before returning to Antoni and Melanie.

"Natalie, you must make time if you want to find *the one.*" He says it as if we should all be combing the apps for the love of our life with every spare moment that we have. Tapping Mel's leg, he gestures to her to move on to the next gown.

"Careful with the pins, love. I'd hate for them to poke you!" As soon as she disappears, he rounds on me once again.

Before he can continue his monologue on love, I interrupt, "Ok, well, that's enough of that, I think. Today is about Melanie, so can we just… not talk about me?"

He throws me a look as I plaster a sarcastic smile on my face. The silly expression does the trick because he laughs, returning his attention to the costumes.

Mel reappears in a new gown, and the two of them continue to work through the dresses for her set list. There are so many—at least eight different outfits, with multiples of each item to last the duration of the tour.

When I think the two of them have wrapped up, several hours and several glasses of champagne later, Melanie comes out in a gown I haven't seen before. It's black and nude, the bottom half is a full satin skirt, flowing down her body, making her look like a princess. The top half is form-fitting, with flowers woven into a mesh fabric. It gathers at her left shoulder, covering her arm in a full sleeve design, leaving the opposite shoulder and arm bare. A large black flower on the shoulder completes the look.

It's stunning.

"Melanie, this is amazing! What's this one for?"

"This is my Grammy dress," she says excitedly. She spins slowly on the pedestal, showing off the flare of the gown as she twirls.

"I think that's my favorite, Mel," Knox's voice comes from over my shoulder. I twist, setting my empty champagne glass on the table beside the couch, noting both Knox and Jake staring at my sister's dress, subtle smiles on each of their faces.

I turn back toward Melanie, watching as her face lights up. "Mine too. I don't think I've ever had an event dress I've loved as much as this one."

As if we don't already have enough going on with the tour kicking off in just over a week and the Gunner article release, this weekend is also the Grammy Awards. We had a long discussion about Mel's attendance, given everything going on, but she really needs to be *seen*. The fastest way to change a narrative is to put yourself in the public eye, so skipping such a high-profile event would not be a great look. The security at events like this is usually tight, so, all things considered, her team decided it's still a must-attend event.

Melanie isn't nominated for any awards this year. Her newest album released last fall, well after the Grammy eligibility deadline, but it's still a big deal in the music industry. Melanie and Knox, along with Asher and a couple of their support team members, will leave in just a couple of days on a plane out to LA, where they will attend the event. They'll get back just days before we leave for Glendale to kick off the tour.

A very chill week right before we take off.

"I can't believe I haven't seen this one yet. I love it. You look so good in it."

She beams over at me. "Thank you!"

Her hip dips as she grabs the dress in her hand on either side and does one more quick twirl.

"Yours is done too, love," Antoni gestures to the rack of dresses Melanie's been using. "I finished the last of the alterations, so you can try it on if you want to jump into the fitting room."

Instead of making the cross-country trip, Dex and I accepted an invitation to a Grammy viewing party at the Nashville Soho House. It's obviously not as special as attending the event out in LA, but it's still a big to-do, hosted by the elite club. Everyone dresses to the nines as if we were attending the awards ceremony, and there are several rooms of viewing set-ups. Dozens of us in the area will be in attendance.

I shimmy excitedly, thrilled to get to try my gown on one more time. There aren't many occasions that call for a publicist to wear a ballgown, but when they do, I live for it.

Hopping off the couch, I make a beeline for the overstuffed rack of dresses. I snag the black bag with my name on it and haul it into the dressing room with me.

I make quick work of shedding my skirt and top. Carefully removing the protective fabric, I slide the green velvet dress off the hanger and wiggle myself into it. The material is fitted, possibly too fitted, clinging to my curves like a second skin. I can't reach the zipper, so I pop my head out from behind the curtain, grabbing Antoni's attention for some help.

He breezes over, dipping inside the room with me as I turn, offering him my back to fasten the dress into place. He hums as he does, dropping two hands onto my shoulders when he's finished and spinning me around.

"Look at you," he coos, his hands coming together in front of him.

"It fits like a glove," I say, running my hands down my sides as I watch my reflection in the mirror. The sweetheart neckline of the dress dips low between my breasts, the green fabric hugging my body as it falls over my hips, splitting into two where my hip meets my thigh.

"Of course it does. It was made for you." Antoni smiles behind me before backing out of the small space, holding the curtain to the side to allow me to slip through as well.

I gather my dress in my hands, careful not to drag it on the floor as I make my way over to where Melanie stands on the platform, her face lighting up as I approach her.

"Oh, my god, that is fantastic!" She says enthusiastically, stepping down from the elevated platform and sweeping her hands out in front of her, gesturing for me to take her place.

I do, gingerly stepping up. As soon as I'm situated, Antoni appears behind me, holding two tall heels in either hand.

"Wrong color, right height, but these will work for the moment." He kneels before me as I shift the dress, exposing most of my leg as I do so. I rest my hand on Mel's shoulder as Antoni helps me into the shoes, taking his time to adjust the buckles as he does.

I scan the room while I wait, watching the many assistants and designers flitting about, pinning dresses and making notes about alterations. My eyes make their way to the wall behind the couch, where Knox taps quickly on his phone. Jake, on the other hand, has his hands tucked into the pockets of his jeans, his eyes focused firmly on me.

My breath catches as he runs his gaze over my figure. From the floor, Antoni taps my ankle, signaling to shift my stance so he can help me with the second shoe. The fabric of the dress swishes in front of me, concealing one leg while slowly revealing the other. Jake doesn't miss a beat as he tracks the movement, following the line of my leg upward until his eyes meet mine.

I see his throat bob, the only sign of movement from him as he stands there, eyes burning into me. I can feel the heat racing along my skin, worried I'm about to turn beet red in front of everyone in this room.

Thankfully, Antoni cuts off our staring contest when he pops back up, a big smile on his face as he appears in front of me. "There you go, love! Take a spin in the mirror while I check the side seams for you."

I do as he says, turning quickly as the dress follows my movement, swirling around my legs. I let Antoni fuss over the fit as I watch in the mirror. Excitement thrums through my veins, although I can no longer tell if it's from the dress or the man behind me, whose eyes I can still feel on my back.

Maybe that wasn't lust in his gaze.

I mean, he appreciated Mel's dress too.

But he wasn't looking at her like *that*.

I force my eyes to look anywhere but over my shoulder, fixing them on the bottom half of the mirror.

It takes a few minutes, but eventually Antoni decides he is satisfied with the dress, and he lets me go. I make my way back to the fitting room, purposefully keeping my attention from the wall where Jake stands as I do.

Antoni follows me, freeing me from the zipper before he steps out. It takes me a minute to remove the ridiculous shoes Antoni chose for the quick fitting, but once I do, I bag the dress back up, and then make my way back to the couch. I busy myself with snagging the champagne glasses we were using, taking them over to the kitchenette.

"You are not washing my glasses. Put them down right now." Antoni laughs as he comes up beside me, taking the glasses from me and setting them on the counter.

"I was just trying to be polite." I argue.

"You're a guest, Natalie. We can handle the dishes." He grabs my hand, pulling me back toward the fitting area. "Do you want me to take this dress out for you? Or do you want me to have it delivered with Melanie's?"

"No need to deliver either of them, Antoni. We can take them with us." I shuffle over, grabbing my dress off the rack. I drape the long bag over my arms, turning back to the couch as Melanie emerges, her own dress in a white garment bag.

I'm debating how to grab our purses, my hands already full, when Jake steps around me.

"Here, I'll take this. You worry about those." He nods toward the couch before he leans forward, carefully reaching to take the dress from me.

Sliding his arms under the oversized bag, his fingers wrap around my elbows instead of the fabric, pulling me into him. He dips his head, his mouth dangerously close to my ear. "For what it's worth, you might not make time for *that dating shit,* but there's not a man on this planet who wouldn't give you anything you wanted in a dress like this."

I tilt my head back, meeting his eyes, warmth shining in them. The lump in my throat keeps me from responding with words, but the shivers rolling through me are impossible to hide.

I feel his fingers pull back from my skin, shifting to take the bag from me. I drag my hands out from under the dress as I break eye contact, stepping away from him.

The vacuum surrounding us breaks, the sounds of the room crashing into me as I blink myself back into reality. I can feel color flooding my cheeks, unsure what to do with myself after a statement like that.

Knox calls Jake's name, and I force my attention back to him, catching his eye one last time before he turns away.

I quickly grab my purse, passing Melanie's off to her, noting that Knox has taken her dress bag from her as well. Hugging Antoni on our way out, we follow the two men toward the front door.

I head straight for the SUV, throwing the door open before climbing inside, just as the other three make their way to the vehicle.

I can hear Melanie joking with the guys outside the window, her muffled jest just barely audible. "Does dress hauling fall under the 'other duties as assigned' in a bodyguard's job contract?"

The sound of laughter grows louder as the rear hatch opens and each of the guys loads in a dress. I busy myself with checking my email on my phone, not wanting to think about whatever the hell that was that just happened inside.

But try as I might, the only thing I can think about on the drive back to the office is the look in Jake's eyes as he watched me in that dress.

FIFTEEN
JAKE

My jacket swings behind me, hooked on two fingers and draped over my shoulder as I jingle my keys in my pocket while I wait outside Natalie's apartment door. When no one answers, I knock for a second time. Several more moments pass as I stare at the closed door in front of me. I'm about to knock a third time when the door is finally pulled open, Dex filling the doorway.

"Hey man, sorry about that. I was trying to help Natalie with her dress. Come on in." Dex slides out of the way, holding the door open for me as I cross the threshold.

I've been here every morning since Knox moved the team around and made Natalie my responsibility. Her apartment is always pristine, clean and well-organized. My house is clean, mostly because I don't have much decor and I'm rarely there. Natalie's apartment is the kind of clean that is also clearly lived in. It's carefully decorated, with items adorning every shelf on the walls and every cubby in her storage cabinets.

I take in the now familiar space as I cross the small entryway into the open living room. The apartment is distinctly Natalie, a collection of neutral items spread around, with a couple of plants to break up the warm cream colors.

Gently tossing my jacket across the arm of the couch, I turn to face Dex, who is standing at the opening to Natalie's hallway, checking the time on his gold Rolex.

"Who's gonna tell her we're supposed to be out of here in five minutes?" He looks over at me, knowing damn well neither of us is going to tell Natalie she's borderline late.

Natalie's voice comes from the other side of the apartment. "I'm not late! I just need to find my—"

There's a large clattering noise, followed by a soft "fuck" floating down her hallway.

Dex's fist comes up to cover his mouth as he chokes back his laughter, yelling, "You good in there?"

Natalie appears in a doorway at the end of the hall, two tall gold heels dangling from her fingertips, the dark velvet dress dragging on the carpeted floor behind her as she makes her way toward us. Coming to a stop in front of her brother, she situates her hands on her hips, gold bracelets jingling on her wrist. She throws a sharp look at him as he stands there, still trying to contain his laughter.

Just like at the fitting the other day, the sight of Natalie in that dress short-circuits my brain. The way her creamy skin contrasts the dark fabric as it flows down her body has me in a chokehold, the entirety of her leg on display in her current stance. Tonight though, her red hair spills over her shoulders in soft curls, long gold earrings peeking out from between the strands.

I know this is crossing a line. There's absolutely no reason for me to be paying attention to details like *this*, and yet, here I am, fucking gone at the sight of this woman with her hair down, looking like a goddamn goddess.

I can feel my cock swelling in my pants as my mind conjures up images of what I could do with that red hair wrapped around my fist—

The loud clatter of keys falling to the floor snaps me out of it, my attention cutting to Dex, who has bumped into the side table behind him. Clearing my throat, I inhale deeply, but before I can turn away, Dex catches me. His laughter coming to an abrupt halt, a raised eyebrow directed at me. Deciding it would be wise to take myself elsewhere, I grab my jacket off the arm of the couch and move further into the living room.

Behind me, I can hear Natalie and Dex talking, but the blood rushing in my ears makes it hard to hear the details of the conversation. I put my jacket on, busying myself with studying the framed display of pressed pennies Natalie has on the shelf over her couch. I can't make out the details from where I stand, but the nine neatly arranged pennies make my lips tip up at the thought of her carefully organizing them in the frame one-by-one.

By the time I have my jacket buttoned and mind back in the present, Natalie has both of her shoes on. Dex slides his own tux jacket over his shoulders, ushering Natalie out the door in front of us. He turns to me just as I approach the door, a sharp look coming from him as he meets my gaze. An unspoken warning passes between us.

I do my best to keep a straight face, maintaining a look of innocence until he turns to catch up with her. I run my hand down the front of my jacket, smoothing it over my chest as I blow out a long breath, waiting for the door to click behind me before I follow them.

As I watch Natalie's hips sway several yards in front of me, I realize I need to get it together, and fast, or this entire tour is about to go sideways.

Thirty minutes later, our driver pulls up in front of an older brick building. The lights inside the building illuminate the drive we're on and much of the sidewalk below it.

I slide out of the vehicle ahead of Dex and Natalie, the street relatively quiet given the security check at the corner entrance. Credentials are required to even proceed this far. A few other cars line the avenue, their doors opening and shutting as people hop out and wander along the sidewalk toward the main entrance.

Dex steps out in front of me, buttoning his tuxedo jacket before holding out a hand to his sister. She accepts, stepping one golden-heeled foot out of the car at a time.

I follow the two of them along the sidewalk to the front entrance, where Dex provides all three of our names to the bouncer.

Following behind them, I can hear the low hum of voices and telltale signs of laughter as we move further inside, taking in the space.

As we approach the end of the hall, the room opens up into a massive sitting area. Groups of people gather around, mingling with one another. We weave through the room, Dex and Natalie stopping frequently, greeted by friends and acquaintances. Some conversations are a quick acknowledgment; others take several minutes before we move on. I give the two some privacy, keeping them in my line of sight, but not breathing down their necks.

Scanning the crowd, I can see that I am far from the only bodyguard here. Many of the people are present with their own quiet shadows.

Dex excuses himself to greet someone across the room as Natalie takes a seat at one of the recently vacated tables. She's barely seated when a loud "Natalie!" comes from behind us. My head snaps around, catching sight of Indy and Austin as they make their way toward us.

Natalie is immediately on her feet, wrapping Indy in a hug, before she shifts over to Austin to offer him the same greeting.

When Natalie releases him, turning her focus to Indy, Austin pivots in my direction, a hand held out in greeting.

"Austin. Good to see you again."

He smiles at me, his bright white teeth flashing in my direction, as he stands next to me.

"You too. I thought you guys might be here tonight."

It's quiet for a minute, the two of us standing awkwardly side-by-side before he says, "I'm glad to see there are no hard feelings there."

He gestures over to Indy and Natalie, both of their heads thrown back in laughter. "I felt bad turning down an offer like that for the tour promotion."

I watch the two women deep in conversation, smiles plastered on both of their faces. Genuine smiles, not Natalie's usual PR smile. She's so animated and bubbly tonight, not a side I get to see of her often.

Or *ever*, I realize as I think about it.

"No," I say, turning my head away from the girls. "I think she gets it."

Austin takes a sip of his drink, his eyes meeting mine as he rambles on. "To be honest, it was a really intriguing proposition. It's not something we've been offered before, but the logistics of it, for six months? We couldn't justify the effort needed to make that work."

"Understandable. That's a long time to be gone." I desperately wish I had a drink of my own to get me through this conversation. Small talk has never been my thing.

"I know Natalie well enough. She's probably on to Plan C or D, isn't she?" He chuckles, the ice in his glass clinking against the sides as it moves.

My gaze trails back to the girls, still chatting in front of us. Without taking my eyes off Natalie, I answer Austin's question.

"I'm sure she will be soon enough. I think she's scrambling a little with this one. Her protectiveness of her sister is... admirable. She was really hoping for a band-aid, a way to fix the damage from the article." I pause, realizing I don't even know where this is coming from.

He hits me with a look I can't decipher, his glass coming up to his lips just before he replies, "I think we're all loyal to those closest to us, though, aren't we?"

I return my gaze toward Austin. Clearing my throat, I shove my hands into my pockets. "That's true, but I think it's more than that for her. It seems like she fills a parental role for the three of them. She sees a problem, and she has to fix it. It's like she can't settle herself until those two are taken care of first. I don't have that kind of relationship with my family, so I can't imagine the weight she feels, bearing the responsibility like that."

He drums his fingertips on the side of his glass, gazing off just over my shoulder. I feel awkward talking about this with him, so I shift gears, talking about the Grammy Awards he's attended in past years. I keep the conversation going as I continue to watch the surrounding area, chatting with Austin for another fifteen or twenty minutes, before guests in the vicinity begin to move toward the various viewing rooms for the start of the awards ceremony.

Dex makes his way back to Natalie and me, weaving through the crowd.

"Ready?" He looks down at Natalie, a broad grin on his face.

"Yes, one second. I want to refill my drink." She wiggles the empty champagne glass in his direction before turning toward the bar, the line lingering as others do the same. "You can go with Indy and Austin if you want; you don't have to wait for me. It might be a minute."

He looks at me, a silent question passing between us.

"I'll stay with her." I confirm out loud. He nods before turning to follow Austin and Indy as they head across the room.

Natalie and I make our way over to the bar, joining the end of a long line. I place my hand on her lower back as I encourage her to step in front of me. Leaning down as she passes, my lips close to her ear, I whisper, "You look gorgeous tonight. I should have told you that hours ago."

She looks up at me from under her lashes, the color in her cheeks deepening. "Thank you. You clean up alright yourself."

I watch as her gaze roams over my tux, making her way back up to meet my eyes.

"Not too bad, huh?" I smooth my hand down my jacket before sliding my hands into my pockets, a smirk fighting its way onto my face.

It's quiet for a moment, the line moving slowly forward.

"Have you ever been to one of these before?" Natalie's eyes scan the room as she asks.

"I have not. Awards show? Yes. But nothing like this event here."

"It's kind of a unique experience. Like a movie premiere, but no red carpet." She laughs.

"Yeah, I had no idea. It's really nice in here."

It's quiet for a moment before Natalie turns to face me. "Mel mentioned you guys replaced her cell phone. Something about tracking software?"

My head snaps in her direction, surprised by the question. "Uh, yeah. It just seemed like there might be more to the press situation. Knox thought it was probably a good idea."

I clear my throat, resisting the urge to tug at the collar of my button-down shirt.

"Interesting. That's a new one, I think. We've never had that problem before." Her eyes don't leave mine as she talks, and I'm starting to panic she might know more than she's letting on.

"Yeah, well—you can't be too careful, you know?"

I'm offered a reprieve from the conversation when Natalie reaches the counter, placing an order for a fresh drink. I take a second to get my shit together, realizing one question about cell phones is not the end of the world. This Gunner situation needs to be handled before I lose my mind completely. Unfortunately, tonight is neither the time nor the place, so I shelve that problem once again.

Fresh drink in Natalie's hand, we leave the main room, heading to the viewing room. I follow behind her as she enters the theatre.

Natalie moves down the aisle to her seat with ease, the building designers having left plenty of room for walking between the rows in oversized dresses.

I watch as Natalie settles into her seat, scanning the space as she looks for me. When our eyes connect, I shrug my shoulder toward the back of the room, letting her know I'll be against the far wall if she needs me. At an event like this, I probably *could* grab a chair, but I don't like having my back to the exits. I can't see what's happening behind me.

She gives me a small smile before turning to Indy, who is sitting behind her.

God, she's gorgeous.

The thought hits me again as I settle into my spot for the night. I'm finding it increasingly difficult to do my job well when the one person I'm assigned to protect continues to command every shred of my attention. It's bordering on a liability, my physical inability to drag my eyes away from her.

I watch as Natalie is once again all smiles, laughing as Indy says something to her, throwing her head back, red curls cascading over her shoulders as she does, and I know I'm in deep shit.

Two hours later, with the ceremony just over halfway through, I see Natalie stand from her seat. She steps quickly and quietly down the row, into the aisle. I can see her mouth moving, though I can't audibly hear the "excuse me's" I know she is whispering. She makes her way up the side stairs, the low lighting on the carpet gleaming off her shoes as she holds her dress up away from her feet. Making her way to me, she leans in to let me know she's heading to the restroom.

I follow closely behind her as she makes her way back down the now-dim hallways. We weave through the building, making our way to the far corner and down a long hall. I watch as she slips into the women's room, continuing a few more steps before I turn, leaning against the floral wallpaper to wait for her.

A large group makes its way toward me. The noise in the small hallway amplified, a cacophony of voices bouncing off the surrounding walls. I shift, shrinking out of the way as much as possible to let them pass. Several women enter the restroom just as Natalie reappears.

With little room to maneuver, she shifts over in front of me, turning her head to catch my eye. I nod, indicating for her to take the lead as I follow. We reach the end of the hall, and suddenly she's pushed into me. Her entire body flush against mine as someone collides with her, rounding the corner without so much as a forward glance.

"Hey, watch it." I push at his shoulder, separating him from Natalie, my opposite hand coming up instinctively to land on her waist. I can feel the curve of her hip against my fingers, the force of her body pressing against mine as she leans into me, the smooth velvet of her dress like lava flowing under my hands.

The guy takes a step back, his hands coming up in a defensive gesture. "Whoa, hey. Ok. I was just heading to the bathroom, man."

"I don't care, *man*." I bite out, irritation spiraling through me, even as I distractedly run my thumb up and down Natalie's hip. "Pay attention to what's in front of you."

I glare at him as he drops his hands, hustles around us and moves away, his eyes locked on mine for several long steps before he turns around and makes his way through the door.

"Jake." I hear Natalie's voice from in front of me. She twists, the smooth feel of the fabric sliding under my grasp as she does. She looks up, eyes meeting mine as she says, "It's fine. Let it go."

Instinctively, I pull her in, my hand tightening on her back as I do. Her hands fall to my chest as our eyes meet, a soft gasp slipping out of her.

The noise snaps me out of it, making me realize what I'm doing. I quickly take a step away from Natalie, clenching my fist as I clear my throat. "We should… get you back."

I run my hands down the front of my suit jacket, the cold satin of the lapels a stark contrast to the feel of Natalie under my palm. She looks at me, a confused expression painted on her face before she wipes it away and continues to the viewing room.

I follow, two steps behind her the entire way, my body suddenly on fire. My mind is a million miles away as it races with thoughts about the redhead in front of me.

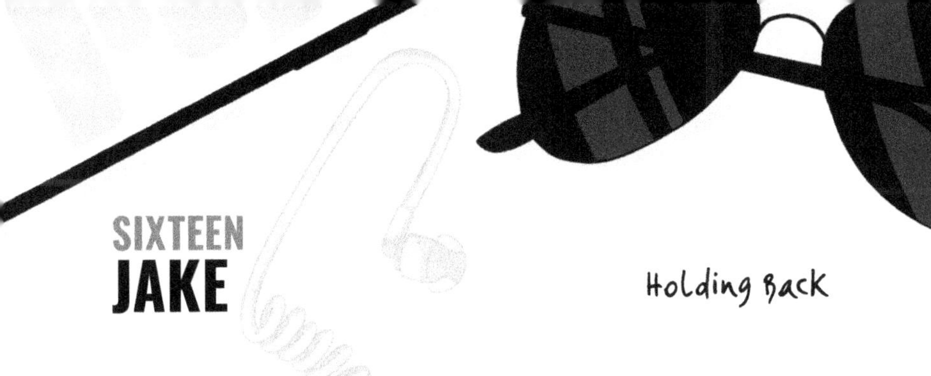

I've spent the past couple hours trying to forget the feeling of Natalie under my hands, but infuriatingly enough, nothing is working. With every move she makes, my body reacts.

I don't know what is happening to me, but every line I've ever drawn for myself has somehow been erased, even the remaining dust of those promises completely gone. By the time the car drops us off at Natalie's apartment at the end of the night, I am ready to combust. My mind is a mess. I'm agitated, needing to escape her so I can think straight.

I follow Natalie through the lobby, waiting for the elevator, which takes several long minutes to make an appearance. When it arrives, Natalie makes her way inside, shifting to the corner when I step in to join her. The smell of her perfume engulfs me, and I can't escape it. I stare straight ahead, watching my reflection in the doors in front of me. The lift crawls at a glacial pace, taking forever to make it to Natalie's floor.

When the door finally dings, sliding open, I let out a long exhale, stepping out into the main hall, and allowing Natalie to pass by. She makes it to her door, digging in her small bag for her keys before letting herself in.

"Alright, well I will see you in the morning." I say from the threshold.

"Jake, wait." I stop, not turning around. "Can you… I can't reach the zipper on this dress. Dex had to get me into it."

I scrub my hand down my face, my heart hammering in my chest with that request.

Yeah, sure. I'd love to undress you.

That's not going to be a problem for me at all.

But I'm not an ass, and as much as I want to escape this self-created hell I've made, I can't. With a quiet sigh, I turn back, following her into her apartment. The door clicks shut behind me, a charged silence settling in around us.

Natalie crosses the entryway, clicking on the lamp on her side table, a soft light illuminating the room in an amber glow. She drops her purse and keys and bends awkwardly to undo the straps on her heels at her ankles. I watch her struggle; the tight fit of the dress makes her reach difficult.

"Here," I say without thinking, taking one step forward and dropping to a knee in front of her. The smooth velvet of the dress flows against my wrist as I push the fabric away, reaching for her. Wrapping my hand gently around her ankle, my fingers slide along her skin as I pull her foot toward me and loosen the strap. I slide the shoe off her foot and drop it on the carpet before moving to the other shoe.

"Thanks," she whispers as I catch her eye, pulling myself back to my full standing height. She holds my gaze before slowly spinning in place. "The zipper is tucked underneath the fabric at the top of the dress."

I sweep her hair up and over her shoulder, the touch setting every nerve in my fingers alight. Taking liberties I shouldn't be, I trail my hand over her now-bare shoulder blades before sliding down to her dress.

I hear her breath catch, wondering if she feels the same insistent ache that I do.

Moving the fabric holding the zipper in place, I wiggle it free from its hiding place. I can feel the heat of her body seeping into mine as our skin touches. The zipper sticks, catching on the lining, and I tug gently at it.

"Sorry, this is not coming out." I grit my teeth, from the exertion of the zipper or the stress of the situation; at this point I'm not sure.

"No worries. Dex had a hell of a time getting it zipped up." She shifts subtly, causing my fingers to slide further between the fabric of her dress along her skin. I can feel my blood racing through my veins, my cock stiffening in my pants, and it's highly likely I will lose my goddamn mind before I make it out of this room.

With another less than gentle tug, the fabric finally lets go, the zipper moving freely. Pulling at it, the dress falls open as my knuckle grazes the skin of her back. I consciously coach my breath out of me, trying, and failing, to keep my mind in check.

When the zipper stops, I let my touch linger at her waist longer than I should. I watch as her shoulders move; her rapid breathing giving her away. After several impossibly long seconds, she spins, clinging to the top of her dress with one hand, the other hand holding a fistful of the train. My fingertips graze the surface of her dress as she pivots, meeting my gaze with those liquid caramel eyes, the desire in them palpable.

My grip tightens on her waist. The smell of her lingers around us, peachy with a hint of oranges. It's vaguely reminiscent of the prosecco she was drinking all night, but sweeter, more intoxicating. I lean in, trying to take in more, mere inches between us now.

"Thank you." Her words are soft, barely a whisper between the two of us. When she rolls her lips together, her eyes searching mine, I can feel the last tether of my sanity pulling taut.

She moves to step back, but I tighten my fingers on her hips, instead pulling her into me, our hips meeting in a barely there brush. That last bit of contact, the feel of her beneath my hands again, has my brain short-circuiting and before I can stop it, the truth comes spilling out. "I can't fucking think around you."

"What?" The unexpected confession has her eyes roaming my face, like she's trying to decide if I'm being honest or not.

"I. Can't. Think." I repeat slowly. "When I'm around you like this, I can't do my job. I can't focus." I pause, scanning her face as she takes in what I'm saying to her.

Weighing the risk, I continue, "I'm supposed to watch out for you. Instead, I can't watch anything *but* you. I spent most of the night fighting with myself, trying and failing to keep my eyes off of you. To keep my mind on the job."

Her tongue darts out, licking the corner of her lips. My breath ghosts across her lips, her whole body trembling as it does. "I can't do it anymore."

Her lips part as she takes in what I'm saying to her. "Do what, Jake?"

She looks up at me from under her thick lashes, and I dip my head further, hesitating, my lips nearly touching hers. I wait for her to react, to pull back, but she doesn't. Instead, she leans in almost imperceptibly. I feel a change in the tension, sparks igniting in that movement.

"Hold myself back." Before I can think better of it, I slide my hand to the back of her neck. I pull her to me, my lips crashing into hers with a rush of adrenaline pulsing through me. She meets my touch, pushing up into me.

She drops her train, her hand slipping up behind my head as she holds me to her, her mouth parting for me as she lets me in. She bites my lip, dragging it between her teeth, before she lets go, coming back for more.

I'm lost in her. Finally, *finally*, feeding this frenzied ache that has been all-consuming. The overwhelming need to ruin her fills me. She presses her body into mine, tightening her grip on my neck. The kiss turns frantic, damn near desperate when a low moan spills from the back of her throat. I can't get close enough, feel enough of her...

My phone vibrates in my pocket moments before the ring of the incoming call cuts through the sound of our heavy breathing, the loud noise interrupting the moment.

I curse silently under my breath as I loosen my hold on Natalie, pulling back from her as I rush to mute the device. The movement seems to wake Natalie up from a trance, because she breaks contact, suddenly looking at me with nothing but horror in her big brown eyes.

The look on her face feels like ice in my veins. She drops her head, staring down at her feet as I take a step back, putting space between us.

My phone goes off again, the fucking thing demanding my attention. I pull it out this time, catching the number before I power the device off, a heavy knot of unease forming in my stomach as I come to my senses, realizing what a catastrophic decision that was.

"I... fuck. Natalie, that was a mistake." I wince, pinching the bridge of my nose, the words leaving a rancid taste in my mouth even as I say them. "I'm so sorry."

Her head snaps up, her eyes meeting mine with a fiery glare as she clutches tightly to the top of her dress, the material bunching under her fingertips.

"Yeah, wow. I... oh my god." She stammers as she turns away from me.

"No, I didn't mean..." I backtrack, feeling my skin crawl as I watch Natalie pull away from me.

"No, you're right." She pivots back to face me. "You're right. Fuck, this was... really stupid. You should go."

She gestures with one hand at the door behind me, leaving no room for argument.

I nod, agreeing with her as I shove my hands in my pockets. I take her in one more time, watching as she stands there, her expression a mixture of fury and... disbelief.

"God, I'm sorry, Natalie."

She doesn't say anything, but the look on her face is all the dismissal I need. I turn, heading out without a look back, the click of the door shutting behind me barely audible over the racing of my heart.

She altered my entire brain chemistry the day she collided with me in the coffee shop. I don't understand the hold she has over me.

But I have to figure it out because *this* cannot continue.

I power my phone back on as I make my way toward the elevator, Gunner's name tied to the string of missed calls and text messages reminding me exactly why I need to stay as far away from Natalie as I can get.

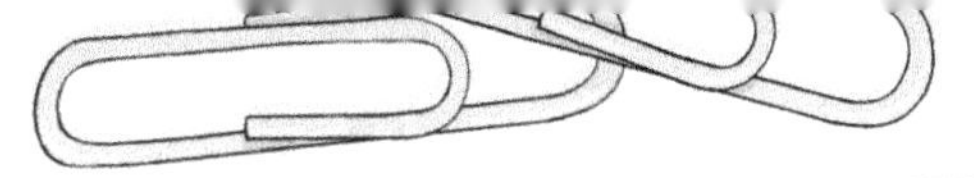

SEVENTEEN
NATALIE

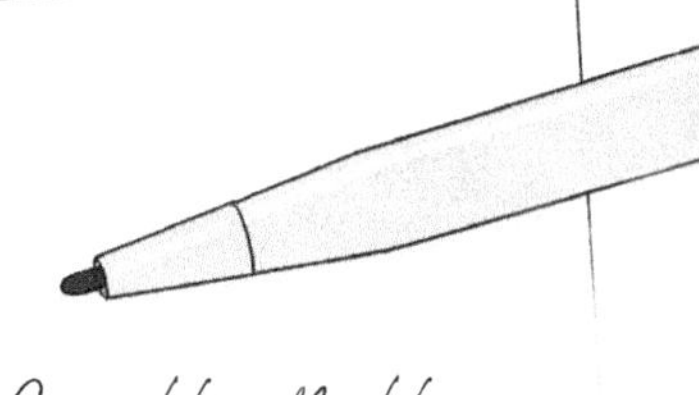

I drum my fingers on my desk as I stare at the mess of text that is my inbox, desperately trying to focus on work this morning, and not Jake sitting across the room from me. The Grammy event yesterday was a huge distraction. It was meant to be just another event on a calendar full of them.

But I can't stop my mind from flashing back to how the night ended. Jake's hands on my hips, his fingers in my hair, the way his lips felt on mine…

Jesus, that kiss?

It was reckless.

It was stupid.

It was really fucking hot.

What it was is a serious lapse in judgment.

I grab blindly for my coffee, bringing it to my mouth as I take a long drink of the now lukewarm liquid. Despite my best efforts, my eyes flick to Jake, who sits in the corner of the room, keeping to himself. We've said all of two words to one another this morning, a quick 'good morning' when he showed up. It's awkward as hell, but honestly, what else is new with us? We haven't had a normal interaction since the day I ran into him.

Before I can look away, he turns his head, his eyes meeting mine. Assuming it's an invitation, I watch as he stands, making his way across the office.

He's wearing his usual outfit: jeans, a fitted tee and that damn leather jacket. I'd love to see his closet. I bet it all looks the same. It's annoying that he doesn't even *try*, and he still looks fucking good.

He comes to a stop on the opposite side of my desk, resting his palms on the wood just two feet in front of me. I stare at him blankly as he stands there, my chin tilted up in his direction. The smell of his cologne floats in the air around us, mixed with a hint of the peppermint from his gum, and god, I want to kiss him again.

No, Jesus, Natalie.

We hold each other's gazes for an uncomfortably long moment before he speaks. "I feel like we should talk about last night—"

Oh, please, not this.

"We really don't have to do that." I wave my hand in the air, gesturing between us. "We can just write it off and pretend it never happened."

His eyes run over me as he contemplates my response. I want nothing more than to avoid this whole discussion right now. There's no point in trading excuses when we both know nothing can happen between us; we're supposed to work together, for fuck's sake. I really don't want to hear him say how much he regrets it. For some reason, the idea that he wants to take it back hurts to think about.

"At the very least, I owe you an apology. I was out of line. You'd been drinking—"

I scoff, cutting him off. "Yeah, none of that. I was well aware of the colossal mistake we were making, Jake."

A smile tugs at the corner of his lips. "Yeah? That seems out of character for you. Intentionally making a mistake?"

I grit my teeth. *Shit, I shouldn't have admitted that.* "Ah, you're right. I was hammered."

He laughs out loud, and I'm taken aback by the sound, more than a little smug I pulled that out of him.

Before he can reply, my phone vibrates, Austin's name flashing across the screen of the device lying on the desk between us. I ignore it for a moment, determined to close this conversation so we can just move on. "Honestly, Jake, we're good. A moment of insanity that meant nothing."

He swallows before nodding his head. His response is a quiet "sure" before he steps away, making his way back to the couch.

I snatch my phone off my desk, taking a centering breath before I hit the green button.

"Austin, to what do I owe the pleasure?" I say, bringing the phone to my ear.

"Hey Natalie. How's it going over there? Everyone good after last night?"

"I think so, a little tired today, but we're here." I chuckle awkwardly, wondering why he's calling.

"Good, good. Listen, I'm calling to talk about the tour. I think Indy and I are willing to reconsider."

He's willing to reconsider?

I lean back in my chair, going completely still. My breath catches in my throat as my pulse races. For the first time all morning, I focus my full attention on just one thing.

"That's—really?!" I hear myself ask him. I'm not sure how to react to this, unsure what would have caused him to reconsider when he seemed so sure before that it was off the table for them. My mind takes off, racing with thoughts and ideas... this phone call changing everything.

Austin laughs across the line this time. "Yeah, we are. We talked about it more, and we think it's probably too substantial of an opportunity for us to pass up. At least in its entirety. I'd like to discuss amending a few of the terms, and we're going to need some accommodations staff-wise, but we're open to making this work if you're still interested in having us."

"Absolutely we are! That would be amazing." My face breaks out into a huge smile as I shuffle through my desk for a pen and clean paper to take notes, a lightness I haven't felt in weeks coming over me. Jake catches my attention as he moves on the couch, our eyes meeting as I mouth, "They're in!" excitedly, forgetting I'm supposed to be irritated with him for a moment.

He cracks a genuine smile at my enthusiasm, grinning even as he shakes his head at me. "How did you manage that?"

I wave him off, turning my attention back to Austin. "What terms are you hoping to change? I can run them by the team lawyer. We need to move quickly... you know we leave at the end of the week, right?"

"We do. We're willing to make that work for us."

Austin and I spend the next twenty minutes running through a few of the changes to the terms of the agreement that he and Indy would like to see; none of them too egregious. I'm so eager to make this work that I offer a blanket agreement to everything he asks for, not even bothering to negotiate.

They can't offer us the full tour, but they offer the first six weeks—and I am more than willing to take whatever we can get. They also have a stipulation for hiring a tech team to work with them—supplemental team members who can help with editing and production for the project so they don't have to ask their own staff to rework their entire lives for the six weeks as well. It's an obvious request now that he mentions it and something I wish I had thought of in the initial offer.

I'm scribbling hastily as I make a note of everything they're ok with and what we need to change to accommodate them. When we've hashed out all the details, I feel like I might be on cloud nine, the events of last night completely forgotten and my excitement at this plan coming together so potent, it feels like that coffee had about twelve shots of espresso in it.

"Well, ok! All of that sounds like it's doable. I'll get on the phone with the legal team and see if we can get a contract over to you. I'll let Dex know immediately too so travel arrangements can be made."

I pull up my calendar, the rest of the week completely full of color-coded blocks. "We should meet up in the next day or two to address any questions and make sure you have what you need. I'm sure you'll need time to decide what you need from us, as far as the show plans."

"Yes, that would be great. Indy has already started outlines, but I know she has several ideas she wanted to run past you. We probably should have just agreed in the first place. Now we're all scrambling to pull this together in a week." He laughs. "Just send me a couple of options, and Indy and I will make one of them work."

I pause, contemplating my next question before asking it, but the high of this unexpected win has me deciding to throw caution to the wind, the words spilling out of my mouth before I can overthink them, the desire to know *why* too consuming. "What made you change your mind?"

Austin hesitates, as if he's unsure what to say. Several long moments pass before his voice comes across the line again. "I realized that sometimes the reason for doing, or wanting, something can be more complicated than what the bottom line tells us. When you presented the idea, I was focused on the logistics, the workload, and the influx of activity this would bring to myself and the team. I was business-oriented, looking at the black and white. But I think the two of us have more in common than I realized. Jake mentioned something last night about how you're putting this together for your sister, to take care of her more than any of the other reasons to hire us. Well, it hits close to home for me. I know what it feels like to watch your sister struggle and not know how to fix it. I, uh... I'm in a similar situation with my own sister. Different circumstances, obviously. But I understand where you're coming from. And, well... I don't know. Call me soft, I guess, but it hit me just right. And this is mutually beneficial enough, it feels wrong not to help."

I'm stunned, unable to think of a response to that. I don't know what I expected his reasoning to be, but it wasn't *that*. Or that Jake, of all people, would play into the decision.

"That's really considerate of you, Austin. Thank you so much." I can feel the tears forming in my eyes as I blink rapidly, refusing to be emotional over this. "I will get all of this sent through and let Dex handle the logistics from here. I'll send over some times for us to meet this week before we leave."

"Will do. Talk soon, Natalie." The line goes dead.

I sit in silence, staring at the phone in my hand for several moments. I look up, finding Jake standing next to me again.

"Do I get to say, 'I told you so?' or is it too soon for that?" He asks, a devilish smirk painted on his lips.

"You didn't say anything, smartass." I toss my pen at him.

"Oh, I did. In the woods." He points at me, shaking his finger before bending down to retrieve the pen from the floor. "I said you'd figure it out."

"I mean, I don't really think I *did* anything here. They just... changed their minds. What did you say to Austin last night?"

"I only made a comment that you were worried about Melanie." He sets the pen down on the desk, leaning forward. His eyes scan my face, sincerity lacing his voice as he says, "Whatever changed their minds wasn't what I said; it was because of you."

A huge grin spreads across my face as the realization sinks in.

I fucking did it.

Austin and Indy are in. The behind-the-scenes show is a go. I can leave for this tour knowing I have a plan to tackle these residual PR problems from Gunner's stupid article.

I feel like a weight has been lifted off my chest and, for the first time in weeks, I can breathe. Even the stress of this *thing* between Jake and me feels lighter now. Looking up at him, his lips turned up at the corner as he walks away, and I feel in control again.

I can handle this.

Fuck, I can handle *him*.

I take a deep breath and refocus on the papers in front of me, throwing all my effort into getting the details together for Austin and Indy as quickly as possible.

THE
TRACKS

AUSTIN: Welcome back to *The Tracks!* We have a very exciting episode today.

INDY: The *most* exciting episode today.

AUSTIN: That's right. We have a very special feature coming up that we can't wait to share with you.

INDY: And by coming up, we mean it's starting in less than a week!

AUSTIN: You know what else is starting in less than a week?

INDY: I don't know, Austin. You tell me.

AUSTIN: Melanie Bennett's Peripheral Vision Tour kicks off one week from today in Glendale, Arizona!

INDY: That's right! Melanie is kicking off a six-month tour across the US. You know, Austin, I wish we could be there. I bet that's really going to be something.

AUSTIN: Oh, I'm sure it is. Imagine being there for the whole thing? Going behind the scenes on tour, following Melanie around as she travels the US? Getting all the inside scoop about the tour, the set list, the venues...

INDY: How cool would that be?

AUSTIN: Extremely. You know, someone should make that happen. That's really something people would want to see, don't you think?

INDY: Oh, absolutely. How cool would it be to be the one that gets to show all the fans? To be the ones to take everyone behind the scenes, spend time with Melanie? To go on tour?

AUSTIN: That sounds amazing. You know what—one second.

[Background static comes across the airwaves, buttons being dialed, and then, a phone rings.]

CALLER: Hello?

AUSTIN: Melanie? It's Austin and Indy from *The Tracks!* How are you?

MELANIE: Austin! I'm great. How are you guys?!

AUSTIN: Well, we're good. We're good. Listen, Indy and I had an idea. How do you feel about a real-time special feature of the Peripheral Vision Tour?

MELANIE: Like, you coming on tour with us?

INDY: Yes! What if we brought our mobile streaming setup and followed you around while you're on tour?

MELANIE: Are we talking about filming the shows?

INDY: Not exactly. We were thinking more along the lines of a behind-the-scenes documentary? A chance for the fans to see how a tour is put on, everything that goes into it, a chance to spend some time with you?

MELANIE: That could be fun! Can you guys be ready in a week?!

AUSTIN: Ready and waiting...

MELANIE: Let's do it!

MUSICMAVEN0989: Wait—so, the show is just covering Melanie Bennett for six months? No one wants that.

THETRACKSPOD: @MusicMaven0989 Our usual content is still being aired! We're adding a segment to the weekly shows for the duration of the tour. <3

KAYDEWREADS: Are you doing an episode with Gunner Greene? Because that's whose story I want.

CASMARTA: YESSS! Behind the scenes sounds amazing! I cannot wait for this.

THETRACKSPOD: @Casmarta Neither can we!

JUNIPERSAIDSO: Oh, come on. Really?

EIGHTEEN

JAKE

Crossing A Line

Before I can finish knocking, the door to Natalie's apartment swings open. Natalie stands in front of me, with a hand on her hip as if she's been waiting for hours.

I double-check my watch.

Nope, I'm right on time.

"Thank god you're here." She grabs my arm, pulling me inside the apartment as she shuts the door behind us.

"Miss me, Princess?" She lets go, dropping her hands to her hips as she spins to face me.

"What did I tell you about that stupid nickname?" She narrows her eyes at me, expression stony. "I need your help."

"Listen, I don't have a shovel, so if you need me to bury a body—"

"God, you're a smartass. No, not today." She takes off across the entryway, still talking as she goes. "I may have... overestimated how much I need to bring today. I need your muscles."

It's been three days since I stupidly kissed her after the Grammys, and things have been *off* between us. Not that they ever found any semblance of normal, but after the trip to the woods, it felt like we'd reached a truce. A place where we could both drop the defensiveness and just... be. But in the wake of the kiss, all that tension seems to be back.

I follow her through the living room. She's considerably shorter today, having forgone her usual power suit for a tight black pair of yoga pants and a loose-fitting sweater that slides off her left shoulder, exposing the entirety of her collarbone. My eyes trail the smooth skin, taking in her casual appearance.

Her red hair is pulled into a loose ponytail, tendrils of the shiny strands slipping from the hair tie, framing her face. She looks good every day in her pencil skirts and high heels, but dressed like *this*? Barefoot, padding across her apartment in the dewy morning light. She looks carefree, effortlessly beautiful...

She looks devastating.

I can feel my cock swelling in my pants as I watch her—a problem that is becoming more and more frequent, it seems. Of-fucking-course we can't be normal around each other; I can't even keep my fucking dick under control. I clear my throat as I turn away, trying to find anything to focus on that will clear my head.

I scan the space, noting Natalie's bags lined up along the wall next to me. There are just two suitcases; not nearly as many as I would have expected for six months on the road. I turn toward her, now standing in her kitchen, to ask her what she meant by *overestimating* when I see a stack of canned coffee as big as she is in the kitchen next to her.

"What... uh—what is that?" I gesture to the coffee she's currently resting her hand on top of. "You packing all of this for yourself?"

"You want to drink shit coffee for months on end?" She quirks an eyebrow at me.

"Well, no. But I'm pretty sure it was someone else's job to stock the buses, was it not?"

"It was, but I checked the supplies and the coffee they got is garbage. I got a replacement." She says it matter-of-factly, like it should be obvious that she would make sure everyone else was doing their jobs to her standards.

"What happened to liking 'pretty much all coffee'?" I quote her from the day I bought her a hot coffee.

"That is not a blanket approval of all coffee in existence. The assistants got the cheapest coffee known to mankind for the tour bus. If I have to be at my best for months on end, I want the good stuff." She taps the cans again gently.

"Let me guess, you left these for me to haul downstairs?" I smirk at her.

"I called down to the front desk; they're going to bring a cart for you." She pops her hip, a smile pulling at the corners of her lips.

I cross my arms as I lean back against her cabinet. "Oh, for me? How nice of you."

"I'm thoughtful like that." A sharp knock comes at the door. "Perfect timing!"

She spins on the linoleum flooring, her ponytail swishing behind her with the movement. The sweet, fruity smell of her shampoo hits me as she breezes by to answer the door, leaving me alone in the kitchen.

I scrub my hands over my face, taking a deep breath before she's back, cart rattling behind her.

It takes a few minutes to load the mountain of coffee, but getting it downstairs and into the waiting car is relatively painless.

I wish I could say that for the rest of the tour, but I have a sinking suspicion that months on the road with Natalie will be anything but painless.

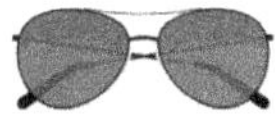

The first day on the road is uneventful. Natalie found a home for her ungodly amount of coffee, but I'll be honest—it was nice to have about three o'clock when the afternoon slump hit. Austin and Dex both caved and took naps, but I tried to hold off, knowing sleeping on the road was going to be a bitch.

Turns out I was right. I've been tossing and turning for at least half an hour, unable to get comfortable. Rolling onto my side, I check my phone; the screen lighting up the small space of the bunk I'm on. It's 3:53am. Way too early to be awake, but apparently sleep just won't be happening anymore tonight.

Rolling carefully over the edge, I sigh as my feet drop to the ladder. Silently, I move to the floor and pad through the dark hallway. The rows of bunks on either side of me are quiet, the rustle of the fabric drapes my only company. The soft glow of the under-bunk nightlights illuminates the path as I make my way to the living room of the bus.

Given the early hour, I fully expect to find the space empty, but as I clear the doorway into the living room, the sight of Natalie on the far couch, her face lit up by the glow of her computer perched on her lap causes me to stop short.

She's curled up on the seat, her feet tucked beneath her, bare legs hugged together. She's wearing a pair of pale pink satin pajamas, the shorts far too short. Her tank top has slid precariously down her right arm, causing the front of the garment to drape dangerously low across her chest. She seems unbothered by her state of undress, but the sight has me doing a double take.

I shift uncomfortably on my feet as I debate backing out of the room and making a dead sprint back to my bunk. Without consciously deciding to, I clear my throat, inadvertently catching her attention. Her head snaps in my direction, eyes going wide as she spots me across the space.

"Oh, sorry!" She shifts quickly on the couch, pulling her laptop closer to her chest as she does.

"No need to apologize." Deciding I'm in it now, I take a step forward, keeping my voice low. "I didn't mean to interrupt."

"You're not interrupting. I'm just... not great at sleeping. Once I'm up, I just lie there and think about all the things I need to accomplish. Instead of running around in my head, I usually just get up and do something about it. It's been worse than normal lately with the tour stress."

I hum under my breath as I settle onto the couch beside her. "Well, we all know you're more than prepared."

She smiles at me. "Still, there's always something that needs to be done. Especially with the mess Gunner made dropping that article."

As I pivot toward her, I realize I want her take on the situation. I *need* to know how she views Gunner and Melanie's relationship. I still haven't really figured out how I feel about all this new information I've been presented with about Gunner, but something inside me is desperate to know how Natalie feels. It's apparent Gunner was wrong about Melanie, but I'm struggling to figure out how I could have been so wrong about him. "We've never really talked about that... not the contents, anyway. Knox made it sound like this article isn't out of character for Gunner?"

She stares ahead quietly for a few moments before she talks, her voice low. "No, not really. I mean, him making a big public display? Not surprising at all. But for him to stoop this low? I didn't think he would actually drag Mel through the mud to pad his own ego."

"It seems like not very many people like him," I hedge.

She laughs quietly to herself before answering, "Around here? No, not all we. We all see the real Gunner Greene."

I let the silence linger while she decides what to share next. Her fingers trace the perimeter of her laptop, idly dancing around the lid.

"I had my hesitations about him when Mel brought Gunner home for the first time, but she seemed happy—over the moon, even. I didn't have a valid reason for anything I felt; I just… got bad vibes, I guess. So I kept them to myself. In the first year after they were married, things were great. She was truly happy; both personally and professionally. But Gunner slowly started showing his true colors; the more successful Mel became, the more the scales on his skin shone through. And about a year ago, Mel showed up on my doorstep at 2am, suitcase in hand, and one long story falling from her lips."

We're treading in dangerous water, Natalie and I. I don't want to stop her; I want to hear what she has to say, but I should not be getting in this deep. There's already too much she doesn't know.

Against my better judgment, I keep quiet, letting her continue.

"We stayed up the entire night, Mel spilling everything about her life with Gunner. Letting me see behind the façade and the mess that she'd been dealing with. I felt horrible for not knowing. She insisted she did her best to hide how awful he truly was on purpose, but I still hold on to the guilt. It's my job to look out for her, and somehow, I never even noticed. Not really.

"I'm sure you know this, but Gunner is an owner of the record label that Mel records under. When Mel hit it big with her fourth album and that first big tour, Gunner saw dollar signs. She wanted a break after that. Some time just to enjoy her success, but I guess that's when things got really bad. He had told her she wasn't allowed to slow down, that she was going to be too old to be successful in the industry. He just kept pushing her harder; she obliged, and before long, Mel was a shell of the person she had been, all of that light snuffed out. Her passion for music was smothered in the suffocating smoke of Gunner's ambition." She stares straight ahead, clearly remembering the situation a little too thoroughly.

"You can't blame yourself for what you didn't know. It seems like Gunner might be good at hiding who he truly is, or maybe he's better at only showing you what he wants you to see. And even if you had known the whole time, Melanie's a big girl; you can't hold yourself accountable for the choices she makes."

"I know... I just... I felt like I should have seen it? You know?"

"I get it. You shoulder a lot of responsibility for her, and even Dex. You know they're full-grown adults too, right?"

"Of course I fucking know, Jake. It's not something I can just turn off. Once we lost both of our parents, my focus became singular. Even though I was just eighteen, I was suddenly responsible for providing for two other people. I was so concentrated on getting Melanie and Dex through high school, and then college. I shed the sibling role on the day of the car accident. And I haven't been able to turn it back on since.

"On her first tour several years back, I saw the light in her eyes. I saw her find genuine joy for the first time in her life, and I promised myself nothing, and no one, would take that away again. *That* was all I ever wanted for both of them, and she finally had it. And now, she's back in the trenches with Gunner. He's ruining everything she's worked so hard for. This role gets blurry. The line between sister and publicist is a gray area."

I nod my head like I understand even though I very much don't. I have such a thin relationship with my own siblings, one-sided phone calls and voice memos sustaining it for the last decade. None of the effort ever made by me. Gunner is the closest thing I've had to a friend, but even that is paper thin, I'm realizing; it's never been a genuine relationship.

"She left Gunner immediately after that night at my apartment, started breaking their lives back into two, and threw herself into planning and preparing for this new tour. Now, she's so close to being free from him again, to being back on that stage where she found herself. I won't let him take that from her. I will fight him tooth and nail to get her through this… I'm just afraid of fucking it up. To miss something again."

I take advantage of the shift in the conversation, knowing her part in this is something I can honestly engage with. I turn toward her, seeing the outline of her features in the dim lighting of the bus. "You're not fucking anything up, you know. Not even close."

She smiles timidly, but doesn't look my way.

"I'm serious, Natalie. Remember what I said by the river? You are a force to be reckoned with. You have taken on this entire scandal, in addition to PR for an entire fucking tour, and you haven't missed a beat. Even when you thought your plan had failed, it didn't. You still pulled it off."

She turns toward me now, meeting my eyes. "I just… want it to be enough, you know? I need it to feel like I'm worthy of the trust, the role."

"It's more than enough. You have earned your position. Hell, I don't know if there's a publicist in any industry who works as hard as you do. You just need to give yourself permission to accept that. To know you're doing the best job you can and that it's ok to put yourself first."

Her eyes gloss over. "That's… Thanks, Jake. That means a lot."

"I'm just saying what everyone here is thinking, Natalie. I know I'm still new here, but I can tell how valued you are. No one wants you to burn yourself out for them."

Her eyes shine as she looks at me, a look of adoration painting her features. "You're not so bad, you know?"

"Oh, I know. Glad you're catching on."

She laughs before meeting my eyes, serious again. "Sorry I thought you were an asshole. Sorry for treating you like one."

"You can stop apologizing to me anytime now. I probably earned a good amount of that attitude, anyway. But I've spent enough time with you to understand where you're coming from. I see you, Natalie."

A single tear slides down her cheek. I wipe it away quickly, snatching my hand back as soon as I realize what I'm doing.

"If you ever need someone to have *your* back, I'm here. No conditions, no strings. Just say the word."

The look of vulnerability in her eyes is all I need to know how much she needed that. Needed someone to be there for her.

And I mean it, I can and will be.

But as we say our good nights and both slide back into our own bunks, the realization that I've gotten in too deep, muddied the waters too much, crawls over me. I'm not sure how Natalie is going to react when she realizes what I've been hiding from her.

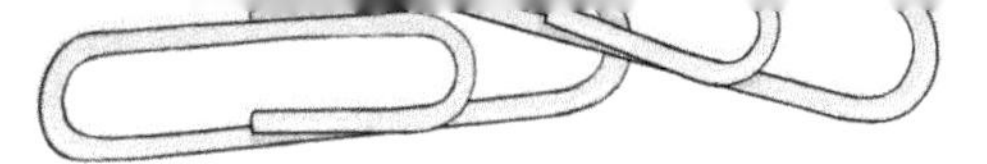

Melanie and I use most of the second and third day of our drive to Glendale to do some planning with Indy and Austin for The Tracks shows. With ample hours of nothing to do but sit and chat, it's the perfect time to give them some backstory and help them plan the episode lineup.

We've been going through the tour logistics, chatting about the calendar, what the PR events will look like, and mapping out a general idea of what they want to highlight for the last several hours. As we're wrapping up, Indy leans in, "Ok, so if that's all the technical stuff out of the way. Can we talk about the good stuff?"

I can hear Austin laughing beside her as he excuses himself, his part in the planning done. She ignores him; looking conspiratorial, her eyes shifting between Melanie and me.

"Absolutely." I say brightly. "What did you have in mind?"

"I want to know about the show. Austin and I talked about weaving behind-the-scenes details into each episode, maybe highlighting something different about the show each time we air a new podcast or vlog, something that will be more show focused and less directly about Melanie. I want to start with the behind-the-scenes of what planning was like and how the tour is going to play out, what kind of input you had on everything."

"Oh, that's brilliant." Melanie says excitedly. I smile beside her, loving the idea. I knew bringing these two on board was the right choice. Indy is so creative and thoughtful. Adding a focus on the themes of the tour itself will be a great inclusion. It makes the whole idea seem more intentional, like we were always going to have someone with us and this isn't a Hail Mary I just threw together.

Indy pulls out a new notebook from her backpack, rifling through it until she finds the page she was looking for. "Ok, so what can you tell me about the concert itself? Anything about the set list or the production? Is there anything specific you *want* highlighted that we should focus on?"

Melanie mulls this over for a minute, absentmindedly snacking on a cookie as she does.

"Well, the premise behind the show is probably the most important one," she begins. "The set list is organized so that it tells a story. I think it'll be obvious from the way the set and costumes change, but we can go through that if you want to start there, and then you'll know what to expect if you want to plan around it."

"I love that. That's a great idea." Indy writes quickly.

"The premise of the show is different visions, basically," Mel begins. "We named it the Peripheral Vision Tour as a play on the term. Peripheral Vision is literally what's happening outside the focus of your vision, in this case the focus in my life. Less about the actual who, what, when of a moment and more about the *feeling* of the moments. Imagine it being that hazy sort of vision that lives on the edge of what's happening right in from of you."

"Well, that seems deep... and really appropriately timed." Indy laughs.

"Now more than ever," Mel agrees, continuing on. "It's a hard concept to explain, but I'm hoping the show layout tells the story and people leave the concert with a full understanding of why I chose Peripheral Vision."

We spend the better part of the afternoon talking through the set list, the themes for each act, and looking through more photos, before we finally call it quits.

"This is... wow," Indy says. "I don't even have words. I'm so excited to see this live."

"Thank you," Mel replies. "It's been a labor of love. I've spent the last, god, almost two years now developing all of this with my team. The fact that we're just days away from it being a reality is mind-boggling to me."

"I bet." Indy caps her pen, closing up her notebook. "I need to nail down specifically how I'm going to organize this, but I'm loving the idea of hitting each stage of your show during the series too. We could slowly work our way through the storyline, each episode providing more details about the different stages. We could align the vlog content to fit it too..."

Her pace picks up speed as she fires off ideas for the segments, how they can tie these show details into the portions we worked on earlier that center on Melanie. Indy is so insightful, so thoughtful. They have a single teaser episode out for Melanie's feature, and already the plans are bigger and better than I ever expected.

We wrap our discussion up, and I put my computer away, settling into the couch. I smile as I turn my attention out the window, feeling an odd sense of peace as I feel everything come together.

I only hope this feeling lasts once everything is in motion, and the tour has officially begun.

We arrive at the hotel late that night; the sun having set several hours ago. I wait patiently for my luggage to be offloaded and then make my way inside. Dex is already standing in the entryway with his assistant, passing out room keys. I make my way up to them, struggling to free a hand from beneath my tote bag and the jacket slung over my arm. Before I can maneuver enough items to free my hand, Jake reaches out in front of me, snagging my card, before grabbing his own.

"Natalie and Jake. Two birds, one stone. Gotcha." He crosses our names off his clipboard as he continues talking, "Natalie, you're in Mel's suite with her. Asher, you're also on the top floor."

He adds the last part as Asher joins us, Dex stretching his hand out to pass off one more keycard before the three of us turn toward the elevators, slowly making our way toward the correct floor. Melanie is nowhere to be seen, but I assume she had a driver take her and Knox around to the service entrance. We do our best to keep her location under wraps for as long as possible when we travel. Sometimes we get away with it; sometimes we don't. The bigger she gets, the harder it is, because now people recognize her team too from time to time. It's easy to figure out that where her staff is, so is she.

When the elevator stops, Asher heads in the opposite direction from Jake and I, his room at the other end. Jake and I wander quietly toward the far corner, where the door to Mel's suite is. With my card still in his hand, Jake reaches around me to tap my card on the reader. He scans the card once, twice, three times, the little red light blinking angrily at us each time.

"I think there might be something wrong with your card." He looks at me, wiggling the card in the air as he does.

I sigh heavily, shifting my weight as I balance all of my stuff and my two large suitcases. I take the card from him, scanning it myself for good measure, but the door isn't any happier with my own attempt to get inside.

"C'mon, you can wait in my room until we get this sorted out." He pivots, walking back the way we came, past several doors before approaching his own. He swipes his card and the reader immediately lights up green for him, a loud click signaling the door has unlocked.

He enters the room, holding the door wide as I lumber my way through with my luggage. I shove the large rolling suitcases off to the side before dropping onto the far bed, my things falling from my arms with a loud thunk onto the hotel room floor.

"Tired, Princess?" He lifts one eyebrow, his lips tugging up into a smirk.

I heave myself up onto my elbows, glaring at him. "I really fucking hate that nickname."

"I know you do." He turns away, but I offer a polite middle finger to his back before I roll over, pulling my phone out of my pocket. I dial Dex, hoping to get a replacement key card, but his voicemail picks up.

Cancelling the call, I try Melanie, but her phone rings through to voicemail as well. I'm sure she's not even up here yet, but it was worth a shot.

Switching gears, I pull my text messages up before firing one off begging Dex to fix my keycard and another to Mel asking how long it's going to be before she's in our room. I send a follow-up message to both of them, letting them know where to find me before I flop back down.

I can hear Jake rustling around on the other side of the room, but I remain where I am, listening to the hum of the air conditioner while I wait for someone to respond. My eyes grow heavy as I lie there, staring at the black screen of my phone. I don't have the energy to fight sleep right now, so I don't, letting the lull of the air conditioner pull me under.

A loud knock wakes me sometime later, the plush white bedding tucked beside me. Rolling over, I notice the pillow tucked beneath my head as the hotel room door opens. I'm too groggy to pay attention to the two deep voices echoing in the room. I realize I should probably get up, but the travel fatigue has hit hard, and the idea of moving my body feels akin to climbing Mount Everest at the moment. Turning away from the door, I pull the covers up under my chin, just as Jake's deep voice grows closer.

"No, that's fine, I can help her. Go get some rest."

The bed shifts as he leans down beside me, his hand on my shoulder. "Hey, Natalie, Dex brought you a working key. You can get some sleep in your own bed now."

Eyes closed, I keep my back to him. "Do I have to?" It comes out half question, half yawn.

I can hear Jake chuckle. "Yeah, you don't wanna spend the night with me. Here—"

Before I can process what's happening, Jake has me scooped up, including the comforter currently wrapped around my body. He carries me over to the door, leaning forward carefully to pull it open with one hand before he turns, moving out into the hall. My arms tighten around his shoulders as he carries me down the hallway and into Melanie's room. I don't remember the door opening, or entering the separate bedroom, but the next thing I know, he's settling me into the clean bed, his warm body pressed against mine as he leans over, placing me on top of my own fluffy duvet. Far too soon, the warmth of his presence is gone, and all I'm left with is a cold pillow, an extra blanket, and a hazy thought that maybe I might like to spend the night with him.

The next time I wake, the sun is streaming through the blinds. I throw the covers off, my feet hitting the soft carpeting as I make my way over to the closed door. I push it open to find Melanie sitting at a small kitchen table across from where I stand, a bowl of cereal in front of her, the spoon halfway to her mouth.

"Morning Nat," she says sleepily, her hair disheveled and her mascara from yesterday smeared into a smoky eye that actually looks impressive and not raccoon-like.

I stifle a laugh, taking her in.

"Um, good morning. Where did all my stuff come from?"

"Jake brought it in after he lugged your sleeping ass to bed," she says matter-of-factly. "You weren't answering your phone, so Dex brought your card up for Jake."

The memory of last night flashes through my head. I might have been half asleep, but I definitely remember curling into his chest as he carried me out of his room and into my own, like I was a doll and not a full-grown woman.

A shiver runs through me at the memory of him over me on the bed right before he left. I push the image away as I dig through the tiny kitchen for a bowl and spoon of my own. Finding both, I sit down across from her at the table and pour myself breakfast.

"What's on the agenda for today?" She asks, knowing I have both of our schedules fully memorized.

"Well, lucky for you, the only rigorous thing is rehearsal later this afternoon. I didn't book anything press-related until tomorrow, and the stage crew won't have the final setup ready for soundcheck until tomorrow either. So you get a nice slow day to recoup from the drive over."

She kicks back, feet up on the chair across from her.

"Well, don't get *too* cozy. We have a team meeting in about fifteen minutes."

She groans quietly.

"I mean, you can take it in your pajamas. I don't know what you're whining about." We both laugh as we finish our breakfasts, polishing off our bowls of cereal just as a knock sounds on the hotel room door.

Before either of us can move, the lock beeps and an entire crew of people comes barreling through the door. The quiet room becomes a cacophony of noise, everyone talking over one another. Knox, with Jake, Asher, and Chase files in. Dex, with two of his assistants and one of mine, as well as Indy and Austin, all make their way through the space. Mel's manager is the last one to arrive, making a beeline for the couch before anyone can steal it from him. Our team fills the small living room, chatter and laughter rippling through the air, and suddenly, anticipation is racing through me.

This is it.

It was one thing when we all loaded up on our buses, but it's another when you're all in the same room, everyone here for the first official meeting of the tour. I get a little giddy at the thought of the next six months.

I reach over, grabbing Mel's cereal bowl before I stand, taking both of our dishes to the sink nearby. I place them next to the drain, giving them a quick rinse before I follow the crew into the living room, watching as everyone finds a place to settle in.

"Should we dive in then?!" Dex looks around, waiting for Mel to join us in the living room before he gets started. "Morning, everyone. Glad to see we're all awake and… *present* this morning."

He crooks an eyebrow at Melanie, sitting in her pajamas.

"Hey, the email from Natalie didn't say this was a formal meeting. I brushed my teeth, even if I'm not dressed yet." Melanie laughs.

"Fine, that's fair. These aren't formal meetings. Wear your PJs if that's your thing." He chuckles, looking around the room. "The first morning in every city will look something like this. We just want an opportunity to bring all our teams together, make sure everyone is on the same page, and rehash the events of the week. I know Natalie has already sent off the schedule in an email, so we can run through it and answer any questions you might have."

He rattles on, covering the key highlights of the week, the timing of rehearsals, show day schedules. I jump in when he's done, highlighting PR events for the week, special requests from the venues, and other important information our teams might need.

"Before we all get too entrenched in to-do lists and pre-show prep of the next couple of days, Mel wanted to do a little something to thank everyone, a little pre-celebration if you will. Thursday night, we have an exclusive event just for cast and crew at The Drunken Cactus. Let your teams know they're invited; full details are in your email, but we just want to take the night, enjoy ourselves a little..." I trail off as Dex catches my attention.

"Key word: A little, Dex. It's not an all night rave; it's a kick-off party." He grins at me, shrugging.

"I didn't say a thing." Everyone laughs, a low murmur of voices sounding around us.

"You don't have to." I pivot my attention back to the group. "Anyway, if you have questions about the party, or any of the events, you know where to find me."

With that, everyone gathers their things, breaking into smaller groups to chat, making their way back out of the hotel room. I watch as they all disperse, the collection of people dwindling until it's just a handful of us. Knox and Jake are chatting in the far corner of the room, and Austin stands off to the opposite side, his laptop tucked under his arm.

"Alright, well, I'm going to get ready and head over to the stadium. Our shipment of PR packets should be waiting for me, and I want to get everything lined up."

Mel smiles as she drops onto the now empty couch. "Austin and I are going through scripts for the podcast for the next week."

"You two have fun."

I make my way back to my room, fishing out my makeup bag before setting up shop in the adjacent bathroom, getting ready for the day.

I'm showered, hair dried, and putting the finishing touches on my mascara when Jake comes into the room, a soft knock on the bathroom doorframe drawing my attention away from the mirror.

"Coffee," he says, placing a cup on the counter next to me before stepping back, keeping a respectful distance between the two of us.

"Oh, thanks! You didn't have to do that."

"Had time to kill. Needed a cup myself." He takes a sip of his coffee.

"I'm almost done here, and we can go. I just need to trade my pajamas for real clothes."

"I don't know; casual suits you." I watch as his eyes scan over me, my bare legs on display in the shorts I'm wearing. It was too hot to put real clothes on after my shower, so I'm standing in my pajamas as he takes me in.

I avoid his eyes when they finally return to my face, knowing my cheeks are turning red. I busy myself with adding an extra coat of mascara as I change the topic. "Thanks for getting me to bed last night. Sorry for making extra work for you."

"Don't mention it."

"Still, that was sweet of you." I throw my mascara into the makeup bag, zipping it up before turning to look at him.

"Just doing my job."

"Taking women to bed is part of your job description?" He smirks at that. I know I'm pushing it, but the high of the morning has me feeling bold.

"If I'm taking a woman to bed, I promise you the last thing she'd be doing is sleeping, Natalie." His gaze heats as we stand there, tension sparking to life between us.

"I'll be in the living room," he says, breaking the charged silence, before turning and stalking away, leaving as quietly as he came.

I watch him go, the door to the bedroom closing behind him, before I snag the cup of coffee off the counter, a perfect vanilla latte greeting me.

TWENTY
NATALIE

Not My Best Idea

On the morning of our first official event, I throw open the door to my bedroom, bounding out into the kitchenette.

Mel barely acknowledges me when I enter the room, her nose buried in her phone as I make my way over and plop down across from her at the table.

"Anything good happening in there?" I ask, gesturing to the phone.

"No, my lawyer emailed this morning."

I cringe, my stomach sinking as I ask the next question, "And what did she have for you?"

"Nothing good." She groans. "Gunner is appealing the latest filing. He's unhappy with yet another set of terms and conditions. At this point, I'm convinced I could give the man every single thing he wants and he would still find something to bitch about."

"They'll get this hammered out, Mel." I try to reassure her, even as rage bubbles up inside of me. Of course, Gunner would try to ruin the first actual day of the tour, intentionally or not. *What isn't he out to ruin?*

"I'm really having a hard time believing that lately." She stares past me, out the window behind my back.

The guys choose that moment to make their way into the room, the beep of the hotel door interrupting us.

"Good morning, sunshine." Knox sings as he makes his way over to us. He stops short when he sees the looks on our faces. "Oh, shit."

Melanie offers him a half-hearted smile as his head swings between the two of us.

"Should we come back?" Knox asks hesitantly.

"No, there's no reason to leave. It's just Gunner. It's always Gunner." Mel heaves a sigh that I feel inside my own chest, the ache permeating. I hate when he gets to her like this.

"Of course it is," he glances at me, the concern I feel etched in his own features. "What did he do this time?"

"More arguments about the divorce paperwork," I provide. "The usual bullshit."

Knox groans, scrubbing his hand down his face. I catch Jake's eye, a look of confusion painted on his face.

I glance away, redirecting my attention toward my sister, wishing we had time to get her out of this funk. Our schedule today is absolutely jam-packed. "Listen, Mel—"

She holds up a hand, cutting me off. "Let's not do this, ok? I'm going to just... let this one go. I don't have time right now to deal with Gunner, with any of it."

Her eyes meet mine as she silently pleads with me. Letting things go is not my forte, but we all have a lot on our plates, and this day needs full attention from both of us. If she wants to ignore this right now, I'll let her.

She turns her attention to Knox. "I'm here for a few more hours this morning, if you have something else you'd like to do. The hair and makeup team should be here any minute to get started."

"Nope, I'm here," he says, dropping onto the couch behind us.

"I am not here, unfortunately. I have to get down to the stadium to set up the media room for today." I slide over, giving Mel a quick hug. "But you know how to reach me if you need anything."

I pivot, staring Knox down, "and you know to call me if she lies about it."

He chuckles quietly. "Yeah, I do."

Reluctantly, I leave Mel and Knox, hating that I can't do more to help her out.

Later that night, the SUV drops Jake and me off outside the entrance to a restaurant in Glendale where we're hosting the tour's first influencer event. Just as I'm getting out of my own car, Mel's SUV drives up, Knox and Asher climbing out before her brunette hair appears, Mel in full glam for her first big event.

I make my way over, offering her a quick hug before the guys usher us toward the building. At first glance, she seems in better spirits than she was this morning, laughing and joking with me. I instantly feel better, hoping for the best for tonight.

The restaurant is a tall white building with a pair of hot pink double doors below the neon sign spelling out the name. Just as we approach the front doors, they swing open, a young man ushering us through.

I grin to myself as I take in the space. The event planner and I have been working on this for months, and it looks even better than I expected. I wanted something special for the first official PR event on the tour, and this will definitely do it.

We spent this afternoon at a local radio station, Melanie doing a series of interviews there, but tonight's event is the one I've really been looking forward to, the one that really feels like the tour kick-off.

"Oh good, you made it!" I hear a shrill voice coming from the other side of the restaurant and turn to find the restaurant's event planner making her way toward us.

"We did! This place looks fabulous. You've outdone yourself."

"Oh please," she swats at me, "it was the least I could do. We're so excited to have Melanie hosting her influencer dinner here. We're huge fans of your music, Melanie."

Melanie smiles, pulling her in for a hug in greeting. "I'm thrilled to be here! This is going to be so much fun."

We make our way through the restaurant, a small table set up in the middle of the room for Melanie to do one-on-one meet and greets. A full six-foot backdrop is standing tall behind it, a blue and purple celestial theme to match the tour vibes shimmers under the restaurant's bright lights.

I help Melanie get situated at the table, making sure she gets some food before any of the guests arrive. Once she's taken care of, I meet with the venue staff, double-checking with the hired bouncers that they have the list of attendees so they can man the doors for the evening.

It's not long before Indy shows up. She has a large equipment bag over her shoulder and a huge smile on her face.

"Oh my god, this place is gorgeous," she squeals as she makes her way over to us. "Look at how perfect this is!"

"It is, isn't it?" I agree. "I booked it because the vibe of the restaurant alone is to die for. We barely had to do anything at all to have the perfect setup for tonight."

She sets her bags down in a booth near us and starts digging through them, coming up with her video camera and the attachable boom mic.

"You're going to have so much content." I watch as she gets the camera operating, the red light blinking on as she pans around the room.

"Oh, I know. It's going to be a lot for the producer to sort through, but thankfully, that's someone else's problem. I'm just here to film it and ask the questions." She laughs. "You can ignore me. I'm going to get shots of the space, and when I come back, I'd love to get some of the two of you working. Austin will be around in just a few minutes here so he can do the camera work for our interview, Melanie."

"That sounds great." She agrees excitedly.

We watch as Indy finishes finagling with the camera gear before she heads off across the restaurant, filming detail shots of all the decor before I shift my attention, ready to focus on making sure tonight goes perfectly.

The next several hours pass in a blur, influencers arriving well before six, when we start a continuous stream of speed interviews for Melanie. I shuffle people through, offering each of them three questions and a photo op. They all have their own cameras for photos and videos, taking their turns with Mel before moving through the restaurant, visiting with other guests and grabbing a bite to eat.

When things finally taper off, I find a window of opportunity to sneak down the back hallway. I pass Indy on the way, quietly filming my sister sitting with two young girls, maybe eight or nine, at her table, chatting animatedly about unicorns, if I heard correctly.

Collapsing on a bench outside the restrooms, my feet are screaming at me; these gorgeous new heels were not a great idea for an event of this length. I close my eyes, leaning my head back on the wall as I take a quick second to myself.

The bone-deep exhaustion sinks in as I listen to the hum of activity in the other room. The long day is catching up to me quickly, and I sigh as I realize this is the first of many, many days just like this. After spending so many months planning the tour, actually kicking it off is something else entirely.

A handful of minutes pass before I hear the shuffle of boots heading toward me. I crack one eye open as Jake approaches.

"Scoot." He says shortly, bumping me with his hip as he drops onto the bench beside me. I oblige, shifting over to make room for him next to me.

"You look dead on your feet." He leans back beside me, his thigh against mine on the bench.

"Mmm, yeah." Still not moving my head, I lift my leg, shaking my foot as I gesture to the shoes. "These were new before this trip. Not my best idea."

I can feel his shoulders shake as he laughs under his breath. "We've been on the go for hours, and this is the first time I've seen you stop for a break. Have you eaten anything today?"

I sit up at that, meeting his eyes as he shifts on the bench, the warmth of his body against mine disappearing as he rotates to face me.

I hesitate. "No. Well, I had a protein bar for lunch."

"Natalie." His voice comes out low and deep. The reprimand not sounding at all threatening, but a shiver runs through me, anyway.

My entire body heats as I occupy myself with looking everywhere but at Jake. We've both carefully held each other at a distance the last few days as we've tackled one event after another. The chaotic schedule has had us barely talking, all of our time spent together since arriving in Glendale occupied with work.

It's been easy to avoid the tension between us that's been near constant since the night of the Grammys. If I can physically keep myself far enough away from Jake, it's possible. If I can keep my mind occupied with work, it's possible. But with him in my space like this, neither of those things being an option, his presence is the only thing I can focus on.

I clear my throat as I shift the topic. "We'll probably only be another hour or two. I hired a crew to clean up after this, so as soon as Mel is done with all the guests, we're free to go."

"Is that reassurance for me, or yourself?" He tips his head in my direction.

"Little bit of both?" I offer sheepishly.

"Natalie!" Indy's voice comes barreling down the hall toward me, and I lean forward, finding her standing several feet down, where the hallway begins. "Can you come help with something?"

"Absolutely." I grimace as I stand again, my feet screaming in protest.

"Have you considered tennis shoes?" Jake asks, standing beside me as he moves to follow me back out into the restaurant.

"That wouldn't be very cute now, would it?" I make my way down the hall, ignoring the persistent ache in my feet.

"You could wear a potato sack and you'd still look good. Maybe you should consider that it doesn't matter what you look like; it matters how you feel."

I don't reply to that, instead making my way toward Indy and Melanie, unwilling to turn around because I know the second I do, he'll see the smile on my face.

TWENTY-ONE

NATALIE

It's nearing midnight by the time we make it back to the hotel. My feet hurt like hell, and my entire body is sore.

Clearly, I am not in the right shape for this tour.

I groan as I drop my tote bag onto the floor, slouching into the nearest chair. Mel falls onto the couch nearby, and we both lie there lifelessly for a few minutes before my stomach rumbles loud enough to wake the dead.

"Hungry much?" Knox asks as he passes through the living room. I jolt upright, my heart racing at his unexpected presence.

"Where did you come from?"

"We've been here as long as you have. I had to grab my stuff I left in here this morning." He laughs as Jake comes up behind him. I must really be out of it if I don't even remember the guys following us in.

"I'm gonna order a pizza if any of you are hungry. I need to eat something, or I will never sleep." Jake scrolls on his phone as he talks, directing his offer to no one in particular.

"I'm done for the day," Mel says through a huge yawn. She drags herself up, rubbing her hand down her face. "I need to get some rest before tomorrow. If I'm this tired today, I'm a little concerned for the actual show."

"You'll be flying high on adrenaline; you'll be good to go," Knox says as he lends her a hand to help her up from the couch. He waits until Mel has bid us all goodnight and shuffles off to her own bedroom before he says, "I'm going to pass. I had about half a dozen tacos at the event. Those things were good, man. You should have gotten some."

"Yeah, clearly I missed out." Jake looks up from his phone, his eyes meeting mine. "Looks like it's you and me, Natalie."

"Oh, no. That's ok. I should really get to bed, too." I brush him off.

"We all heard your stomach. Don't make me eat a whole pizza by myself."

I laugh at that, caving. "Fine, fine. If you insist, I'll help you."

"That's the spirit. Do you want to eat in my room so we don't keep Melanie up?"

"Probably a good idea." I look down at my skirt and blouse, realizing how uncomfortable I am. I shoo the guys out of the hotel room, promising to meet Jake over in his room in a few minutes.

After a quick shower and a change into cozier clothes, I make my way down the hall and tap on Jake's hotel room door. I wait a moment, and when he doesn't answer; I knock twice more. Fishing my cell phone out of my pocket, I dial his number, but he doesn't pick up.

I'm getting concerned when the door finally swings open and Jake stands there, water dripping from his hair, the droplets landing on his shoulders and cascading down his body.

His shirtless body.

Jesus. Who knew he was hiding… all of that?

I swallow as my eyes track a droplet from his shoulder down his arm, over some interesting tattoos I've never seen before. A forest of trees wraps around his bicep, a river flowing down the inside of his arm and cascading toward his elbow. Above the tree line, four birds fly, wrapping around his shoulder where they disappear. I tilt my head as I scan the scene. It feels familiar, but I can't put my finger on why. My eyes snap back to his when he starts talking. "Sorry, I lost track of time. The pizza should be here any minute though."

He steps back, holding the door open for me as I carefully pass him, the scent of his body wash hitting me as I do my best not to stare at his chiseled abs as I make my way into the room.

"Feel free to steal my bed again. I'll be out in just a couple of minutes." He gestures to the unmade bed across the room before closing himself in the bathroom.

Though the idea of crawling into his bed crosses my mind, I opt instead for the tiny table across from it, dropping into the closer of the two chairs sitting next to it, trying to remind myself we have a *working relationship* and nothing more.

I check my email while I wait for Jake to re-emerge, the bathroom door opening just as a knock sounds on the hotel room door.

Jake pivots in that direction, greeting the pizza delivery guy in the hallway. He's forgone the usual black attire tonight, shockingly, instead choosing a white t-shirt and gray sweatpants. The fabric of the tee clings to him, showing off the sculpted muscles of his back. The lighter color reveals hints of ink peeking through the fabric.

I quickly drop my eyes back to my phone as he moves to close the door, pizza box now in hand.

He places the food on the table between us, with a stack of napkins on top.

"I don't have Melanie's accommodations, so I hope you're good with eating out of the box."

I grab a napkin, unfolding it to create a makeshift plate. Jake just chuckles to himself as he grabs for the remaining stack and flips the box open.

We're quiet for a few minutes while we both eat, me over my napkin plate, Jake in the seat across from me, hunched over the box. It should be the most unattractive thing in the world, but somehow *even that* looks good when he does it.

Girl, you have got to get it together.

"Good call on the pizza." I say as I finish up, wiping my fingers and tossing the used napkin onto the table in front of me.

"I know," Jake looks at me, the left side of his mouth tipped up into a smirk, like being right has made his whole damn night. He adds his trash to mine, scooping the mess before he stands up, shuffling across the room to dump it into the trash.

In an effort to keep his ego in check, I add, "I mean, you didn't *have* to force-feed me. I'd have been fine."

I'm talking to his back, but I see his shoulders shake before he turns around. "Probably. Doesn't mean you should make it a habit of starving yourself."

"It's not intentional."

"I know that." He sits on the edge of the bed facing me when he returns.

"Don't get too cocky there. You sound like you know me better than you do."

"I might know you better than you think."

I scoff. "Sure you do."

"Natalie." The way he says my name does something to me, turning the stone walls I keep in place into a gooey gelatin, sliding into a pile of nothingness. "I know you put everyone and everything before your own needs. I know you work yourself to the bone to prove a point; one I'm happy to remind you doesn't need to be proven. I know you're organized; meticulous to a fault. But also one of the most thoughtful people I've ever met."

Warmth bubbles up inside me at the unexpected list of observations. "Ok, ok, point made. You're like some undercover supersleuth."

"No sleuthing required. Just paying attention." The sincerity in his voice only intensifies the warm feeling, an ache forming in my chest. His eyes meet mine, and he doesn't move, holding my gaze for far longer than usual.

"Right," I clear my throat. "I'm glad you know me so well. I feel like I know nothing about you."

"What did you want to know?"

"I don't know... what's your favorite food?"

"Cinnamon rolls." He smiles. "There's a bakery right downtown in Nashville, a block over from The Brew, that makes the best cinnamon rolls I've ever had. You should try them sometime."

"Maybe I will. That sounds amazing."

"Oh, they are. What else you got for me?" He leans forward, resting his elbows on his knees as he looks at me. "I don't have a favorite color. I'm not really into dogs or cats if you want to know my favorite animal. I'll pass on long walks on the beach—"

"More of a smartass who likes a stroll in the woods."

"That's right." The full-on smile he is wearing does things to me. Playful Jake is rare, and I'm not ashamed to admit I like this side of him.

A lot.

"You never said why your parents moved away from there? New job or something?"

"Uh, no. Not exactly." His smile falls as he leans back, resting his palms on the bed behind him, t-shirt pulled tight over his chest.

We've hedged around this before, but the desire to know something *real* about Jake wins out over any hesitation I have about pushing for more. "What do you mean?"

"There were… too many memories in that house. And my mom needed to get out. I think she thought a fresh start might fix us." He takes a deep breath. "I don't usually share this with people, but…"

"It's ok, Jake, you don't have to share. I'm sorry I—"

"No, that's the thing, Nat." He swallows, his eyes meeting mine. "I want to share. I just… I don't talk about it. Ever."

That catches me off guard. I know his family isn't something he talks about, but I didn't realize it might be because it was too hard for him. I sort of assumed he just didn't talk about them, the way he doesn't open up about much of anything.

"I was twelve when my youngest brother died."

I involuntarily suck in my breath. "Jake, I had no idea. I'm, God—"

"No, it's fine." He pauses before he continues. "Well, it's not. It's just… I haven't spoken to a single member of my family since the day I moved out. That was over a decade ago now."

"What happened?" My heart breaks for the man sitting before me, the little boy whose entire life was shaped by tragedy.

I get it.

I lived it.

"We were home alone, fucking around outside in the pool. My parents were at my older brother's baseball tournament. I stayed home with my two younger brothers. My youngest brother, Gabe, slipped on the wet cement. He fell into the pool, hitting his head on the way down. I got him out as quickly as I could, but he was unconscious for too long, and neither of us at home knew CPR. He died before an ambulance ever showed up.

"I... I was in charge. I was supposed to keep them safe while my parents were gone for the day... and I... didn't."

He's quiet for a moment before he continues. "It broke my mom. She never really recovered from the loss. My parents ended up separating a couple years after that. I don't think my dad ever forgave me. I moved out the day after I graduated high school, and I haven't been back since."

"You were just a kid. You can't blame yourself for that."

"Yeah, but age doesn't change the facts of the situation. I was responsible. His death is on me."

"Jake," I shift in my chair toward the bed, scooting closer to him, taking his hand in mine, squeezing tight as I look him in the eyes. "You were a kid in a horrible situation, who did the best he could. You're not responsible for what happened. It was an accident, and I hate that you've lived your entire life believing you're at fault for that."

His eyes scan the room, looking anywhere but at me as I keep going. "I'm so sorry your parents never told you otherwise, but you can't hold responsibility for something like that solely on your own shoulders. That's not fair."

"I mean, I didn't really give them the chance. After the accident, I made myself scarce around the house, spending as much time with friends as I could, or when I was older, working. I left for the Army as soon as I was old enough and I've never gone back. Never... never reached out."

"That doesn't make it ok." I'm angry for him, hurt that someone's parents could essentially just *abandon* their child after something like that. "They never reached out to you?"

"My brothers call from time to time. I've never answered. It is what it is."

I study Jake's face, seeing the sadness etched in his features, the loneliness he's learned to wear like a second skin.

"I think we can safely say you've accomplished the goal of getting to know me." He laughs, but it's forced.

"Jake, I really—"

"Natalie." He meets my eye again. "Don't apologize. I told you because I wanted you to know. I don't really know why—"

He trails off, a rush of affection running through me at the confession, a strange feeling of pride that he feels comfortable enough to confide in me.

"Well, thank you. That means a lot."

It's quiet for a while before he shifts the topic, instead talking about the first show in two days.

I humor him, jumping into the conversation with a little more enthusiasm than I typically have at one o'clock in the morning.

But as we talk, me sharing what I'm looking forward to most, the previous conversation closed, I realize we're *still* holding hands.

I Think I Like You

The bass from the music vibrates my body as I lean against the wall of The Drunken Cactus the night before the first show. My eyes scan the crowd made up entirely of Peripheral Vision Tour cast and crew. The third floor of this building has been reserved for the evening. The bouncers provided a very specific guest list by Natalie for tonight's tour kick-off party.

It's a bonus that the venue security is also working this event because it makes my job that much easier. And with the way my head has been fucked lately, I need all the help I can get.

I've done other full-time contracts like this, dozens of them, and never once have I had an issue keeping my focus on the job. It's like the more time I spend with Natalie, the more of my attention she demands. Not explicitly, but the way I'm attuned to her—finding her in a room, watching her while she works. It's definitely over the line of professionalism. And somehow, I have to get back on the other side before I do something I regret.

Or she gets too deep, and I've got a bigger mess on my hands than just my personal feelings. She still has no clue I know Gunner, that we have a relationship of our own and the closer I get to her, the more the guilt of that secret eats at me.

I watch Natalie now, from across the room, her head thrown back in laughter as she chats with Melanie and Indy, along with some of Melanie's dancers. Tonight, she's chosen to wear a form-fitting pair of black jeans and a little white top that hugs her breasts, flaring out just above her hips. With her fiery red hair down, soft curls surround her face. I watch the way she interacts with the girls, deep in conversation. One hand is occupied by her drink, but the other fidgets with the bottom of her shirt, adjusting the hem where it meets her jeans.

As if she can feel my gaze, she lifts her head, her eyes meeting mine. I hold my drink up to her, in a toast from across the dance floor, Natalie responding with her own beverage as a broad smile crosses her face. My drink is soda, never any alcohol while on the clock, but the way Natalie freely offers me such a wide grin, I know she's got more than just pop in her own glass.

As I stand there watching, Indy tugs Melanie and Natalie out onto the dance floor. They're absorbed into the crowded space, disappearing from my line of sight. I make my way around the edges, watching as their heads bob in the middle of the room. Knox and Austin are both leaning against the far wall, talking, so I make my way over, taking an open spot next to them.

"How's it going?" I ask, raising my glass to my lips as Knox shrugs in reply.

"Oh, it's going." He takes a sip of his own drink.

"Hey Jake," Austin offers a half wave from the other side of Knox.

"Hey Austin." I lean against the wall, crossing one foot over the other as I relax onto the brick. "Goddamn man, all these events are kicking my ass. I didn't realize how on the go we would be."

They both laugh as Knox turns my way. "Buckle up, Buttercup. The Bennett girls don't have a pause button. Thought you might have learned that by now."

"Oh, I'm aware. Doesn't mean I can't hope for a break every once in a while."

Austin chuckles as he leans forward. "Good thing this is a road tour then, isn't it? Guaranteed day or two each week where you have nothing to do but sit on your ass and watch the scenery. At least, that's the part I'm looking forward to."

"That's true." I agree. A loud catcall from the center of the dance floor catches our attention. We look over to see the entire group taking a shot before the DJ turns on Melanie's latest release. The squeals and yelling from the girls ratchet up to a nearly unbearable level as Melanie and her dancers, Natalie, Indy, and several others I don't recognize, break out singing along with Melanie over the speakers.

It's been close to six weeks since I started working with Melanie, and I'm feeling confident all the information about her I've learned from Gunner over the years was complete bullshit. Much like the article he released.

I don't know what to do with this information, but I haven't spoken to Gunner in a couple of weeks, so I'm inclined to keep ignoring the situation for now.

For as long as I can, honestly.

My attention zeroes in on Natalie, her red hair flowing behind her as she tips her head into her sister's and the two of them belt out the lyrics to the song as Dex comes up behind them, slinging an arm over each of his sisters' shoulders. I watch the three of them laughing together, clearly enjoying this moment.

Natalie and I both have tragic pasts, childhood wounds that altered our paths irrevocably. She stepped up when their parents died, keeping the three of them close, hyper-focusing on how to move forward after an unthinkable tragedy.

If I hadn't been at fault, I wonder if I would've handled it more like Natalie. We have a lot in common, the two of us. The difference is that her need to protect and take care of people is personal: she's looking out for her siblings. Mine is a lot more generic: a contract to fill the void in my life. As if helping someone else can somehow make up for the mistakes in my past.

A lead weight settles in my stomach as I process those thoughts. An unsettling feeling that maybe, after all this time, I'm realizing what I'm missing out on, what could have been.

And maybe, after all this time, I'm wishing it were a possibility for me to have it back.

"I think I'm probably ready to call it a night." Natalie yawns as she makes her way over to me a couple of hours later, lifting the arm holding her wineglass, using the back of her hand to cover her mouth as she does.

"Yeah, partied a little too hard?" Her eyes narrow at the question.

"I'm happily buzzed, thank you. That's a great time to end a party." She finishes the contents of her wineglass before spinning on her heels, heading over to deposit the empty cup on the bar top.

"If you say so," I follow along, making our way along the dance floor. We climb our way carefully down three flights of stairs before winding around the building and into an SUV waiting for us.

The drive back to the hotel is only ten or fifteen minutes, but *happily buzzed* Natalie has a hard time keeping her eyes open.

"Did you have a good time tonight?" I ask, hoping to keep her awake long enough for her to get herself upstairs.

Not that I wouldn't love an excuse to get my hands on her again, but I know better.

"I did. That was a lot of fun. I need to do that more." She settles into the seat, the intoxicating scent of her wrapping around me in the backseat of this vehicle.

"Do what?"

"Go out. Get a drink. Have fun."

"You do have a habit of working an awful lot."

The car is dark, but I can tell she has her eyes narrowed at me once again.

"Just stating the obvious," I chuckle.

She yawns again before tipping her head back. "You have a great laugh."

I'm not entirely sure I heard her right.

"Me?" I ask, stupidly pointing to myself.

"Yes, you." She shifts slightly towards me. "I barely ever hear you laugh. You should do it more."

I tip my head in her direction as she continues talking. "I like it. Your laugh. I think I like you. Not gonna lie, when Knox made you my bodyguard, I really thought this was gonna be a disaster. I can't focus when you're around."

The confession spills through the back seat of the car in a barely audible whisper.

"Is that so?" I can't stop the tug on my lips, and even though it's dark, I scrub my hand over my face so she can't see the stupid-ass grin on my face.

"No, you're so distracting. And you have no idea."

That pulls a quiet laugh out of me. She's going to be upset with herself tomorrow if she keeps talking like this. "You're kinda drunk, you know that?"

"I'm fine." Her half-hearted argument dies when her head lolls to the side, landing on my shoulder. She curls up against my arm, resting motionless for several long moments before she says, "I think I lied."

Against my better judgment, I respond, knowing damn well sober Natalie would not be this open with me. "About what?"

"I do like you. More than I should." She shifts in her seat, closing her eyes as she kicks her legs out beside her.

"All good, Nat. I like you too."

She's quiet for a long time, her breaths evening out as we make our way toward the hotel, but before she falls asleep, she lets one more truth slip. "I wish you didn't regret kissing me."

The confession lands somewhere behind my ribs, sharp and unexpected. And though I don't acknowledge that last shared secret, I do spend the rest of the night thinking about it.

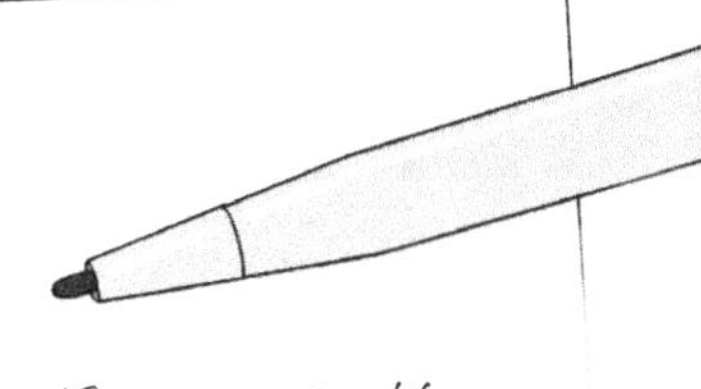

On our way to the final soundcheck, I take Jake in as I sit across the vehicle from him, watching from behind my dark shades. He is relaxed in his own seat, elbows propped on his knees as he leans forward, scrolling aimlessly through his phone. His usual black leather jacket is gone, replaced instead by an official security jacket for today. Still black, of course, but this one is a windbreaker jacket. The soft fabric makes a swishing noise as Jake pockets his phone, shoving both hands into the pockets instead. A small Shield Security logo is embroidered on the chest next to the zipper, with a bold "Alder" in gray letters beneath it.

The jacket falls open at his sides as he sits back, a tight black tee clinging to his chest beneath it. I watch the way his chest rises and falls as he breathes; the muscles moving as he does.

I let truths slip that I shouldn't have in my hazy, buzzed state after the cast and crew party last night. I wish I could take back telling him those things, but instead I'm just pretending nothing happened last night. Like I don't remember.

As if I could forget.

I've stopped wondering when this is going to pass. This attraction? Weird infatuation? Obsession? Whatever it is, it's apparently here to stay. What I need to figure out now is how to fucking deal with it because constantly thirsting after someone is really going to be a problem for me.

Melanie clears her throat to my left, and I jump, caught off guard by the noise.

"Hello, earth to Natalie." She pokes my ribs.

"What?"

"I said, are you going to come backstage when the show starts?"

"Oh, um, I can. I will!"

"You can watch the show opener from the main stage. The front scaffolding stays open for the first part of the set so you can see the stage from both sides. I thought it might be cool for you to see it, since I assume most of the shows you'll be in the VIP tent."

"Yeah, for sure." I'm trying to focus on the conversation, but I can feel Jake's eyes on me and it's distracting as hell.

Thankfully, the car pulls up to the stadium entrance at that moment, maneuvering through a gated entrance, down underneath the facility to the private parking bay. I'm immediately preoccupied with making my way through the stadium, Mel and I following behind Knox and Asher as we weave our way through the building.

Soon, the five of us find ourselves backstage, behind the main stage entrance. The doors are swung wide right now, with a plethora of activity happening on the other side. I wander onto the stage to see the venue from this viewpoint.

The elevated floor sprawls out before me, a giant diamond making up the furthest stage out in front of us, one long rectangle forming the main stage behind it. Lighting hangs overhead, dozens and dozens of lamps and tracking pieces rigged to the ceiling, none of them turned on yet.

It's so cool to see everything in the quiet lull before the chaos of the event picks up. Most of my time here this week was spent in the media room, prepping for the journalists set to arrive in just a couple of hours. I haven't made it down to the main bowl before now to take it all in.

"Jake, we have a problem." I can hear Knox's voice coming from behind us. I spin on my feet to see him heading in our direction from the main stage, phone to his ear. "Chase can't find the security director for the stadium, and he's got a crew of t-shirt people wanting to know where they're supposed to report."

"And this is our problem, how?" Jake asks from beside me.

"Because we're the only security in the building at the moment, it would appear." Knox makes no effort to hide his annoyance. "I can't leave Melanie, who needs to start the soundcheck. I don't really want to have Asher off on this either. I'm not comfortable with just one of us on Melanie."

"I'll take care of it." He flicks his eyes to me. "Are you ready to get over to the media room? We can head that way, and I can see if I can problem-solve this."

I nod as Knox clasps Jake on the shoulder. "Thanks, man."

He wraps up his phone call, telling whoever he's talking to that Jake is on his way. We make our way back across the stage, retracing our steps through the building into the main hall once again.

We arrive at the media room and I make my way inside, dropping my tote on the front table before turning back to face Jake.

"Are you ok if I leave you here while I run down to the security offices?" He scans the room as if he's making sure nothing is going to pop out at us.

"Yes, Jake, I'm fine. I can handle fifteen minutes alone."

As he promises to be back, I realize that fifteen minutes alone might just be the thing I need to clear my head, get my focus where it needs to be before this concert starts.

"I've got the venue lights going down in five. Tech, are we ready to roll with the opening sequence?" There's yelling coming from all directions as I hustle down the main aisle backstage, making my way toward Mel. I meant to be back here with plenty of time to see her before she went on, but I got stuck in the press room answering questions for much longer than I anticipated it taking. I thought I could just usher them all out to the stadium floor, and they'd disperse, but apparently not without a couple hundred questions about the performance first.

I weave through the crew, Jake hot on my heels. Backstage is a flurry of noise and activity; the buzz of opening night completely electric.

I approach a group of Mel's backup dancers and I know I've found the right area. I squeeze around the perimeter of their waiting spot, careful not to interrupt, and make my way near the front entrance of the stage. Nodding to the lighting technicians, I duck under some scaffolding and finally spot Melanie talking to her sound engineer, up front, right behind the main door. Even over the noise and chatter of the backstage activities, I can hear the dull roar of the crowd through the heavy doorframe.

"MELLY." I squeal in excitement as I launch myself at her and wrap her up in a big hug.

"You did this." I pull back and gesture around me, waving my hand up and down in front of me toward the door, the chatter of the crowd loud even through the thick metal. "THIS. Is all because of you." I poke her gently on the shoulder, and she grins wildly at me.

She looks ethereal in the costume for her opening number. It's the same sparkly black and silver outfit I saw her in at the costume fitting, but it looks even more perfect under the dim lighting of the space. She shimmers in the lights dancing through the cracks of the scaffolding, reflecting off the sequins and tinsel in her dress.

"Melanie! Curtain call in three minutes." A voice booms from behind us, making Mel and I both jump.

"You've got this!" I quickly hug her once more, and then squeeze her hand before I turn away. I wave over my shoulder at Jake and we tuck ourselves into the far left scaffolding to watch my sister's opening from behind the stage. We're back far enough to be hidden, but close enough that I can see her whole entrance.

I hear the countdown audio start out front and, moments later, the lights go out. Every single one of us backstage disappears from what would be the crowd's line of sight, absorbed into the darkness.

Melanie stands up front, with her back to me, lit up from a row of track lights immediately behind her. The mic is in her right hand, resting lightly at her side. Her hip is popped, knee bent, and her chin tipped up to the night sky.

The doors in front of her roll slowly open, as smoke billows from the fog machines positioned on either side behind her. I see the crowd coming into view, thousands of lights flashing and sparkling outside in the stands; the noise surging to a deafening roar. Mel begins the choreography, and her backup dancers sashay past us, out onto the stage to join her.

I'm lost in a trance, watching everyone move on the stage in front of me. I watch the dancers floating around my sister; the choreography absolutely magical. When the first song ends, she transitions seamlessly into the next, and I use this opportunity to head to the VIP tent so I can watch the rest of the show from the audience.

I gesture to Jake to follow me, and we weave ourselves back through the stage area, slipping out the side entrance, and hurrying around to where the VIP tent stands. I flash my ID to the venue security guards outside the tent, and Jake and I enter. There's seating in the tent, but no one is using it. Everyone has congregated at the front, behind the safety barriers, crooning to get a better look at each of the performances. I join them, threading through the clusters of people until I reach the front.

As we press ourselves forward, I can feel Jake's presence behind me, and I realize this tent was probably a bad idea. Backstage had more breathing space. The tent is so full of people, all vying to see the first show, that Jake's body is nearly entirely up against mine.

As we settle in against the barrier, I hear my name yelled from the left, Indy and Austin making their way over to us, fighting the crowd not willing to give up their coveted spaces up front. Eventually, Indy finds a spot beside me, with Austin on the far side of her.

When we first talked about it, Indy had wanted to use her backstage pass right out of the gate tonight, but I convinced her and Austin to enjoy a show first, to see it in action before they started filming content for the series. I understand the thrill of diving into something headfirst, but even *I* know something like this is meant to be enjoyed. At least for a show or two.

The energy of the stadium is contagious, racing through me as I watch my sister and her team on stage. Everyone is fully immersed in the songs, singing and dancing along, oblivious to anything but Melanie's presence on stage. The choreography, the theatrics, the entire production is absolute magic. I'm enraptured, taking it all in, one song at a time.

By the third or fourth song, Indy and I have abandoned all decorum, singing along just as loudly as everyone else in the tent behind us. It's a unique kind of high, screaming your sister's lyrics with twenty-five thousand other people. I feel giddy, and so fucking proud, as I watch her on stage, having the time of her life.

Jake is jostled into my back, his hands coming up to grip my hips as he fights to maintain his balance. I can hear his voice in my ear, feel his breath against my neck as a low "sorry" breaks through the noise of the concert. Despite the number of bodies in here, and the sheer overstimulation, the only thing I can focus on right now is Jake. His chest is flush against my back, my ass pressed against him. I can no longer think about the incredible show my sister is putting on. Instead, my brain short-circuits and all I can think about is the body against mine.

I try to throw all my focus back into the music, but I notice Jake doesn't move away; doesn't move his hands. His grip tightens as I dance in front of him, almost as if he doesn't *want* to let go.

Undecided if I'm testing my patience or Jake's, I take a step back, forcing Jake back a step as well, allowing the crowd to close in front of us along the barrier. We slip into the mass of people, nothing more than two bodies in a sea of thousands.

Without the front row view, that also means it's harder for anyone outside this tent to see us now. I take this moment of freedom to move my hips to the music, feeling the growing evidence that Jake is enjoying this as much as I am. Heat pools between my legs as I try to act unaffected, pretending to be lost in the music, despite the circumstances. It's a weirdly intimate moment, trapped between all of these people. But despite the proximity, none of them are paying any attention to either of us.

The last song of the middle set of the concert comes to an end, and the crowd breaks out into a loud round of cheers. I join them, throwing my hands up as the lights go down. Melanie and her crew are blanketed in darkness while they switch sets. As I stand on my tiptoes to see over the people now in front of me, I feel Jake's fingers slide up my side, brushing the bare skin along my waistband beneath my shirt.

I pause, but I don't say anything out loud, instead, pressing back against him, a silent acknowledgment of the change in position. When I don't move, Jake's right hand joins his left, now both with a firm hold on my bare skin.

If I weren't already warm from the dancing and the sheer number of bodies in this tent, the heat currently coursing through my veins would have given me away in an instant. We stay that way for the entire third act, Jake's hands roaming my bare skin, though respectfully sticking strictly to my hips and stomach, never higher, and, *fucking hell,* never lower either.

I'm so distracted I don't realize the show has ended. The crowd in the tent swelling as everyone tries to get the best view of the final bows. I watch Melanie on stage with her dancers, and I know without a doubt she killed it, even though I didn't actually see the last few songs.

The stadium lights kick on as everyone disappears from the stage, flooding the interior of the tent with light. We make our way toward the exit with the crowd, moving at a glacial speed as all of us try to leave the tent at the same time. It's not until we're finally through the small, gated fence, that the crowd opens up, cool air rushing around us, that Jake drops his hands, taking two big strides away from me.

But despite the distance, I can still feel the fire burning where he had his hands on my body.

TWENTY-FOUR

JAKE

Goddamn Blackout

There's doing your job and then there's... *whatever the fuck that was.*

That was not doing my job.

That was... every ounce of common sense I have leaving the building. Every professional expectation just, non-existent.

I took liberties I should not have. There was no reason for me to even *stand* that close to Natalie. Absolutely no reason for me to have my hands on her...

... and yet, I did.

And fuck if I didn't like it.

We enter the green room, my mind a million miles away. It's ironically a very non-green room built into the back of the stage, just a few feet from the stairs that take you up to the entrance to the main stage. The space is meant to be a room for Melanie, the dancers, and special guests to wait before a specific appearance in the show.

Tonight, the room is prepped for an end of the show celebration; several ice buckets are situated on the end tables, bottles of champagne chilling in them for the crew. A few small standing tables have been added as well, also donning ice buckets and champagne glasses.

The crew files in slowly, the noise in the space growing as the crowd does. Natalie head towards the far side of the tent, finding Indy and Austin on a bench with Dex. I watch as she plops down next to them, a big smile on her face.

Slipping off to the side, I step out of the way, taking in a big lungful of air as I attempt to realign my brain with other parts of my body. In all my time as a bodyguard, I have had no issues keeping my personal life separate from my professional one. I've never once crossed any sort of line, physically or emotionally; never even felt *tempted* to cross the line. I need a pause, a reset, *maybe a lobotomy.* I'm not sure how we went from being at each other's throats to kissing to... whatever *this* has become, but I do know the crux of that issue has been *me.*

Professional as fuck, Alder.

Melanie enters the room to a deafening roar of applause. Every person standing, cheering for the star of the night.

I watch as she makes her way through the crowd, stopping to greet the cast and crew as they congratulate her, showering her with praise and attention. It's clear that everyone working with her loves her. I've heard nothing but praise of Melanie this entire week.

The clinking of a glass pulls me out of my thoughts. The crowd grows silent as everyone turns toward Dex, the source of the noise.

"If I can have just a second..." his voice rolls through the room, loud and deep. "I just wanted to say thank you to every person in this room. Tonight's performance would not have been possible without you, and your dedication to this tour, and to Melanie, is deeply appreciated."

Melanie slides up beside him, holding her glass in the air as well, as she picks up where Dex left off. "It's really impossible for me to convey how thankful I am, that we all are, for each one of you. Tonight was a dream come true for me, for many of us in this room, and I only have this privilege because of everyone working tirelessly around me. So thank you for being here, for supporting me and this team, for being a part of this journey... and cheers to another twenty-three weeks of shows just like tonight!"

A loud chorus of "cheers" echoes around the room, glasses bobbing through the air, before a round of applause breaks out, the team celebrating their much-deserved success.

Hours later, with the concert venue fully prepped for the next show tomorrow, and many, many tired people dispersed, I'm following Natalie down the hall in the hotel.

We enter the stairwell, Natalie taking the steps at a brisk pace, despite the bitter exhaustion I saw on the drive back here. I catch up to her, grabbing her elbow. She pauses abruptly on the landing before turning to face me.

"Hey, can we talk for two seconds?" I ask, loosening my grip. She shakes me off with a sigh.

"About what? I really just want to get to bed. I'm exhausted."

I rub the back of my neck. "I know, I just… think we need to address the tent—"

"Here? Now?" She gestures around the empty stairwell, a look of incredulity on her face.

"Listen, I don't know what's wrong with me. I'm doing stupid shit and I—"

"If you want to have a conversation just so you can write off your behavior, I don't want to hear it, Jake." She crosses her arms, her gaze narrowed on me. "You're a grown-ass man who has full control of his actions. You either mean to do it or you don't. Do not start with the back and forth."

I scrub my hand over my face. I get her frustration. I'm fucking annoyed with myself too. "That's the thing… there shouldn't *be* any back and forth. It never should have happened."

"You've said that before, remember? I *know* that none of this should be happening." She raises her voice. "But I'm not the one instigating. *You* kissed me. *You* had your hands on me."

She steps forward, poking me in the chest with her finger.

Grabbing at it, I wrap her hand in mine as I tug her toward me. I grit my teeth, but the confession slips out anyway; the words spilling from me before I can grab them back. "I know, Natalie. But I don't know how to fucking stop."

"What?" Her eyes go wide as I finally give her something real.

"I have no self-control around you." I continue slowly. "I can't think. You scramble every thought in my head. You walk into a room, and you demand my undivided attention just by being there. I'm in a goddamn blackout, and nothing exists except for you."

I press her back against the wall. Dropping her hands, I prop my forearm against the wall and box her in, forcing her to meet my eyes. My voice is low as I say, "I've been doing this for almost a decade, and nothing has been as dangerous to me as you are."

Her breath catches as she shifts, dropping her gaze, her chocolate brown eyes roaming my collarbone, my neck, anywhere but my face, as she considers what I said.

"Tell me how to make it stop." I put my left hand on her hip, just as I did earlier, my thumb slipping onto the sliver of skin between the fabric of her blouse and skirt. I don't even fight the urge to feel her smooth skin beneath my hands, rubbing the pad of my thumb along her waistband.

"I... I don't know, Jake," she whispers back, looking up at me through her lashes, giving me her full attention.

"Then tell me that this insatiable urge is all you think about, too."

"Does it matter? Does it matter whether I agree or disagree? Because we both know nothing can happen. I can't be with my bodyguard, Jake. You can't be with your *client.*"

I watch her throat bob as she swallows, her eyes still fixed on mine. The desire swirling in them so potent it takes everything I have not to crash my lips to hers.

Instead, I do something equally stupid, leaning in, running my nose down the column of her neck, before making my way back up, whispering into the shell of her ear, "I know that. I do, but the thing is, Natalie... I don't care."

She tips her head back, a rush of breath leaving her as she pushes herself flush against me, every nerve ending alight.

I feel her hands pressing against my chest. Leaning back, I take in the planes of her face. Her hazy eyes watching me. The deepening pink in her cheeks, telling me what she won't say out loud... that she's feeling this too.

"Jake, seriously. This is..."

She trails off as I take her jaw between my thumb and forefinger, tilting her head back.

"It's what, Natalie?"

She stares at me, her teeth digging into her bottom lip.

I repeat my question. "It's what... Natalie?"

Instead of waiting for a response, I press my lips against the corner of her mouth. A kiss that's barely there. A tease meant to leave her wanting as badly as I do.

"This is..." I feel her breathing, heavy against me as I wait for her answer. "A terrible idea."

She arches, seeking friction, and a low moan tumbles out of my throat.

I let go of her chin, pulling my arm off the wall as I slide both of my hands down the sides of her body, feeling the curve of her breasts and the dip of her waist before running my fingertips over her thighs. I grab ahold, squeezing the backs of her legs, lifting as I press her back into the cement wall while she wraps her legs around my waist, her core grinding against my cock.

I've been half-hard all night, but that first roll of her hips makes my dick stiffen painfully inside my pants. She lets out a gentle moan as I kiss along her jaw, taking my time making my way to her lips.

Her hand reaches up, surprising me, as she cups the back of my head and forces my mouth back to hers, a quiet mewl coming from her as our lips meet. She squirms in my hold, and I dig my fingers into the flesh of her thighs, straining to keep myself in check.

The kiss is needy, desperate. Fueled by days of pent of up frustration and denial. The way she moves against me tells me she's just as desperate as I am.

My entire body aches at the feel of her against me. I slide my hand down the outside of her thigh and up along her leg, beneath the fabric of her skirt. She rolls her hips again, and I pause, just short of the apex of her thighs.

Pulling back from her, my chest heaves as I look her in the eyes.

"Tell me to stop, Natalie." I whisper, kneading my fingers into her thighs.

Her response is low, a whine slipping from her as she shifts her body, my fingers coming dangerously close to her core.

"No."

I groan. Any thought I had of holding myself back completely evaporated with that single syllable. I let my fingertips slip beneath the elastic of her underwear, teasing her as I slide my hand slowly up, feeling the moisture collecting on the pads of my fingers.

"Jesus, you're already soaked, aren't you?"

She cants her hips in response, forcing my fingers to slide right through her core and up to her clit. Tilting her head back at the contact, she rests it against the wall, and a low chuckle escapes me.

Watching her come undone might be my new favorite thing.

"It's always like this." Her voice is strained, the admission broken by a shuttering breath.

"Like what?"

"This ache. Around you. It's constant." I drop my head into the crook of her neck as her fingers dig into my shoulder blades. She hisses between her teeth, her nails digging half-moons into my skin, even through the fabric of my shirt.

I run my tongue along her collarbone, feeling her shudder against me as I rub my thumb against her clit. Working small circles against the sensitive flesh, I slide my fingers down, teasing her entrance.

"Oh, my god." Her voice is gravel in my ear as she moves against me. "If you don't…"

She trails off as I pull my fingers away from her core, gathering the wet material of her thong and tugging on it.

"If you want my fingers, these have to go." One last tug on the scrap of fabric breaks it free from her hips. I ball up the torn thong and shove it into my pocket.

Her head snaps down, brown eyes wide. "Jesus, Jake."

I don't acknowledge that, instead sliding a finger into her, her core immediately clenching around me.

"That's what you wanted, isn't it? You were dying to have my fingers inside your tight fucking pussy."

My name is her only response as her back leaves the wall, arching further into me.

"Say it again," I say, withdrawing my fingers, feeling her chasing my touch. "Say my name and I'll give you more."

She whines, but I hear a husky "Jake" in my ear, my cock twitching painfully at the sound of my name leaving her lips. I press into her, imagining the feel of her around my dick while I thrust two fingers inside her, giving her exactly what I promised.

"Good girl." I say, my thumb finding her clit, her entire body writhing against me. The only sounds in the stairwell are her quiet pants and the wet slide of my fingers as they move in and out of her.

It only takes several quick thrusts before I feel her clenching around my fingers, her entire body going taught as she comes with a soft cry, her orgasm rolling through her. Her hands cling tightly to my shoulders as I work her through it, my fingers and thumb moving in tandem as the waves roll through her. When her breathing slows and she slumps back against the wall, I slip my hand out, carefully wiping my left hand on my shirt.

I watch as she leans against the wall, the swell of her breasts rising and falling, my cock painfully hard against my zipper. I can feel the pre-cum leaking from the tip, but refuse to acknowledge my own needs right now.

"Fuck," I say, as I trail a line of soft kisses along her jaw and down her neck once more. "You look incredible when you come."

I feel her legs loosen around my waist, gently setting her back on the ground. She shimmies her skirt down, adjusting it so it falls smoothly against her legs once more.

"I—holy shit, Jake." Her eyes meet mine, her cheeks flushed, as she anxiously pushes her hair back off her face. The tiny flyaways looking both adorable and untamed.

I run the fingers of my right hand along her cheekbone, crooking a finger under her chin as I drop one more kiss to her lips. It's slow and gentle, exactly the opposite of every kiss before this.

She settles two hands on my shoulders, putting space between us as she breaks the kiss. "I, um, should probably go. That was—"

Her eyes search mine, but I wait for her to continue. "Wow. That was… We probably shouldn't make a habit of this. You know?"

I nod, not wanting to agree, but knowing it's the right answer here. "Yeah. You're right. That's…"

"... a bad idea." She says with more confidence in her voice now.

"Right." Before I can get anything else out, she's gone, slipping under my arm and hustling up the stairs. I stay rooted where I am in the stairwell, listening to the door slam on the next landing as she enters our hallway, no doubt already halfway back to her room.

A sinking feeling of dread rolls through me as I stare at the closed door on the landing above. Things were complicated enough before tonight; the secret I'm keeping from her already poised to ruin whatever tenuous relationship we were forming.

Now we've entered new territory; a place where there isn't any room for secrets, and I've brought a giant one across that line with us.

THE
TRACKS

INDY: You did it! The first show is in the books. How do you feel?

MELANIE: Relieved.

AUSTIN: I can only imagine. Tell us what it feels like performing for a crowd of 25,000 people?

MELANIE: It feels… surreal. It's almost overwhelming to stand on a stage in front of so many people, individuals who are living and breathing your music with you. It's still wild to me that so many people know my songs and can sing the lyrics.

INDY: I can tell you, as a member of the crowd, you can feel it in the air. You can feel the collective heartbreak in the sad songs, but you can also feel the electricity in the angry ones.

MELANIE: You totally can. And we—myself, the dancers, the band— feed off that energy. It's like nothing I've ever experienced.

AUSTIN: What's your favorite part about performing?

MELANIE: I think it's the shared moments, Austin. You've got a stadium full of people—from all walks of life, all different ages, all different paths to get here—and we're all relating to this one song in that moment. We're all bringing different emotions and memories to each song, but it's so cool to see everyone my music has touched.

INDY: Your first stop on the tour was Glendale. How did you like it?

MELANIE: Oh, I loved it. Arizona is one of my favorite places, so getting to kick the tour off there was a dream. It's still winter in Tennessee, so escaping to the warmth of Glendale was more than welcome.

AUSTIN: Yeah, no hurt feelings that this tour kicks off in the South. We're all very happy to ditch the cold.

INDY: And it's a great time of year to visit too; the temperatures are justtt right!

MELANIE: They absolutely are. And let's be honest, no one wants to be outside in Arizona summers. They were definitely a great early choice.

AUSTIN: So, where are we off to next?

MELANIE: Texas! We will be there for the next two weeks, first in Arlington and then in Houston.

AUSTIN: What are you looking forward to most in the Lone Star State?

MELANIE: We have our first official meet and greet happening while we're there. I'm really looking forward to meeting the fans before the shows.

INDY: And we can't wait to be there to experience it all with you. I can't wait to see what kind of trouble we can find in Texas.

AUSTIN: I'm sure you can't.

SOLARBLOOMS: I was there for opening night! Wowww! Melanie is amazing!!

MUSICMAVEN0989: It's still wild to me The Tracks is spending SIX months covering this tour. You have nothing better to do?

MEGHANREYNOLDS: Ok, but Melanie had a room full of influencers at that PR event, and her focus was on the two little girls. How sweet was that?!

MUSICMAVEN0989: @MeghanReynolds I'm sure she knew she was being filmed.

HRHANASTASIA: @MeghanReynolds YES! I saw that too. It was ADORABLE.

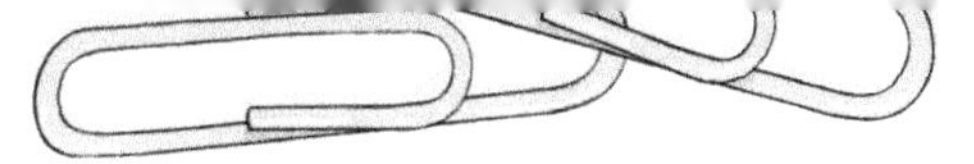

TWENTY-FIVE
NATALIE

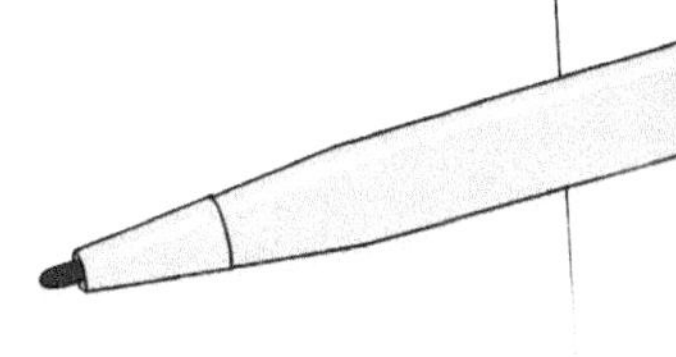

"Jake," I say again, annoyance in my tone this time. His head snaps up from his phone as he turns to look at me. "I asked if you have the contact information for the director at the stadium. I want to get in early tomorrow if it's possible."

He nods, acknowledging me this time. "Yeah, I can get it to you. Give me five."

It turns out coming on someone's fingers makes the relationship with them... complicated. The pseudo-friendship Jake and I had built has completely crumbled in the aftermath of the moment in the stairwell. All the pent-up sexual tension has just become hostility, and it's somehow even more annoying than being worked up all the time. We're both being short with one another, when we're not flat out pretending the other doesn't exist.

It's made for a very fun week.

Thankfully, night two in Glendale passed in a complete blur. I didn't even slow down to enjoy the show on the second night. I busied myself with running through the crowd, offering a few upgraded passes as an excuse to keep myself occupied, and showing people around. Jake and I were so busy hurrying from one place to the next, we didn't even have to pretend to ignore each other; we just naturally did.

The three-day drive to Arlington was a bit more tedious. I spent most of the trip laser-focused on helping Indy and Austin, discussing future episodes, deciding on how to tie Mel's performance into the ideas she had for the rest of the shows. I think my attention to detail was overwhelming them, because by day two they were both trying to table any further planning conversations for later in the week.

Instead, we spent the rest of the drive combing through the early episodes, which aired over the first week of the tour, reading comments and related articles about Melanie and the show. The response was fairly positive, with decent viewership, but nothing groundbreaking. It was a bit of a letdown; I had put a lot of hope into the results of the initial airings, but Austin and Indy tried to assure me we're just getting started and the more we put out there, the better it will get.

I redirect my focus to Jake. "Actually, if you want to just give the director a call for me, that would be great. I can concentrate on finishing up here."

Another nod is all the acknowledgment I get before he stalks off.

We're out in front of the stadium, tucked behind a roped-off queue and a fourteen-foot banner that makes a wall between the public and those here for the event. My team is working on getting the merch tables all set up and ready to go, while I'm getting the spot where Melanie will sit arranged. I sigh as I return to assembling the large photo backdrop, wrapping the fabric pieces over tubing to stand tall behind Mel and her fans at today's meet and greet.

"Alright, he said any time after nine is fine." Jake makes his way back over to where I'm working, sliding his phone into his pocket. "He'll be near Gate B, so just call when we show up."

"Perfect, thank you." I don't even look up, refusing to acknowledge him when it just feels so fucking awkward.

At exactly three, we open the gates and allow the fans to flow through the welcome banner and into the queue that winds its way over to where Mel and I stand. We spend the next couple of hours moving through the process: greetings, photos, merch handoff.

It's going well until I turn to move down the queue and find myself face to face with Jake. This is the third time I've nearly crashed into him this afternoon, and frankly, I'd just like some space.

"Do you have to breathe down my neck?" My voice betrays my irritation with him.

"Just doing my job." His tone is also clipped.

"Well, I'm trying to work, and you're constantly in my way." I crane my neck to stare him down, but I can't see anything behind his stupid sunglasses.

He shuffles to the side, sweeping his hands dramatically out in front of him. "After you, ma'am."

I throw him a look. "Is there literally nothing else you could be doing? It's a big event. I'm sure they need help somewhere else."

"You're kind of my job though, aren't you?"

"Fine. Can you just... I don't know. Stand on the other side of the barrier? So I can at least have a clear walkway?"

I suspect he throws me a glare, but again, sunglasses make it impossible to tell. Eventually, he strides off, and I don't bother to watch him go.

The next hour passes blissfully, the thorn in my side now removed. I'm talking to a group of fans, eager for their chance to meet Melanie, when a couple of young guys, maybe in their early twenties, get a little too comfortable waiting in the line nearest to where I'm standing.

"Daaamn, you wear that skirt well." I can hear the cat call from behind me, but choose to ignore it, not sure who it's directed at and not at all caring to engage assholes. I'm immediately uncomfortable though, shifting on my feet as I wait for the line to move.

I guide the next few people forward through the makeshift gate to the last stretch of the line, keeping an eye on the people beside me as I do so. Just a couple of minutes pass before I hear another snide remark.

"Seriously, you look like a snackkk, mama."

I pivot around, catching the eye of a guy standing with two of his buddies, who are snickering quietly from behind him.

"Great, thanks. Can we keep the commentary to ourselves?" I ask politely before pulling my attention from him to answer a question from a couple beside me.

"Oh, she doesn't want to hear the commentary I'm keeping to myself." I think he intended to whisper that, but he doesn't seem to understand volume, or doesn't care to. I shrug him off, moving further over through the line, putting space between the guy and myself. My skin prickles as I feel his gaze following me, but I let it go, knowing he'll be out of my hair soon enough.

Unfortunately, the line continues to move, and before I realize it, he's once again immediately behind me. I feel the unwelcome touch of someone's hands on my ass and I jump, whirling around to face him.

"Excuse you. You need to keep your hands to yourself or you will find yourself removed from the premises. Is that understood?" I am immediately seething, feeling uncomfortable and exceptionally angry.

He runs his eyes over the length of my body, and my skin crawls. He holds his hands up as he says, "Ah, it's all good. No hard feelings."

"Maybe for you," I huff under my breath as I turn to walk away, looking for Jake, or any of the security team. Before I can take more than a single step, a hand wraps around my arm, pulling me roughly in the opposite direction.

"What was that?!" The creepy bastard has my upper arm in a vice grip, his face right in mine. I try not to wince as the acrid smell of his breath washes over me.

"I... it was... nothing. Take your hands off me." I try to push back at him, but he doesn't move. With my right arm trapped in his hand and my left arm clutching my clipboard, I can't reach my earpiece to call for help.

I shift again, trying to shake my arm loose, but it doesn't budge.

"Nah, I think you had something to say to me, didn't you?" A bit of spit lands on my collarbone, and my stomach rolls. I snap my head away from him, trying to put as much space as possible between his face and mine.

Before I can take another breath, Jake moves into my line of sight. I swear he takes just one step to close the distance between the two of us, even though we're too far away for that to have been possible. I feel a warm hand wrapping around my waist, pulling me gently to the side as the guy squeezing my arm is suddenly lifted off the ground, one large hand closing around his throat and hauling him up, away from me.

The dickhead immediately releases my arm, his grubby fingers clawing at the hand holding him. I watch as Jake moves beside me, his hand sliding around my back in a comforting acknowledgment as he steps between us, depositing the guy back on the ground.

"What the fuck, man?" The guy is clutching at his throat, his eyes as wide as saucers as he stares at Jake.

Jake's expression remains blank, his posture relaxed as he crosses his arms in front of him, the width of his body shielding me entirely from the guys in front of him. I can barely see what's happening over his shoulder, but I can clearly hear the vitriol in his voice as he says, "You have three seconds to make your way to the nearest exit before I help you find it."

The guys immediately take off, all of them leaving the line and heading around the perimeter toward the front gate without looking back.

Jake turns to face me, his eyes scanning over me before he grabs my hand and pulls me gently through the crowd behind him.

"Knox, there are three guys busting ass for the main entrance. Make their acquaintance and call me in ten. In the meantime, Natalie's on a break. Someone cover for her." I hear him growl in surround sound as his voice floats over his shoulder in front of me and simultaneously vibrates through the earpiece to our teams.

We hurry through the crowd, Jake's head whipping back over his shoulder every few strides as if to check on me. We leave the main area, heading to the back of the enclosed lot where a small trailer is stationed. He strides over to it, yanking the door open before stepping aside to usher me in.

I climb the stairs, entering the private space set up for Melanie for her breaks. Dropping my clipboard onto the table, my pen clatters loudly onto the cheap plastic surface.

The door snicks shut as Jake takes the three steps in one giant stride, coming to stand immediately in front of me.

"Are you ok?" He hooks his sunglasses on his shirt, eyes wide with concern as he takes me in. His scent overwhelms me in this tiny space, the familiar amber and cedar notes of his cologne making me feel inexplicably comfortable, despite the circumstances.

"I'm fine, Jake."

Jake's eyes soften as he watches me, tugging on my hand as he leads me over to the couch. I drop into the corner, grabbing a pillow and squeezing it in my lap as I replay the last fifteen minutes over in my mind.

I am fine. *Technically.*

I'm just grossed out. I feel the need to shower the invisible slime off my body; erase all traces of what just happened entirely.

But physically, I'm fine.

The situation could have been so much worse, but... it wasn't.

Jake sits next to me, his thigh grazing mine as he leans forward, resting his forearms against his knees, staring straight ahead. I run my eyes over the giant "Security" emblazoned on the back of his black nylon jacket, the same one he wears for every event and show.

We sit in silence for a few minutes, the muted noise of the meet and greet continuing without us humming outside the trailer. I pick delicately at the embroidery on the pillow, not sure what to say, or do, in this moment.

Eventually, Jake shifts, tilting his head toward me. "You don't have to be ok right now, Natalie. There's no one else here. It's just you and me. But I need you to be honest. Are you sure you're ok?"

The softness in his tone catches me by surprise. Dex and Mel check in on me all the time, but this feels... different. I've never had someone look at me the way Jake is looking at me, his eyes penetrating as he watches me.

I choke up at the gesture, the concern spilling from him, and my eyes well without my permission.

God, this is stupid.

Why am I about to cry right now?

I. Am. Fine.

I repeat the mantra over and over in my head as I nod at Jake, but my body betrays me, a rogue tear slipping from my eyelashes and streaking down my cheek.

"Come here." Jake shifts, reaching for me, and without even thinking about it, I go, folding myself into his arms, burying my face in his shoulder. All the animosity I've felt since Glendale has disappeared, his presence feeling more like a relief than anything else right now. His arms wrap around me, holding me tight.

I. Am. Fine.

I. Am. Fine.

I. Am. Fine.

I continue the chant, as if it will rebuild the shields Jake has somehow crashed through. The adrenaline of the incident is wearing off, and I can feel the physical weight of the anxiety bearing down on me.

Usually at this point in a breakdown, I throw myself into something, anything to take my mind off the situation, but as I sit here with Jake, I don't have the option.

I don't know if I want it.

Maybe... I'm not fine.

"You don't have to be fine." Jake's arms tighten around me as he rests his head against mine.

I suck in a choppy breath as I realize I wasn't thinking that last sentiment; I said that out loud.

All at once, the entirety of the situation becomes too much. I'm too worked up. Jake's being too sweet. And the fact that I'm not alone, that I can't pep talk myself out of this, crashes into me.

I have to face these emotions head-on.

And I don't know how to do that.

So I cry.

Every fissure of stress and anxiety comes rolling out of me, coursing down my cheeks, and settles onto the nylon of Jake's coat beneath me.

I don't know how long we stay like that, huddled up on the tiny trailer couch, but Jake doesn't move once. He's there the entire time, holding me tight and reminding me I'm not alone.

JAKE

There's That Word Again

That night, in the silence of my hotel room, I realize I fucked up.

Shit, I fucked up.

I sit on the edge of the bed, staring at my black shoes as I run my feet back and forth across the burgundy carpet, following the striations in the design.

The guilt eats at me as I replay the events of the afternoon over in my mind.

I let my guard down.

I walked away.

And what happened when I did? Another man put his hands on her.

And the parallel to sixteen years ago rips through me like it was just yesterday. When I let my brother get hurt on my watch.

I let my guard down.

I walked away.

And that time? He died.

And while Natalie's physically fine, this situation very different from the one with my brother, the guilt doesn't dissipate with that knowledge because I did the one thing I promised myself I would never do again; the one thing I have worked tirelessly to avoid for my entire career.

And I was *stupid.*

So fucking stupid.

I let her get under my skin. I've never had someone get me as riled up as she does. Things have been so weird since we made out in the stairwell in Glendale and for the life of me, I could not focus on my job. My mind was clearly other places, I let her push me away.

I *walked away* intentionally.

And once again, I put someone I care for in danger.

More than the parallel to my past though, *that* is the realization that has me spiraling.

I care about her.

I run my hand through my hair as I shift on the bed. The long strands tangle between my fingers as I heave a sigh, cupping the back of my neck with my hand.

I knew I was attracted to Natalie, obviously. But what dawned on me as I watched someone else putting his hands on her is that I *care* about her. This isn't just physical attraction anymore. She's worked her way into my system. Through a crack I didn't know I'd left open. I saw red as I made my way over to them this afternoon, all logic in my brain completely evaporated and my sole focus was on getting her away from him.

The proper procedure would have been to detain the man, but I couldn't bring myself to walk away from her. I let him go, hoping Knox would have the time to head him off. That he stopped the guy is kind of a moot point when I let him go knowing I didn't care what happened to him, as long as Natalie was fine. That's going to be a fun discussion when corporate finds out.

I sat with Natalie for longer than I meant to, hiding out in that tiny trailer until the event ended. At one point, she tried to convince me she needed to help the cleanup crew, but I won that argument, taking her back to the hotel and encouraging her to take a night off.

After making sure she was securely back in her room, I headed down to the local police station to give my statement and relieve Knox of the duty of cleaning up my mess. What they actually needed was a chance to talk to Natalie, but hell if I was letting them anywhere near her today.

Or ever.

Knox was surprisingly supportive when I met up with him after that. If it had been my team member saying 'fuck the protocol', I wouldn't have been as understanding. His primary concern was also Natalie's well-being, so at least we were on the same page. He did stick me with filing the incident report, but it feels like getting off scot-free, to be honest.

A knock at the door snaps me out of my thoughts, pulling me unceremoniously back to the present. I push off the bed, making my way over to the door as the knocking grows louder.

"Yeah, yeah, I'm coming." I groan as I reach for the handle, pulling the door open to find Dex standing there, Knox and Asher standing side-by-side behind him.

"Uh, hi?" I say awkwardly, not sure what's happening here.

"You have time for a drink?" Dex asks as he fishes his sunglasses out from inside his jacket.

"Now?"

"Yeah, now. You're not working, right?" He quirks a brow at me, knowing damn well if I'm hiding in my room, I'm off the clock.

"No, Chase is on the schedule tonight. Obviously..." I gesture to the rest of the team standing behind him.

"Great, let's go."

My eyes flick to the door next to mine. Natalie's door. I debate stopping in before taking off, but what else is there to do that I haven't already done?

A large hand comes down on my shoulder, turning me toward the exit.

"She's fine, man. Let's go," Knox says as he steers me away from the rooms, leading me out of the hall and into the elevator.

The bar Dex leads us to is just down the block from the hotel, a quick walk away. We enter through the large oak doors, the light from the open door illuminating most of the space, the smell of fried food hitting me as I cross the threshold.

We make our way toward the back, my boots sticking to the floor as we weave our way through the bar. After we all place our orders, the guys dive into a conversation about the upcoming events on the tour. I don't really care to take part in this one, so I sip my beer, letting them carry on the conversation around me. When the first round is nearly gone, Dex slides out of his side of the booth, tagging me on the shoulder as he does.

"Come help me grab the next round."

I look around, watching the servers delivering drinks to the other tables, but decide not to ask questions.

We make our way over to the bar, but instead of joining the line, Dex swings around the line entirely, stepping off to the side.

"Listen, Jake, I don't want to make this weird, but I just wanted to say thank you for what you did for Natalie today."

I clear my throat, appreciating the sentiment, but not really wanting to talk about it. "No problem. Just doing my job."

Dex crosses his arms as he stands next to me. "Yeah, but you didn't *just* do your job. I talked to Natalie, and she told me what happened after you pulled the guy off her. You took care of her."

There's that fucking word again.

Care.

I don't want to care.

"Um, yeah." I run my hand across my jaw, scratching at the beard growth there. "I wasn't going to just leave her after that."

"I know. I appreciate it. Natalie is annoyingly independent. She would rather handle everything silently, on her own than ask for help. She can be hard to reason with." He laughs to himself, and I can't help the twitch in my lips at that statement. "I'm just glad she has you. That you know when to push back. You can see when she actually needs help and just refuses to ask.

"I don't just mean with today. That was... Jesus. Terrifying. But really, this entire tour is... a lot. And she's gonna wear herself thin. I can tell her that four hundred times, but she's never going to listen to me. It's just... nice that she has someone else who sees it too. That looks out for her."

I stand awkwardly with my hands in my jacket pockets, not really knowing what to say to that. I don't do this kind of thing, having deep conversations—and now it's happening twice in one day?

He claps me on the shoulder. "That's all. I owed you that. I just didn't want to make things awkward at the table."

"Yeah, of course."

With that, he walks away, joining the line at the bar. I make my way over to him, waiting a couple of steps back from where he stands while he orders another round for the four of us.

We spend another couple of hours at the bar; the guys working their way through several rounds of drinks. I take a slower pace, but still find myself feeling more upbeat by the time we make it back to the hotel.

I'm not even buzzed, so it wasn't the beer, but a night out with the guys feels... *good*. I don't have many friends, but being included felt nice. It felt like I belonged, even though I was definitely a broody asshole all night.

I shrug my jacket onto the chair nearest the door as soon as I cross the threshold of my hotel room.

God, I need a shower. And sleep.

My phone buzzes in my pocket, and I pull it out, a text from Gunner popping up again on the screen. Cursing silently, I open it, but instead of entertaining Gunner with a reply, I pull open his contact and hit block.

At this point, Gunner has caused enough fucking problems, clearly told enough lies. I'm not entertaining his shit anymore.

I power the phone down and shove it into the desk drawer beside me. My eyes scan over the interior door beside me, the one that connects my room and Natalie's.

Unlike in Glendale, where the hotel was big enough to have multi-room penthouse suites and Natalie stayed with Melanie, this hotel is smaller, forcing Natalie into a room of her own. It definitely felt like an annoyance when we first got here, but after today's events, I'm glad she's right next to me.

Against my better judgment, I open my side of the door, finding hers already cracked. I knock, waiting for a reply, but none comes.

I push through into the space; the room bathed in the glow from the bathroom, the door ajar and light turned on. I can see Natalie in bed, curled into a tight ball, her hands under her pillow, and red hair spilling wildly across the white linens.

I stand there for a moment, taking her in before I realize this is a creepy fucking thing to do. Especially today, when she's probably had enough leering men to last her a lifetime.

I back out slowly, but she stirs as I do, her eyes opening.

"Jake?" Her voice sleepy and quiet.

"Yeah, sorry. The door was cracked." I gesture over my shoulder. "I didn't mean to wake you."

"No, no, it's fine." She brushes the rogue strands of hair away from her face as she sits up. "I was looking for you earlier. I just… didn't really want to be alone."

The confession hits me somewhere in the middle of my chest, a balloon inflating behind the cage of my ribs.

"Sorry, I was out with Dex and the guys. They wanted to grab a drink down the road."

"Oh," she says quietly, "I like that."

"You… like that?" I ask, confused.

"Yeah, you guys being friends. It's cute."

"I am not cute, you weirdo." I chuckle quietly at the sleep-addled thoughts spilling from her, much like her drunken secrets. She's softened around the edges, more gentle like this.

"You're very cute." The comeback has my eyes widening, a reaction she can't see from her vantage point.

"Glad you think so." I want to tell her she's cute too, but as the thought crosses my mind, I realize how fucking gone I am.

Cute, really?

The balloon pops, leaving me feeling deflated and vulnerable. I take two steps back, making my way through the door between our rooms as quickly as I can.

"No," I hear her say as I move away, "Can you stay?"

"What?" I'm not sure I heard her right.

"Will you stay? Just for tonight? I keep waking up. I can't get comfortable." I can hear the pleading in her voice. Today must have *really* shaken her up if she's actually asking for help.

I remember what Dex said tonight, and everything I've seen over the last two months. She might have people who *would* be there if she asked, but she doesn't ask. She doesn't want to burden anyone, ever.

With that, my decision is made. I can't tell her no, not when she's opening herself up to the idea of allowing someone to be there for her.

"Yeah, I can stay. Let me just change my clothes."

I hear a little hum as she plops back down onto the pillow.

Trading my jeans for a pair of pajama pants and fishing out a fresh shirt, I'm back in just a couple of minutes. I click the lights off as I cross between our rooms, detouring to Natalie's bathroom to do the same.

"Nat?" I ask quietly as I pad my way across the dark space, making my way to the opposite side of the bed but she doesn't reply, already out.

Lifting the edge of the comforter, I climb into bed. I'm damn near falling off the edge, but I'd rather hit the floor than accidentally get too close to the middle.

I'm nearly asleep when a soft hand brushes my upper arm. I turn onto my back, finding Natalie curling up immediately next to me, her entire body flush with mine as she flings her arm over my stomach and her leg across both of mine.

I curse softly as I lie there, staring into the darkness at the ceiling. I don't know what to do about this. Staying away is apparently too difficult. Getting close though… might be too dangerous.

But I don't move, and I don't move her.

TWENTY-SEVEN
NATALIE

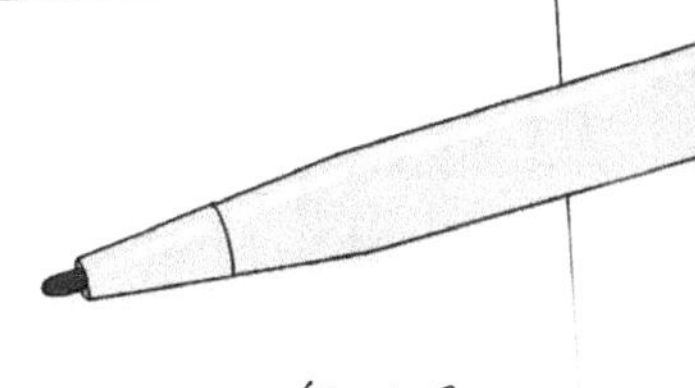

I wake up the next morning, sprawled across a very large, very hard pillow. I crack my eyes open to find myself peering up at Jake's short beard, his chest rising and falling beneath my head.

Oh, shit.

Shit. Shit. Shit.

I pull back carefully so I don't wake him, easing myself to my pillow across the bed. I scrub my hand over my face as I turn away from Jake, putting my back to him as I stare at the wall beside me.

What did I do?

I remember asking him to stay last night. I was sleepy, and it's hazy, but I do remember. What I don't remember is him agreeing. I was so out of it; I had clearly lost all common sense.

I shift slightly as I shuffle through yesterday's memories once again.

It was so unexpected, the way Jake handled everything. I've never seen him lose his cool like that.

When we had the whole paparazzi run-in after Gunner's article dropped, he handled the situation completely differently. He was calm and collected the whole time - laser-focused on the situation and our surroundings.

But this time, he was focused entirely on me. I was shocked when he sent the guys running. Apparently, no spare fucks for what became of them after that. I've never had someone show that level of concern for me before. It was weird to be the one looked after, instead of being the one making sure everyone else was ok.

And I think it cracked something open inside me. This weird feeling of warmth that seeps through my veins when I think about how protective he was over me. I can't seem to control the feeling, even though I'm sure I'm overthinking it.

He is a bodyguard after all. He was just doing his job.

The bed moves beside me, and I turn to look over my shoulder, Jake's eyes meeting mine as I do.

Although, I don't think doing his job involves being my teddy bear.

"Morning," I whisper.

He rubs his eyes with his hand, a muffled "morning" coming from him as he does.

I hear a knock on the door to my room and sit up in a bolt of panic. Melanie's muffled voice comes from behind the door. "Natalie, open up!"

My heart jumps into my throat as I look over at Jake lying in the bed beside me.

"Go!" I hiss at him. "You have to go!" I fan my hand out toward the open adjoining doors dramatically as he stares blankly at me.

"Jake, for fuck's sake, go!" I bolt upright and out of bed as the hotel room door opens; a loud metallic clang coming from the door.

"Nat?! You have the safety lock flipped. Are you up yet? Let me in!" Melanie's voice is loud and clear through the opening in the door now.

"One second!" I yell across the room to Melanie. Jake still hasn't moved. I grab my pillow and chuck it at him. The fluffy fabric smacks him square in the face as he makes no attempt to stop it from hitting him.

"Shit, sorry. Sorry." He stammers, untangling himself from the sheets before hustling across the room. He throws one last look in my direction before slinking through the adjoining doors.

I take my first breath since I heard Melanie at the door as I straighten the pillows on Jake's side of the bed. I make my way to the door, flipping the safety lock before swinging it open.

Her eyes go wide as she stands before me.

"Uh, Nat? Did you know your white tee is basically see-through?"

My eyes drop to the outfit I'm wearing, and sure enough... The top I picked out last night is threadbare and damn near sheer. My nipples clearly visible through the material of the shirt. I flush as I realize why Jake needed to be goaded out of bed.

"Jesus fucking Christ."

Despite the awkward morning in my hotel room, the rest of the week goes smoothly. The shows in Arlington the next two days are flawless. There are no hiccups to deal with. Melanie and her crew kill it on stage, and the new Tracks shows are seeing a spike in viewership.

Jake and I seem to have reached a truce after everything. We both drop our snappy attitudes and clipped conversations, falling into a comfortable camaraderie that is new to us.

Somewhere in the aftermath of the fan situation, or our slumber party, we independently decided that the hostility was unnecessary, the tension irrelevant. The last week has been easy. I feel comfortable with him, and I think he feels the same with me.

Everything is going swimmingly when we arrive in Houston the following week. Wednesday night, following an afternoon of interviews at two local radio stations, the team decides to take a group outing.

Indy booked us the VIP area at a local dueling piano bar for tonight. The lounge is a trendy second-floor loft that overlooks the platform on the main floor where the pianos are staged. We can see the performers, two pianists and a drummer, with no crowd interference.

I make my way over to the wrought-iron railing, leaning against the cool metal as I watch the performers warming up down below. It's an eclectic group of people on stage, but from what they've played so far, they sound great together.

My thoughts are interrupted when a man grabs the mic and begins talking. "Welcome to Houston's most popular dueling piano bar, The Dive!"

The crowd cheers, drowning out the host as Mel slides up next to me, her hip bumping into mine in greeting.

"They look like they're having fun, don't they?" She asks, gesturing at the band on stage below us.

"They really do."

We chat for several minutes before Austin wanders over to join us. As soon as he does, Mel shifts away from me, falling into conversation with him. Smirking to myself, I turn to give them some space, watching the performers on the stage again.

Before long, Jake's scent surrounds me. I don't turn, but I feel him to my left as he leans his body up against the rail next to mine. As per usual, my body is well aware of his presence, lighting up at his proximity.

He doesn't say anything, doesn't move closer, just stands next to me listening to the music down below. We stay like that for several songs, the people around us coming and going. Neither of us acknowledging the other, yet wholly aware of their presence.

I heave a long sigh before glancing over at him, once again finding him already staring at me.

"You do that a lot," I say, taking a sip of the drink in my hand.

"What?" he asks, those dark brown eyes piercing.

"Stare at me."

His mouth tips up. "It's my job. I'm supposed to pay attention."

"Just how closely are you watching me, Jake?" I smirk from behind my glass.

"Too close," is all he says before turning his gaze back to the entertainment below. I do the same, trying, and failing, to keep my eyes on the stage below us.

I realize I've finished my second drink. Absentmindedly trailing my fingers through the leftover condensation on the outside of the glass, I feel Jake's arm brush mine and my entire body lights up.

This stupid awareness is *constant*.

An all-day struggle.

I take a quick step away, aiming for the bar to replace my empty glass. It's like I'm sixteen again, giddy over a boy who has no idea the effect he's having on me, instead of a grown-ass woman who is more than well aware men only lead to trouble.

I thank the bartender for my refill just as a hand slides over my lower back. I don't have to turn to know it's Jake.

Desire courses through me, and frustration rolls in right behind it. My mind races, an idea coming to me. I've had *just* enough alcohol to decide to throw caution to the wind.

My eyes scan the surrounding crowd, watching my friends and co-workers chatting, dancing, and enjoying one another. They're in their own worlds, having the time of their lives.

Turning away from Jake, I slip through the VIP area, heading for the back stairwell. I glance quickly behind me before opening the stairwell door, and sure enough, he's a handful of paces behind me.

I smile to myself as I make my way down the stairs and out onto the crowded main floor of the bar. Weaving in and out of people, I move toward the dark corner in the back, hiding amongst the crowd, a floor below anyone we know or work with.

When I finally stop, I turn and come face to face with Jake.

"What are you doing, Natalie?" his expression is lined with confusion. Bodies move around us, swaying to the upbeat song currently being played.

"Dance with me, Jake." I turn, putting my back to him as I swing my hips to the beat of the music.

"I don't dance." He's trying to argue, but I grab his arm, wrapping it around my waist as I back up, aligning our bodies.

"You do right now." I hear a low chuckle spill out of him, but I don't turn to look. A few moments later, feel his body moving with mine.

We're silent for a minute before I tip my head back, talking to him over my shoulder, "For someone who doesn't dance, you're doing just fine."

"I said *I don't dance*, not that I can't dance." He leans down, his lips brushing against my ear as he replies. "There's a difference."

"Where did you learn to dance?" Part of me is curious; part of me wants to keep him here, his body wrapped around mine, his voice low in my ear, our own little bubble in this crowded room.

"Sometimes you need to be a bodyguard without looking like a bodyguard." His hands move over my hips as he talks. "I've got lots of tricks up my sleeve."

I look up, catching his eye, a mischievous glint in them beneath the dance floor lighting. I take a long pull of my drink before I refocus on the music and the people nearby.

For several songs, we stay like that. The music moving through the room; the crowd boxing us in; and the feel of Jake's body aligned with mine.

I can feel the ache building inside me, the tension tightening between us the longer we stay there. So far, we've avoided talking about whatever this is between us, mostly at my insistence.

I can feel the third drink kicking in. My glass now empty, the alcohol in my system making me just loose enough to have this conversation without overthinking what I'm about to do.

I spin, Jake's hand remaining on my hip as I do so. "Listen, you're right."

He raises an eyebrow, his fingers tightening their hold as he pulls me into him. "Am I now?"

"We can't keep doing this."

He sighs, "I know."

"It's a terrible idea." I slide my free hand up his chest and over his shoulder, my fingertips gripping delicately at the back of his neck. "You're my bodyguard. If we got caught, we'd be in deep shit."

"We would." He agrees, but he doesn't move.

There's a long pause as the mass of people move around us.

"I don't know how to stop it though." My admission is low, barely audible over the noise of the room, but I know he heard it.

"We could... not get caught," he offers, his hands snaking further around my back.

My heart races at the possibility of this being something, but I know it's a bad idea. My head swims. I started this conversation, but I realize I wasn't planning on this ending anything between us. Still, I push back, knowing the mature thing to do is at least try. "Absolutely not."

"Why?" He's smirking again, the tilt of his lips an enticing invitation. "Afraid of breaking the rules?"

"No, mature enough to know some rules are meant to be broken. And this," I gesture between the two of us, "is not one of them."

"You're right." He lets go, backing away a step. The loss of his touch hits me like a punch to the gut, and I feel the ache within me intensify.

He's right. My gut instinct *is* right.

We... *can't.*

My eyes scan over Jake as he stands in front of me, hands on his hips, his eyes currently searching the room around us.

I'm so tired. Tired of fighting this insatiable lust I feel every time I'm in Jake's presence. It's with me from the moment I wake until the moment I go to sleep and, frankly, I can't deal with it any longer. I don't want to think about this man anymore... I just...

His eyes snap back to mine when I call out to him. "Jake?"

"Yeah?" He steps close again, closing the gap he just created.

"I'm tired of following the rules." I whisper, pulling him closer.

Surprise lights in his eyes. I step back into him, pressing my body to his as his hand drops back to my hip, like it's the most natural thing in the world. My breath catches as my eyes bore into his. He's staring at me, his look hazy with lust.

"Fuck it," I breathe, slamming my lips to his.

I can feel his hesitation, the shock of the action rendering him motionless for a beat... then two. I don't think he expected I would actually give in. Holding my lips to his, I wait for him to move, but he doesn't.

Just when I think I've fucked up and gotten too bold, his arms slide around my back, grip tightening as he leans into me, meeting my kiss with equal fervor, the warmth of his body seeping into mine as we meld into one. I lick across his bottom lip, tasting him, encouraging him to open, and he does, taking my tongue with his.

I roll my hips, feeling him grow hard against me, loving the knowledge that he is just as affected by this as I am. That he wants this the same way I do. I pull back, noting the pink tint to his cheeks under the dim lighting.

"Come on, we can't stay here. Someone's gonna notice..." He tugs on my hand, leading me off the crowded dance floor.

"Where are we going?"

A slow smile crosses his face as he looks back at me over his shoulder. "Back to the hotel."

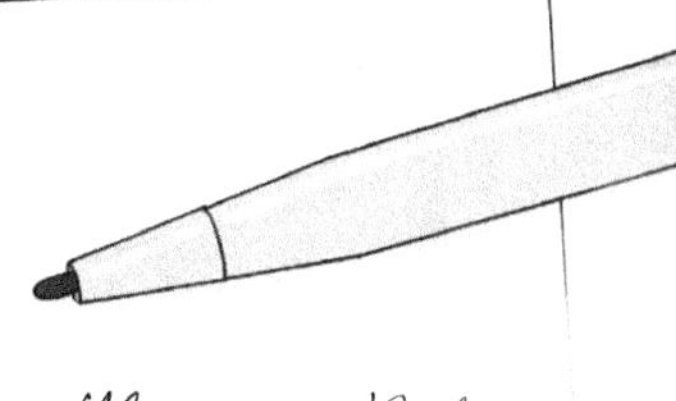

Manners, Red

Jake tells Knox and Mel I'm not feeling well and calls a car before we sneak out to head back. I try to remain composed, but internally, I am a ball of nerves. The last thing I want to do is jeopardize either of our jobs, but... I also can't say no. I can't stay away.

Clearly, I've tried.

When the car drops us off in front of our hotel, we make our way through the lobby and into the elevator. The doors have barely closed before Jake is on me. There's a stark contrast between the cold metal of the elevator wall at my back and Jake's warm body, pressing into me as he guides me backwards.

It's been so long since I've been with someone.

Embarrassingly long.

His hands weave through my hair, tugging at the elastic holding my bun in place. He shakes it out, my hair tumbling down my back as he runs his fingers through the strands. I shudder as I feel his lips ghosting over my ear and down my neck, excitement pooling low in my belly.

"I love this." His voice is quiet.

"My hair?" The question comes out breathy.

"Yeah." I feel his fingers working through the ends as he gathers the strands in his fist, wrapping my hair around his hand twice before flattening his palm against the base of my neck and tugging gently. He tips my head back, my spine arching. I meet his eyes as it does. "It wraps so nicely around my fist."

Oh.

I catch a devious smirk playing across his face before he drops his lips to mine, my mind melting as we come together.

His fingers urge my head to meet his, his hips pressing into mine. Anticipation races through me, knowing there's nothing stopping us tonight. There's no hesitation, no holding back. I'm nearly delirious with need by the time the elevator dings and we reach our floor, my entire body aching to be touched.

When the door chimes, opening, Jake unwinds his fist from my hair, carefully tucking the strands behind my ear before turning and gesturing for me to lead the way out of the elevator. I move quickly, fishing my key card out of my bag as I go.

We make our way down the hall, just a handful of steps between the elevator and the first of our two rooms. He grabs my hand, tugging me back toward the nearest door, his door, and pressing me against it.

His fingertips dance along my hip as he scans the card I didn't even see him pull out, and the door swings open behind me. We both stumble into the room, Jake's hands never leaving my body.

"Should we… talk about this?!" I ask, turning in his hold so we're face to face.

"What do you mean?"

"Like, um. Rules. There have to be rules." I can barely think with Jake's hands on my body. My mind is already twelve steps ahead, desperate to be under him.

"Of course there are rules." Jake drops his head, kissing my neck, the smooth press of his lips running along the tender skin. "What are you thinking?"

"No one finds out. I mean no one, Jake."

He pulls back, his hands sliding up my side as he looks at me. "That's a given. There's a lot on the line here."

"It doesn't have to be a one time thing, but—"

He smirks. "Of course there's a but."

"But I think we acknowledge what this is. It's not a relationship; it's just a fling. This doesn't continue past the end of this tour." I tighten my grip on his shoulders, making sure I have his full attention.

"I don't know if you've met me, but long-term isn't my thing." The honesty in his eyes tells me we're on the same page.

"I'm aware. That's why I'm saying, hard stop in September. When the time on the road ends, this does too. We can fool around for a few months, but we go our separate ways when we're done."

He nods. "Fair enough."

Before I can move, I feel Jake's arms snake around my waist, pulling me back into him. His hands run the length of my body, skimming down my sides, until they stop at my hips. He tugs my blouse out of the skirt it's tucked into. "Can I fuck you now?"

I nod this time, my heart racing with the way his eyes burn as he looks at me, desire burning through every limb in my body.

"I have thought about this… so many times." He says, his fingers working through the buttons on the front of my shirt.

"Have you?" I ask, trying to keep my voice even as he pauses, my shirt gaping open, the fabric pulling wide to reveal the lacy white bra I have on underneath. I can hear a low groan escape Jake's throat as he runs a finger down from my collarbone along the inside of the shirt and over the curve of my breast.

"I've lost count of how many times I've fisted my cock in the shower while I think about what you look like underneath these fucking tops. What you wear under those goddamn skirts."

His fingers pinch my nipple through the thin fabric of my bra before he makes quick work of the buttons that remain, slowly sliding the shirt off my shoulders when he's done.

He palms my breasts, squeezing them in his hands, running his thumbs along the under wire as he drops to his knees in front of me, leaving a trail of soft kisses down my body as he goes.

The sight of this man on his knees before me does something to me. My breath quickens as I take him in, those brown eyes penetrating, his hands moving over me. I run my fingers through his hair, an acute desperation rolling through me now.

But Jake takes his time, exploring every exposed inch of my stomach, every path his fingers trail leaving nothing but a visceral need in their wake, before he finally finds the zipper on the skirt. In one swift tug, he has the entire thing on the floor at my feet, and I'm standing in front of him wearing nothing but my white bra and thong and my red heels.

I drop my hands to his shoulders as he takes me in, his palms sliding down the outside of each leg as his gaze drops to my shoes and then running back up and cupping my ass as his eyes lock back on mine.

"Fucking hell." It's a mumble I can barely hear before he's standing quickly. He picks me up and throws me over his shoulder. A loud squeal leaves me at the unexpected way he tosses me around. He pivots, taking two quick strides across the room before gently tossing me on the bed, and crawling over my body until he's positioned on his forearms on top of me, still fully clothed. The warmth of his body wraps around me, and *god*, he smells so good.

"This feels a little... unfair," I start as Jake drops his lips to mine, silencing me for a moment. His tongue dips inside my mouth, and my fingers thread around the back of his neck as I hold him close to me. "I have no clothes on, and you're fully dressed..."

He chuckles under his breath, taking his time with me before he leans up, one arm reaching behind him as he pulls his shirt over his head, tossing it off to the side before claiming my mouth once more.

"Better?" he asks between kisses. He's thorough, diving into my mouth, leaving me breathless before he cuts across my cheek and down my neck with a trail of hot kisses and lingering nips.

"Getting there..." I hook my fingers in the belt loops of his jeans and pull on them. I can feel his smile against my skin, but he continues working his way down my body. He drops kisses across the cleavage spilling out of my bra, pulling the fabric away before taking the stiff peak of my nipple into his mouth. I arch my back at the sensation, shivers running through me as he works his tongue over me.

Too soon, he's trailing his tongue over my stomach before he eases himself back off the bed. I prop myself on my elbows as he reaches to unbutton his jeans. His eyes never leave mine as he slowly slides the denim off his hips and drops it onto the floor, leaving him standing before me in nothing but a pair of tight boxer briefs, the bulge of his dick undeniable.

I lick my lips, enjoying the view as he wraps his hands around my ankles and hauls me to the end of the bed.

"Jake!" I squeal, but his hands back on my body turn the squeal into a moan, his thumbs rubbing the crease where my thighs meet my hips. His fingers slip under the damp lace of my underwear, skimming along the apex of my thighs.

"Fuck, Natalie." His voice is low, gravely as his thumb slides through my core, gathering the wetness and then back up over my clit, where he applies pressure.

My legs move of their own accord, coming up over his shoulders as I writhe under his touch. He smirks, removing his thumb, instead hooking two fingers on either side of my thong and pulling it off. He leans back, tossing it onto the desk, before grabbing both ankles and placing my legs back over his shoulders.

I'm suddenly feeling very self-conscious in front of him, laid completely bare like this. He doesn't give me time to dwell on the feeling though, as his hands trail up over my legs and he kisses his way up my inner thigh, the rough scratch of his facial hair making me nearly incoherent.

"These fucking heels," he murmurs as reaches up, his right hand toying with the strap on my ankle.

His hands work their way up my legs, wrapping around my inner thighs and spreading me open in front of him. With no hesitation, he leans in, running his tongue up my center, the pads of his fingers digging into my legs as he pulls me into him.

"Jake..." His name falls from my lips, a plea, a cry for more tumbling from me as the sensation of his tongue working through my core unravels me. He works in an alternating pattern of flicking and sucking that has me writhing beneath him.

"You like that, Natalie?" He pulls back, his eyes shining in the dim light of the hotel room. "Do you like my tongue on your pussy?"

Jesus, the mouth on this guy.

"Y-y-yes." I can't quite get the word out, my brain hazy with pent-up lust. His tongue runs along my seam again, a barely-there touch that has me aching for more, my hips leaving the bed.

"Sorry, what was that?" He asks, a devilish grin playing across his lips. "I need to hear you say it."

He's staring at me, the lust in his eyes so potent I can hardly stand it.

"Yes, Jake. I like you eating me out."

"Good." He starts, running his nose along my inner thigh as he says it. "Because I fucking love the taste of you."

With that, he pulls my clit into his mouth and sucks. Hard. My back arches again, but he moves his hands over my hips, forcing me into the mattress.

It's too much. His hands on my body, his tongue splitting me open, dipping inside me. The hold he has on my body makes his control absolute.

The pattern causes the pressure to build, my thighs tightening on either side of his head as I try to hold off the impending orgasm. It's too fast, too soon to feel this close to the edge.

As if he knows how precariously close I am, he adds two fingers to his pattern, moving them inside me in tandem with his tongue moving across my clit. It takes only moments before that familiar wave is cresting through me, my entire body rolling with sensation as I come on his tongue.

"That's it," he murmurs as he works me through it, licking until I'm spent, flopping back on the bed as he shifts in front of me. He carefully slides each of my heels off before he crawls up the bed and scoots me back onto the pillows behind us.

I let my head flop into the pillow, my breathing labored and my body spent from what is possibly the best orgasm I've ever had. The ones I give myself are... perfectly fine, but nothing like the one from Jake's tongue. The aftershocks roll through me, and I swear I feel them in every inch of my body.

He looks so smug, staring down at me as he shifts himself up the bed next to me.

"Hey, Jake?" I lean up, catching his eye as he falls onto the pillow next to me.

"Yeah?"

Before I say anything else, I push myself up, throwing my leg over his hips to straddle him, two hands falling to the top of his briefs.

"Can I?" I ask, watching the way his arm flexes under the ink of his tattoos as he reaches for me, the muscles defined and delicious. His hand wraps around the back of my neck as he pulls me down to him, our chests flush, our noses touching. I feel the clasp of my bra open under his touch, and he slides the garment off, adding it to the growing pile on the floor. His eyes search mine for a moment before he brings our lips together, a kiss so all-consuming I can feel the flames ripping through my body. I'm desperate to have him, and as much as I love kissing him like this, that's *not* what I want to be doing right now.

I push up off his chest, rolling my pussy across his dick as I ask again, "Can I take these off?" I snap the band of his underwear.

"Jesus," he says it in a low, gruff voice, hands on my hips as he moves me over him once more. "Fuck, whatever you want."

It's my turn to smirk as I tug the fabric down his legs, his cock bobbing free. He is *not small* by any means, and the asshole knows it, mischief dancing in his eyes as he watches me, watching him.

I shove his briefs off to the side, taking my time to run my hands up his body while I am in control. He's laid out before me like a fucking model, hands now perched behind his head, hair mussed from my fingertips, abs rippling with each breath he takes.

It's ridiculous, to be quite honest, and I tell him as much.

He just chuckles at me, reaching for my arms, but I bat him away.

"It's not your turn." I say, dragging my fingernails across his stomach as he quirks an eyebrow at me. "I really just want…"

My thoughts trail off as I take him in my hand, gripping the smooth skin of his shaft. I toy with him, running the pads of my fingers along the thick vein on the underside of his dick, circling it slowly around the head as I trace the ridges of his cock.

I look up to find Jake's head tipped back, his eyes closed.

"I'm sorry, am I boring you?" I tease, pulling my arm back, craving the feeling of him watching me while I have my hands on him. His eyes pop open as he props himself up, pulling himself to a sitting position while he cradles me in his lap.

"Fuck no." He whispers, his palm coming up behind my neck and squeezing as he pulls me toward him. "You can do that all night if you want to."

I brush his nose with mine, ghosting my lips over his. "I don't."

His mouth catches mine, and we're momentarily distracted as we swap kisses, the gentle playfulness turning into something untamed.

Jake shifts me in his arms as he reaches over the side of the bed, rifling through a suitcase just off to the side. He comes back with a condom, wordlessly holding it out to me.

I smile, taking it from him and ripping the foil open. I take my time, rolling the latex down over his thick shaft. When it's on, I climb back into his lap, wrapping my arms behind his neck as his close around my waist, two hands holding me tight, his grip anything but delicate.

"How do you want to do this?" he asks, but the only answer I give him is to move myself over his dick, running myself along the rigid length as we both heave matching sighs.

He loses patience before I do, taking his cock in his fist and holding it taught.

"Such a tease." He rubs the head of his dick roughly against my clit and I fold into him, clinging to his shoulders.

"Fuck me, Jake." My voice is low in his ear.

"Manners, Red."

I shiver as his cock meets my clit again, grinding down on his shaft. The nickname, though I've heard it many times throughout my life, hits different coming from him like this. It's delicious, almost dirty, the way he says it.

I love it.

"Jake." I'm whining now, and I don't even care how pathetic it sounds. I might actually combust if I don't feel him inside me.

"That's not the word I'm looking for." He slows his rhythm, dragging the head of his dick through my slick center, taunting me.

"Please. God, Jake. *Please* give me your cock."

"There we go." I hear his voice in my ear, but I'm completely incoherent as he notches his dick inside me and urges my hips down onto him. "You're so pretty when you beg."

We move slowly, Jake letting me take the lead.

The burn is exquisite.

I work him into me one inch at a time, needing a moment to adjust. It's been a long time and I'm not about to ruin anything by rushing it.

"Fuckkk," his voice is a low moan in the air between us, his eyes fixated on where we're coming together.

It doesn't take long. I'm so wet that he's fully seated in no time at all, the stretch the best kind of painful.

His hands work their way up the side of my body, his head dipping to take my nipple into his mouth. He lavishes my breasts with attention as we sit there. I'm overwhelmed with sensation as he laps at one side, while his fingers pinch and twist at the opposite nipple.

It's too much, the stretch, the stimulation, the ache to move urging me forward. I shift my hips forward, feeling him inside me as I do, and the thin string of restraint snaps.

I press my hands into his shoulders, forcing him down on the bed as I lift my hips and roll them back, trying to tame the incessant need racing through me.

I take in the pink of his cheeks, the veins in his neck, as I move on top of him. His fingers dig into my hips as he holds me to him, and I'm going to have bruises tomorrow, but the idea of his mark on me is so enticing.

Sooner than should be possible, I can feel the waves of another orgasm cresting again.

"Jake, I'm going to…" Before I can get the full sentence out, he sits up, flipping us over so I'm pressed into the mattress beneath him, the building pressure interrupted as he shifts, breaking my rhythm.

"JAKE." It comes out a cry of half anger and half lust as he thrusts into me so hard, I shift up the bed.

"This one is mine, Red. You can make yourself come on my cock next time, but this one? I'm taking it. It's mine." He snaps his hips, holding me in place this time, my entire body alight with the fire in his eyes, the demand in his voice.

His pace is hurried, his breathing labored as he moves inside me. I arch into his touch, craving more. He's quick to notice the silent plea, one hand dropping from my hip to rub on my clit, the other sliding up my stomach to toy with my nipples.

That combination does it, my body hurtling back toward the edge and flinging itself over without so much as a pause.

My orgasm rolls through me, my pussy clenching tightly as Jake continues to move, each wave carrying me further away until I'm a hazy, delirious mess of limbs.

"Fuck, I'm gonna come. Natalie..."

"Do it, Jake. Come. In me." My sentences are choppy; my breathing erratic.

He doesn't need to be told twice, his orgasm roaring through him before the last word has even left my mouth. I watch as he slows his movements, his head tipped back, his skin pink from exertion. He collapses forward, falling gently over me, as he tries to catch his breath.

We stay like that, the room silent except for the sounds of our heavy breathing and the soft rustle of the sheets when we move.

When he rolls off me he doesn't pause to lie in bed, instead continuing until his feet hit the floor and he makes his way to the bathroom. He comes back a few moments later, crawling in next to me as he pulls the covers up over us both and tugs me into his chest.

"Are you a cuddler, Jake?" I ask, the unexpected gesture causing a pinch in my chest. *Why is that so cute?*

"No, I hate cuddling." He tightens his arm around my waist, hand splayed across my stomach as he drops a kiss to my shoulder blade. "I'll let you go in a minute, if you want out of here."

He sounds exactly how I feel: exhausted and satisfied.

"I... think I'm good." I turn my head into the pillow, just to be sure he can't see the smile that crosses my face.

God, he's too much like this.

It's sweet. And adorable.

And cute Jake, who apparently comes with sexy Jake, is a dangerous combination.

A soft knocking jolts me awake a short while later, the rap of knuckles on the door pulling me out of the sex-induced haze and causing panic to course through my veins.

"Jake!" I hiss. "There's someone at your door."

I shake his shoulders, two brown eyes popping open to look at me. The knocking starts again, and this time he bolts upright, muttering under his breath as he jumps out of bed in search of a pair of pants.

I follow his lead, wrapping the sheet around me as I race to collect my clothing from the floor. When I've gathered all the pieces, I slip through the adjoining doors, being careful to close them behind me.

I hear the loud click of his hallway door as I do, my sister's voice floating through the room.

"Hey! We just got back. Is Natalie ok?"

"Yeah. She just had a stomachache. She went to bed as soon as we got back."

Guilt fills my stomach like a leaden weight as I listen to Jake lying to Melanie for me. Mel and I don't keep secrets; we don't hide things from one another. And here I am, sleeping with my bodyguard behind her back.

"Oh, ok. I didn't want to risk waking her; I just wanted to make sure everything was ok. It looks like I woke you instead. Sorry."

"All good. I don't mind."

"Alright, well thanks, Jake. We'll see you tomorrow."

I don't hear his reply, but I can hear the heavy door close behind Melanie. A few moments later, the adjoining door I'm eavesdropping at swings open, Jake standing there, wearing nothing but a pair of joggers.

"You answered the door to my sister wearing that?" I gesture to the gray fabric, revealing way more than is appropriate.

"Yeah, well, I was short on time. Get back in here." He tips his head toward his side of the door.

"This is such a bad idea." I plop down on the edge of the bed, keeping the sheet pulled around my body. "There are too many eyes on us."

Jake sits down next to me, the bed dipping under his weight as he leans into me, dropping his lips to my shoulder before moving them up the slope of my neck.

"We already spend all of our time together." His teeth tug on my earlobe before he leans away, meeting my gaze with his. "No one's gonna notice anything different. We just need to be smart about it."

He pauses, hesitating before he lowers his voice. "Unless you're saying you don't want this, then we can call it right now."

"No, no, I want to. I just don't want anyone finding out. You could lose your job."

"I could." He brushes my hair off my shoulder, tugging the sheet out of my grip and letting it fall away from my body. "But I think that's a risk I'm willing to take."

He pushes me onto my back as he climbs back over me, the eager glint in his eye telling me he's nowhere near done with me.

APRIL

SUN	MON	TUES	WED	THUR	FRI	S
		1	2	3	4	5 Houston Sh
6	7 Day Off!	8 Day Off!	9 9a Team Weekly	10	11 New Orlean	12
13 NOLA Drive →	14	15 9a Team Weekly	16 Tampa Baseball Event	17	18 Tampa	
20 Tampa Drive — beach? →	21	22 9a Team Weekly	23 Atlanta Station Interviews	24	25 Atl	
27 Atlanta Drive — →	28 Day Off!	29 Day Off!	30 Day Off!			
Nashville! →						

THE
TRACKS

AUSTIN: You're a month into the tour now. Tell us what it's like!

MELANIE: Busy. Very, very busy. It's a continuous cycle of travel, PR events, rehearsals, and shows. But I love it.

AUSTIN: What does your downtime look like? Do you get any time off while you're on the road?

MELANIE: It mostly involves sleeping. No, but honestly, we don't get much free time. We have our first actual break at the beginning of next week, and I'm so looking forward to it.

INDY: What are you doing on your off days? Anything fun?

MELANIE: Well, I really love trying to do something local. Visiting local restaurants, seeing a tourist attraction, shopping at small businesses, things like that. I'm so fortunate to get to travel the country on this tour; I'd love to see as much as possible. It's hard with the limited schedule, but we try to make it work.

INDY: A lot of your PR events overlap with that idea too, don't they?

MELANIE: They do. Obviously, we stop in to see local radio stations as much as we can. We do a lot of meet-and-greets, but we really like getting out into the community when we travel. We also try to keep each location unique when we can.

AUSTIN: Are there any upcoming PR events you're most looking forward to at the future tour stops!?

MELANIE: There are honestly so many. Natalie, my publicist, is amazing at what she does. She has so many great events in the works. When we're up in Massachusetts, we have an afternoon event at the Boston Gardens that I'm really excited about. We also have an event at the Cincinnati Zoo that will be super fun.

AUSTIN: Sounds like it's a lot of hands-on events?

MELANIE: It very much is. We're trying to get out, spend time in the cities we're passing through, make a memorable event of every place we stop. I really want to be in the community, interacting with fans. Obviously there are some limitations to how much I can do, but we try really hard to make it happen.

AUSTIN: So, what's next? What's happening after your break?

MELANIE: We're down in New Orleans for the next two shows. I've never been there, so I'm excited to visit somewhere new.

AUSTIN: And what's on tap while you're in the city?

MELANIE: Undecided on that, Austin. The prospect of time off has me counting sheep. Once I get some sleep, I definitely want to venture out and do something fun.

AUSTIN: Sounds like there's no shortage of dull moments.

MELANIE: No, absolutely not. There's always something going on.

INDY: Well, I, for one, am so excited! I might have to send Austin back to the office when our time on this tour is done and keep tagging along by myself because this sounds like fun I don't want to miss.

MELANIE: We'd love that. [laughter] Sorry, Austin, sounds like you're taking one for the team here.

AUSTIN: Aren't I always?

KATAKLYSM.69: Poor Austin. He's so outnumbered on this tour.

NOVAFAERIEREADS: Why didn't you cover Melanie donating to the women's shelters? She's done it in all three cities so far!

CRUNCHYCUCUMBERCRUMBBOB: She may not want that publicized. She's getting a lot of attention right now. This may have been something she wanted to do privately, without the press making a big deal about it.

JUNIPERSAIDSO: With her ex-husband's accusations, you would think she would WANT people to know she's doing nice things.

CRUNCHYCUCUMBERCRUMBBOB: That's probably the very reason she doesn't share it.

JUNIPERSAIDSO: Missed opportunity.

TWENTY-NINE

JAKE

Nice Work, Dumbass

I used to be able to follow the rules I made for myself. I keep my life cut and dry: I go in, do my job, and leave. Everyone and everything stays behind, where it belongs. I don't stay in one place too long, and I sure as hell don't form connections to anyone I'm working with.

Leave it to Natalie to be the one who has me breaking every boundary I put in place. From the moment she crashed into me, she's been under my skin. At first, it was more like a thorn, but now…

It's been almost a week since that night in my hotel room, and I'm struggling to keep my hands to myself. My days have become a challenge; forced to be in her orbit, unable to do anything about it with all the eyes on us.

We had three more nights in Houston after the night we snuck out of the bar, and Natalie found her way into my bed every single one of them. Unfortunately for us, the bus trip to New Orleans put a swift stop to that. And this week, she's back to sharing a room in her sister's suite.

Fucking high-end hotels with their multi-room penthouse suites.

As a result, it's been days since we've been able to do anything more than have a casual conversation, and the ache to touch her is getting harder to contain.

I growl under my breath as I jam the button on the coffee maker in the hotel lounge. The device sputters to life, the hot liquid rattling into the paper cup in my hand.

"Well, good morning to you too, sunshine." Knox comes up beside me, clapping a hand on my shoulder as he swings around me, leaning against the counter beside the machine.

Today is the first of two days off for the tour crew. For the first time since we left Nashville, the schedule is free of all obligations: no PR, no rehearsals, no shows. I don't for one second think that means we'll be relaxing in the hotel rooms though. I already heard Indy in the hallway this morning plotting a group outing.

"Morning," I say, more to my to-go cup than to Knox, as I lean to blow on the scalding hot coffee.

"Still good if I give Asher the next two days off? Sounds like the girls are planning to spend their time off together, so he might as well take the days while he can get them."

"You're the boss."

"And you're a grumpy bastard. Maybe I should make you take it off and have Asher fill in for you instead."

I huff under my breath, but my mind takes that idea and runs with it, debating what I could do with two days off and Natalie in my hotel room. The image of her under me, her lips parted as she comes around my cock...

Hot coffee spills over the side of my cup and onto my hand, the scalding liquid landing on my skin with a harsh bite.

"Fuck." I switch hands quickly, shaking the coffee off. A napkin appears in front of me, Knox's hand waving the white square in my face. I snatch it, setting the coffee on the counter as I dry my hands.

"Clearly, you're having a good day." The asshole laughs to himself as I throw him a look. I toss the napkin in the trash and collect my coffee cup, snapping a lid on this time. "Anyway, heads up that we're leaving at noon. The girls planned a lunch or something."

I nod in acknowledgment as Knox flags down Dex across the room. He's gone before I can reply. I turn to leave the lounge, making my way toward the door just as Natalie and Indy come crashing through it, the two of them laughing loudly.

I stop in my tracks, taking them in. Natalie's in jeans and sneakers, a combination I don't think I've seen from her before. She's got a black MBM t-shirt on, the logo of Melanie's music company splayed across her chest in white. Her red hair bounces on top of her head, tied up in a ponytail with a goddamn bow.

Fuck, she looks good.

I can, and often do, go months without sex, but three days without having Natalie and I think I might be losing my mind. Shaking my head,

I force myself to refocus. I'm acting like I've never been with a woman before, and I don't know what the fuck is wrong with me.

The girls make their way over, smiles plastered on their faces.

"Morning, Jake!" Indy chirps as they come to a stop a few steps in front of me.

"Morning." I answer her, but my eyes are focused on Natalie next to her, doing her best to look unaffected.

It's cute.

"Are you grabbing breakfast?" Indy prattles on as I pry my eyes from Natalie, shifting them over to her.

"Uh, no. Just needed a coffee before I hit the gym."

Indy's eyes shift between Natalie and me. I clear my throat before taking a long pull on my coffee, doing my best to look casual and not at all guilty of eye-fucking Natalie in front of her.

"Those waffles are calling my name. So, I'll see you two later." Indy slinks off, leaving Natalie and me alone.

Natalie takes a step forward, the fresh scent of her shampoo pulling me in as she draws closer.

"Morning," she breathes, her eyes raking up over my torso before meeting mine. A small smile stretches across her face.

"Morning, Red." I watch as her cheeks darken at my use of the nickname. It was an accident the first time it slipped out, an unconscious decision in the heat of the moment, but it felt right. And now, well, I like the reminder of that moment. And I like her reaction to it even more.

"Shouldn't you eat something? You know, before you go lift heavy weights and pass out?"

A laugh slips out of me at that. "Worried about me now? I thought we were keeping it low-key. That feels… serious."

I'm teasing, but the look that passes over her face looks a lot like hurt from where I'm standing. Instead of correcting her, I barrel on, "I ate earlier, before I went for a run."

"You run too? Jesus Jake, it's—" She checks her watch, "not even 9am. I thought I had a problem with taking the day off. At least I don't hop out of bed for an early morning torture session."

"I enjoy running; it clears my head. I don't do it all that often, but it's nice to get out when I have a chance."

She scoffs at that. "I mean, clearly it's working for you."

I smirk from behind my coffee cup as I take a quick sip. "I'm glad you think so."

The blush returns to her cheeks as her eyes drop from my face. She scans the room around us, looking adorably awkward.

"I should let you get to the gym. Don't want to interrupt your schedule." She straightens her back, plastering her PR smile on her face, the polite one that looks anything but real.

"Listen, Natalie—"

"Oh, are we going to the gym?" Dex comes up behind us, inserting himself into the conversation. I instinctively take a step back, putting space between Natalie and me.

"We are definitely not." Natalie laughs as she takes a step further into the lounge. "I am just here for breakfast, not torment. You boys have fun though."

She gives a little wave before taking off, her sudden change in demeanor making a lot more sense.

"Mind if I join you?" Dex asks as he turns toward me.

Mind? Yes, absolutely.

I like Dex; he's a nice guy. But the last person I want to be around right now is Natalie's brother. Unfortunately, I don't have a choice except to play nice, so I force a half smile as I reply, "Not at all."

The hotel gym is surprisingly nice. The equipment looks well-kept, and the space is large and open. It's quiet this morning, but I imagine Monday morning trips to the gym are not high on the list of priorities for guests here.

I'm currently spotting for Dex, because, apparently, this trip to the gym is a buddy workout. Dude's so damn friendly, it's really hard to tell him no when he asks for something.

"We can switch." He says as he racks the barbell he's holding before he slides out from under it and snatches his towel off the side of the bench. He stands, wiping his brow before tossing the towel over his shoulder.

I busy myself with adding more weight to the bars before I position myself under them.

"Show off." Dex laughs as he stands over me, taking a long pull from his water bottle.

"Don't worry, bud. Keep practicing and you'll get there."

"Fuck you." He squirts water at me from his water bottle before he finishes his drink and sets it off to the side.

"Dick," I mutter under my breath before beginning my first rep.

It's easy with him, in a way it's never been with my own brothers. I assume the lack of shared trauma has something to do with it, but it's nice. The companionship. Even Knox and Asher are easy to get along with. I don't mind spending time with them.

Shit, I might even consider them friends at this point.

And the thought that used to give me hives now feels… comfortable.

Dex is talking, and I'm unsure how much I've missed, but I tune back in just in time to catch him going on about a ghost tour.

"Melanie was adamant we do something 'fun and touristy'—her words, not mine—and apparently it's a crime to come to New Orleans and not tour the haunted graveyards."

"Well," I grit out through my teeth as I lift the bar again, "that should be fun."

"The girls make the rules; I just follow them. Best just to go with the flow." He laughs to himself as I rack the bar, sweat beading down my temples.

"I hear that's how it goes."

"Do you have any sisters?"

"Ah, no. Just… three brothers." I never know what I'm supposed to say in these instances. I usually shut a conversation down instead of addressing it.

"Mmm, that must have been chaos."

"Probably? I couldn't tell you, to be honest. The memories I have... aren't good ones. My family is nothing like yours."

"Sorry to hear that, man."

"Can't really change the hand we're dealt." I grab the bar and start my second rep.

"No, I suppose you can't." Dex is contemplative before he continues. "At least you didn't have two bossy know-it-alls raising you."

I huff a laugh as I bring the bar toward me. "Who, Natalie?"

"Mmhmm. Melanie really wasn't any better either." He drops his head, looking at me. "Nat looked happy this morning. Her and Indy. I haven't seen her like that in quite a while."

I can't tell if he's directing that at me, or just looking at me while he talks now, so I keep my mouth shut, silently counting my reps as I continue lifting.

"You didn't know her before Sean, but I swear she's never been the same since. I mean, it hasn't even been a year, but things didn't end well there. I feel like she lost part of herself in the split. I've tried to talk to her, but... well, you've met Natalie."

I rack the bar for the last time as a small laugh escapes me. "Yeah, she really loves pillow talk."

I grab my towel, running the fabric across my face as I clear the sweat from my brow. It isn't until I drop the towel that I realize my joke was a little too on the nose.

Dex stares down at me, his face a stony, emotionless mask.

Shittttt.

"Did you..."

"Listen, man—" We talk over one another before he cracks a smile, laughing out loud.

"Did you just make a joke, Jake?"

The relief I feel is palpable. "Uh, yes. Yeah, I did."

"Look at you." Dex slaps my shoulder as I stand and walk past him. He follows me over to the cleaning station, where we grab cloths to wipe down the equipment we've been using. "He does have a sense of humor."

I force a laugh before I busy myself with putting everything back the way we found it.

One week.

I haven't even made it one full week, and I'm already about to reveal one of the most important secrets I need to keep hidden.

Nice work, dumbass.

THIRTY

NATALIE

I'm writing an email politely telling a magazine editor requesting Melanie's statement on Gunner's article to "fuck off," when the hotel room door swings open, chatter rolling in from the hallway when Melanie and Indy come walking in.

"Natalieee!" Melanie bounds over, a little skip to her step as she makes her way through the hotel room. She plops down at the table across from me, brown eyes shining.

"Hey," I say, looking up from the computer. "What are you two up to?"

"Us three? And Dex. And Austin." She says with a smirk on her lips, ticking people off on her fingers as she goes. "I thought we could all go out tonight! Indy scheduled this ghost tour for us. She found a company that does private tours, and we have the cemetery all to ourselves."

I sigh, reaching over to take a swig of my drink on the table. I'm sprawled out in our hotel room, making the dining table into my office for the next few days. Technically, our crew is off duty. The management team left a gap between events this week so we could recharge. We've been running for a month straight, but I can't bring myself to shut it down with everyone else. I still have so many things to do in the coming weeks; I need the time to tackle this massive to-do list. A lot of the PR events for late in the tour are still in the early phases of planning, and getting ahead on those would be amazing.

So far, with one glaring exception, the events have gone perfectly. That means that all the planning and preparation is working. That also means now is not the time to slow down.

"Well, that sounds like fun for you all." I say, arching an eyebrow at my sister. Gesturing at the computer in front of me, I add, "I have a boatload of work to catch up on, so I think I'll probably use the next two days for that."

I smile at her, knowing she's about to argue with me.

"Come on, Natalie. This is literally the first day off we've had in a month. Please come with us?"

I look over her shoulder at Indy, who holds up two hands in front of her. "Not my idea! I was just fulfilling the wishes of the pop star."

Melanie scoffs playfully. "Yes, the pop star demands. Please, Natalie? One fun outing? We don't get very many of these days."

She throws me puppy-dog eyes—knowing damn well I rarely tell her no. "I agreed to lunch already. I'm taking the afternoon."

"So what's a few more hours? Take the night too."

I sigh, and Melanie's grin widens. "Finnneee. Fine. But you remember how I feel about ghosts, right?"

She laughs. "It will be fun! You'll be fine. All of us will be there. It's not *real*; it's just a tourist attraction."

I am entirely horror-averse. It's the unknown, really. I hate shit I can't control or predict.

Scary movies? Absolutely not.

Thriller novels? Nope.

Ghost tours? Lord, help me.

Before I can argue, the door swings open again and Knox stands there, knocking on the doorframe like he didn't just use a key. Jake stands over his shoulder, still in the hallway, and my heart kicks into high gear at the sight of him.

There has been no sneaking around since we left Houston. Trying to play it cool on the bus to New Orleans was nearly impossible. And now we're at the hotel, and instead of sneaking into his room every night, I'm stuck imagining what I could be doing instead while I share a room with my sister.

Needless to say, I'm a little frustrated. And a lot annoyed.

I'm also back to hyper-fixating on my behavior around him because I'm worried someone might pick up on the body language between us. I'm constantly overthinking the things I'm doing. Am I laughing too much? Looking his way too often? I'm apparently a fucking kid again, and it's exhausting.

Honestly, I'm doubting my decision to throw caution to the wind and take what I want because, apparently, I can't focus on anything but him now.

My train of thought is interrupted as the guys come to a stop right in front of us.

"Still going to lunch? The car is outside for you." Knox looks between the three of us, waiting for confirmation.

"Oh, yes!" Melanie claps her hands. "Perfect timing. You good to go, Natalie?"

"Sure, I can save this problem for another time." I close the windows, secretly glad for the reprieve from dealing with reporters, and flip the lid shut. I stand, gathering my purse before I follow the girls to the door. Knox takes off down the hall with Mel and Indy on his heels.

Jake takes his time closing the door before we make our way down the hall behind them. I watch as they round the corner in front of us. As soon as they disappear, Jake's hand reaches out to grab mine, and he pulls me back into him.

I spin as his hand comes up behind my head, angling my mouth to his as we crash together, a rush of need pulsing through me at the contact. The kiss is short, a few heated seconds, but there's an urgency to the movements.

Too soon, he lets go, stepping back as he brings his thumb up, running it over his bottom lip while he watches me.

"Sorry, I just… Hey." His lips tip up as his eyes blaze.

"Hi," I tug on the lapels of his jacket, pulling him back into me for another quick kiss. I could easily get lost in this, lost in him, but before I do, my anxiety kicks into overdrive. "We should go… before they notice."

"Yeah, yeah." He gestures ahead, and I turn, rounding the corner to catch up to the group ahead of us. I dip my head as a smile spreads across my face.

We arrive for our reservation at a rooftop bar just outside downtown New Orleans about thirty minutes later. The waitress shows us to our table, tucked back in the corner of the roof. It's nice and private, with a gorgeous view. I can immediately smell the food in the kitchen, the rumbling of my stomach reminding me how hungry I am. Jake and Knox make themselves scarce, dipping off to the side.

Indy, Mel, and I slide into our chairs, natural wicker colored seats with black and white patterned cushions. I sling my crossbody bag over the seat, settling in as I look around.

Our chairs are sitting around a natural wood table, with matching greenery spanning the center of the table, small candles enclosed in glass flickering gently in front of us. The New Orleans skyline sits behind us, off in the distance.

We study the menu in comfortable silence, each of us ordering a large drink when the waitress comes back to check on us.

"A sit-down meal feels so nice," Melanie says as she shifts in the chair, getting comfortable. "I'm already over the catered meals. It's nice that we have them, don't get me wrong, but eating on the run is a lot less enjoyable."

"You've had enough sandwich spreads?" Indy laughs.

"This is a nice change," I agree. "The view is incredible."

"Would have been a great clip for content, but I was trying to give us a break." Indy laughs. "Naturally, that would be the case."

"Isn't it always?" Mel chimes.

"I love and hate this job. To get the best content, you almost always have to be on, tuned in, thinking of opportunities, but it makes it so hard to turn it off and just enjoy doing things."

Mel and I hum in agreement, our roles being very different in actuality, but the sentiment fitting perfectly.

"So, Ind, I saw the email come through on The Tracks numbers this morning—it looks like everything is going really well?" I unroll my napkin in front of me, setting the silverware off to the side as I place the napkin in my lap.

Melanie perks up at that. "Wait, what?! No one told me!"

"This is me bringing it up." I laugh, "It just hit my inbox before you came to get me for lunch."

"Ah, yes!" Indy claps her hands. "The last few episodes have really had a pop in viewership. I think people enjoy the content. The comments section certainly is."

We spend the next little while discussing the commentary surrounding the show, all of it overwhelmingly positive. The Tracks is seeing record-high viewership; every concert on the tour has now sold out. There weren't a ton of extra tickets available when we left, but what remained was snapped up within two episodes of The Tracks airing the tour shows.

I feel a smug sense of satisfaction as we talk through the positive impact the show is having on both parties. I *knew* this was the way to go, and to see it coming together like this, proving I was right to my team and The Tracks team? It feels amazing.

"It's a bummer we're down to two weeks on the contract. I don't really want to pack it up and call it quits just yet."

"We could talk with management, ours and yours," I offer. "If it continues to do well, it would be in the best interest of both parties to keep going. I'm sure Dex can flex accommodations; he's made it work so far."

"I mean, I obviously can't make the call myself, but sign me up. I'd love to stay on. The team has really found a groove with us on the road and the office staff doing our other segments now. I can't see them being upset about an extension."

"Let's see what we can do. I want to pull the numbers I got into a report, but I'll use that as ammunition when I pitch the continuation of the series." I pull out my phone, adding a time block to my calendar tomorrow to meet with Dex and get the ball rolling. He'll have to coordinate with Austin, but the idea of prolonging the show has me excited.

I spend a few minutes adding some thoughts to a note on my phone, while Mel and Indy chat beside me.

When I look back up, Indy is fidgeting with her napkin, looking over her shoulder, her eyes tracking the guys behind us before she turns back and changes the topic completely. "Can I ask your opinion? While it's just us?"

"Of course, on what?" I ask, shifting my chair to face her better.

"I have a… situation. A personal situation?" She laughs and continues, "I know this is like, not girls' night or anything…"

"Babe, it's always girls' night around here. Spill." Melanie winks as she teases her.

"Well, I… I sort of slept with someone? It was weeks ago, and it was a one-time thing, and to be honest with you, I didn't see it going anywhere."

"On the tour?! Wait, full stop. I want details." Melanie is leaning forward, fully invested in this story now. "Who was it?"

"What? No, no. It was before the tour started." She pauses as the waitress appears, dropping our drinks off. We order a round of apps to share before she disappears again.

"Spill, Indy." I laugh at the serious expression on Melanie's face. "We never have good gossip like this; let's hear it."

Indy takes a drink of her margarita before she continues. "It was someone I met at a club. I was positive it wasn't going to be a big thing, but now…" She picks at the straw wrapper in her hand, pulling it into tiny pieces.

"I can't stop thinking about him. I haven't gone a single day since we slept together without catching myself daydreaming about him. That's… not normal, right?"

Oh, girl. I feel your pain.

I wish I could say as much out loud. God, it would feel good to talk this whole Jake situation out with the girls.

I chew my bottom lip as I think it over.

No, I can't.

Even if it is just Indy and Mel, there's too much on the line if someone finds out.

Melanie snickers, pulling me from my own thoughts as she says, "Well, normal is relative. It's certainly… interesting. Have you messaged him?"

"No, I don't have his number. He was adamant it was just a hookup. We made that clear before anything ever happened. It's usually not an issue, but I think I'm losing my mind. I'm honestly annoyed at how much time I spend thinking about it."

My eyes catch Jake as I listen to Indy talk, watching as he stands there, his eyes scanning the room.

Yep, it's really annoying when you can't focus on anything but a fucking guy.

"Well, I'm no help, honestly." I shift my attention back to the table before they catch me. "I'm thirty-four and I turn into a teenager when I'm into someone apparently, so… right there with ya." I take a long pull on my straw, the Long Island I ordered hitting the spot.

"I'm sorry, you're into someone?!" Melanie looks at me in surprise. "This is news to me."

Shitttt.

Jake's head snaps toward the table, clearly hearing every word of this conversation. He wiggles his eyebrows at me, and I choke back a laugh.

"No, not like… now." I backtrack, realizing I said too much. "I mean, generally speaking. Like with Sean."

She gives me a look, as if she's debating whether I'm lying, but she doesn't push. "Yeah, well, Sean was a whole stupid thing. Everything there was a mess."

Melanie shifts her focus to Indy. "I think you may have come to the wrong people, Ind. Natalie's sworn off men entirely after her last boyfriend, and I'm in the middle of a divorce."

Indy chuckles, "Well, at least we're all a mess. That makes me feel better."

"It's men," Melanie says. "Men make the mess. Every time."

Conversation shifts as the food arrives, and we spend the next hour talking about anything and everything, except our love lives.

It feels good to get out and do something with the girls, to take a moment to feel normal in the middle of this whirlwind experience. But even so, as we sit discussing whether we'll have time for an afternoon at the beach when we get down to Tampa, my attention drifts over and over, keeping an eye on Jake in my periphery.

THIRTY-ONE

JAKE

You Look Like Mine

"Why did we have to do this after dark?" Natalie asks Melanie, her eyes scanning the city outside the window as we ride to the cemetery for the tour Indy booked. "That seems dumb. You can see things much better in the daylight."

"Yeah, but it loses some of its appeal when you're on a haunted tour in broad daylight, now doesn't it?"

"I hate this," Natalie murmurs under her breath. Melanie doesn't seem to pick up on it, but from her other side, I hear her loud and clear.

It's pretty obvious that Natalie will do just about anything for her sister, whether it's in her own best interest or not. I might admire that more if it didn't seem to wear her down so much. At first, I thought it was because of the whole Gunner situation, but it's really just who Natalie is. She puts herself last every time.

The SUV comes to a halt at the black wrought-iron gates of a sprawling cemetery, tall stone pillars on either side of the arched metal over the entrance. We pile out, our car and the other SUV behind us emptying completely before the drivers take off, parking around the block until they're called back.

We're greeted at the gates by two employees. They usher us onto the grounds, the cracked and aging stone of the main path adding to the haunted cemetery vibes tourists are promised. Lamp posts dot the pathway, dim yellow orbs breaking up the otherwise dark cemetery, bathing the area with ambient lighting and swaths of shadows.

A middle-aged man, significantly shorter than my own 6'3", greets us as we enter. We all circle up as he introduces himself and gives us a brief history of the cemetery we're standing in, highlighting all the famous people buried here and promising to share the haunted tales of the graves as we move through the tour. I cross my arms, trying hard not to roll my eyes at this attempt to be ominous as the guide wraps up his speech and takes the lead, moving us through into the cemetery.

Melanie is right up front, with Dex and Indy on either side of her; Austin and Knox make a row behind them. I'm following along beside Natalie, who is at least two steps behind everyone else.

She's changed out of her jeans and tee from this morning, instead choosing a short skirt that flares out just before it stops mid-thigh. She's paired it with a skin-tight, long-sleeved t-shirt with a low neckline. To top it all off, she's got a pair of calf-high black boots on that are short-circuiting my brain. She looks damn good, although a little cold. As if keeping it together this week isn't hard enough, she chooses an outfit like *this* to wear out.

The afternoon rain has left a crisp edge to the air. You can feel the chill in the breeze as it wraps around us.

We make our way along the narrow walkway. A white wall on our right borders the row of graves we are currently entering, the tall facades of the mausoleums on the left passing by in various constructions of brick and cement designs.

I watch Natalie as the tour guide talks, her arms crossed over her chest, her shoulders tight and rolled up into her neck. I'm trying to decide whether her rigid posture is a product of the cold or just the environment. A stick snaps on the other side of the gravestones in front of us, and she flinches.

"Not a big fan of ghosts?"

"No, not so much." She answers quietly.

We keep going, wandering down one row and up another, each mausoleum different from the last. We stop again as the guide shares another story about the grave we're standing in front of. This one involves a man with a serial infidelity problem who was haunted by one of his wives, but the details are lost on me as I watch Natalie shiver.

I slide my coat off my shoulders, the black nylon swishing loudly in the quiet night air. Natalie's head turns in my direction, and I hold the jacket out to her. Her eyes scan the fabric slowly, as if she's contemplating the offer. I shake the jacket at her, a quiet insistence, and she sighs. Her fingers slide across mine as she takes it from my grip, the now familiar spark following in their wake.

"Thank you," she whispers as she slides the jacket over one arm and across her back. I nod as I watch her fit the zipper together and close it up, her arms coming back together in front of her when she's done.

Natalie stops shivering almost immediately and the tour continues for another thirty minutes; the guide leading us around, sharing more popular tales of the residents of the graveyard. Natalie, however, remains stiff and uncomfortable, jumping at every tiny noise.

As the group winds its way toward another section of the cemetery, I make a quick decision and, instead of following their lead, I grab Natalie's elbow, slipping her into the shadows beside me. I pull her back from the path, in between two mausoleums just as the group disappears around a corner. The unexpected detour makes a small squeal slip from her lips. I slap my palm over her mouth to silence the noise, crowding her against the stone behind us as I do.

"It's just me." Her eyes narrow as she swats at my arm, but she doesn't push me away. I can barely make her out in the dim lighting that spills through the crack in the stone monuments, but I watch as her chest rises and falls as she steadies herself, the sweet fruity scent of her engulfing me.

"What the fuck is wrong with you?" She hisses.

She stares at me, the heat in her gaze morphing as she does.

"My intention wasn't to scare you," I say. I run my fingertip down her temple, following the curve of her cheek and the vein on the side of her neck before slipping my entire hand behind her head. I thread my fingers in her hair and tug, tipping her head up toward me. "It's to distract you."

My face hovers close to hers for a moment before she pushes up onto her tiptoes and presses our lips together. We meet in an urgent rush, her body melting into mine as her mouth does. The nylon of my jacket brushes against me as she slips her arms up behind my neck. I slide my free hand down to her hip, gripping tightly, and lick at the seam of her mouth. She sighs, opening for me, and we kiss for several long moments, the anticipation between us building. Pausing, I can feel her lips tip up into a smile as I pull my head back, taking in her reddening cheeks and the desire in her dark brown eyes.

"Well, consider me distracted," she says in barely more than a whisper, her breath warm on my skin in the cool night air. I trail a line of kisses up her neck to her ear, tugging on it with my teeth as her hands drop to my stomach, her nails scratching at me through the fabric of my shirt.

I roll my hips into her, dropping my hand from her waist to skim up the bare leg of her thigh, inching it up to the hemline of her skirt. She tips her head back as she lets out a small moan, and I take that as a sign to keep going. My fingers creep up her smooth skin, sliding along her outer thigh until I'm cupping her ass, my cock notched right between her legs.

God, this fucking woman.

She's hot as hell when she's buttoned up, wearing her usual outfits with her hair pulled back. She looks confident, in charge. But this? The flowy skirt, the tall boots... it's a different side of her. Sexy as hell and completely irresistible.

"This fucking skirt." I whisper as I trail kisses across her jaw and down her neck, my hands sliding along the bare skin of her thighs beneath the fabric. "And those fucking boots."

I pull back, admiring the creamy skin that meets the dark fabric of her skirt, my own tan skin a stark contrast to both as I grip onto her.

Je-sus.

"Did you put this outfit on knowing that it would break me?" I meet her eyes, the amber glow from the light posts dancing in them. "That I wouldn't be able to keep my hands to myself?"

I hear her breath catch as my fingertips slip under the edge of her underwear. I snap the band I'm toying with against her skin, and she rocks against me in response.

"Maybe," she pants. I dip my head, humming against the skin of her throat at the confession, loving the knowledge that she *wanted* to turn me on. I drop a kiss where her collarbone meets her neck, sucking gently as I do.

"Is *this* what you wanted when you put this on?" I slide my knuckle along her panty line, through her wet center, stopping short of her clit while I wait for her to answer. When she doesn't, I pull my hand back and lift my head again to meet her eyes.

"I asked you a question, Natalie. When you put this skirt on, did you imagine what it would feel like to have my hands on you?"

She moans, rolling her hips into me again, and her eyes pop open.

"Yes." Her response is breathy, rushed. "I did, ok? I think about it all fucking day."

I smile at that, leaning in to capture her mouth again quickly, before dropping to a knee. I run both hands up the outside of her thighs and back under her skirt. Hooking a finger into each side of her thong, I make quick work of sliding it off, tapping her ankle as she shifts on her feet to free the fabric. I pocket it as I slowly stand back up.

"Those aren't yours!" She reaches for my pocket, and I catch her wrists, holding them in my hands between us.

I lean in, my voice low in her ear. "They are now."

Before she can reply, I let my right hand move back under her skirt, over the curve of her ass and along the crease where her thigh meets her hip. I squeeze my hand there before I slide two fingers through her pussy, spreading her open and exposing her to the cool air around us. Her fingers dig into the back of my neck as she grabs hold of me, her hips jerking forward as she searches for more. She tips her head back when I press my thumb against her clit, sliding two fingers inside her at the same time.

"Oh god" she murmurs. I work my hand in a slow rhythm, my thumb circling as I move my fingers in and out. Her hips roll with each slide of my fingers, chasing more.

"Fuck, you feel good, Red. Needy little thing, dripping on my fingers like this." I pull my fingers out, brushing them along the outside of her entrance.

"Fuck... Jake." Her fingertips dig into my arm as she clings to me, arching her back against the brick behind her.

"I like this," I say as I take her in, head tipped back, eyelashes fluttering, aching... *for me.* "You in my jacket, writhing on my fingers, moaning my name..."

I take a deep breath as I sear the image of her like this, in my clothes, into my brain. It hooks onto something deep inside me, a feeling of possession coursing through me. She's got my name on, the logo on my jacket staring at me as she arches her back and, fuck if it's not the hottest thing I've ever seen.

I lean in again, dragging my lips up her neck, pausing at her ear.

"It feels like you're mine, Red. Like you belong to me. This pussy belongs to me." With that, I push my fingers back inside her, dropping my thumb to her clit as I do, working my fingers in tandem as she mewls under me. I can feel her orgasm building, the way she clenches around my fingers.

Moving my free hand to the back of her neck, I cup her head as I bring it forward. I'm desperate to see her unravel at my touch, near feral at this opportunity to touch her after days of nothing.

Her eyes fly open, and I hold her gaze.

"Eyes on me when you come. Let me see you."

Her throat bobs as she swallows, my eyes tracking the movement. I hold her gaze as my hand moves under her skirt, my slow pace not quite enough for her.

"I need more, Jake." Her voice is low, almost pained as it cracks.

I move my hand from the back of her neck, skimming over her skin as my thumb rubs against her bottom lip. I tug, pulling it down as I watch her eyes dance, the need in them potent.

This time when I pull out, I add a third finger to my movements, speeding up when I do. She presses against me with a quiet gasp, clenching around me as I continue.

In a few moments, I feel her cresting, her orgasm moving through her as she grinds into my hand, riding through the waves. Like the fucking queen she is, those chocolate brown eyes never leave mine.

I ease her down, slowing my movements until she's spent, slouched back into the wall, her hips falling away from mine. I slide my fingers out of her, using the thong in my pocket to clean them off, before tucking it away again.

She eyes me, her chest rising and falling as she catches her breath. God, what I wouldn't give to see all of her right now.

To have her right here.

A tightness in my chest makes it hard to breathe as I stand there, taking her in. When her eyes soften toward me, a small smile tugging at her lips, I realize that this might be more than I bargained for. This might be more than just lust and infatuation I feel in the presence of this woman.

"You are not keeping those." She says, the fire I love so much igniting as she stands up straighter, holding her hand out for the underwear.

"I absolutely am." I step into her, leaning into the sudden distraction from thoughts I'm not ready to address. I take the hand she's holding out, capturing it with one of my own before pinching her chin with two fingers with my other. "What's a tourist attraction without taking home a souvenir?"

She opens her mouth to argue, and I drop my lips to hers instead, kissing her slowly, taking my time. When I pull back again, she smiles softly, letting me win that argument.

"Come on," I say, stepping back one last time. "Someone's gonna notice we're missing."

She nods in agreement, and I let her lead the way, meandering back through the cemetery, heading toward the group. As discreetly as I can, I adjust myself inside my pants, trying to hide the evidence of our indiscretion before we round the corner, finding the rest of the group just a few rows over from where we were hiding.

We creep up behind them, Natalie's hands holding her skirt tight to her legs behind her. I chuckle, knowing she's going to be conscious of her missing underwear for the rest of the night. But she looks noticeably more at ease now, much less anxious than ten minutes ago.

Mission accomplished.

We no sooner come to a complete stop when Melanie's head snaps our way, a knowing smile crossing her face as her eyes move between her sister and me. A heavy weight settles into my stomach as I slide subtly to the left, putting extra space between Natalie and me.

I keep my eyes on the tour guide, pretending not to be aware of her scrutiny as I stare straight ahead. It feels like an eternity before she turns back, but the lead weight in my stomach doesn't budge.

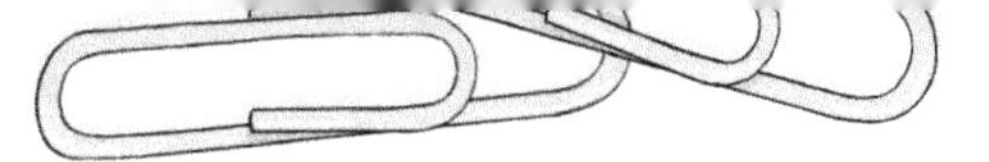

THIRTY-TWO

NATALIE

Do Not Change That

My foot taps quietly on the uneven linoleum flooring of the venue coordinator's office. I check my watch for the tenth time in the last half hour, sighing heavily as I wait.

And wait.

And wait.

"I'll be right back." *My ass.*

The event staff here misplaced the boxes we sent ahead—the ones with the press passes and information packets. The venue coordinator ran off to see if one of his staff could find the boxes for me. Phones exist, so I don't understand why I'm wasting my time sitting in this office, waiting for him to come back when he could just make a few calls and solve the problem while we were both here.

I roll my shoulders to ease the tension building there, but it doesn't do much to stave off the mounting stress. I remind myself there are backups tucked under the tour bus, just in case something like this happens, but I know there's not enough. This is one of the bigger shows, media-wise, and if I can't find these boxes, I won't have enough materials for the weekend. And there is nothing I hate more than being unprepared for something.

I jump, levitating off my chair, when the door unexpectedly opens, anxiety lighting up every nerve ending this morning. Instead of the coordinator I was expecting, Jake's broad shoulders push through the doorframe, a coffee cup in each of his hands.

I immediately feel a sense of relief wash over me as Jake looks over, butterflies swarming in my stomach. Unexpectedly, Knox was the one at my door first thing this morning. He said Jake had a call that held him up, so Knox brought Melanie and me over to the stadium.

As I take Jake in, standing before me in his usual uniform of jeans and his nylon security jacket, my mind immediately rewinds to Monday on the cemetery tour; the two of us tucked between the looming gravestones, his hand between my legs, his voice rough in my ear.

Jesus, that was hot.

I have never done anything like that. I've never even considered fooling around in public. But honestly, that's been my entire relationship with Jake. He does weird things to my head.

I can feel the color in my cheeks deepening as he makes his way into the room, the door slowing closing behind him. He holds one cup out to me as he slides by me, dropping into the open seat on my left.

I smile, taking the cup from him and bringing it to my nose as I inhale the sweet smell of coffee. I take a big sip of the drink, sighing as the caffeine enters my bloodstream.

"This is a pleasant surprise." I gesture, holding the cup up in front of me.

He looks over at me, his eyes meeting mine over the top of his cup as he takes a drink of his own coffee. "Made a pit stop on my way over this morning. Knox filled me in on the mix-up here. Felt like I should bring reinforcements."

"Absolutely the right call. I've been waiting for this guy to return for over half an hour now. I'd leave, but I don't have his information, and I need to know where my boxes are."

"We can fix that." He reaches into his back pocket, pulling out his cell. A couple of quick swipes later, I can hear the dull ring on the call through the phone in the quiet office.

"Hey, Hunter. Jake Alder again." He pauses. "Yeah, good. Yourself? Good. Listen, do you have the number for the venue coordinator? I need to grab something from him, but we're having trouble locating him this morning. Perfect. Thanks, man."

He hangs up, and a moment later his phone chimes. He taps the screen before holding it out to me. "Here you go."

I glance down, finding the coordinator's information, including two different phone numbers for him. I pull out my phone, typing the information in quickly. "Wow, you are efficient. How did you manage that?"

"We have a list of the security contacts at every stadium. I've started reaching out to them before we get to each location. Hunter is who I was meeting with this morning. We were going through the protocols for the shows this weekend, and it took longer than I expected."

"So that's why Knox was flying solo?"

"Yep." He takes another sip of his coffee. "Hunter is the first liaison who has actually had an interest is coordinating with us on security. It was a nice change of pace."

"What does that mean?"

"We are not typically involved with anything the venue security teams do—the training, the protocols, any of it. We operate completely separately, and it's caused more than a few problems on this tour already."

He catches the weary look in my eye.

"Not big problems, thankfully. But gaps that might be big problems. So I've started reaching out to the contacts before we get here, trying to establish a relationship, offering to set up meetings, going through things. It's been a slow roll. Little reception, but Hunter here has been really on board with the idea."

"Oh, smart thinking."

"I know, thank you." He cracks a lopsided smile, his dark eyes meeting mine. "So, what else can I do for you this morning?"

"Smartass." I slap his arm.

"Let's get your boxes. Maybe we can get this setup done early enough to sneak out to lunch or something." He winks at me.

I open my phone back up, hitting dial on the venue coordinator's number. Sure enough, he answers just a handful of seconds later, apologizing profusely for the delay. Apparently, there was another issue that derailed him from solving mine, but he was able to locate my boxes in the team's corporate offices—accidentally mistaken for an official team delivery instead of the temporary event receivable. He promises to have them moved for me within a half hour, and we hang up, both free to go about our business now.

I lead the way, exiting the office as we make our way through the stadium and back to our designated areas for this morning. Jake's right next to me, his hand sliding smoothly over my back. I can feel his fingers running along my lower back, shivers breaking out over my skin as he does.

I'm setting up the media room, missing boxes finally in the correct location, when my phone rings. I look down at where it's resting on the table, my brother's name flashing across the screen.

"Hey Dex, what's up?"

"Hey, I'm just getting to the stadium, and I have a pile of packages that were delivered to the hotel for our team today. One of them was for you—do you want to come get it? Is this one of the missing ones you were looking for this morning?"

"No, those were the media boxes that were shipped directly here." I scan my memory, trying to decide what would have been shipped to the hotel for me. When I can't think of anything, I tell Dex to just bring it up. I'd rather have it if it's important.

"I'm on my way to a meeting right now. I can bring it over around lunchtime if you can wait."

I debate for a quick minute before making a decision. "Can I send Jake to get it? Leave it with someone on your way through and just let me know. He can head down right now."

Jake quirks an eyebrow at me.

"Ok, sounds good."

"Thanks, Dex." I end the call, dropping my phone back onto the table.

"Uh, what errand am I doing?" Jake asks, coming to stand beside me.

"Can you run down and grab my package Dex brought over? I'm worried it's something I need for today, and with all the missing packages, I'd rather not take a chance. I can text you when he tells me where he's leaving it."

"Yeah," he shrugs his coat off, removing his headset and the wiring for it. "Take this though."

"Why? I have a cell phone?" I usually have a headset connection to the security team during PR events, but the rest of the time, Jake is the only one with a mic to reach them.

"Yeah, but the service is shitty down by the stage here. I couldn't get my phone to connect earlier. I'd feel better if you had this on, in case you need something while I'm gone. I'll grab a spare from Knox or Asher while I'm down there. As soon as I'm hooked up, you can tell me where I'm heading."

"Ok..." I hesitantly take the headset from him, putting it on and threading the wires around my torso so they're not in the way.

"Thank you." He drops a kiss on my forehead before he walks out of the room, leaving me alone with my thoughts and the crackling of the headset as two crew members try to find a spare speaker.

Ten minutes later, Jake's voice comes through the headset in my ear. "Where am I heading, Natalie?"

I check my phone, finding a text from Dex waiting for me. "Main office by the front entrance he said. Front desk staff has it."

"Got it." The line goes quiet again for a few minutes before Jake's voice returns. "Package acquired."

"Thank you! Do me a favor. Will you see what it is?"

"Right now?"

"Yes, please. It's driving me nuts not knowing what I sent to the hotel."

"Switch over to Channel 7. I'll open it."

I do as he says, pressing the button until the channel number is set to 7. "A private channel, how very fancy."

"Well, more private. The entire stage crew doesn't need to hear our conversation." The walkie-talkie beeps as he releases the button.

"I'm just really annoyed because what the hell am I sending to the hotel? How would I even have had that address when I was shipping media—"

I release the button on the device as it suddenly dawns on me what is in that box. The walkie-talkie clatters to the floor, and I swoop down to grab it, jamming the button as I nearly yell into it. "Jake, stop."

After the graveyard tour, where Jake lost his mind over my outfit, I realized I spend all my time in work clothes. It's always pencil skirts and heels, so I thought, since we seem to be getting together regularly, I'd order something... a little more fun. I placed an overnight order that I'd completely forgotten about until *right now.*

"Fucking hell, Natalie." He hisses over the headset.

"That's not for the media, is it?" I ask sheepishly, knowing he's probably staring into a box full of lacy bras and matching thongs right now.

"It better not be." I can hear the tension in his voice.

"Um, surprise?" I say, trying to lighten the mood.

"What did you have in mind with this?"

"I just... um, I thought some cuter things would be... nice, you know? You can bring that back here. Go back to the crew channel."

"Do not," his voice is low, "change that channel."

"Jake, can you just bring that back here? Someone could hear us!" My voice is about two octaves too high as my mind conjures up the image of someone listening to us talking about my fucking lingerie.

"Someone could hear me telling you all the things I want to do to you when you're wearing these outfits?" His voice is low, somehow even sexier in the static of the walkie-talkie.

"Well, no, you're not doing that—"

"I'm not telling you how badly I want to see your ass in this red set? The one with all the strings? How fucking perfect it would look tied up in these bows?"

"Jake!" I can feel the color flooding my cheeks.

"Fuck, Natalie."

"Please tell me you are not digging through that box in the middle of the hallway where anyone can see you? You just said yourself someone *could* be listening…"

"That was before I knew you ordered a whole new wardrobe to torture me with. I'm supposed to *work* knowing you're wearing these?!"

"Well, they were for the next time I could sneak into your room—"

A loud noise startles me as a box is dropped onto the table behind me. Jake stands there, both hands on his hips, his eyes burning into mine. "Yeah, we're gonna figure that problem out real quick."

"Oh, thank god." I feel instantly lighter seeing him standing there. I drop the walkie-talkie before I rush over to the table. "Close that up. I'm going to have to find somewhere to put that until I can get it back to the hotel."

Jake slaps his hand on the top of the box, holding the flaps closed as his eyes meet mine. "You should wear it."

"What? I mean, obviously, that was the point."

"Put it on, Natalie."

"Right now?" I ask. "I'm at *work*, Jake."

He spins the box around, opening the flaps as he digs out the red set with the bows.

"If I have to work all day, knowing these exist, the least you can do is wear them." He tips his head toward the supply closet in the corner of the room, a devious smirk crossing his face.

"Now? Anyone could come in here!"

"I'll watch the door." He winks at me. "C'mon, Red. Please?"

"Jake!" I hiss. "I can't—"

My eyes drop to my phone on the table.

"Fine. But I don't see the point." I'm the one smirking as I grab the items from his hand, feigning reluctance. I carefully scoop my phone up as I walk past.

"Eyes on the door, Alder." I toss over my shoulder as I hurry across the room, slipping into the supply closet. Fumbling for the light, I flip it on. I quickly swap my current bra and underwear for the new set, pausing to take a couple of photos before getting dressed again. It's a bit of a challenge in the small space, but the results are good enough for what I have in mind.

I catch Jake's eye as I return to the table, a knowing look in his glance as I hide my undergarments in the box with the rest of my order, taping it shut before stuffing it underneath a table along the wall.

I'll figure out how to sneak that back later.

"I'm not sure why you're so eager, considering you won't get to see them for a while anyway." I say to Jake as he comes up beside me. He props himself against the table, resting his ass on the edge as he crosses his arms, staring at me.

"That's ok. It'll keep me entertained for the time being." I watch as his eyes travel over my body, my stomach fluttering at the awareness.

"What's entertaining you?" Austin asks, just as he and Indy come wandering into the room, equipment bags on each of their shoulders.

I jump, the unexpected visitors making my heart race. Jake clears his throat, doing his best to look unaffected as he stands, turning away from me. "Uh, organizing the press passes."

He rounds the table, putting himself to work sorting the lanyards into piles as I struggle to hold back my laughter.

Indy shifts her attention to me. "Put the bodyguard to work while he's already on the clock? Damn girl, teach me your ways."

I do laugh out loud at that, watching as Jake chuckles to himself, before turning toward Indy. "Are you here for your badges?"

Indy and Austin both nod as I duck under the table, fishing out my tote bag. I pull out two universal passes I found for them.

"Here you go! I feel bad you have to hunt me down every single week, so I found more of the all-access passes in Dex's stash for you. They'll get you anywhere you want to go, anywhere on the tour. Guard them with your life."

"Ohhh, fancy!" Indy coos as she takes them from me, passing one to Austin. "We're like, official now!"

I laugh at that. "Yes, you are."

I spend the next twenty minutes chatting with Austin and Indy, talking through some options for new content they haven't filmed yet for tonight's show. Excusing myself halfway through, I grab my phone to "send a quick email," but instead, I pull up Jake's text thread, sending off one of the photos I took in the storage closet. I set my phone back down just as his chimes, conveniently throwing myself back into conversation with Indy.

I watch out of the corner of my eye as Jake's eyebrow quirks when he sees my name on the screen. His eyes widen as he clicks on the message.

His head shoots up, looking in my direction, but I keep my full attention on Indy, who's rattling off ideas in front of me.

I can't stop the smirk that crosses my face though, knowing Jake is going to be *very distracted* this afternoon and that I'm the reason why.

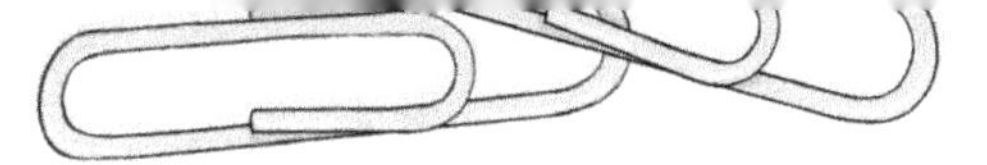

THIRTY-THREE
NATALIE

Late Saturday night, well after the second show for the week has ended and everyone else has called it a night, I'm back in my hotel room, working on prep for the meet and greet in Tampa next week, feeling exceptionally irritated.

I didn't expect to find myself complaining about bunking with Melanie, but then again, I didn't expect to find myself wanting to spend time with Jake either.

I've debated coming clean with my sister. I don't *really* think she'd care that Jake and I are sneaking around, but something's holding me back. We don't keep secrets from one another, but for whatever reason, I want to hold on to this one.

I don't know if I'm worried she'll judge me for sleeping with my bodyguard, but I also feel like I know better. Maybe it's just that if we let anyone in on our secret, it will spoil it a little. Or maybe I'm just hung up on the newness, wanting to keep it for myself.

Whatever the reason, I don't want to tell my sister. Which means I'm stuck here, in this shared room, without the freedom to sneak over to Jake's.

I check Mel's room. The door is shut, the lights still off. She went to bed an hour ago, and it seems like she's officially out for the night. It's not likely she's going to notice what I'm up to right now. She sleeps like the dead after her shows.

Weighing the risk, I gather up a folder, shoving a bunch of blank pages inside it, and sneak out of my shared room, trekking a few doors down the hall to Jake's hotel room.

Quietly, I knock on his hotel room door, my head moving quickly side-to-side as I scan the hallway, just to be safe.

I hear Jake chuckle as he pulls the door open.

"Hi." I say, sliding into the room, brushing past Jake, not even waiting for him to step aside to let me in.

"What are you up to?" He asks, leaning his hip against the desk near the door, crossing one leg over the other, his gaze running over me. I look down, remembering I'm wearing sweatpants with an oversized crewneck sweatshirt that has the tour logo across the front, my red hair in a ponytail on top of my head.

"Um, nothing. I just…" I fidget with the folder in my hands, dropping my eyes. "wanted to see you?"

I cut my eyes back to his face, watching as he tries to suppress the grin that spreads over his face at the admission, but he can't stop his lips from tipping up as he watches me.

"You did, huh?" He pushes off the desk and makes his way across the room, snagging my hand and pulling me toward the oversized chair next to the end table.

I go willingly, following Jake to the seat, where he drops onto the cushion, pulling me down on top of him. I smile as I fall into him; the folder flopping open on my lap. "What is this?"

"It's… work?" I blush. "I thought I should have a reason to visit you. In case Melanie woke up before I got back, or someone saw me…"

"So you brought a folder full of paper?"

"No one's going to look inside. It's believable that I would run a work errand at midnight." He runs his thumb over my hip, feeling the skin above the band of my pants. "I just… these new arrangements kind of suck. It's been a week of people everywhere. I liked it better when we had adjoining rooms in Texas and I could sneak over every night."

He laughs, "Yeah, that was much nicer."

I twist in his lap, turning to drop the folder on the desk behind me.

"Were the ghosts too much? Are you having trouble sleeping all alone?" He tugs on my ponytail as I smile at him, my eyes meeting his.

"No, smartass. I'm fine. It's been like four days."

"Mmhmm… you seemed fine at the cemetery. Totally chill." He squeezes his fingertips on my hip.

"Listen, it's not my favorite activity we've ever done, but I survived." I pull my ponytail over my shoulder as I toy with the ends of my hair. "Thank you, by the way. For the… distraction."

"You're welcome—for the distraction. I'm happy to distract you anytime." He leans down, kissing his way across my neck.

"I'm sure you are. It should be your turn." I laugh as I poke him in the chest. "I owe you, like, several times over now."

His leans back, his face growing serious as he stares at me.

"This isn't transactional, Natalie." He tips my chin up with his finger, making sure he has my full attention before he continues. "I don't do anything with the expectation that it's a favor that needs to be returned."

His brown eyes shine in the dim lighting of the hotel room, and he looks so sincere as he continues, "Everything we do, I want to do. Tell me you understand that, please."

I swallow, my throat feeling tight at the raw honesty, the confirmation that he wants nothing from me. It's rare for me to feel like I don't owe someone something: my time, my money, my attention. Sean was a big fan of making me feel like everything in our relationship was an IOU, and to be honest, I never even stopped to think that's not the way it *should* be.

"Yeah, I do." I pause. "Thank you."

I get comfortable in his lap, shifting so my legs drape over him and onto the edge of the chair.

"I'm surprised you're wide awake." I rub my hands over his shoulders, wrapping my arms behind his neck. "What are you still doing up?"

"I just got back from the gym." He says it as if it's not at all weird that he was at the gym in the middle of the night.

"You… what? Who goes to the gym at midnight?" I ask, incredulous.

"We had a busy day today; it was the first opportunity I had."

I laugh. "Normal people would probably just crash after a busy day, not work out."

"I'm used to odd hours. I've never worked a nine to five."

"Have you always been a bodyguard?" I ask, realizing I don't know much at all about Jake's past, outside the few pieces about his family that he's shared.

"More or less. I was in the army for a while, but my first job after that was in private security. At first, it was more patrolling—campuses, apartment complexes, what have you. It morphed into what I do now over the years."

"Patrolling buildings sounds… fun."

"Yeah, not the best job I've ever had. Working with people is much more entertaining."

"What's the weirdest thing you've ever done on the job?"

He debates for a minute. "I was working for an actress going through a shitty divorce a few years back. She wanted an extra set of eyes on her kids because her husband couldn't be trusted, so I signed a contract with her for several months until eventually he was arrested for his behavior."

"Oh, my god! That's awful."

"That's not the weird part." He laughs. "She took the kids to a petting zoo one weekend, and while we were there, the alpacas escaped their enclosure and charged the boys. I had to scoop them up and outrun a couple of feral animals."

I giggle. The idea of alpacas on the run after Jake is extremely entertaining. "I thought alpacas were friendly animals?"

"Yeah, so did I. I think these ones were just spooked by something. But I certainly never imagined I'd have to rescue someone from them."

"Well, lucky they had you." I toy with the hair at the nape of his neck. "Are all your clients women?"

The question slips out before I can think twice about it, insecurity laced behind the words.

"Not all, but most. Generally speaking, men don't hire help to protect them. We tend to have far fewer things to need protection from."

"That's… fair." I chuckle dryly as I think back to the conversation I had at lunch with Indy and Melanie. "Men really do make all the problems."

"Most of them. Yeah."

I debate my next question before I ask, not entirely sure I want to know the answer, but now that we've gone there, something inside me needs to know the answer. "Have you, um, had a relationship with other clients before?"

I try to laugh it off playfully, but even asking makes my stomach turn.

"No, never." He's completely serious, his eyes boring into mine. "I have never even been tempted before you…"

The relief at that answer is palpable. I feel my stomach uncoil itself as I let out a long exhale. "That's good to know."

"Although I did pretend to date an actress for a while because she needed someone undercover."

"You did not! Who?!" A history of actually dating clients I probably couldn't handle, but a fake relationship? Now I'm intrigued.

"Confidentiality clause. I can't tell you that."

I throw him a look. "Oh, come on. Let me guess!"

"Go for it. But I'm not telling you." He smirks at me.

I throw out several guesses, all of them off the mark. I'm working my way through movies I've seen recently, people I know who are big in the industry, but each guess earns me another shake of his head.

"Wait! Was it that girl from the Weatherman movie?!" He looks away this time and I know I'm right. "Oh, my god! IT IS!"

I'm up and off his lap before he realizes what I'm doing, grabbing my phone off the side table as I pull open the browser to search her name, adding "boyfriend" for good measure.

Jake comes up behind me, wrapping his arms around me to cage me in as he reaches for my phone, laughing. "Do not Google it."

I spin, ducking under his outstretched arms, as I make my way over to the bed, the image search results now filling the screen. Scrolling through the page, I find photo after photo of the actress with a few different guys, none of them Jake. I hit page two as Jake climbs over me, pushing me onto my back as I extend my phone out as far as I can.

"What is it you're looking for, Natalie?" His body covers mine, my breaths coming fast now.

"I don't know," I blush, my eyes tracing the stubble on his face. "Incriminating evidence of the two of you together."

He takes my phone from me, sitting up to hold it out of my reach as he types into the search bar, handing it back just a few moments later.

"Here." I grab the phone from him, looking at the photos on the page. I tap the screen, enlarging the first one. Jake stands in a hotel lobby, his arm around the waist of a gorgeous blonde woman, a huge smile on her face as she looks up at him. "Is that what you wanted to see?"

I feel sick to my stomach, but I force out a lie anyway. "Yep! Look at you two lovebirds!"

Play stupid games, win stupid prizes, right?

He takes the phone from me, tossing it across the bed. "You know what we did that night? Went back to her hotel room and watched Golden Girls reruns until she fell asleep."

"Well, aren't you a hot date?" I tease.

"Not at all. I was only around until her creepy ex got off her back. We were never anything more than friends."

"Really, that's a shame. You'd have been such a cute couple." I don't know why I'm saying this, opening myself up to a conversation I don't want to have.

"She's not really my type." He smirks.

"Oh? And what is your type?"

"Redheads, it would seem." He slips his fingers underneath the bottom of my sweatshirt, running his hands over my bare skin as he drops his lips to my neck. "You, specifically."

Without any hesitation, my body reacts, coming to life beneath his touch. I arch up into him, nipples pebbling and heat pooling between my legs.

"Natalie—" his hands pass over my bra and I smirk as he changes course, suddenly eager to remove the sweatshirt covering me.

I help him along, shimmying the top over my head, watching as Jake takes in the red bra with the bows he was so fond of.

"Fuck, it looks even better than the photo." He toys with the scalloped edges of the cups, trailing his finger over the translucent lace fabric to the clasp between my breasts, one larger bow situated there. He swallows, dropping his hands to the top of my sweatpants as he tugs those down, revealing the matching lace underwear, a coordinating bow tied on each hip.

"You've had this on the whole time and you let me sit there talking about alpacas and a fake fucking date?" His eyes meet mine, the desire in them so potent, I feel like I might combust from his stare.

"You didn't ask," I reply coyly.

"Do you know how many times I got myself off to that photo this week, Red?"

I smirk at that, loving the confession, as I offer him a wink. "You're welcome."

"Fucking tease." He takes my hands in his, pinning my arms over my head as he hovers above me. "Should we see how you like it?"

"Please." The word slips out as I squirm in his hold, aching to be touched. His grip on my wrists tightens as he stares down at me, his tongue darting out to lick his bottom lip.

"I hope you're not tired. Because I've got a lot of ideas right now, and none of them involve sleep."

"You did say the last thing a woman would do in your bed is sleep." He laughs, but it turns out Jake means it when he makes a promise.

"Alder." I'm awaken sometime later when Jake answers his phone in the bed next to me, the clipped greeting pulling me out of a deep sleep I apparently slipped into.

"Noah?" The confusion in Jake's voice has me sitting up. He lets out a long sigh before he stands, scrubbing his hand down his face. I watch as he wanders toward the window, listening intently to the person on the other end of the line.

I decide to give him some space, opting to use the bathroom while he takes this phone call. Padding across the room, I close the door, just as I catch one last sentence: "I... don't know. I'm on a job I can't walk away from right now."

Unease settles in my stomach as the door clicks loudly beside me.

What does that mean?

Who is Noah?

I use the bathroom, catching the time on the clock on the counter. It's 4:14am. Who calls in the middle of the night? I don't want to intrude on whatever Jake's dealing with, but something tells me it's not good news at this hour.

Nosiness wins out, and I peek out the bathroom door, finding Jake sitting on the edge of the bed staring aimlessly across the room. His head turns toward me when he hears me walking in his direction, a small smile crossing his face.

"Hey," I move between his open legs as his arms wrap around me, two hands sliding across my hips, coming to rest on my lower back before he pulls me into him. "What was that?"

His eyes meet mine, a look of sorrow passing quickly over them before he wipes all expression off his face.

"Don't... don't do that. You can talk to me." I move my hands over his shoulders, lacing my fingers behind his neck while I wait for him to respond.

After several long seconds, I see him swallow, his Adam's apple bobbing. "That was... uh, my brother."

"Your brother? I thought you didn't talk to your brothers?"

"I don't. I haven't—My older brother is in the ICU, apparently. My younger brother thought I should know because they're not sure he's gonna make it out."

"Oh my god, Jake. What happened?" I unwind myself from his hold, sinking onto the bed beside him. He drops his elbows on his thighs, clasping his hands in front of him.

"He got into a car accident tonight. My brother didn't share a lot of details; he just... wanted me to know so I could decide if I wanted to be at the hospital or not." He trails off, wringing his hands together.

"Jake. You should go. Knox can figure out security. Here is the last place you need to be right now..."

"I don't know, Natalie. I haven't seen any of these people in eleven years. Do I really want to go? I don't even *know them* anymore. Do they really want me there? What difference is it—"

I cut him off; the panic bleeding into his voice making my chest ache. "Listen, I don't know much about your family situation, but I do know that if you don't go, you will regret it, Jake. If you have this opportunity to go, possibly say goodbye, and you don't take it..."

I let out a breath, thinking about my own past. "I think if you go and you regret it, that's going to hurt a lot less than if you don't go and you regret that choice."

He doesn't acknowledge what I've said as he stares at the floor.

I rub my hand down his back, not really knowing what else to do in the moment.

"I don't want to overstep, but if I had this option with my parents when they got in their car accident..." I clear my throat, trying to dislodge the lump building there. "I wish I had that option. That's all."

Jake looks up, his eyes meeting mine. "No, you're right. I should go. Be there."

It's quiet for several long moments before he speaks again.

"Am I really going to do this twice?" He whispers it, more to himself than to me, but he doesn't have to explain himself for me to understand.

A rogue tear slips from my eye, trailing down my cheek as the reality of one person losing two siblings sits between us.

THIRTY-FOUR

JAKE

Full Of Surprises

Am I doing the right thing here?

Is showing up at the hospital the right move?

It's been too long. The distance, both physical and emotional, is too much.

I'm triple-thinking my decision as I stare up at the towering white doors in front of me, the red Emergency Room sign staring back. I've already put my life on hold, grabbing the first flight from New Orleans to Chicago, where my oldest brother is now.

I tighten my grip on my overnight bag as my chest constricts, the anxiety of what I'm about to do, what's about to happen, threatening to overwhelm me. I'm rooted to the spot, indecision turning in my stomach.

It's not too late to back out.

No one knows I'm here.

A loud ping from my pocket grabs my attention, a second one following immediately after before I can fish the phone out.

I feel the bands around my ribs loosen when Natalie's name flashes across the screen. I quickly swipe the phone open, pulling up the text thread.

RED

Hey. Make it ok?

I'm glad you decided to go.

An involuntary tug pulls at my lips. They're two short messages, an insignificant thing to most, but for someone who has spent his life alone, it's unnerving how settling they are. How comforting *she is.*

ME

Yeah, just got to the hospital.

She texts back in a matter of seconds, clearly holding the conversation open while she waited for my reply.

RED

Good luck.

I'm here if you need me.

The tug grows to a full smile as I shoot off a quick reply and silence my phone, dropping it back into my pocket.

I square my shoulders as I look back up at the entrance, this time putting one foot in front of the other as I make my way inside.

The sterile smell of the ER hits me as I make my way through the doors and across the tiled floor. People are lingering, clustered in small groups or sitting in chairs throughout the lobby.

I approach the desk, shifting uncomfortably from foot to foot. When the nurse gestures for me to move forward, I do, taking one quick step up to the counter, my heart racing beneath my skin.

"Hi, I'm looking for—" Before I can finish my sentence, I hear my name from my left, snapping my head around to find my younger brother, Noah, standing there, his eyes wide with disbelief. "Uh, never mind. Found them. Thank you."

I rap my knuckles on the counter before turning away from the desk and making my way across the brightly lit space.

Noah is standing just a few feet away, dark purple circles blooming under his eyes, ones that look so similar to my own. His hair, not unlike mine either, is cropped close on the sides, longer on top. The same dark, unruly strands looking very much like he's been running his fingers through them. His shirt is wrinkled, a dark flannel that he's clearly been wearing for some time.

"I—Jesus, Jake. I didn't think you'd come."

I come to a stop in front of him, not able to bring myself to meet his eyes. "Yeah, I didn't think I would either."

He doesn't say more, doesn't even hesitate before stepping closer and pulling me in for a hug. It's awkward, his hand holding the coffee, mine clutching an overnight bag, but his free hand finds my shoulder and mine finds his, both of us squeezing tightly to one another for the first time in well over a decade.

"I've missed you, man." His voice is quiet, but sincere. A knot lodges itself in my throat as I realize that, fuck, I've missed him too. He pulls back, meeting my eyes for the first time as he puts a hand on my shoulder. "Come on, I'll take you back."

I follow Noah quietly down the hall where he flashes a visitor badge at an employee just before a set of double doors leading to a second hallway. When we round the corner, I stop short, watching as he makes his way behind a glass wall into a private waiting room in front of us.

Heads pop up as he approaches, eyes cutting past him as they find me, standing awkwardly on my own. I take a deep breath, summoning the courage to face my family before I slowly make my way over to them.

I'm not even three steps into the room before my mom breaks out into a sob, her shoulders heaving as she buries her face in her hands. A woman, presumably Noah's wife, stands off to his side, putting a hand on my mom's shoulder. I've never met her in person, but I remember Noah's call to me last year when he got married. I didn't answer, letting the call ring through to voicemail, but I've replayed the voicemail he left more than once in the time since.

I felt such guilt after my youngest brother died that I left the second I could, walking away from all the people in this room without a second thought. And now here I am, showing up after all this time, making a bad situation worse.

Fuck, this was a terrible idea.

It's too much at one time.

What the hell was I thinking?

I approach slowly, desperately wishing I could just disappear.

My bag has barely left my hand, hitting the cold tile with a soft thump when my mom stands from the bench, making her way over. She stops in front of me, this tiny five-foot-nothing of a woman, looking up at me, eyes brimming with pain.

I'm immediately filled with an overwhelming tidal wave of emotion, an entire childhood of grief and heartache coming back all at once. The little boy who desperately needed his parents, who instead pulled away... and no one ever tried to pull him back.

That's not true though, is it?

You just didn't let them.

The ache in my chest grows as tears fill my eyes.

Fuck. This was not at all what I thought was going to happen.

"Jake..." My mom's soft voice fills the space between us, and without thinking about it, I step forward, wrapping my arms around her and folding her in close.

Soft sobs wrack her chest as she clings to me, the scent of her familiar even after all this time.

When we settle into seats, Noah fills me in on everything that has happened with Matt since they got here. He's been in surgery most of the morning and into the afternoon, with repairs made to several organs. They're having trouble getting the internal bleeding to stop, which is the worrisome part, but he also has several fractures they need to deal with. Apparently, it's all very tenuous, and if they can't stop the bleeding, nothing else can get repaired, and time is crucial.

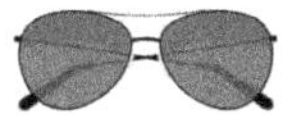

We spend a good chunk of the day just sitting in silence, my mom's eyes finding me every few minutes, as if she's not sure she's believing what she's seeing with me sitting next to her.

Several hours after I arrive, a doctor appears in the hallway, making her way toward our small waiting room. She looks to be about middle age, her dark hair graying at the temples. Air becomes sparse when my mom taps my leg, standing to make her way over to the doctor.

"Hi, are you Matt Alder's mother?" Mom nods once, wringing her hands in front of her as both Noah and I move to stand behind her, Noah's wife folding herself into his side. "I'm Dr. Patel. I just got out of surgery with your son. He's got a long road ahead of him, but I feel comfortable saying it looks like he's going to be ok."

Mom's entire body heaves as she chokes back a sob. I wrap an arm around her shoulder, holding her steady, as the doctor fills us in on Matt's condition. They finally had success in staunching the internal bleeding, which allowed them to get more accurate imaging of his other injuries. The details are lost on me as she talks, the list of issues extensive, but she seems confident that they are all things that can be handled.

"... now we just wait. He should start waking up in the next hour and then we'll evaluate his condition and go from there. I'm working on a comprehensive plan to tackle each of the injuries and surgeries he'll need in the safest and most effective way for him."

The relief is palpable as she leaves us in our private waiting room, the air itself feeling lighter knowing Matt's going to be ok.

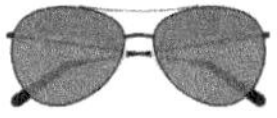

Noah and I decide to visit the cafeteria, desperate for some food. Mom's adamant she doesn't want to leave, so Noah's wife stays back with her.

We wind our way through the halls, following the signs down a couple of floors.

"So, where's Dad?" No use beating around the bush with this one, the one person noticeably absent. I've been itching to ask, but the timing never felt appropriate.

Noah steps ahead of me, reaching out to open the cafeteria door as he holds it for me to follow behind him. "On his way back from China, I believe. He was having trouble getting a connecting flight or something."

"Does he spend a lot of time there?" We join the short line behind the service counters.

"Um, yeah. He's been working there for the past few years. I text him once or twice a month, but we don't really keep in touch that well." I nod, shuffling forward as he does. We don't talk again until our trays are full and we've found a table on the far side of the room, sitting across from one another.

"So what are you doing these days?" Noah asks, unwrapping his packaged sandwich before cutting it in half.

"Private Security. Contract jobs, usually." I keep the details to a minimum, partially because I hate talking about myself and partially because I'd just prefer he not ask too many questions.

"No shit. That's cool." He takes a swig of his drink as I turn the question on him.

"What about you?" I feign indifference, but, surprisingly, I *want* to know more. This weird urge to catch up pushes me to continue the conversation.

I don't know many details about my family. I know where they live. I know Noah got married, and I know Matt is not, but I don't even have social media, so the information I have is incredibly sparse.

"I work for a law firm out in New York now. It's not very exciting work, but I like it. Morgan's family is from upstate, so we moved out there right after we got engaged. I think I might have told you that at some point. I'm sure there's a voicemail." He laughs, but continues. "She works for a school district just outside the city."

"That's awesome. I do remember getting a message about that."

"Ah, so you were listening to them." He smiles before taking a bite of his sandwich.

"Yeah, I... sorry, man. I wasn't in a good place for a long time. And then, I don't know. It seemed easier to... keep to myself."

"I noticed." He wipes his mouth with a napkin. "Good news, I'm incredibly skilled at the annoying younger brother role."

A laugh escapes at that. "I'm glad you didn't cut me out. I'd—"

I swallow, trying to decide what I want to say here.

"I'd like to try. To connect more. I can't really undo the last decade, but maybe going forward—"

"Jake?" He cuts me off, his brown eyes shining in the cafeteria lighting. "I'd love that."

"Cool." It's a lame response, but at the risk of getting choked up, I leave it at that, not really sure how to handle all these emotions suddenly making themselves at home inside my chest.

For a guy who used to be terrified of anything remotely permanent, I'm realizing that reluctance isn't the predominant feeling anymore. I think spending time on tour, around so many *good* people, has shifted my perspective a little. This new feeling is foreign, and a little uncomfortable, but it feels an awful lot like *a desire* to form some connections.

And that's something I honestly never thought I would feel.

I ended up staying in Chicago for the better part of a week. At first, because I wanted to be there through one more extensive surgery Matt had, but then I stayed a few days past that because being around my family felt *nice* in a way I hadn't expected.

On Saturday night, just past midnight, my phone rings, Natalie's face lighting up the screen.

"Hey, Red." I say in greeting, a genuine smile breaking out over my face.

"Hi! How's it going?" The sound of her voice, just those few words, wraps around me, making me feel an inexplicable sense of relief, like walking into the warm rays of the sun after spending too long in the air conditioning. It floods my system, soothing the fraying nerves from the week.

"Better." I settle into a chair in my hotel room, giving her my full attention. "It will be another few days before Matt heads home, but he's recovering from last surgery really well so far, they said."

"Good. I'm so glad to hear that." She sounds exhausted. I've kept her in the loop this week, but with her busy schedule and me in and out of the hospital, any real communication just hasn't happened.

I miss her more than I thought I would.

Apparently, this week has been full of surprises.

"Are you getting to spend time with Matt at all? You've mentioned Noah a few times..."

"Surprisingly, yes. I've spent time here and there in his room. I was a little nervous that showing up would make shit worse, but he seemed happy to see me. He spends most of his time asleep, but we've had a few good chats."

"Good, I'm so glad. And your mom? I know you were nervous about that."

She's right. I had needed another round of motivational texts from Natalie before I tackled a conversation with my mom, but she was more than happy to encourage me to clear the air.

"Yeah, that conversation went well, I think. It was a lot harder to talk to her than my brothers, but I don't know..." I trail off, thinking back on the heart-to-heart I had with Mom. It was heavy, but it felt good to finally talk about everything.

Natalie immediately fills the silence, offering me an out. "You don't have to go into it with me. I was just curious if it went well."

"No, it's not that. I was just—It did go well, actually. She apologized for letting me shoulder all that guilt after the accident. I apologized for just... abandoning them. We both agreed to try harder. To see if we can bridge this gap a little."

"I'm really glad to hear that, Jake. I'm so happy you got this time, although I wish the reason you were there was better."

"Me too. But I booked my flight back today. I'll meet you in Atlanta on Wednesday."

"Oh, really?" She perks up at that. "I'm so excited!"

"Yeah, there's nothing more I can do here. I've stayed longer than I probably should, but…" I hesitate before continuing. "It's been nice. Catching up with everyone. Weird, but nice."

"I can imagine. It will take time. But I'm really glad you opened yourself up to that, that you went."

"I am too." I can hear her rustling around on the other end of the line. "Thank you for encouraging me to do this."

"I didn't really do anything, Jake. You decided to go; I just nudged you in that direction." She chuckles.

"Maybe so, but I wouldn't have done it if it weren't for you. I think I needed this more than I realized."

We talk for a few more minutes before her yawns become so frequent, I'm convinced she's going to fall asleep mid-sentence.

"Ok, well it's my turn to nudge you in the right direction. Go get some rest."

She laughs, but it's lazy and half-hearted now. "I'm so tired. You don't have to tell me twice. I'll see you soon?"

The vulnerability of that question hits me square in the chest.

"Yeah, you'll see me soon. Good night, Red."

"Night, Jake."

We hang up, and as I'm staring at the screen in my hands, I realize that I've had it all wrong all these years.

It turns out I do like having roots.

Someone to call mine.

I just hadn't met her until now.

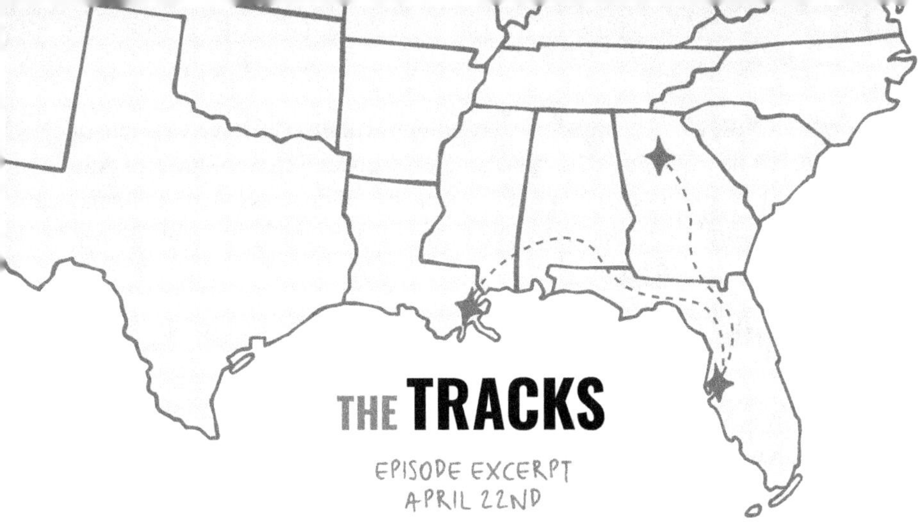

AUSTIN: New Orleans, then last week, Tampa, this week, Atlanta. You're really making your rounds down South, aren't you?

MELANIE: We sure are. [laughter] It's been so much fun though.

AUSTIN: What's been the highlight of these last couple of stops?

MELANIE: Oooh, that's a tough one. You know, we really had a great time down in Tampa. We stopped at the beach on our day off. But throwing the opening pitch at Tampa Stadium last Wednesday was a really fun experience. Can you believe that was the first time I've ever sung the National Anthem?

INDY: Really?! You've never done that anywhere else?

MELANIE: I haven't! I love that I'm getting to try new things on this tour. I also don't think I've ever thrown a baseball before that outing, but I didn't do too badly, if I say so myself.

AUSTIN: I mean—[muffled, sharp intake of breath]

INDY: What he means is you did fantastic.

MELANIE: Thank you, Indy. It's not my area of expertise. I'll agree to that.

INDY: So what's happening in Atlanta this coming week? Do you have more fun PR events lined up?

MELANIE: We actually don't have any big plans. We have a couple of local radio interviews, but that's it for the upcoming city. Our schedule is sort of planned so that one week has bigger events, or formal outings, and then the next week is a little more chill, so hopefully we can all maintain our sanity.

AUSTIN: Solid plan. You do have twenty-three straight weeks on the road, best to pace yourself.

MELANIE: That's right. And we have my hometown show the following week. While Atlanta is certainly not a flyover stop, we are really looking forward to heading back to Nashville after that.

INDY: Do you have something fun up your sleeve for that stop? Any big events you can tease?

MELANIE: Wouldn't you like to know?

AUSTIN: We would, actually.

MELANIE: I guess you'll have to wait and see…

POETRYDRIVE: Cannot wait for the Nashville shows! I have tickets for both nights!

JUNIPERSAIDSO: Ok, but let the man speak because Austin was probably right about the first pitch.

TRAVELGIRL1208: I don't care if she can throw. Did you see the clip of her signing that ball when they returned it to her and she gave it to a little kid in the stands? So sweet!

C.H.MAGICAL: I was there in Tampa! The concert is SO good. I'm trying to get tickets to Atlanta now, but they're a fortune on the resale sites.

THIRTY-FIVE

JAKE

A Little Bit Undone

Fuck, it's good to be back.

Which feels weird to say, but the visit with my family was intense. It was an emotionally heavy week, and truthfully, I didn't realize how much I would miss being around Natalie while I was gone.

I don't miss people. I don't do attachments. The whole thing is a foreign concept to me, but here I am, eager to be back with her. I don't really know what to make of that, but I don't feel the urge to fight against it.

I haven't seen her yet; my flight on Wednesday was delayed twice before being cancelled because of a pilot shortage, of all things. I rebooked for this morning, but that flight was also delayed, and now here I am, Friday's show about to start, just getting back to work.

The low roll of thunder sounds in the distance, and I pick up my pace as I make my way across the stadium. The weather does not look promising. I can see the dark gray clouds moving overhead, threatening to open up at any moment. Everyone backstage is hustling, protective gear being carted through the concourse as tarps and covers are wheeled around the scaffolding and out onto the main floor, the crew working to cover as much area as possible before the impending storms reach the venue.

According to Knox, who called as soon as I'd landed, tonight's show was put on an official weather delay about forty minutes ago, but with only an hour until the actual start time, the stadium is well over half full.

Fans are currently being redirected to the interior, and it's pandemonium. There's not adequate space for thousands of people to loiter on the concourse, so they're spilling through the hallways and filtering into areas that would otherwise be empty or restricted.

I make my way through the crowds, weaving in and out of bodies and equipment as I head toward the green room. The green room at this stadium is, unfortunately, smack dab in the center of the chaos, an independent construction backstage. It's not a storm shelter, and because of the weather warning we're currently under, Mel and her team can't stay there.

"ETA Jake?" I hear Knox's voice in my ear as I push my way through the groups of people crowding the area.

"Two minutes. I'm around the corner." I release the button on my headset, shuffling a couple people to the right as I breeze past them.

When I descend the stairs and reach the green room door, the venue security stationed there nods at me, eyeing the badge I flash in their direction. They allow me to pass, and I make my way into the space, people milling about as they wait for direction. Most of our security crew is already here. Chase and his team are organizing in the back. I spot Dex and Melanie off to the far side and head toward them.

"Oh good, you both made it!" Dex acknowledges Asher and me as we both approach.

"Yeah, sorry. The press room is about as far from here as you can get in this stadium. And with ten thousand extra people here, it took a minute." Asher says as we both come to a stop near the group.

"Is Natalie still over there?" Melanie is the one asking, but my head snaps up at the question.

"Yeah, I left her with the media, who had already shown up. She was doing an impromptu Q&A with the spare time."

"Of course she was." Dex huffs a laugh under his breath.

"She's got Indy and Austin with her." Asher adds.

So she doesn't have security, but at least she's not alone.

"Ok kids, here's what's happening." Knox speaks up over us, the five of us forming a tight circle in the crowded space so he can be heard. "Chase has the rest of this tent under control. All of us will relocate to the locker rooms beneath the stadium. It doesn't sound like a clear path from here to there, so we'll just have to do our best. We're taking Mel out first before the rest of the crew comes, but it's not gonna matter because we can't hide her either way. I have a couple of extra hands outside the door here from the venue staff, but no one here needs to be reminded they're untrained, so let's keep our eyes open."

I mutter under my breath to myself. *God, this is annoying.* Having next to no coordination with the venue security team is frustrating—and why the fuck is there no other route than directly through the fans to get Melanie out of the chaos?

I don't have time to get worked up over things I can't fix, so instead, I focus on the task at hand, as Knox and I lead Melanie toward the exit, Dex and Asher following closely behind.

The noise in the hall is deafening as soon as the doors open, fans screaming wildly for Melanie when she appears. Venue Security clears a path for us as we make our way down the hall, but Knox and I are busy trying to keep grabby hands out of Melanie's airspace. It's slow going with the volume of people converging in the area, but we work as quickly as we can to move from the green room deeper into the stadium. Taking several turns before the noise finally dies down, we make our way down a long, empty hall to the locker rooms we will use a storm shelter.

"Ok, well they were holding out on us." Melanie looks around the opulent space as we clear the double set of doors, the black and red room elaborately decorated for a locker room. The walls are all black, with each individual stall lit up with ambient lighting. Leather chairs sit beneath the team's logo, also bathed in the same mood lighting.

Dex lets out a low whistle as we make our way toward a large leather couch in the middle of the room. "No wonder tickets to the football games are so expensive."

He laughs to himself as he and Mel claim a spot in the middle of the couch. Knox, Asher and I take a minute to double-check the room, making sure there's no hidden fans or anything else we might not be expecting. When we're sure it's clear, we make our way to the couch and join them, the five of us taking in the space for a few minutes before we're joined by the rest of the backup dancers and the band members.

The noise level in the room increases tenfold with all the extra bodies, but there's plenty of seating, so they filter through the room, dropping onto the benches and getting comfortable.

"Can I get a weather update?" Knox's voice cuts through my earpiece about twenty minutes later. Because of the location of the locker rooms, we can't see or hear anything happening outside the stadium, which is great for weather safety, but less than ideal if you want to have any idea what's happening.

"Storm's moving in. The sky has opened up, and the outer edge of the radar is now firmly over the stadium. We have all the fans secured throughout the halls. The stage crews have made their way to the guest locker room."

"Roger. Thank you."

Behind me, the doors to the locker room fly open. Natalie, Austin and Indy come barreling through the doors, laughing and completely soaked through.

"Jesus, Natalie, what in the world?" Dex is up and off the couch in seconds, making his way over to them, and before I can think better of it, I'm up, following behind him.

A wide smile crosses her face as she sees me, an acute ache vibrating through my chest at the sight of her. She wrings out her ponytail, water dripping from her hair. "Yeah, we uh, tried to take a shortcut before the storm rolled in, but it rather abruptly started as we were crossing the main floor. I was trying to avoid being stuck in the media room all night; instead, I ended up getting a shower."

Austin disappears, reappearing at her side a moment later, holding a small stack of towels for the three of them. Natalie takes one, using it to dry off her hair as much as she can.

"I think there are probably dryers of some sort over on the other side of the locker room, by the sinks." I gesture behind me, off the short hallway behind the main area where we're standing.

"Oh, good thinking. Do you want a dryer, Indy?"

"No, I actually have spare clothes in my backpack, assuming those aren't also soaked through. I should be ok." She drops her backpack off her shoulder and starts rifling through the contents.

"Good call. Apparently, I should start doing that." She looks down at her cream blouse, now completely see-through thanks to the rain.

Water droplets fall from her dark purple skirt, landing on the carpet where a small puddle is spreading.

"C'mon. Let's get you dried off." I gesture toward my right, and we move toward the far side of the locker room, the noise of the crowded room growing duller as we round the corner.

"When did you get back?" Natalie asks as she squeezes the water out of her hair with the towel.

"A little bit ago. I texted you on the taxi ride over, but I assume you've been busy."

We come to a stop in front of a large white hand dryer. It's a less than ideal option, but it should work.

"I have. I haven't sat down in about four hours. Here, will you take this?" She slips her tote bag off her arm and hands it over to me. "Hopefully, the rain didn't make it inside. I don't really know if that zipper was meant to be waterproof."

"Do you want me to check?"

"That would be great."

I take the bag from her, dropping to one knee as I open the top zipper. The air dryer behind me kicks on; the loud noise overwhelming in the quiet room. I can feel the warm air blowing around me as I dig through the tote bag, checking that the laptop and all the paperwork inside are dry.

When I can't find any signs of water damage, I close the bag back up, pushing it up against the wall beside us.

I stand, turning back. "Looks—" I'm caught off guard when I see Natalie, holding her blouse under the air dryer, standing there in nothing but a white lacy bra, her cleavage spilling over the top. "—good. Bag... bag looks good."

She looks up at me, her eyelashes stuck together with the weight of the raindrops still on them. Her mascara is running, little black smudges forming at the corners of her eyes. It's messy and disheveled and hot as hell.

I'm dying to put my hands on her, but even removed from the group in this room, anyone could walk in at any time. I clear my throat, shifting as I try to ease the ache of my thickening cock behind the zipper of my jeans.

"Thank you." She watches me adjust myself next to her, laughing. "Sorry, this felt easier than trying to fit my whole body under the tiny vent."

"Hey, don't apologize to me." My eyes trace over her exposed skin.

I move myself between her and the door, careful to block the view of anyone who might come around that corner. She spends a few minutes drying the top before she puts it back on, sliding her skirt off over hips and repeating the process with the bottom half of her outfit.

I shamelessly watch her the whole time, not at all sorry as I take her in.

When she deems the clothes dry enough, she shimmies back into her skirt and turns toward the mirror, focusing on cleaning the makeup off her face with the towel in her hands.

"Did you want to dry your hair?"

"No, it's not worth the effort. I'll just put it in a bun or something." She tugs at the hair tie holding her wet hair up, yanking harshly as she tries to pull it out.

"Doesn't that hurt? Here." I step up behind her, carefully separating the hair tie as I unwind the elastic and gently pull it through the tangle of strands wound around it.

"The rain really did a number on you, didn't it?" I meet her eyes in the mirror as I free the elastic and hold it out in front of her.

"Apparently, I'm a fucking mess." She grabs it from me, slipping it onto her wrist.

Turning her slowly in front of me so we're face to face, I box her in against the countertop, resting a hand on either side of her body as I lean into her. "Nah, you're not a mess, Red."

I run my nose along her cheekbone, kissing the side of her temple before I whisper in her ear, "You're just a little bit undone. Exactly the way I like you."

I hear her breath catch as I drop a kiss on her neck before leaning back, wiping away the last remaining hint of mascara from the corner of her eye. "Is it too forward if I say I missed you?"

She smiles at me. "Not at all. Is it too forward if I say it back?"

"Not at all." I cup her cheek in my hand, leaning in to drop my lips to hers. She presses up into me, deepening the kiss, a soft sigh escaping her at the contact.

I thread my fingers through her hair, holding her to me for several long moments before I pull back, resting my forehead against hers. "We probably need to go. Before someone comes looking for us."

A soft smile spreads across her face. "Yeah, probably."

She grabs my shirt, pulling me back to her for another searing kiss before she hops off the counter. She turns, picking up her bag and grabbing my hand, leading me to the doorway. Before we clear the doorframe, she drops it, stepping away from me.

As I watch her walk into the locker room, a smile plastered on her face as she makes her way to her sister, I realize this feeling is a lot more than lust.

It's feeling like something *real*.

THIRTY-SIX

NATALIE

Well, This Is Awkward

The drive from Atlanta up to Nashville is only about four hours, so by Sunday afternoon we've already unloaded and made our way home. Because it's the hometown show, most of us on the crew will stay at our own places this week. The break from hotel rooms is more than welcome.

I currently have my suitcase open on my bed, carefully unpacking everything so I can do my own laundry for once, when Jake comes into the bedroom, sneaking up behind me and wrapping his arms around my waist.

I feel his lips meet my neck, his breath warm against my skin as he asks, "What are we going to do with three whole days to ourselves?"

We're on a break for the first half of the week, the short travel time between stops giving us a much-needed vacation for a couple of days. Once we're back, we have a huge hometown meet and greet down at the stadium on Wednesday and a special soundcheck event for fans on Thursday. The end of the week is going to be full, but for the first time, I'm really looking forward to taking a couple of days off. The man with his hands running over my hips has a lot to do with that.

"I don't know, but I can probably think of one or two things to keep us busy." I drop the clothes I'm holding, turning to face him as I wrap my arms behind his neck, pulling his face down to mine.

Our lips meet slowly, patiently, in a way we haven't been with each other before. Every time we've been together on the tour, it feels frantic, desperate, and a little hurried, knowing we're sneaking around.

This feels... *different.* Somehow both calming and more intense all at once. Jake picks me up, wrapping my legs around his waist as he carries me to the opposite side of my bed. Laying me down on the clean comforter, he crawls over me, threading his hands in my hair as he tips my head back.

I lean into his kiss, the feeling of his body flush against mine heating me through. I arch my back, desperate for more, when a quiet cough has me freezing.

"Well, this is awkward."

I turn my head toward the door, finding Melanie standing there, arms crossed and keys in hand. Jake eases off me as I frantically sit up, pushing him away.

"I'll, uh—give you two a minute," is all he says before excusing himself from the room, one quick glance back at me before he disappears into the hallway. I hop up, fixing my hair before smoothing out my t-shirt, my pulse racing for a completely different reason now.

Melanie turns to watch him go before she pivots slowly, coming back to face me.

"Just so you know, I tried to call. I also knocked before using my key."

"Yeah, I don't have my phone on me." I offer lamely.

"So I see." She takes a step toward my bedroom door, looking down the hall one more time before shutting it, turning to face me, the biggest grin pasted on her face. "Soooo, how long have you been sleeping with your bodyguard?"

She rushes over to the bed, pushing my suitcase out of the way, as she climbs on the mattress, bouncing on her knees.

I can feel the flames licking my skin as the heat rushes through me.

"I, uh—" She's clearly not mad, but *fuck,* I did not mean for her to find out this way. I clear my throat, rubbing at my temple as I say, "Since Houston?"

"Oh, my god!" She swipes at my pillow, tossing it at me. It bounces off my shoulder and onto the floor. "I *knew* there was something going on! Why didn't you just tell me?"

"Shhh, sweet Jesus, do not *yell.*" I step back over to the bed, sitting down beside her.

"I shut the door!" Melanie's enthusiasm is unbridled.

"Ok, but it's not soundproof."

"Sorry. So why didn't you tell me?!" She whispers it this time, grabbing onto my arm with both hands as she does, pulling me into her.

I can't help the laugh that slips out of me. "I don't know. I was worried that it would look unprofessional, I guess. People already think I have my job because I'm related to you. I didn't really think that adding *sneaking around with my bodyguard* to the list would be a great idea."

"First of all, no one thinks that. And fuck them if they do because you're the best publicist in the industry." She grows serious, pointing her finger at me as she talks. "And second, I would never judge you. I thought you knew that. We don't do secrets, Nat."

"I know, I know. I just… Not telling you had more to do with me than it did with you. I was feeling a certain way about how it looked, and I don't know… a secret seemed like the better way to go. Jake could lose his job."

"Well, sure, but not because of me. I'm not about to rat anyone out here. Plus, I like Jake. I'd rather Shield not fire him. Who knows who they'd send in his place." She laughs at that, and I offer her a half smile.

"At first we were just messing around and there really wasn't anything *to* tell—"

She cuts me off. "Excuse me, I am *always* interested in good gossip."

I quirk an eyebrow at her. "Well, it wasn't supposed to be a thing. It was just supposed to be… taking the edge off."

"Why does it sound like it's not like that at all?"

I sigh, staring at the wall across from us.

"I don't know, Mel. Because it's not. Not anymore. Maybe it never was." I shift on the bed, pivoting to face her, "I really like him. Like, *like him, like him.*"

"What are we, twelve?" Her smile softens as her eyes meet mine with understanding in them. "Listen, it might be a *slight* conflict of interest, but you're not hurting anyone by following your own heart."

"Except myself."

"I don't see how you're hurting yourself."

"Well, not at the moment, but inevitably, it will hurt. When the tour ends and we go our separate ways?" My stomach turns over at the thought, already anxious that we're already approaching the halfway point of this tour fairly quickly.

"Who said you have to break up when the tour ends? Why can't it continue if this is something real?"

"I did. We agreed it was only while we were on the road. When the tour is done, so is this thing between us."

She looks at me as if she can't comprehend what I'm saying. "Ok, but you can change your mind. You're allowed to do that. There's no reason it has to end."

"I might change my mind, but he specifically said he's not a relationship guy, Melanie. He doesn't do commitment and strings. He's probably going to take another job and end up halfway across the country."

"Have you talked to him? Told him any of this?"

I let out a half laugh. "No. Absolutely not."

"You might start there then. Seriously, have an actual conversation about this with him and see what happens."

"The last time I made plans with someone for anything permanent, he slept with someone else. I'd rather not do that again."

She takes my hands, a stern expression on her face. "Natalie, Jake is not Sean. Those two could not be more different."

"I know." I let out a long sigh. "I'm just... scared, I guess."

She drops my hands, sitting up. "And that's fair. But love is scary. Sometimes you've just gotta... do it."

"Oh, no." I stand up, smoothing my hands down the front of my shirt. "This isn't love."

"Sure, babe." Melanie smiles, standing herself before she paces toward the door. "You keep telling yourself that. Should we go put them out of their misery? I'm dying to know what Jake told Knox and Asher while we were in here."

"Oh, my god." I cringe as I follow behind her, forgetting my sister doesn't travel anywhere on her own. "Jesus, the entire crew is going to know, aren't they?"

"Nah, it's not the whole crew you need to worry about, Natalie." She grins as she opens the door and heads down the hall. "It's Dex."

"Shit. He's never going to let me live this down once he finds out, is he?"

"Not a chance."

I can hear her laughter following her down the hallway as she goes.

When Melanie and I make it back to the living room, all three guys are sitting there, watching baseball on the TV like it's guys' night in my apartment.

"So what did we decide for dinner?" Knox looks up at Melanie and me from where he's perched on the couch.

Melanie pulls her purse up over her head, turning to drop it on the entry table behind where she stands. "Natalie and Jake are in for pizza if someone wants to order for us."

Melanie winks at me as she takes a spot on the couch.

"Yep! Pizza sounds perfect!" I cringe internally at the false cheer in my voice, deciding I might need a minute to pull myself together. "Let me see if I have any water or anything left in the kitchen, but you'll need to add drinks if you want something other than that."

Knox pulls out his phone and busies himself with ordering as I excuse myself to the kitchen to find drinks. I hear Jake stand, offering to help me as he does.

I round the corner into the kitchen, making a beeline for the pantry, where I find an unopened pack of bottled water sitting on the floor. I fish out several, spinning to find Jake, standing behind me, both hands gripping the trim along the top of the doorframe as he leans into the small space.

"How'd that go?"

I'm distracted by the muscles rippling in his arms as he leans forward, my eyes tracing the lines of his forearms up to the intricate tattoos wrapping around his biceps. "Um, what?"

His mouth tips up into a grin. "I said, how did that go? With Melanie?"

He drops his hands, taking the water bottles from me.

Oh, right.

"It was fine, actually. Better than fine? She was so excited." Jake steps out of the way, and we both leave the pantry as I shut the door behind us. "What did you tell Knox and Asher?"

"Nothing." He rests his hip against the countertop beside him. "They just made a comment about how Mel must have found you and then plopped down and turned the game on."

"Easily distracted. Well, that's convenient."

"Just like someone else, apparently." He smiles at me as he says it.

I blush at that, hesitating for a moment before I ask, "Do you think we need to tell them?"

"No, I don't think so. Better we don't tell more people than we have to."

"Right." That was a stupid question. Mel's words are still tumbling around in my brain, that maybe this is something real.

It can never be anything *real* when he's still working for us.

No matter how much I might want it to be.

THIRTY-SEVEN

JAKE

You Look Well Fucked

I snap the buckle of the bike helmet beneath Natalie's chin, tugging gently on the strap to keep the helmet securely on her head. Her brown eyes look up at me, a smile pulling at the corner of her lips.

"Ready to do this?" I ask, and she nods hesitantly, turning away from me. I smack her butt, covered in a pair of tight jeans, and she jumps, hands coming out behind her to protect herself as she giggles.

We spent last night at her apartment, but I brought her back to my place this morning for brunch. We're spending our day off taking a ride on my bike, which took a little convincing, but eventually Natalie agreed it might be fun.

I round the bike, grabbing my own helmet off the shelf along the way. I pat the seat behind me, beckoning Natalie over. She gingerly climbs on, her body sliding into place behind mine as her arms wrap around my waist.

Turning the ignition over, I rev the engine before the garage door slides open. I take it easy as we make our way out of the neighborhood, passing rows of neutral-colored, cookie-cutter houses, making our way toward the side roads to head out of the residential areas and toward the Tennessee country.

I can feel Natalie's arms around my waist, tightening through the turns as she holds on. The sun hits my black jacket; the late April rays warming me through. We ride for close to an hour, taking in the views of the green, rolling hills, tiny houses peppered in the distance.

I slow the bike as I approach a turnoff, a sharp left finding us on a dusty dirt road. At the end of the dead-end road, I slip around the familiar bridge-closed sign and slow to a crawl. Meandering down the trail, I come to a full stop in front of a rusted barrier, blocking the entrance to the well-worn wooden bridge.

"I don't remember it looking like this in the winter." Natalie says, looking at the overgrown area. Trees line the roadway, thick with leaves and branches; all of them towering above us. In front of us, the bridge stands, and I grab her hand, leading her through the branches, ducking under the low-hanging ones and weaving our way toward it.

"It didn't. And we parked way back on the main road. My truck can't wind all the way into the woods here."

"We're not… going out on that, are we?" she asks, her eyebrows raised in concern.

"Just trust me," I say to her, a smirk tilting up on my lips as I help her up and over the rusted-out barrier.

The bridge wobbles as I set her down on the worn wooden planks, her eyes going wide with concern.

"I promise it's fine; it's just old." When we get to the middle, I stop, turning her to stare out over the guardrails in front of us, looking down as the river ebbs and flows around a large down tree right in the middle. The river bends to the right in the distance, the trees swallowing the water as it disappears around the bend.

"This is… gorgeous." She says, her hand still clasped in mine as we stand there.

"I thought you might like it in the spring."

We stand like that for a few more minutes before I wordlessly turn and continue across the bridge. It's short, only half a dozen car lengths, and before long we've cleared the other side.

I maintain my lead, padding carefully through the overgrown grass, a small path jogging down toward the river through two trees directly next to where the bridge starts. It's a little steep, but we work our way carefully down it, stepping over branches as we go. After just a couple of minutes, the trees thin out and the hill levels off. We step out into a small open area, a log laid down along the river bank; the spot I was aiming for.

I lead Natalie over, dropping to sit on the far side of the log as she takes the seat next to me. We both take in the area, listening intently to the sounds of birds chirping, a woodpecker in the distance hammering into a tree, and the soft rustle of the leaves moving in the surrounding breeze.

It's peaceful and calming.

Just the way I remember it.

I'm really glad I had the chance to bring her back here in good weather because nothing compares to the sense of belonging I feel out here.

I watch the river flow in front of us; the water moving at a fast clip as it flows downstream.

"Little different from the first time we were here, isn't it?"

"Considerably warmer." She laughs. "It looks so pretty with all the trees filled in and the grass as green as it is."

"It's quite a view." I say honestly, looking directly at her as I do.

She looks over, smiling softly at me.

Something shifts inside me, this feeling that I've felt more and more in her presence. It's a weird sense of rightness that has come and gone in the last three months, but right now, sitting here with Natalie on a log in the woods, sharing my favorite escape, that feeling seeps into every broken crevice in my chest, filling the empty spaces with warmth. The emptiness I've carried around with me for so long feels... smaller, less consuming. As I watch her red hair rustling in the wind, I realize I might be in love with her.

She scoots closer, dropping her head to my shoulder. I wrap an arm around her as I sit with that thought for a moment, just long enough to realize there's no *might* about it.

I *am* in love with her.

And I don't even begin to know what to do with that revelation.

We spent a couple of hours down by the river before we made our way back home, the afternoon one of the most enjoyable I've had in years.

We grilled steaks for dinner before Natalie slipped off to take a bubble bath in my Jacuzzi tub. I debated joining her, but she doesn't take time to do things for herself, so I opted to wait, *somewhat patiently*, for her to do her own thing.

Instead, I'm sitting in a chair in my bedroom, sipping a nearly empty glass of whiskey when she comes out of the bathroom, wearing nothing but my shirt, her bare legs on full display.

"Christ." I murmur, watching as she makes her way over to me. She does a little twirl as she comes to a stop between my spread legs, her hands resting just above my knees.

"Thanks for this," she says, as she runs her hands up my thighs.

"For what?" I ask, finishing the whiskey before I set it off to the side, reaching out to pull her into my arms.

"For the day away. It's been… really nice."

I wrap one arm tightly around her waist as I pull her into my lap, her bare pussy settling onto the gray fabric of my sweatpants, notching my dick right where it wants to be.

She runs her hands over my bare shoulders, sliding them down my arms as her fingers trace the ink there.

"You've never said what this is for." She moves her nails over the trees on my arm. "The bend in this river looks like the view from… the bridge."

Her eyes meet mine as my lips tip up into a smile. "Yeah, because it is. I had the tattoo drawn from a photo I took on one of my trips there about seven years ago."

The pads of her fingers follow the flow of the river up my arm, a collection of trees on either side wrapping around my bicep. Along the top of the tree line, four birds fly in a sky that covers my shoulder.

"Are these four birds meant to be for you and your brothers?"

I run my free hand up her arm and through her red hair, combing my fingers through the wet tresses as she settles her weight onto me. "Yeah, they are."

"This is so beautiful, Jake. I mean, I know I've seen it before, but I never really—It's striking how much it looks just like the view you showed me today."

"Yeah, the artist is incredibly talented."

She dances her fingers up, wrapping them around my neck as she shifts in my lap.

"You look fucking good in my shirt, Red." She smiles coyly, her eyes lighting up as I pull her lips down to mine, whispering against them. "I might like this better than all that lingerie you bought."

She meets my lips with hers, the soft pads brushing up against my own as she opens for me, allowing my tongue inside her mouth to explore. A low moan rolls out of her, her hands moving from my shoulders to the back of my head, holding me to her.

I slide my hands down her body, over her curves covered by the white cotton of my shirt. When I meet the bare skin of her thighs, I work my hands underneath the fabric as I trace her soft skin up her sides, stopping when I reach her rib cage, the pads of my thumbs brushing the underside of her breasts as she rolls her hips into me.

"Jake—" She pants into my mouth, her fingers tightening in my hair.

"Take this off." I release my hold, dropping my hands as I pull on the bottom of the t-shirt.

She smirks as she pulls away, pushing out of my lap and taking one step back before turning away from me. It's a quick moment before the shirt is lifted and over her head, Natalie tossing the fabric onto the floor beside her as I take in her ass, following the line of her spine up and into her hair before she spins, turning back to face me.

"You are perfect. You know that?"

She smiles again, taking another two steps away as she makes her way toward my bed. She rounds the right side, patting the white duvet as she puts a knee on the bed, crawling toward the middle. "Come here."

My dick swells painfully in my pants as I do what I'm told, making my way to the side of the bed, still fully dressed. I climb onto the bed opposite her, standing on two knees as I meet her in the middle, the redheaded vixen smirking up at me as she moves her hand down my chest, sliding her fingers into the waistband of my sweatpants.

Slowly, she pulls them down, my cock bobbing free as the fabric releases it. A mischievous grin plays across her face as she drops onto her hands and knees, her lips meeting the head of my dick.

A low rumble escapes me as her tongue licks at the underside of my dick, working from the base to the tip before slipping it into her mouth.

Her tongue trails over the head, the sensation so fucking good. I gather her hair into my hand, holding the makeshift ponytail so I can watch her mouth as it moves over me.

That only lasts a few minutes before I can't take it anymore. I slide my free hand down to her ass, giving it a firm squeeze before I tug on her hair, guiding her backwards as she takes her mouth off of me.

It takes everything in me to maintain control as she whimpers, but if we don't put a pause on this, I'm going to come in about four seconds and that's not exactly what I had in mind for tonight.

I tug her upright, sealing her mouth to mine, the intensity of this kiss exponentially higher than the one a few minutes ago in the chair.

I let her control the pace, meeting each of her fervor'd kisses with one of my own, my hands exploring her body. She shifts in front of me, pushing down on my shoulders, forcing me to the mattress before she climbs atop me and shimmies her way down my body.

Before I can react, she has my pants off, tossed onto the floor where she left my shirt, and my dick is back in her mouth.

"Natalie—"

She cuts me off, cupping my balls as my eyes roll back into my head. I slide my hands down her back, holding her to my body as I cave, thrusting up into her open mouth.

She moans around my dick, and I nearly come, remembering why I had pulled her off. I reach for her, her head snapping up to meet mine as I lay on the bed, anticipation racing through me.

"Get up here." My voice is rough, a low growl as it leaves my throat.

She stares me down, her mouth still just inches from my twitching dick.

"Up." I tug again on her arms, and she moves up my body, her spread legs open over my chest.

I tug one more time.

She laughs. "I am up!"

"No, all the way. I want your pussy on my face… your hands on my headboard." I smack her ass to punctuate my demand. "That wasn't a request, Red."

My hands close around her hips as I lift her up, a low squeal leaving her, before I'm lowering her down, her knees landing on the pillow on either side of my head.

"Jake, seriously—" I tighten my fingers on her hips, pulling her down onto me, my tongue splitting her open just as her hands fall to the headboard in front of her. My grip on her hips holds her where I want her, my tongue sliding through her core as I cut my way through her pussy, lapping at her before nipping gently at her clit and repeating the pattern once… twice.

She rolls her hips, moving her body over me, the folds of her pussy rubbing wantonly against my face as I smile into the movements.

Her hands release my headboard, and she drops them to meet my own, still firmly on her hips. She loosens my grip, taking my fingers in hers as she twines our hands together, lowering them to the bed beside me as she moves over my face.

A rush of desire rolls through me as she squeezes her hands in mine, a long, low moan coming out of her as she continues to move.

Fuck, she is a dream.

She looks like a fucking queen like this, taking what she wants, using me for her own pleasure. I don't even think she realizes how fucking sexy she is.

She picks up her pace; her echoing moans becoming breathier, faster.

It's too damn much; the movement, the sounds pushing me quickly toward my own climax.

I let go of one of her hands, moving to grip my dick, squeezing to the point of pain at the base of my cock to hold off the impending orgasm. I refuse to come until I'm buried inside her.

I flick my tongue over her clit one more time and she comes undone, hips rolling, head thrown back as she utters my name.

It's the single sweetest sound I have ever heard.

Unable to restrain myself, I run my hand over my cock. I stroke myself to the sound of her orgasm as I work my tongue through her, lapping at every pulse as it moves through her.

Her movements slow as she comes down, her hips rolling slowly as she shifts off to the side, turning over onto her back. I follow her, resting on my forearms as my body hovers over hers. A smug smile crosses my face as I take in the hazy look in her eyes, the pink tint to her cheeks and the sweat glistening on her forehead.

I drop my lips to hers, brushing them against her as I whisper, "You look well fucked, Red."

I don't let her respond before I press our lips together, savoring the moment as she presses into the kiss, completely undeterred by the fact that my face was just between her legs.

I glide my hands down her body, cataloging every inch of skin as I run my hands over her, wanting desperately to remember every detail.

When I reach her hips, I drop back onto my heels, taking in the sight of her lying before me, spread open for me like a fucking goddess as she waits for me to make the next move. I lean toward the nightstand, but her hand catches me.

"I—I don't want anything between us. Can we skip the condom?" She bites her lip, but she has to know by now I'd give her anything she asked for.

"You sure? I mean, I'm clean, I—"

"I'm sure," she says, more confidently this time. "I have an IUD. I just… want you, Jake. All of you."

Fuck.

I nod as I shift back between her legs, giving my dick a couple of hard tugs before I move the head through her core, both of us sighing heavily at the contact.

I notch my cock into her, meeting her eyes as I slide home in one swift movement. She arches up into me, a low moan leaving her as she does, her tits on full display for me. I palm one, pinching her nipple as I rock my hips back, moving inside her.

"Jesus, Natalie. You feel like—" I trail off, unable to form a cohesive sentence as I move inside her, feeling her tightening around me with each thrust.

"Like what?" She's panting, skin shining in the dim light.

"You feel like mine." I say as I drop my lips to hers, our pace becoming frantic as we work to time our kisses with each of my thrusts, the movements growing frenzied as we both climb higher.

"Jake," she whines. "Fuck, I'm gonna come again."

"Do it, Red. Give me another one." I lean back just enough to watch her as I move, sweat rolling down my temple as she comes undone, my name on her lips once again, her head tipped back in ecstasy.

I will never get enough of this.

Of her, under me. My name uttered in that throaty way.

Her, in my bed. In my life. Permanently.

A thought that would have scared me shitless just a handful of months ago now spurs me on.

I follow her cues as she comes down, slowing my thrusts until she's spent, panting underneath me.

"I can't—" she pants, catching her breath, "Oh my god."

"I'm not done with you," I smirk as her eyes widen. "Flip over."

She does as I ask, slowly turning over on the bed, her head on my pillow as she sticks her ass up.

I run my hands down her sides, squeezing my fingers into her hips as I move over them; the sight of her ass in my hands nearly has me coming undone already.

"I won't take long. You're gonna do me in." I'm panting too, near feral for the woman in front of me.

She wiggles her ass in front of me, and I laugh, fisting my cock as I slide it through her cheeks. I tilt my hips as my dick slips into her, her pussy dripping as she takes me again.

I grab onto her waist, moving quickly as I pick up right where I left off, seconds from coming, but desperate to hold off for just a minute longer.

When I can't, I fold myself over her body, both of my hands finding a breast as I pinch, tugging on her nipples just as my orgasm tears through me. I can feel her clenching around me as a third one finds her as well, both of us cresting, riding the high of coming together before we collapse on the bed.

I'm careful to hold my weight off her as I roll to the side, gathering her in my arms while we lay there, spent, panting, and sticky with sweat.

"Jesus Christ, Natalie."

"That was—" she doesn't finish her sentence, but she doesn't have to.

"Yeah, it was."

We catch our breath before I drag us both out of bed and back to the bathroom for a quick shower.

Thirty minutes later, as we slip into my bed together, Natalie once again tucked into my arms, I'm positive that nothing has ever felt like this.

I've never wanted anything the way I want *this.*

And nausea rolls through me as I realize we agreed to sneaking around, agreed to sleeping together for the length of the tour, but we never agreed on this being any form of permanent.

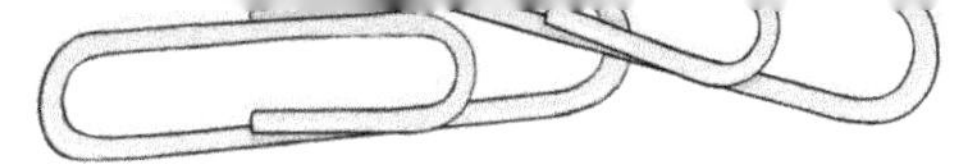

THIRTY-EIGHT

NATALIE

Thanks For The Concern

We wander the streets of downtown Nashville, coffee in hand, as we enjoy one last morning together before we head back to work. We decided not to cook for ourselves, instead heading to a diner downtown. When we finished eating, neither of us were ready to go home, where we'd have to pack and get ready for tonight's rehearsal, so instead we're wandering aimlessly.

It's kind of fun to be a tourist in your own city for once. I don't take time just to *enjoy* things, and this week has me appreciating how fucking nice it is.

We make our way past a visitor shop, one of those cheesy ones with a sign in the window that reads, "Get your Nashville Swag here!" I cringe, running my eyes over the gaudy display of all things emblazoned with "NASHVILLE" across them.

Jake pauses, tapping on the glass. "Hey, they have one of those machines."

Behind the mannequin in the hoodie standing directly in front of us, I can see a pressed penny machine tucked into a corner against the wall.

"Yeah, so?" I look over at him, a glint in his eye.

"C'mon…" He turns the corner, ushering me inside the door.

"What are we doing?" I hiss as he tugs me through the store. "Oh, for the love. I do not need a Nashville pressed penny!"

"Sure you do. I guarantee you don't already have one in your collection."

"No, I do not. Because I *live* here. I don't need a token to remember my hometown."

"You don't want a token to remember the time your sister sold out the stadium in your hometown on her cross-country tour?" He asks, one eyebrow cocked at me.

"I, well, no. I wasn't collecting tour-stop pennies..."

"Maybe you should."

I meet his stare with one of my own before I laugh, caving. I pass my coffee off to Jake and dig in my purse for spare change. Grabbing the shiniest penny I can find, I put the money into the machine. I contemplate my options for a moment, finally settling on a simple one with the guitar on it. The skyline is appealing, but this one feels more appropriate for the purpose of the week.

I turn the crank, watching as the coin slips through the machine, the plates pressing it into a long, flat oval. A few moments later, a loud clink sounds in the tray below me, and I reach down, pulling out my newest penny.

It has raised dots running around the edge, the large guitar in the middle. The word "Nashville" is printed above the guitar and "Tennessee" below it.

"Do you want one? I think I have enough change to get another..." I ask Jake, as he watches me study the penny before I slip it into my pocket.

"Sure, why not?" He shrugs.

I quickly press a second penny, handing it over to him. He takes a moment to admire it before slipping it into his pocket as well.

It feels a little childish, but I can't help the little bubble of excitement expanding within me as we make our way out of the store and continue down the street.

We wander hand-in-hand for several blocks before my eyes catch a head of wavy blonde hair heading in our direction up in front of me. As quickly as it came, that bubble pops, my heart jumping into my throat. I can feel it trying to claw its way out of my body as each step brings us closer together. Before I can even think of an alternative to running into him, Gunner is standing right in front of us, his eyes searching me, lingering on my joined hand with Jake's, before they shift over to him.

"Well, Natalie. What a surprise this is!" Gunner drawls, that fake Southern accent grating on my nerves. I never did like that about him. I can feel Jake stiffen beside me as Gunner addresses me.

"Hi, Gunner. Nice to see you." I clench my jaw, trying not to say what I'd really like to share with him.

"What are the two of you doing out this morning? Aren't you supposed to be on tour?" His eyes once again shift between the two of us.

"We are, actually. Melanie is playing in Nashville this weekend."

"And this is how you're spending your time?" His eyes shift to Jake as he says that. "Wondering the streets with your... staff?"

"I don't think that's any of your business—who I'm with or why." The venom coating my mouth is dying for a chance to escape.

"Oh, I think it might be." Gunner's eyes shift back to me. "You'd be surprised what I can make my business around here, Natalie."

"Oh, I would be entirely unsurprised, I'm sure." Jake squeezes my hand. I can't tell whether it's a warning or something else. Either way, I'm not interested in hanging around with Gunner. "Well, as fun as this has been..."

I move to step around him when he speaks again.

"You should be more careful, Natalie." Gunner's eyes shift to Jake.

"Careful about what?" Bile creeps into my throat as he watches us, making me uncomfortable.

He's still maintaining eye contact with Jake when he says, "Who you spend your time with. Who sees you."

I give him a scathing glare. "Noted. Thanks for the concern."

I walk away, desperate to put space between Gunner and myself. Before I can get far enough away though, he calls out behind us, "It was really nice to see you again. Give my love to Mel."

I hasten my pace, hustling down the block and around the corner, finding Gunner's eyes still on us as we round the building, stepping out of his sight. I stop short against the side of the building, snapping my eyes up to meet Jake's, who has remained silent this entire time, his usually tanned skin a decidedly paler color.

"What the hell was that?" I ask out loud, more to myself than to him. His eyes hold mine, but he doesn't speak. He just stares at me as we stand there on the sidewalk.

"He was always a little off-putting, but he's never been downright creepy before. I don't know what the hell his problem is."

Jake clears his throat before he speaks. "Probably just, I don't know, angry about the divorce? Angry in general?"

"Yeah, probably." We continue down the sidewalk, unease still feeling like a block of lead sitting inside my stomach. My sudden nausea has me tossing my unfinished coffee into a bin as we pass by, not wanting to finish the nearly full beverage.

We make our way back to Jake's truck, both of us silent on the ride back to his house.

MAY

- Detroit baseball collab?
- call zoo coordinator

SUN	MON	TUES	WED	THUR	FRI	SA
				1	2	3
						Pittsburgh Sh
4	5	6	7	8	9	10
	9a Team Weekly		PA Station Interviews			Philly Sh
11	12	13	14	15	16	
Philly Drive →	Day Off!	9a Team Weekly	NJ Station Interviews			Jersey
18	19	20	21	22	23	
Jersey Drive →	Day Off!	9a Team Weekly	Boston Gardens Night			Foxbo
25	26	27	28	29	30	
MA Drive →			Zoo Event			
Cincinnati Drive →						

pennsylvania stops:
confirm station schedules
108.6 wants TV interview

jersey & foxborough:
gardens PR packets for influ.
passes for zoo event

Chicago:
call the
schedule

AUSTIN: Tell us about the hometown show, Mel.

MELANIE: Oh my gosh, it was so much fun! We did an extended meet and greet on Wednesday. On Thursday, we did a special sound check with a mini performance. And then, of course, the shows on Friday and Saturday. The special guests we had each night were such a great surprise. The fans really loved it.

AUSTIN: They sure did. There were some big names on that stage with you. Madison Grace? Cameron Clover? There was so much raw talent in that stadium, it was ridiculous.

MELANIE: Yes, there was. It's so weird to me the reception we get when my team reaches out to put things like this together. I'm still not used to the overwhelming excitement that we usually get in response.

INDY: Well, I mean, I can see why everyone would be so excited. Who *wouldn't* want to perform with Melanie Bennett?

AUSTIN: Well, you might find me on that list. I lack the musical talent required to share a stage with Melanie.

MELANIE: [laughing] We could get you up there doing something else. How do you feel about pyrotechnics?

AUSTIN: Yeah, no thank you.

MELANIE: There's always a stagehand position.

INDY: [more laughter] Now we're talking. Put the man to work.

AUSTIN: Why don't we just… move along. Where are you off to next, now that the hometown show is done?

MELANIE: We are heading up the east coast, Austin. We're doing a bunch of shows in the Northeast in the next few weeks.

INDY: Oh, that's one of my favorite areas.

MELANIE: I know; I can't wait. We have four shows in Pennsylvania before we stop in New Jersey and Massachusetts. I'm really eager to get to the zoo event in Boston.

INDY: That's right! Oh my gosh, so am I! So what do we have to look forward to in the three weeks before that?

MELANIE: We have another exciting influencer event when we're in Pittsburgh. This one is being hosted at a floral shop, and we're inviting local small business owners to hang out with us for the night. I love supporting the communities we travel through, so I'm really looking forward to this one!

INDY: I am so glad we decided to keep going with our tour coverage. I cannot wait to be there for that one.

AUSTIN: Florals? For spring? Groundbreaking.

MELANIE: Did he just—?

INDY: [laughing] Yes, yes he did.

KAYDEWREADS: Austinnnn. The jokes, man.

SOLARBLOOMS: I am so glad you guys continued this series!! The BTS has been amazing! Melanie has quickly become one of my favorite artists.

FANCY_PENELOPE17: Seconding this! How do we get this for all the big tours?! I need to see Cameron Clover with six months of behind-the-scenes coverage when his kicks off!

PERIDOTPAGES: I was never a regular viewer before this series, but I am now! Absolutely love this.

Know Him, Know Him

"I could get used to this," I say to Natalie as I curl myself around her, dropping a kiss to her bare collarbone, wrapped up in the hotel bedsheets.

She hums in response. Her fingers trace the scruff of my beard as we lie side-by-side in my bed in Pittsburgh.

Running into Gunner last week was not the ending to our time off I would have hoped for. We went back to my house, silently collected our things, and drove downtown to the stadium. I didn't bring up the awkward meeting with Gunner, and neither did she. I still don't know how I made it through that conversation without being addressed, but I continue to thank some fucking deity for the luck that got me through that one. I had somehow managed to forget he even existed in the chaos of the last month, but coming face to face with him was a real wake up call.

The fact that he didn't address me still doesn't sit right. I spent both of the hometown shows looking over my shoulder, expecting to see Gunner around every corner, waiting for him to come find me.

But he never cropped up. And we left Nashville on Sunday, making our way north to the first of two stops in Pennsylvania. Pittsburgh, fortunately, has us staying in a hotel where Natalie has her own room, so late at night she's been creeping into mine and we picked up right where we'd left off.

The more this happens, the more I crave it, and I don't know what to do about that. My eyes rake over the redhead beside me, her hair sleep-mussed and her eyelids heavy. She looks fucking good tucked into my blankets, curled up into my side.

She *feels* good in my life.

The reappearance of Gunner has my stomach in knots, and I know I have to come clean with her about him before I try to make whatever this is between us into something permanent. I owe her the truth, and I know I can't put it off anymore.

I lean forward, dropping a kiss on her forehead. "I'm gonna get coffee brewing so we can get over to the stadium."

Her hand snakes up, wrapping around my neck as she stops me from pulling away, instead bringing my face back to hers, our lips meeting. I meet her eagerness with my own, sliding my hands under the covers and running them the length of her torso as she opens for me, her tongue meeting mine.

"If we start this now, I'm not stopping it." I smile through the kiss, an audible sigh leaving her as her fingers tighten in my hair. "We're already bordering on late."

I squeeze my fingers on her hip, pulling back far enough to meet her eyes.

She rolls away, flopping back onto the bed as she dramatically throws one arm over her face.

"Fine." The word is barely a mumble, the single syllable drawn out into half a dozen as she relents, clearly annoyed by the presence of morning.

"We can pick this up tonight." I lean down, dropping one more kiss on her lips for good measure before I roll away, my feet hitting the carpet.

Right after we talk.

"Are there any of those donuts left?"

I chuckle as I turn back to face her. The box of donuts from earlier this week is empty on the counter across the room. "There are not, but we can stop on our way over there if you want."

"Can we? Is it on the way?" She smiles at me when I promise to make time for a stop. It's not even remotely close to the stadium, but I pull up the bakery on my phone as I make my way across the room, placing an online order for a box of donuts to go.

Several hours and several donuts later, Natalie is prepping the media room for tonight's show. It's just before lunch, with a long afternoon of prep still before us.

My phone rings, the muffled sound coming from my back pocket. I fish the device out, seeing Connor's name flashing across the screen. Unease washes over me, the sinking feeling in my stomach telling me this is not good.

I look over at Natalie, who's humming to herself as she shuffles through her press packets. "Hey, I have to take this. I'll be back in a few."

"I'll be here." She wiggles the folder in her hands at me before refocusing on the task at hand.

Stepping out into the hallway, I hit the green accept button. "Alder."

I hurry away from the conference room, my steps carrying me as far down the hall as I can get before Connor's voice comes over the line. "Jake, Connor. You got a minute?"

"Sure, what's up?"

"Got an interesting phone call this morning. Gentleman says he saw you looking a little *too* comfortable with your client out in Nashville."

I stop dead in my tracks.

That motherfucker.

"Seemed adamant the interaction was unprofessional. How he knew your relationship to Natalie, I don't know, but Jake, you know we have a strict no fraternization policy. Unless you can tell me this claim is bullshit, unless you can *prove it,* I'm in a tight spot here."

I swallow, weighing my response. As much as I'd like to argue against Gunner, I know I can't. Instead, I take a deep breath. "I, uh—I can't do that."

A long sigh comes over the line. "Care to explain the situation to me?"

"Not much to explain, sir. It wasn't something I planned on happening… it just… did."

"Of all the women—"

I cut him off. "With all due respect, I'm aware of the rules. This wasn't a careless decision."

Connor is quiet for a long minute before he talks again.

"I see. Well, unfortunately, the circumstances of the situation and the intricacies of the relationship won't change the outcome here. But I appreciate the honesty. It kills me to do this. You've been one of the best employees I've had in a long time. I know Knox has found you invaluable on this tour."

I hear movement in the background before he continues, "Your contract with Shield is terminated, effective immediately. I'm going to ask you to remove yourself from the team as quickly and efficiently as possible. Knox is already aware of the situation and will step in if need be."

"That won't be necessary." My jaw aches from the force of my teeth clenching. The last thing I want is a scene. "I can be out of here in a couple of hours."

"Appreciate it. I'll send a formal email with your letter of termination and the next steps for returning the Shield equipment. You have my number if you need anything in the meantime. Disappointing end to this relationship, Jake."

"Yeah." Unsure what else I could say to make this better, I trail off. I'm not about to apologize for something I don't regret, even if this current situation is less than ideal.

"I'll be in touch." A final click echoes over the line as he disconnects. I stare at the phone in my hand, debating my next steps.

"Care to tell me what the fuck is going on?" Knox's voice carries down the hallway, his heavy steps moving toward me as I turn to face him.

He comes to a stop in front of me, arms crossed, feet wide, like he's looking for a fight.

"Um, no, not really." I move to pass him, but he grabs my arm, stopping me.

"Well, that's too damn bad because I'd like an answer."

"There's nothing to share, Knox. Natalie and I have been sneaking around, Shield found out, and now I'm done." I wince as the words roll off my tongue. *Sneaking around* is the truth, technically, but trying to label it as *just sex* feels wrong.

"That's not what I'm talking about. I know the two of you have been sleeping together. I'm talking about Gunner Greene calling Shield to rat you out."

There's an ominously long pause. "How do you know Gunner, Jake?"

I swallow.

Shit.

"Doesn't everyone know Gunner?" It's a cheap line, but I'm digging for scraps here.

"Don't bullshit me, Jake. Gunner's an ass, but he doesn't do things just for shits and giggles. If he's calling your boss to tell him you're sleeping with your client, you've done something to him personally. Which means you know him. *Know him,* know him. So I'm going to ask you again, how do you know Gunner?"

My eyes scan the room, looking at anything and everything but Knox. At this point, what do I have to lose?

Heaving a long sigh, I tell the truth. "I was friends with him."

Knox looks stunned. "I'm sorry. I must have heard you wrong. It sounded like you said you're *friends* with him?"

"Yeah, sort of—" He cuts me off.

"Don't you think that's something you should have mentioned at some point?!"

I exhale, knowing he's absolutely right. "It is, yes. I just—the timing was never right."

Knox's jaw tenses, his face stone cold fury. "What is that supposed to mean?"

"At first I didn't say anything because it didn't really matter. I didn't know I was working for Melanie when I took the job. I learned that on day one. So I kept it to myself. I wasn't here to complicate shit. I had a job to do. By the time I realized I *should* come clean, the article had dropped. And that seemed like a shitty fucking time to share that kind of thing, so I didn't."

"And the months since then? No good moment to let Melanie know you're buddy-buddy with her fucking ex? To tell Natalie?"

"I know, Knox. I fucked up. I'm aware."

He scoffs at that. "How long, Jake?"

"How long, what?"

"How long have you been friends with Gunner?" He holds his posture, arms crossed, feet spread in front of me, one hundred percent the intimidating bodyguard he's hired to be.

"For fuck's sake, we're not *that* close."

"Just answer the goddamn question." He's seething. Rightfully angry, but a little scary, if I'm being honest.

"I went to high school with him, but you should know—"

Before I can finish that sentence, before I can explain anything to him, Knox's right fist connects with my cheekbone, the force of the blow sending me stumbling backward. I'm barely able to stay on my feet, but I hold my balance. My hand comes up to cover my face, pain radiating through my cheek, the sting of the punch catching me off guard.

"What the fuck!" Knox yells as he shakes out his fist. "Are you kidding me right now?"

"I wish I were." It's a barely audible mumble.

"Jesus Christ. And here I was, thinking *we* were friends."

"We are friends, Knox."

"Bull-fucking-shit. Friends don't lie to their friends. We're apparently nothing more than former co-workers."

The accusation hurts, salt in a reopened wound, one I didn't realize had healed. "I get it. I should have come clean months ago, but I can promise you, we're not buddy-buddy, man. I haven't even talked to the guy in months."

He scoffs. "Yeah, sure, ok."

"Would you just let me explain myself?" My face fucking hurts, but it pales compared to the ache forming in my chest.

"Yes, please do. Because I'm interested in hearing how you fucked both my sisters over in one go." We both turn to find Dex standing several feet away, hands on his hips, a look of raw fury in his eyes.

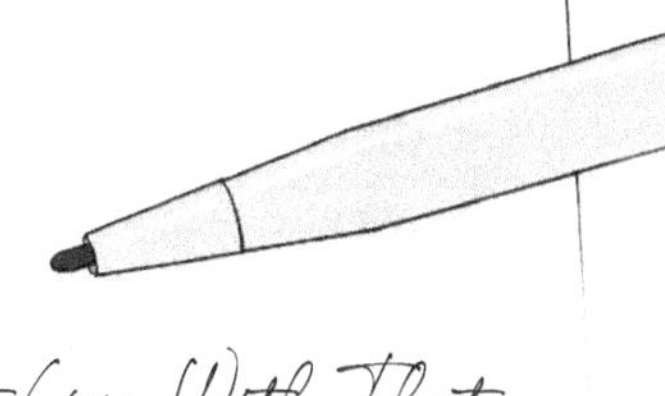

I Can't Live With That

"Have you seen Jake?" I ask Dex as I come up next to him. "He was with me this morning, but he got a phone call around noon and took off. He made it sound like he would be right back, but I haven't seen or heard from him since. His phone is off."

Dex clears his throat. "Uh, yeah. Here, c'mon."

He tugs on my arm, hauling me after him as he takes off across the concourse, moving through the stadium. Dropping my arm, we walk side-by-side for several minutes, the noise of the pre-concert prep dulling as we make our way further into the stadium. He swings around a corner and into a random office, gesturing for me to enter.

I throw him a look, confused why we're here, of all places. "What's going on?"

He shuts the door behind me before he moves to sit on the empty desk in the middle of the room. "Do you want to sit? You should sit."

"What? Why in the world... Dex? You're being weird." I watch as he fidgets with his hands, clearly uncomfortable.

"Listen, I have to tell you something. Two things, actually."

My stomach turns. I don't like when he dances around things like this because it's almost always bad news. Dex is straight to the point, no bullshit.

"What?"

"Well, first, I know about you and Jake."

I can feel my stomach drop clear out of my body.

"You... know about us?" My voice is quiet, my mind spinning with the implications of what this means.

"Did Gunner call you?"

"Why the fuck would Gunner call me? Of course not." He looks appalled. "I've known about you two for a while now. You're not as stealthy as you think you are. To be clear, I don't have a problem with it; that's not why I'm telling you. My feelings about the situation aren't relevant."

"Then why are you telling me, Dex?"

"It turns out I'm not the only one who knows." My breath catches in my throat, a thick band tightening around my chest, making it impossible for air to flow properly.

"Who else knows?"

"Shield. Jake disappeared on you because he was fired this morning. He wanted to come find you, but Knox asked him to leave."

I drop into the chair beside the desk, the room spinning as I try to make sense of what Dex is saying.

"If you want me to pull someone from your team to deal with this, I can. I know it's a lot at one time…"

My mind immediately goes into work mode, planning the next steps, how to neutralize the issue, how to get Jake un-fired. It's several long moments before I realize what Dex said.

"Why would we need someone from the team? I can fix this. I can call Shield—"

"Because, first of all, it's a conflict of interest, Natalie. And two, because you don't *need* to be the one dealing with it. Let someone help you."

"Rude of you to suggest I can't handle this…"

"I'm not suggesting anything! I'm telling you that you don't *have to*. You shouldn't have to!"

"Listen, Dex, can you stop—"

"Can *you* stop? Because I'm not done here."

It doesn't seem possible my stomach could twist itself into anymore knots at this point, but it does. "What do you mean you're not done?"

"There's more."

"More… what?"

"Jake was…" He pauses, taking a deep breath before he continues, his voice lower. "Jake knew Gunner."

"What do you mean? He knew Gunner? Like he worked as a bodyguard?"

"No, not as a bodyguard."

"Then I don't understand! What is going on, Dex?"

"I know. Listen, I've only known for an hour. I had no idea about any of this before then. Apparently, Jake's known Gunner since high school. They were friends."

The entire world stops. I can hear the screeching of the brakes as everything comes crashing into me. My chest tightens. A lump the size of a golf ball crawls into my throat and…

I will not cry.

I will not cry.

I will not cry.

Dex ducks down to my eye level, hovering in front of me, resting his arms on the chair around me. "Breathe, Nat."

"I… don't understand."

"I know. I don't either. I got very few details before Knox saw him out."

Panic claws at the inside of my chest.

Jesus, Melanie.

All this time… she's had someone from Gunner's circle *with her*.

"Dex! He's been here… the whole time! He's been here for *everything*. Oh my god, Melanie. Does Melanie know?"

"No, Natalie, breathe. Please. I'm not worried about Melanie right now."

"How are you not worried about Melanie? What if that's why he was here? He was reporting back to Gunner!"

Dex puts his hands on my shoulders, squeezing tightly as he looks at me. "I'm trying to figure everything out. I haven't had enough time to get all the details yet. Let me worry about Melanie. I need you to *let me do that*."

"What?" My mind is such a jumbled mess right now, I'm struggling to string a single coherent thought together.

"I just want you to worry about yourself, ok? Not problem solving anything for anyone else right now."

I nod, unsure what else to do at the moment.

"Dex?" My voice is barely more than a whisper.

"Yeah?" He drops his hands, leaning back to look at me.

"What if he was just using me... to get to Melanie?"

The tears start in earnest now. Uncontrollable waterworks cascade across my cheeks as I break, every moment between us running through my mind. Every word he said being turned over because how do I know what was true? Was any of it?

Dex leans in, his arms coming around me. "We'll figure it out, Natalie."

I don't reply; I can't. Instead, I just nod as I fall apart in front of him.

The car pulls up to the hotel, barely rolling to a stop before I have the door flung open. I step onto the brick drive, the sharp bite of my heels clicking on the stone as I make my way inside. I can hear Dex talking to the driver behind me, but I don't pause.

As far as afternoons go, this afternoon was the worst I've ever had, by far. Dex and I hid out in that office for about an hour before I tried to go back to work. I managed to pull it together for my staff meeting, but I bailed right after, accepting that I'm far too distracted to focus.

Jake was asked to leave the tour but apparently stayed in town, booking a room at this new hotel several blocks away. Dex, angel that he is, somehow found the hotel Jake booked once he left the stadium this morning.

Jake doesn't know I'm coming, but I couldn't put this off. I only have a small window before the concert starts, and trying to get back into the stadium in time will be an absolute bitch, but this cannot wait.

I'm so pissed, but also so fucking hurt, and I can't sit on this ledge waiting to tip over. I have to see him. I have to have some sort of explanation for all of this or I will absolutely lose my mind.

Making my way to the entrance, the bright lights of the lobby spill out onto the drive as I approach the revolving door. The cool air hits my skin as the door spins, chilling the light sheen of sweat on me and making my skin clammy.

My chest aches, a lead weight pressing down on me. *This* is why I don't bother with getting close to someone, why I prefer to rely on myself. Because in the end, no one else is truly reliable. You give them all these important pieces of yourself, and what do you get in return?

Fucking heartache.

Betrayal.

A load of shit.

I take a deep, steadying breath as I press the button for the elevator, Dex coming up behind me. He opens his mouth just as the lift arrives, but I silence him, my hand held up as I step in and press the button for the sixth floor.

"Not right now, Dex."

His mouth snaps shut as his eyes meet mine, the concern in them palpable. I know he thinks this is something he can help me with, but it's not. He's here as a favor to Knox and his team, not because I wanted his input. Technically, I'm still on their contract. I should still have someone with me. But, fuck if I'm bringing anyone else into this mess right now. Dex convinced them he could handle it for an hour.

The ride up to Jake's floor takes a small eternity, the elevator moving at a snail's pace. When the lift dings, I step out, following the signs that point me to his room number.

As I step in front of his door, the tightness in my chest worsens. I might *actually* be sick. Never in my life have I felt like this.

God, when Sean and I broke up, I felt nothing. I was absolutely devoid of any emotion. And the lack of feeling is so much more preferable than this.

This inescapable feeling of cracking in half, of being pulled apart at the seams, the pain worsening with each unraveled thread. I'm terrified to consider the difference right now, why the pain I'm feeling at the moment is nearly suffocating, when leaving the man I thought I was going to marry was nothing.

I think the answer might devastate me.

I suck in a long breath as Dex's hand closes over my shoulder.

"I'll be right here." He gestures vaguely to the hallway beside me, and I nod in acknowledgment, not trusting myself to speak right now.

With another deep breath, I knock, staring blankly at the orange wood before me.

Several seconds, or possibly an entire lifetime, pass before I hear movement behind the door. With a loud click, the door swings open and Jake stands there, the look of relief on his face plain as day.

"Hey." His eyes meet mine, a thousand thoughts passing silently between us as we stand on either side of the threshold. I feel Dex's hand slip off my shoulder as he steps aside. Jake's eyes flick to his for a moment before coming back to mine, apparently unconcerned with Dex's presence.

"Did you want to..." He opens the door all the way and I slide past him, careful to keep as much distance between our bodies as possible. I take several quick steps into the room before turning to face him, his attention pivoting between me and Dex, who is still behind him.

Dex steps in, leaning toward Jake as he whispers something I can't hear, his back turned to me. He moves back, grabbing the door handle beside Jake and tugging the door with him. He meets my eyes one last time before he murmurs, "Right out here."

The door clicks shut; the noise vibrating through the room. The hum of the air conditioner behind me fills the space between us as we stand there, awkwardly looking at one another.

Despite the reason I'm here, I somehow already feel lighter, the anvil on my chest easing just from being in his presence. And it makes me furious.

How dare he do this to me?

How dare he waltz into my life, crack me open, and then leave the pieces shattered on the floor?

I hope like hell it hurts now that he's walking all over them. I hope it cuts deep and leaves a mark. It's the least he deserves.

I take a few moments to take him in, his hair disheveled, sticking up in all directions. A deep purple bruise blooms under his eye. From Knox's punch, I assume. I will admit to feeling a touch satisfied when Dex told me Knox hit him.

I pivot away from Jake, stalking toward the window. When I turn around, an entire room between us now, he hasn't moved.

"Well?" I ask, my voice dripping with ire.

"I just…" He runs his hand through his hair, tugging at the strands as he tries to find his words. "Jesus, Natalie, I don't even know where to start."

"The beginning is probably a good place to start, Jake." I cross my arms over my chest, my face a perfect mask of indifference. "You know what? No, I actually don't care where you start. It's not going to make a lick of difference, but go on. Let's hear it."

He sighs, the pain in his eyes clear as he drops his hands to his hips. He takes two steps forward before I hold out my hand. "No. You can talk. But do not come over here."

He nods, licking his bottom lip as he does.

Fuck him for being attractive even when I want to hate him.

"I need you to know this," he gestures between us, "was never the plan."

I scoff, the reminder cutting deep. "Oh, believe me, I am aware."

"I don't mean it like that, Nat. I—, fuck." His eyes glance up at the ceiling before finding mine again. "I wasn't here in service to Gunner. I didn't even know what the job was until the first day in the office."

"No? How convenient for you."

"I wasn't here as a spy, Natalie. I know the guy, but we aren't even that close."

"Sure, ok. So, the plan wasn't to get info for Gunner and bail? Were you even actually *working* for Shield?"

"Of course I was! You're taking this way out of context. I knew Gunner. I didn't work for him. I wasn't a fucking informant."

"Oh, my god. *That's* why you settled for working under Knox, isn't it? So you had as little responsibility as possible and were free to fuck off for Gunner."

"That's not it at all." He sounds irritated now. I'll admit, it sounds far-fetched even as I'm saying it, but believing he always had bad intentions feels better right now. Believing he was never the guy I thought he was hurts less.

"Of-fucking-course you did; you needed the in."

"Would you please let me explain? We're so far off the rails. I know that I should have told you months ago. I'm aware I fucked up."

I don't answer, my mind reeling. He takes my silence as permission and takes a deep breath before continuing. "I knew Gunner, but we were not *friends.* Gunner and I went to high school together. When my brother passed, I fell into the wrong crowd, Gunner's crowd. It was a coping mechanism. They had the answer to my problems, a way for me to escape the hell I was living in."

"Cool, so he was your dealer? That seems like a weird thing to keep hidden, but go on." I'm being callous, but I'm too hurt to care. If he wanted me to be nice, he should have extended the same courtesy.

"No—I mean, yes, but no. We talked after that. I left for the army as soon as I graduated. Gunner reached out from time to time, and he was the only person I kept in touch with from my old life. When I got out, I had no job. No place to live. Gunner helped with both."

I scoff. Gunner being nice? Playing savior? That seems a little off-brand for him, but still I remain silent, letting him continue.

"He called after I got this job. I still don't know how he found out, but he's Gunner. He has his ways. He asked me to find dirt on Melanie to give him an edge in the divorce, and I told him no. I was never once passing information to him. He is completely separate from my life here. I know it's too late, and the damage is done, but I cut him out. I blocked his number. I'm not even talking to him anymore."

"How noble, Jake. And at what point was that? When we started sleeping together? When we agreed to sneaking around? Because sleeping with me and being friends with my sister's abusive ex felt too slimy? Was *that* the line?"

"No, I realized who he was well before I realized I had genuine feelings for you." He looks away, defeated.

He takes another step closer to me. "I take the work that keeps me on the road, away from home and out of my own damn head. And for most of my life, Gunner was the only person I thought was any sort of a friend through that. I see it now, obviously. It was never a friendship for him. And it was a crutch for me."

"Oh, you've realized the error of your ways? You should have told me months ago, Jake. You should have mentioned it when you started the damn job. Were you even going to tell me? Or at this point, were you just hoping I'd somehow never find out?"

My voice is low, barely above a whisper now. I'm teetering on the fence between anger and despair and, honestly, I don't know which way I'm going to fall when this is all said and done.

"Of course I would have. I *wanted* to tell you so many times, but the timing always felt wrong. I thought... I thought there would be a right time."

"When the fuck would that have been, Jake?"

"I really don't know. But then everything happened with Matt, and we finally had time to ourselves when I got back... I just... I forgot for a minute. And that's not an excuse, I know. It's not. You should have already known."

"Of course, you just *forgot.* I don't think you ever actually planned to tell me. I trusted you. I gave you pieces of myself that I don't share with anyone else. And you gave me bullshit in return."

"I didn't, Red. None of this is bullshit. Not telling you was a fucked up choice, but *this* is very much real." He lets out a heavy sigh, running his hands through his hair before leaving them on his head.

"Don't... you don't get to use a cute nickname right now."

He exhales. "I have spent more than half my life keeping people out. Every relationship I had prior to this tour was surface level, at best. They can't even be called relationships because I refused to open up. To form any connections at all. Not even with my own damn family. And then you waltzed in and crumbled every fucking wall I've built without even trying. I never stood a chance. Every moment between us was real."

I let the tears fall now, the effort of holding them back too much for me in this moment.

"As touching as that is, Jake, it doesn't matter." I swipe at my cheeks, trying desperately to get this out before I fall apart completely. "The fact of the matter is, you hid things from me. You hid a relationship with my sister's disgusting ex-husband. And I... I can't live with that."

The anguish on his face hurts, but I refuse to let it change my opinion on the matter. We were doomed from the start, and before I knew all of *this,* I did know *that*... I'm just the one who ignored it.

"I have to go. I have to be back before the show." With my head down, I make my way across the room, brushing by him on my way to the door. His fingers close around my arm as I pass, halting me in my tracks.

"Natalie..."

But I don't have it in me to hear him out any longer because there isn't anything that's going to change my mind. I shake my arm free from his grip as I pull open the door, stepping out into the hallway without a single glance back.

I breeze by Dex, stalking straight past the elevator as I make my way to the stairwell. The bright light bouncing off the stark white walls hurts my eyes, the tears still streaming. My steps echo through the empty space, the noise somehow deafening. I make it down the first flight of stairs, coming to a stop on the next landing. I know without even turning around, Dex is already there, two steps behind me.

Before I can open my mouth, before I can even react, he moves, the protective arms of my brother wrapping around me as every last piece of my carefully constructed armor crumbles and I fall apart.

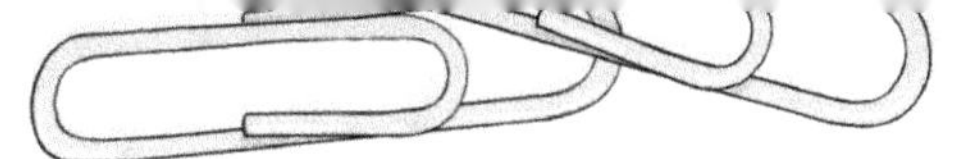
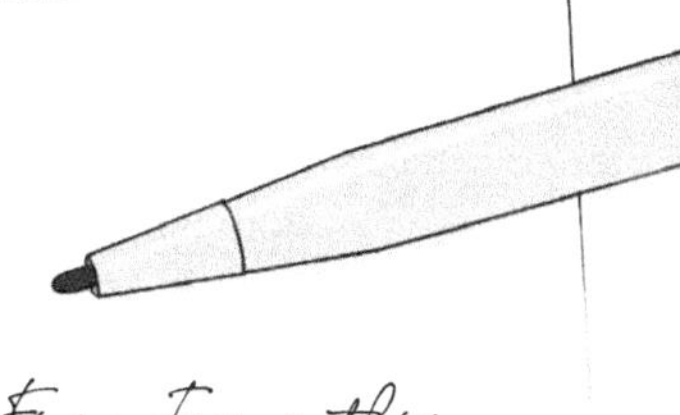

FORTY-ONE
NATALIE

Fried Food Fixes Everything

Somehow, I make it through both shows over the weekend. I spent two full days just going through the motions, putting on my PR smile, but my enthusiasm was not there. Avoiding my sister was nearly an impossible feat, but I managed it.

I want nothing more than to crawl into bed and sleep until this pain ends and my heart miraculously heals itself, but unfortunately, duty calls, and I don't get the luxury of taking time to mope. I thought working through this mess would fix me; it usually does. But not this time.

By the end of the second night, I'm dead on my feet. I'm so physically and emotionally drained from spending two days in my own head that I don't even wait for Dex in the green room to head back to the hotel. At the first available moment, I call a car to take me back, holing up in my hotel room. I keep the lights off, fumbling around in the darkness as I find sweats and a hoodie to change into.

I just want comfort, and right now that looks like a fluffy bed and my baggiest clothing.

I climb under the covers without even taking my hair out or washing my makeup off. My mind races, everything that went said, and unsaid, between Jake and I running laps around my brain.

I'm so fucking frustrated by everything that has gone down. Frustrated that he lied. Frustrated that I fell for him. Frustrated that I let myself get into this situation when I had told myself, after Sean, it was never happening again.

Just.

Fucking.

Frustrated.

Tears well in my eyes, and even that is frustrating because *how is there anything left to cry?* I have cried more in the last few days than I have in the last few years.

I hear the door to my room open, the soft light from the hallway illuminating the dark space. My back is to the door, so I can't see for sure who is checking in on me, but common sense tells me it's Melanie. She and Dex are the only two with the ability to get a key to my room. It's quiet for a few minutes as I lie there, unmoving, waiting patiently for her to back out of the room again.

Finally, when the hinges on the door creak again, I let out a long, low breath.

"Nat?" The bed dips as my sister's voice breaks through the silence. She settles onto the duvet right behind me, careful to keep her distance.

"Hmm?" It's obvious to both of us I'm awake right now, so I don't bother faking any differently.

"Everything ok?"

"Yep! Fine. Good. I'm just... exhausted tonight. It's been a long week."

"Do you want to talk about it?"

I try not to laugh. Do I want to discuss the fact that my life is falling apart in the middle of this cross-country tour?

No, no, I do not.

"All good, Mel. Nothing to talk about."

The bed shifts again as she stands, and I think I'm in the clear as I hear her shuffling around the room. But a few moments later, the covers lift and Melanie is sliding into bed, lying on her back right next to me.

"What are you doing?"

"Just lying here..."

"Why?"

"I just want to be here for you, even if you don't need anything from me."

My heart aches at the confession. "Really, Mel, I'm fine."

My voice breaks on the word fine, betraying me.

"Ok, I'm cozy though, so I'm going to stay here." She turns on her side, her position identical to my own now as we both lie staring at the same wall.

Several long minutes pass while neither of says anything.

I roll over, shifting to my left side as I lie on the bed facing my sister. It's so dark in here I can barely make out her features, less than a foot away from me, tucked under the white duvet on the bed. "Maybe… maybe I want to talk about it."

"I'm all ears."

"Why are men the worst?"

She laughs at that. "I wish I could tell you."

"When did Dex tell you?"

"After the show last night. You didn't think you were avoiding me all on your own today, did you?" I can hear the smile in her voice.

"Fuck, I'm sorry. I should have told you myself. I just… I didn't want to say anything before the show, and then avoiding you felt easier." I can see her nod in acknowledgment. "How much did he tell you?"

"Very little, actually. He told me Jake was fired. And that he was apparently friends with Gunner, but he did not elaborate."

A soft sob escapes me. Apparently, basic respect and a modicum of privacy are too much for me to handle right now.

I take a deep breath, taking a few moments to collect myself. "I just feel… blindsided, Mel. He's been with us essentially every fucking day for almost four months now. And there wasn't a single opportunity to mention he was *friends* with Gunner?"

"You have every right to feel hurt, Nat. To be angry about it. Dex said he took you over to see him?"

"He did." My chest throbs at the memory of the look on his face, but I push it down. The last thing he's getting from me right now is empathy. I heave a long sigh before I fill Melanie in, rehashing everything Jake shared yesterday afternoon. She listens quietly, her full attention on me. It's silent for a while after I finish, Melanie's eyes searching mine.

"I'm going to say something, but I just want you to listen." She pauses, brushing a rogue hair out of my face for me. "I want you to have this information because I think it matters."

I raise an eyebrow in her direction, but in the dark, I don't think she can tell.

"Gunner is, unfortunately, a charming and cunning person. He has a way of making you seem invaluable, while maintaining complete control of the relationship. I think maybe it's important to acknowledge the influence Gunner likely had over Jake, based on what he told you." She pauses, thinking before she goes on.

"I'm not taking Jake's side, but it's worth considering that when Jake had no one, Gunner positioned himself to look like the hero. And that's not an easy shield to see through. Jake being in security is beneficial to Gunner. Think of the people Jake knows, the places he's been, the things he's familiar with. I can easily believe Gunner kept Jake close enough that when Jake became useful to him, he was there—waiting to take advantage. That's what men like Gunner do. The world is theirs to manipulate, and they're disgustingly talented at turning the people around them into chess pieces."

My stomach turns over at her suggestion, not wanting to offer Jake any sort of benefit of the doubt.

"I'm in no way excusing the omission because he could have—and should have—handled it better. But I think it's probably worth looking at the full scope of the relationship. Just... coming from someone who's been there."

"I just don't see how this is something I can forgive him for."

"Maybe you can't. And that's fine too." She shifts, rolling onto her back.

"Why aren't *you* angrier? Why are you lying here being kind and understanding and not... forming a riot?"

"Oh, don't get me wrong. I'm fucking pissed at him. But I can be angry as hell and still understand. I'll forgive him eventually... maybe. But in this case, I can see his side of it too." She tips her head back in my direction. "If you're holding on because you think he wronged *me,* please don't. I shouldn't be part of the equation. It's about the two of you. What *you* feel for him and how he's treated *you.* If he can make it right with you."

I take in what she's saying to me as the door opens again, Dex appearing in the light of the hall that shines through the opening.

"Can I come in?" He asks. Mel gestures for him to enter with a wave of her hand, sitting up and turning on the light next to the bed as she does, the door shutting softly behind Dex.

He holds up a white takeout bag. "I brought reinforcements."

That makes me laugh. "You two are ridiculous. Neither of you needs to be here."

Dex kicks his shoes off, climbing onto the end of the bed before crossing his legs and dropping the bag into his lap.

"And yet, here we are…" He pulls out three containers, one full of fries, one full of deep fried mushrooms, and one full of sauces. "I heard fried food fixes, well, everything."

I sit up now too, the smell of the food causing my stomach to rumble.

"Sounds like that's a yes then."

A watery laugh slips out of me as I reach for a fry, feeling immense gratitude for my siblings. And though nothing really dulls the ache of being lied to, Dex is right. The fried food helps.

Sunday afternoon, Melanie and I, accompanied by Knox and Asher, meet up with Dex for an early dinner just outside the city. Our bus doesn't leave until late tonight, and when Mel suggested a sibling dinner, I reluctantly agreed. Anything to feel normal right now.

We settle at a table in the far corner of the restaurant. I watch as Knox and Asher find themselves a little alcove to the left, tucking themselves away as they chat with one another, an ache vibrating through my chest seeing the two of them.

Jake should be here.

I quickly shake the thought, knowing that dwelling on what happened, and what should be, will not make anything better.

"And for you, ma'am?" The server is staring at me expectantly, her notepad poised in her hand.

"Oh, um, I'm sorry. I'll have whatever she's having." I gesture at Melanie, having no clue whether they ordered drinks, a meal, or both. Truthfully, I don't care to decide either way.

The server smiles at me softly before she walks away.

I realize I've tuned out again when Dex moves his hand in front of my face, waving at the air as he says my name.

"Jesus, Natalie. Hello?"

I snap my attention over to him. "Yeah. Sorry. I'm here."

"Barely," Dex mutters.

I scrub my hand over my face. "I just, god, I'm sorry. I'm focusing. I'm focused."

"You've never been less focused, Nat." Melanie laughs as she picks up her water, hiding her face behind the oversized glass.

"Anyway, I was telling you to check your email." Dex gestures to the cell phone on the table, lying face down.

It's not even on. Jake sent me two texts yesterday morning, and I turned the damn thing off so I wouldn't have to deal with him. I have no interest in what they said.

I sigh as I power the phone on, tapping my fingers on the white linen tablecloth as I wait for the logo screen to disappear.

Eventually, my home screen loads. The photo of Melanie, Dex, and I on the night of her first show lighting up the screen.

"What am I even looking for, Dex? Personal? Work? Is it from you?"

He snatches my phone from my hand, scrolling through the endless list of emails that need my attention. Eventually, he finds what he's looking for and taps the screen, handing the phone back to me.

I take it from him, studying the message on the screen. It's a confirmation email for a flight leaving tonight, in four hours to be exact, heading back to Nashville. And it has my name on it.

"What is this?" I glance up, looking from him to Melanie, trying to figure out what the two of them are up to.

Mel's smile softens as she meets my stare. "A ticket home. So you can take a minute and decompress. Find some peace and quiet and deal with this however you need to."

"I'm *dealing* just fine, thank you very much."

"Are you though?" She asks.

"Some things are just too big to bury in work, Nat." Dex's hand lands on top of mine as he squeezes gently. "This is not a bad day, or an event gone wrong. This is a big deal, and you deserve to take the time to work through it."

I look over the ticket information again. "I can't just take four days off in the middle of the fucking tour, Dex. I have commitments. We have events this week."

"We know. But your team is more than capable of handling everything. They can get Mel through a single week of events without you."

I scoff. "Glad to know I'm needed."

"You are, Natalie. Just… not right now. *You* need you right now. You'll be in Philly on Friday well before the show starts. Take the time off."

I swallow down the lump in my throat as I meet each of their eyes.

"I… don't know what to say. Thank you seems inadequate."

"Thank you is more than enough, Nat." Dex thanks the server as she places our plates in front of us.

"Focus on you, Natalie. Take some time and allow yourself to *feel* instead of just pushing it off, ok? I'll book you a rage room, if you want. I've always wanted to do one of those."

Melanie's offer makes me laugh.

"No, I don't think I'm up for that. Thank you, guys, honestly."

And even though I don't want to, can barely force myself to, I manage to eat half my plate of food.

# FORTY-TWO
JAKE

Gravel crunches under the tires as my bike rolls slowly down the dead-end dirt road that leads the way to my escape. I let the bike idle as I come to a stop in front of the rusted-out bridge, taking in the view.

It's hard to believe that just two weeks ago, I was here with Natalie. It feels like a different time. A different place. So much has changed in that short period of time.

I know I screwed up. I've known it for a while, to be honest.

It was stupid to just ignore the problem.

I got comfortable with Natalie. After years of holding everyone at arm's length, having someone there for me, someone I wanted to be there for, fucked with my common sense.

I knew from the day I started unraveling Gunner's two sides that it was not a little misunderstanding. It was never something that was going to be swept under the rug.

I also knew that falling for Natalie would never end well, and I did it anyway. The truth is, I couldn't have stopped myself from falling even if I had tried.

Falling for her was inevitable.

Unavoidable.

I have no doubt in my mind she was meant to be mine with the way she slid so effortlessly behind every wall I had put in place. I spent over a decade keeping people out, and in a handful of weeks, she burrowed so far into the core of who I am, I couldn't cut her out if I wanted to.

So instead of doing the right thing, I did nothing.

Jesus Christ. I was somehow so wrapped up in Natalie I *forgot* Gunner existed. And now I'm in a mess of my own making with no idea how to get myself out of it.

The irony is that for the first time, I actually have friends, people I could have turned to, who I could talk to about this, and I fucked them over too.

Yet another reason I have a history of walling myself in, keeping myself from getting close to anyone and anything. I can recognize it as a pattern of self-destruction, but I don't know how to make it fucking stop.

I scoff at myself as I shut the bike off and pull my helmet off my head. A breeze rustles the strands of my hair; the May air warm. The sun is bright, but the uncomfortable smog of summer hasn't set in yet.

I slide the helmet onto the handlebars as I swing my leg over my bike. Winding my way through the trees, I take the side path down to the riverbank where Natalie and I came the first time I brought her out here.

It's funny that this has been my place for so many years, so many trips and different reasons for the visits. But now my two favorite spots out here hold the memories of her and me, and I'm not sure a million more visits would erase them, however momentary they were.

I slump down onto a log, leaning forward, my elbows propped on my knees as I watch the river moving in front of me.

My mind races as I sit there, turning the options over in my mind, ways to make this right. A simple apology won't be enough, not for a person like Natalie. And truthfully, it shouldn't be. I owe her more than that. I broke her trust, but I also broke Dex and Melanie's trust, and somehow, I have to prove to all three of them I can earn it back.

What I need to do is prove that my relationship with Gunner was insignificant, but I don't really know how you'd *show* someone that.

The frustration only grows the longer I turn over my options, the sun dipping lower in the sky, amber light bathing the woods in its warm tones.

My phone vibrates in my pocket, cutting through the silence. I fish it out, seeing my brother Noah's name on the screen.

Scrubbing my hand down my face, I debate answering. *Now* is really not the time for brotherly bonding. But I remember I promised myself, and him, I would try.

"Hey Noah." I do my best to keep the exhaustion from seeping into my voice.

"Jake. How's it going?" I debate how to answer that, trying to decide just how honest I want to be with someone I truly don't know. I wait a beat too long because Noah responds to himself before I can. "That good, huh?"

"No, it's good. It's fine. You know the usual." I cringe at my response, hating how fucking fake it sounds, even to me.

"Yeah, seems like it."

"I just—it's been a long week."

"Anything I can help with?"

"No, man, it's just something I have to figure out. What did you call for?"

"Mostly just to see if you'd answer." He laughs at his own joke. "I didn't know how serious you were about reconnecting, figured it was worth a shot."

"I meant it. I'd love to visit again. Maybe after I get this mess cleaned up, I can make some plans." The feeling of defeat weighs heavily on my chest as I try to even think past tomorrow.

"You sure you don't want to talk about it?" I appreciate his offer, but this whole thing is so new. It's the first time we've talked since I saw him in Chicago. I can't just unload a truckful of my stupidity on the guy.

"I don't—nah, I'm good. I won't do that to you." I try to laugh it off.

"Listen, I get it. This is awkward, but we've gotta start somewhere, right? All those years aren't gonna make up for themselves. Maybe unloading on a near stranger is what you need right now."

"It feels… weird." I hedge, trying to decide if I'm really about to give in to this ridiculous idea.

"Nah. Your obsession with those dot candies? The ones that come stuck to paper? That was weird." We both laugh at the memory I'd forgotten, the lightness between us a welcome change.

"Fair point." I take a deep breath, running my palms over my jeans as I try to decide where to start, how to catch Noah up on the entire fucking mess that is my life right now. After another gentle insistence from Noah, I decide just to start at the beginning, no holds barred, and lay out the entire situation for him. The relationship with Gunner, the job with Shield. Melanie and Natalie. The entire tour. I talk more in the next thirty minutes than I have in the last year, Noah quietly chimes in, letting me know I've got his full attention.

It feels good to get this off my chest. Sharing the burden with someone else for a minute. It's fucking strange to have my guts splayed out to a man I barely know, but he's the one with a wife. The one who's got his shit together.

And at this point, what do I have to lose?

When I've wrapped up, Noah blows out a breath. "Wow, you do have a mess on your hands, don't you?"

I choke out a half laugh at the brutal honesty. "Little bit. And now I have no idea how to even begin to make this right."

"Well, if you want to fix things with Natalie, fix them with her siblings first."

"What do you mean?"

"No woman is going to forgive you if you're fucking over her family. I'm making assumptions here, but considering all you said, it sounds like they're pretty close. So, if you've fucked them over, you gotta fix that first."

"I... did. Yeah."

"So... undo it." He says, like that's it. That's the answer.

I scoff. "Yeah, ok. I'll just erase it all. Great plan."

"You said her sister is still in the middle of a nasty divorce, right?"

"Yeah, sounds like it."

"And Gunner specifically asked you to spy for him?"

"Yes?" I answer, not sure where he's going with this line of questioning.

"Then here's what you do: You call Melanie's lawyer and tell her what you have. Offer witness testimony."

"You can do that?"

He huffs a laugh. "Yes, you can do that. When divorces get messy enough, lawyers can actually seek witnesses to strengthen their case."

"Why does that sound too easy?"

"Well, there's no guarantee it will accomplish anything. Or that it will undo any of the damage you did in hiding the relationship from them. But it sounds like Gunner is trying to falsify information against Melanie to sway the settlement in his favor. I'd bet their business arrangement, or even the prenup, has carve-outs for malicious behavior or ill will. Like I said, it might not *do* anything, but it's worth a shot if you really want to fix this. If nothing else, it clears up the nature of your relationship with Gunner for them."

"What kind of law do you practice?"

He laughs. "I work in mergers and acquisitions. This is not my wheelhouse, but I think you have enough information here to be dangerous."

"Shit, if I knew you'd have all the answers—"

He cuts me off with a laugh. "Hardly have any answers here, man. Just a different perspective."

"Yeah, I guess so."

"The ball is in your court this time; let me know how it goes."

"I will. Thanks Noah."

"Anytime, Jake."

When the call disconnects, I feel lighter than I have in days. Noah's right. One phone call may not change anything, but having a plan in place feels like progress. If I can do this for Melanie, then I can focus on how to make things right with Natalie.

I scroll through my phone, deciding there's no point in delaying. When I find the number I'm looking for, I hit send, waiting for an answer.

The call connects; the harsh tone exactly what I expect in greeting. "Jake. This is a surprise."

"Hey, Dex. I need your help."

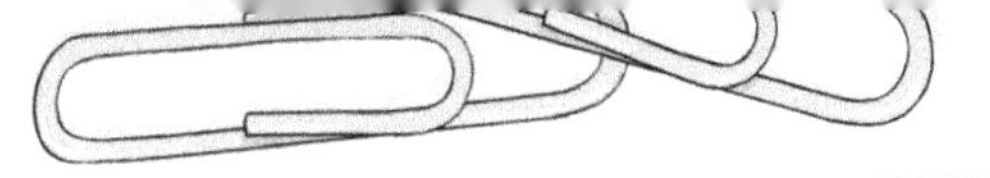

FORTY-THREE
NATALIE

Out Of My Comfort Zone

It's near midnight when my plane lands on Sunday back in Nashville. Exhausted and emotionally fraught, I'd like to claim temporary insanity as the cause of the tears that broke out when I found a driver and car waiting for me at the airport.

I've always been the caretaker. Ever since our parents died, it has been my job to make sure my siblings were taken care of. Yes, of course they get the occasional meal, show up with coffee... I have very kind and considerate siblings. They were by my side when I went through my nasty breakup with Sean, but this?

This attention to detail and level of forethought are almost overwhelming. I'm so full of all these emotions I don't know what to do with that being cared for feels like too much.

I rein it in for the drive home, keeping myself in check long enough to lug my shit into my apartment and collapse onto my bed. I can't be bothered to grab a shower or even change out of my clothes.

As soon as I'm in the comfort and quiet of my own space, the last two weeks come rushing back to me, every abysmal moment and painful memory of what I thought I had and how it immediately came crashing down rather remarkably slams into me and I collapse under the weight of holding myself up.

I climb under my covers, have a good cry, and sleep for the next sixteen hours.

The bell jingles over the door of The Brew as I enter through the front door. It's a weird feeling, not only being back here, but being back here alone. The Brew is my favorite place to come with Mel, and we always slip in through the back door, but today, I'm just another face in the crowd. A regular Joe, and honestly, it feels nice.

I spot the privacy setup near the back corner, and the little balloon inside my chest inflates just a touch. I love that they're still holding space for us, even though we let them know we wouldn't be back for several months.

I make my way toward the front counter, stepping into the line on this busy Wednesday morning.

It's been two full days since I flew back to Nashville, and I won't lie. They were rough. I left my bed only when my body required me to, surviving on the saltines that were just about the only thing left in my pantry.

This morning, I woke up feeling marginally better and a hell of a lot more put together after finally getting a shower. I guess there's something to be said for letting your body rest. Waking up with an appetite and a desire to rinse the grease out of my hair felt like a small victory, so I decided to brave the real world and grab breakfast at my favorite place.

Before I left, I took my time in the bathroom, drawing a bubble bath, finding my nicest shampoo and conditioner. I even lit a candle and turned on some music to really give this fresh start my all.

When it's my turn, I quickly greet the cashier before placing my order and sliding my card through the reader. Shuffling off to the side, my eyes scan the café as I wait for my name to be called.

I watch as a little girl runs back and forth from the mug display to a man that I assume is her parent several times, her blonde pigtails bobbing and her yellow princess dress swirling around her legs as she spins, a soft giggle slipping from her as she bumps right into the small table below the community events board. The handouts on the table tip precariously over the edge, fluttering to the ground and scattering at her feet. Two tiny hands come up to cover her mouth as she realizes the mess that has been left in her wake.

I take a couple of quick steps in her direction, bending down to help collect the fallen flyers. The little girl's dad scoops her up, corralling the child before bending down to lend a hand as well.

"Oh, I've got these! You have your hands full."

He smiles down at me. "Are you sure?"

"Absolutely. It'll take two seconds."

"Thank you so much. C'mon, princess, let's take this tornado somewhere else." He straightens up, carrying her back to their own table.

I shuffle the flyers back into presentable piles, sorting them into two stacks. Scanning the designs as I sort, I note that one flyer is for a pole class in downtown Nashville, tonight.

I scoff at the ridiculous idea of me trying to pole dance. I can barely dance with my feet on the ground. It would be comical, to say the least.

I leave the pole flyer next to the line dancing flyers and head back toward my waiting spot near the counter just as I hear the barista yelling next to me, but it's not my name they're calling.

"Jake! French Vanilla Cold Brew!"

My heart stops beating and my breath catches in my chest. My eyes dart around the café, looking for Jake, but as a man I don't recognize reaches for the coffee cup, I realize it's not *my* Jake.

The sobering feeling of disappointment washes through me. A heavy feeling in my stomach weighs on me at the realization that every Jake from here on out will never be *my* Jake.

And just like that, I feel stupid all over again for thinking there was ever a Jake that was mine.

When I make it back home, any appetite I may have had is completely gone. I toss the food into the fridge and take my coffee to the couch, where I collapse onto the cushions.

That familiar urge to busy myself rears its head. It's been literally a handful of hours since I left my bed, and already I'm itching for distraction, something to occupy me.

I take a sip of my coffee as I lie starfish across my couch. I could go find my phone. I haven't powered it on since I got in the other night. It's probably teeming with messages that need to be answered, problems that need to be solved.

I feel a pinch of excitement in my chest at the idea of having a purpose, something to do. Someone to help.

Melanie's voice in my head reminds me that throwing myself into work for others isn't taking care of myself though.

There has to be... something. What the fuck do people do if they're not working? I'm used to being so overrun with tasks to accomplish that the prospect of having any amount of time for myself is overwhelming.

My mind flits back to the flyer from the coffee. The pole class tonight downtown.

I couldn't.

Could I?

It would be laughable at best. I'd probably make a fool of myself.

But... so what if I did? Maybe I should use this time to try something new. To do something I would never normally make time for, much less fathom even attempting. I can't remember the last time I went to a gym or any kind of fitness class.

Because you're too busy taking care of everyone but yourself.

I hate it when Melanie and Dex are right. It's time I did something for myself. I sit up, making my way across the room for my laptop before returning to the couch. I power it on and wait as the colorful circle loops around, loading the home screen.

A quick Google search tells me the class starts at seven. I take my laptop back to my desk, jotting the address down on a sticky note before I power the computer off again.

I grab my coffee and my purse, heading out of my apartment. With an entire day in front of me to do anything I want, I decide a new outfit for a new hobby is a good place to start.

What the fuck was I thinking?

Go to a pole class. It'll be fun!

God, I'm fucking dumb.

My arms scream at me as I grab onto the pole and lift, exactly like the instructor demonstrated. But somehow I just look like a baby koala trying to scramble up a tree that's too tall for it.

Actually, that's not true. I'm sure koalas are born with the ability to climb. They probably look graceful from the first moment they're out of the womb.

Fuck my life.

A low groan escapes my chest as my palms slip down the metal pole, the sweat making my hands slick.

"Use your legs more." I jump as the instructor comes up behind me, a smile on her face as she gestures to the pole in front of me. "You're trying to do too much of the lifting with your arms; use the muscles in your thighs to help you grip the pole and give your arms a little relief."

I nod in acknowledgment, reaching up, wrapping my left leg around the pole again, but this time, squeezing my thigh muscles as I step forward and swing around the pole.

"That's better! See how you hold the bar more evenly with both halves of your body?"

"Yes, much better." I mutter, though I do feel a little more accomplished having stayed on the pole for this full rotation. I had way more success with the walking portion of this class. We spent the first fifteen minutes learning how to walk while holding the pole, and *that* was something I could understand. Throwing my body around this thing and trying to look elegant?

Beyond me.

The instructor calls for a quick water break, and I plop myself down on the side wall, popping the lid on my new water bottle.

I brush the sweat-soaked strands of hair out of my eyes as I take in the space. The class is nearly full; apparently, the free class offer for new attendees is a good selling point. Close to two dozen women stand around the room, talking quietly among themselves.

"First class?" A gorgeous blonde with a waist-length ponytail sits down beside me, water bottle in hand.

"Yeah, how can you tell?" We both laugh.

"It's different, isn't it? Everyone makes it look so effortless and beautiful, but it's a lot of work."

"How long have you been doing this?" I gesture to the room in front of us.

"About a year. I come twice a week. It's been a really nice way to let go, and the group of girls here is really fantastic."

"That's awesome. I don't take classes of any type, so this whole thing is new to me."

"Really, why not?"

"No time."

"You know, I said that too. But when you find something you love, you somehow find the time to make it happen."

I think back to this summer, sneaking around with Jake, and I realize she's entirely right. If I *want* to make time for something—or someone—clearly, I can. I have just never given myself permission.

"I suppose that's probably true. I'm Natalie, by the way." I hold out a hand, the professional in me ever present.

She returns the handshake and offers a genuine smile. "Isla."

We spend the rest of our break chatting, eventually swapping phone numbers so we can keep in touch.

"Alright y'all! Let's start the second half of this class!" The instructor's voice carries through the open space, interrupting us.

We both close up our water bottles and make our way back to our respective poles.

I spend the remaining time in the class trying, and mostly failing, to learn the techniques the instructor demonstrates. By the end, though, I feel immensely proud of myself.

I may not have done it *well*, but I did it. I tried something completely new and totally out of my comfort zone. And for the first time in nearly a week, I thought about Jake for only a single moment while I did it.

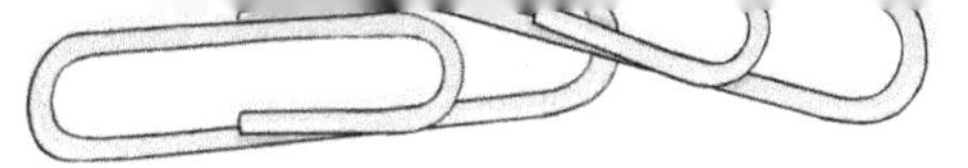
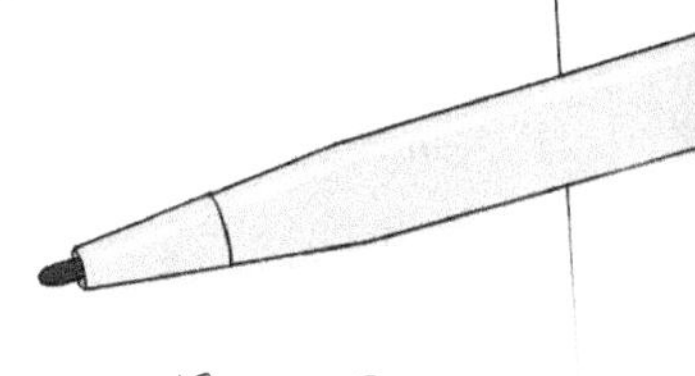

FORTY-FOUR
NATALIE

It takes a good hour for me to get through a routine shower when I return home from the pole class. I'm really glad I tried something new, just for the hell of it, but tomorrow is going to be absolutely miserable when I try to pull myself out of bed. Muscles I didn't even know I *had* ache right now.

I shake my towel out, hanging it over the bar before I make my way back into the living room. Deciding to continue on my trend of doing things for me, I light a few candles and grab my favorite vinyl out of the cabinet, turning on the record player before I detour to my desk, grabbing my phone.

For the first time in four days, I power it on, but work is not my intention. I find several messages from Mel and Indy—funny little quotes and several sassy cat memes from Indy and I can't help but laugh to myself. I'm searching for the perfect one to reply with when Indy's face pops up on my phone, a photo of her and Melanie I took at the graveyard tour and assigned to her contact.

Without hesitation, I hit enter, watching as the photo turns to Indy's real face, a huge smile lighting up the screen.

"Hey, Nat!" Her bubbly personality is constantly present; a trait I love about her.

"Hey, Ind. How's it going?"

"It's good! Busy. Mel crushed her interviews today."

"Oh good! I'm glad to hear that." It occurs to me that I didn't even stop to think about what was on Mel's schedule today, I was so busy shopping for new workout gear. I feel a stab of guilt for not thinking of her, but then I remember *this is what she wanted.* I'm supposed to be thinking of myself.

"What are you up to? Are you in for the night?" I watch as Indy sets her phone down on the hotel room coffee table, sitting back against the couch as she gets comfortable.

"Yeah, I am. I just got out of the shower." I quickly fill her on the pole class, which has her in stitches.

"Oh my god I would have paid money to be there. Take me with you next time."

"I don't think there's going to be a next time. I can't fathom putting my body through that again."

"You're thirty-four, Natalie. Not ninety-four."

"Yeah, and that's about a decade too old for that shit." We both laugh as I cross the room, flipping my record and turning the volume down. Before I can settle back into the couch, my doorbell rings.

"That's... weird. I don't think anyone even knows I'm in town?" I trade looks with Indy, who just shrugs. "Hang on, I'm putting you down while I go get that."

I set her on the arm of the sofa as I trek through the entry way, opening the door to find a delivery boy standing there, giant giftbag in hand. "Natalie Bennett?"

"Uh, yes?" I clear my throat, confused. "That's me."

"This is for you. Enjoy!" He shoves the oversized bag into my hands before marching off, job apparently done.

"Thank you?" I'm talking to myself as I kick the door closed. I take the bag over the couch, grabbing my phone as I plop down. On the screen, Mel is now sitting alongside Indy, both of them with giant wine glasses in their hands.

"Mel, hi!"

She waves at the screen. "Hey, Nat. Whatcha got there?"

I situate the phone on the table in front of me, watching myself in the tiny mirror image in the corner. You can hardly see me behind this obnoxious bag. "I... don't know? It was just dropped off."

"Open it! Let's see what it is." Indy claps her hands in encouragement.

I can't help but laugh at her as I set the bag at my feet, pulling out all of the excess tissue paper in the bag. When I can finally see the contents, tears spring to my eyes, unbidden.

"This is from you two, isn't it?" I pull out a gigantic bottle of wine, my favorite kind, along with half the contents of the candy aisle and some of my favorite chips. My couch is littered with my favorite snacks when I turn back to the screen. "You guys!"

Mel and Indy exchange conspiratorial glances before Indy says, "Maybeeee."

"Free time is hard to come by on this tour, but we really wanted to have a girls' night. We took a gamble you didn't have plans while you were at home." Melanie laughs.

"Well, you'd be right. Apparently, I'm about to eat my weight in chocolate."

Indy pulls out a basket of snacks, very similar to the ones scattered around me. "Perfect. Me too then."

I excuse myself to find a wine glass, taking the opportunity to find a tissue while I'm up. The thought that these two people, who I see on a daily basis, wanted to surprise me with a girls' night is borderline too much for me to handle right now.

When I return, the two of them are whispering to one another.

"So how's it going?" I settle in against my couch. "Have I missed anything this week?"

I watch as they exchange a look before Indy hops up, racing out of the screen. I can hear her voice as she moves away from the phone, "No work talk, Natalie. It's girls' night!"

"Fine." I glare at my sister, knowing the two of them mean well, but being annoyed, nonetheless. "Full catchup when I get back?"

"Yep! Absolutely." She takes a drink of her wine just as Indy comes back with a remote in hand, queuing up a movie on their end. I do the same, syncing up my play time with theirs.

I cuddle up under a blanket, grabbing for the nearest snack, with the girls on the phone propped in front of me. I can't help but feel immensely grateful for the world's best friends as we settle in. And for the first time in an entire week, I don't think about Jake until the next day.

My suitcase clatters along behind me on the tile floor of the Philadelphia International Airport. For being first thing on a Friday morning, the space is not as congested as I would have expected it to be, but I welcome the calm crowds.

As much as I hate to admit it, Dex and Melanie were right. The time off is not something I would have given myself permission to do without their push, but I feel excited this morning, looking forward to getting back to work. But most importantly, my head feels clearer, my heart a little lighter.

Truthfully, I don't know how long it's going to take me to feel whole again after this entire disaster with Jake, but I found some much-needed clarity on the situation. I'm just going to focus on *me* and hope that the rest of it takes care of itself. It's all I can do going forward.

Coming in at the last gate, I have a long walk to get myself to the correct pickup area where a car is waiting to take me to the crew's hotel. I'm debating a quick pit stop for a fresh coffee when I see a pressed penny machine tucked against the wall just a few feet in front of me.

Before I can think better of it, I shuffle my belongings over in front of the machine, fishing out a penny and the change needed to operate the machine from my purse at my side.

It still feels childish to be collecting pressed pennies, but if I'm honest with myself, I love doing it. I love my little collection, flipping through my books and seeing all the places I've been. It might be too late to collect all the tour stops now, but fuck it. I can start today, right now, with the Liberty Bell design being pressed onto a shiny copper penny as I crank the handle on the machine.

The penny falls into the dispenser, and I fish it out, holding the copper oval out as I take in the bell, with the city name printed neatly underneath it. The design even printed perfectly centered, which almost never happens.

I smile to myself as I slip the penny into my wallet before I continue my trek through the airport, a little zip of energy racing through me as I make my way outside and into the waiting car.

I weave my way around the concourse several hours later, making my way down to the main floor. It looks like the soundcheck hasn't started, so I'm just in time.

It takes a few minutes before I spot Dex's head, just a handful of inches higher than most of the people surrounding him. I cut through the crowd, making my way toward him.

"Morning," I sing-song as I come up beside him. Shifting his attention over to me, a big smile lights up his face.

"Natalie!" He leans into me, wrapping me in a hug with the arm not holding his clipboard as he drops a kiss to the top of my head. "You look good. Did you get some rest?"

"I did. Thank you. I think the time off was good for me."

"I told you it would be." He's still smiling as he pulls back. "Mel just took off with the band to start the soundcheck."

"Oh, ok. I'll find her after. I have a meeting with my team in about an hour to catch up."

"Oh, good timing."

"What did I miss while I was away? Anything good?"

"Good? Uh, nope." He clears his throat. "Nothing good. Nothing new."

I throw him a look. "Why are you being weird?"

"Not weird at all. Just nothing to share." We start walking, Dex's long strides making me walk at a brisk pace just to keep up. "Well, actually, Knox is gonna have Asher work with you now, so he can catch the new guy up to speed as quickly as possible."

"The new guy?"

"Yeah, Shield moved guys around to replace Jake."

My breath catches. A wave of sadness rushes through me, deflating the happy little bubble I've been floating around in.

Of course they'd replace Jake. That's obvious.

"Right. Ok. Well, I can work with Asher." I feel a small sense of relief at that actually, finding comfort in knowing I don't have to work with anyone new.

"Yeah, I told Knox you'd appreciate that."

"How… is he?" I hesitate to ask, not really wanting to bring Jake up, but I'm not the only one Jake lied to.

"Knox? He's fine. I mean, all things considered. Hitting Jake probably cleared up most of his frustration with him." Dex chuckles to himself.

"Oh, good. That's… good." I really wish it was that easy for me. I don't know, maybe I should try it. "Do you know what he told Asher? Or any of the team?"

"I think he just told them Jake quit. He respects your privacy, Nat. There's only a handful of us that have any other pieces of the story."

I nod as we continue to move through the venue, Dex clearly on a mission to get to where he's going.

"Alight, well, I'll leave you to it. I need to go find Jamie before I show up at the staff meeting."

"Ok. I was going to say—" He stops abruptly, turning to face me. "Shit, sorry. We're ripping the band-aid off."

Before I can work out what that means, a tall man with dark brown skin comes to stop in front of us.

"Hey, Caleb." Dex greets the man with a wide smile. "This is Natalie. She's the PR manager for Melanie. You'll probably end up working on many of the events with her and Mel."

"Hey Natalie, it's nice to meet you." He sticks his hand out in greeting.

"Nat, Caleb is the new Jake." I can see Dex scanning my face as I greet Caleb, but I'm careful to keep my PR smile firmly intact as I meet his reach with mine.

"Hi, it's a pleasure. Welcome to the crew."

We chat for a few minutes, trading niceties, before I excuse myself, hustling off to find a quiet room where I can be by myself before I have to face my team.

It wasn't the worst thing in the world, meeting Jake's replacement. At least I handled that surprise better than the one at The Brew.

Baby steps.

I don't have to have my shit together, but at the very least, I know I can make progress.

Even if it's in baby steps.

FORTY-FIVE
JAKE

The week ends much better than it began. It took some convincing, but I got Melanie's lawyer's information from Dex. He had to do a little digging for me, which took a couple of days, but when I called Thursday morning, they were receptive to what I had to offer.

I laid out what I could share with them over the phone, and Melanie's team said they'd be back in touch to collect an official statement. If it goes to court, I may have to testify, but the threat of damaging Gunner's reputation might be enough to get him to cooperate.

With that plan in motion, I can turn my attention to the one that really matters: how to make it up to Natalie. I really don't know the *right* thing to do here. What I need is time—time to make it up to her, prove to her she can trust me.

I think it over, debating what my options are as I shake out my duffel bag, deciding I need to get around to washing all the clothing I brought home from the tour last week. I'm sorting the clothes into piles when the pressed penny from the morning in downtown Nashville with Natalie falls out onto the floor, the dark copper making a metallic sound as it bounces off the tile floor of my laundry room.

Bending over, I scoop the penny up, turning it over in my hand. I run my thumb over the embossing, a smile tugging at the corner of my lips. I pivot, putting the penny safely on the shelf before I finish sorting and start the washer.

I'm walking into the kitchen when my phone rings on the island, Dex's name flashing across the screen. I quicken my pace, grabbing for the phone on the third ring.

"Hey, Dex." I'm surprised to hear from him, given everything, and I'm instantly worried something bad has happened. "Everything ok?"

"Hey, Jake. Yeah, everything's good. Listen, I was calling because I need a favor."

"Ok." He could ask for just about anything right now, and I'd figure out how to make it happen. But I suspect he knows that.

"Knox and I have been talking. The new security guard is good, but he's a little more… single-focused. He doesn't have the eye that you do, or the intuition, and he can't manage a liaison role with his security role."

"That's not all that surprising. I got a little carried away with all the things I was doing at every stop."

He laughs. "Right, so there's a gap in our team now. We need a person who can coordinate with venue security, who can handle the details of the venue and the contacts more thoroughly. We need an actual security liaison on the team."

"And why are you telling me this? Did you want me to send you recommendations? Knox could give you Connor's number?"

"I don't want Connor. And I don't want recs."

I'm confused about why he's calling, then. "I don't—"

"I want you, asshole. I want you to come back on this tour and pick up where you left off, only this time, your sole focus is on venue coordination. You'd be part of the Melanie Bennett Tour Management Team."

"Work for you?"

"You can call me Boss Man; that's fine."

I scoff at that. Of-fucking-course. "Dex, I don't think—"

He plows on, ignoring me. "There's a catch."

I'm quiet while I wait for the other shoe to drop.

"You have to fix your shit with my sister first."

The tiny bubble of hope that sprung up in my chest at his offer deflates as quickly as it surfaced. "Dex, that's not gonna happen. I don't really see Natalie being willing to forgive and forget anytime soon."

"You might be surprised. Fix it, because I really need you here, Jake."

"Wait—Dex."

"Yeah?"

"Why are you doing this?" I'm so confused right now.

"Doing what exactly, Jake?"

"Offering me this job? Shouldn't you be like—Team Natalie?" It sounds stupid, but I'm genuinely surprised he's reaching out to *me* after everything.

"Because I've been watching you with my sister for months, Jake. She needs someone like you, prioritizing her. Helping her prioritize herself. And while I do think that withholding secrets is stupid as fuck, I also feel like you didn't mean to hurt her by doing it. So if she forgives you, that means she trusts you won't do it again. And you're really fucking good at your job, man. I need you."

I laugh at that. "That's a lot of assumptions to be making right now."

"It is. Don't make me regret it."

With that, he hangs up, leaving no room for debate or argument.

I think over his proposal. Bridging the gap between the team security and the venue security would be a nice gig. All the perks of working on tour and a lot less work than being a bodyguard, to be quite honest. And I'd still get to be on tour with Natalie.

The problem is, I still don't know how I'm supposed to make things right.

FORTY-SIX

NATALIE

Melanie passes me the bag of Twizzlers, holding them out to me from where she's sitting on the couch, wrapped up in a blanket. I'm on the floor beside her, my back to the couch, facing Dex, who's lounging in the chair across the coffee table from us.

Tonight's show went well. I was busy. Melanie was on fire. And all things considered, it was really good. We're back at the hotel now, the clock on the hotel living room desk reading 1:15am.

"My lawyer called again today," Mel says casually as she bites off a large piece of the red rope in her hand. "I guess Gunner might end up settling after all. Not having to go to court would be so fucking nice."

She flops back onto the pillow behind her.

"Wait, what? Seriously? Why didn't you tell us that sooner?"

"We were all busy. I got the call on the way over to the stadium and then didn't see you for a bit. Anyway, I'm telling you now."

"That would be amazing. What got him to change his mind?"

"My lawyers called his and said they were gathering witness testimony. And I guess it spooked him. So, honestly, we can thank Jake."

That catches me off guard. "Jake... why?"

Mel exchanges glances with Dex across the room, her eyes going wide.

"I... assumed you knew."

"Knew what?" I look from her to Dex. "What would I know!?"

"I..." Mel trails off, and I see Dex shaking his head.

"What the fuck, you guys?"

"Jake didn't tell her," Dex says to Melanie, still leaving me in the dark.

"I got a call while you were off, from my legal team. Jake contacted them to see if he could provide a character witness in the case. He was willing to testify if they wanted, go on the record about Gunner trying to spy on me."

"Why would he do that?" I ask, confused beyond belief.

"Because he feels bad, Natalie. I really don't think he ever had malicious intent. And as much as it's helping me, I think it's more so for you."

"How is that for me?"

Melanie raises an eyebrow at me. "Because he's well aware you won't forgive him if you feel like he's wronged me."

"Well, he's right there. He can fix it all he wants, but I'm not about to just forget what he did."

"I think in this case you might consider forgiving him, Nat."

"I just… it seems too easy. To just let him off the hook."

"I think he's beating himself up enough for the both of you." Dex chimes in as he reaches over, making grabby hands for the Twizzlers I'm holding.

I hand them over the coffee table, leaning forward. "And how would you know that?"

"I may have… had a couple of calls with him." Dex hedges, snatching the candy from me.

"What the fuck? Has everyone here been talking to Jake but me?"

"Hey, I didn't talk to Jake. I talked to my legal team." Mel bites off a chunk of her candy.

I roll my eyes. "Close enough."

"I called him, yes." Dex clarifies. "Well, he called me first. I called him a few days later."

"Why?"

"Knox is having a hell of a time managing security with him gone. The new guy is a good bodyguard, but he's *new*. He doesn't have Jake's experience. All the gaps he'd bridged for us are showing. I don't have anyone on my team I can spare—or who has the knowledge needed— to do what he did. So I called Jake."

"And how is Jake going to help you?"

"I offered him a job as a security liaison."

"YOU WHAT?" I blink, staring at my brother as I try to process all the information being thrown at me.

"Calm down. It was a conditional offer." He shoves the rest of his Twizzler in his mouth before he fishes a new one out of the bag.

"Conditional on what?"

"Your approval."

I'm so confused, not comprehending why my brother would offer Jake a job behind my back. "My approval?"

"That's what I said. I'm not hiring someone that you can't stand to be around. But I thought you might…" he trails off, letting the sentence hang open between us.

"Might what, Dex?" I ask through gritted teeth.

"Might have had a change of heart about him."

"In a week? I don't think so."

"Well, to be fair, I also assumed he would have told you he went to Melanie's lawyers. Clearly, I was wrong about that."

"I haven't taken a single phone call or answered any texts from him since he was fired."

"Well, maybe you should," Mel chimes in from behind me, but I don't acknowledge her.

"I don't understand how the two of you can just forgive and forget like this isn't a big fucking deal."

"We're not forgetting anything, Natalie. But he's a fucking human being. And people make mistakes. It's what you do in the aftermath of those mistakes that defines who you are as a person." Dex pauses, the crinkling of the candy bag the only noise in the room. "Am I pissed at him? Yes. And I probably will be for a while. I think we all will. But do I think he's a bad person who wanted to hurt either of you? No, I truly don't."

As he passes the candy back to me, I can't help but wonder if maybe I am being too hard on Jake, if the hurt is overriding my ability to consider the fact that he's trying to make it right.

I'm currently holding myself together with a very tenuous thread. I don't know if I have any more of those left to offer. If I give him a chance to prove I can trust him, is it worth the risk of getting hurt again? Will I survive it if I do?

I guide the group of photographers around the front of the stage on night two in Philadelphia.

"The left side here will have the best viewpoints of the third act. She spends a lot of time moving around the stage, but the power poses you're going to want to capture will be when she pauses on this side facing the audience. You'll have unrestricted access if you cut right through here," I walk them through the barriers. "Be sure the press pass is visible and acknowledged by Security before you do it or you'll find yourself back out front on the sidewalk real fast. Our guards down front don't mess around."

There's a round of chuckles from the group. "I think that's about it, unless anyone has any questions for me."

No one does, so I let them go on their way, freeing them to move around the main floor until the fans show up.

I'm dead on my feet today. Mel, Dex, and I went to bed not long after the discussion about Jake last night, but I spent hours tossing and turning as I mulled over the information they shared, their opinions on the whole situation. It seems like a cop-out, to just forgive and forget, make up with him. I don't even know if he *actually* wants to be together. We've never talked about it. We've never discussed whether there is a future for the two of us.

I sigh as I scrub my hand over my face, desperately in need of a nap. Or maybe just some caffeine. The energy drink in my purse back in the media room is calling to me, so I decide to take a quick break, making my way across the floor and back onto the concourse, Asher following along quietly in my wake.

The last two days have been all right with him. He's quiet, keeps to himself mostly. I didn't ask if he knows what happened with Jake, and Asher hasn't brought him up either.

"I'm just going to head over to the media room and grab a quick snack before everything gets too chaotic in here," I tell Asher as we close in on the hallway I'm heading for. "You're more than welcome to join me, but if you want the chance to take a break of your own, now might be the time."

He nods at me. "I think I will. Been dying for a bathroom break."

"Oh my god, Asher. You don't have to watch me like a hawk. Please take bathroom breaks when you need them." I laugh.

"I know, I know. But you were way out in the middle of the stadium, and I was just waiting until the timing was better."

He waves me off as he continues down the concourse toward the men's room. I make my way past the concessions, hanging a right at the sign that reads "front offices."

I'm only a handful of steps down the short hallway when I come to a complete stop, Jake's tall figure leaning against the wall, his head ducked low, halfway between me and the room I was aiming for.

My stomach bottoms out, that sudden feeling of complete loss of control convincing my body we're now at the top of the highest drop on the world's tallest rollercoaster instead of firmly on the ground, standing in front of my... ex-something.

We never defined what we were to each other, and here I am, my fight or flight in full-fucking-force at seeing him again for the first time since everything unraveled.

"What—" I look around the deserted hallway. "What are you doing here?"

His head snaps up, and his eyes meet mine, so many unspoken words passing between us. "You didn't answer my calls. Or texts."

"No, no, I did not. Been a little busy."

"Or you've been avoiding me."

He pushes off the wall, his hands tucked into the pockets of that damn leather jacket as he makes his way toward me. He comes to a stop a few feet in front of me, the dark circles under his eyes evident. The bruise on his cheek from where Knox hit him fading to a greenish-yellow color. His facial hair is messy, his usually neat neck peppered with new growth.

I swallow, my throat dry. "Little bit of that, too."

"Can we talk?"

"I don't think there's really anything left to talk about, Jake." I sidestep him, making my way into the media room.

"I think there probably is."

I head for the closet on the far side of the room, fishing out my tote bag and finding my energy drink. While I'm in there, I grab a couple of my snack bags before shoving the whole thing away. I take my time, in absolutely no rush to head back out into the room and face this conversation with Jake. When I can't reasonably stall any longer, I shuffle back into the conference room, dropping into a seat at the table, across the space from where Jake stands, hands still tucked into his pockets.

I fight with the plastic on the bag of crackers I'm trying to open, my attention too shot to actually open the bag correctly. Jake wanders over, taking the bag from me, pulling it carefully open, and handing it back before sitting on the table, just a foot away from me.

"Thank you," I mutter without looking at him.

"Natalie, please." His voice is so soft, so tender, so unlike him that I can't hold on to my cold shoulder, turning to look at him.

"Jake, I really don't—"

"Just let me get this out, ok?" I nod, and he continues. "I *know* I fucked up. I let you down, and I let Melanie down. And I know that, more than anything, her and Dex's well-being is the most important thing to you.

"I can't go back and change what I did. Keeping Gunner a secret wasn't supposed to be malicious. It was a poorly handled omission. I should have dealt with it the day I met Melanie."

"You should have." I sigh, not knowing where that would have eventually landed us, but confident that having that knowledge upfront would have changed... *probably everything.*

But it's also unlikely I would have looked twice at a *friend* of Gunner's.

I shove the thought away, changing the conversation. "Thank you for calling her lawyer. You didn't have to do that."

"I know that, but I *wanted* to. I want to do whatever it takes to make this right between us."

"I appreciate the gesture, but I don't know that it changes anything between the two of us."

He nods. "I can't change the past, Nat. But I'd really like it if there were a future for us where I could prove to you how sorry I am."

The pain in his eyes cuts through me.

"There are a lot of things I don't know. A lot I've never dealt with. I'm great at my job. Really fucking good at physical protection, but this emotional stuff is all new to me. I've never cared about what someone else felt or thought the way I care about you."

Tears well in my eyes.

"I've never missed anyone the way I've missed you." A single tear streaks down my face, Jake wiping it away. "I should have tried harder, even if the timing was shit, to be honest with you, with Mel.

"I'd say I'm sorry a thousand times if I thought it would help." He's quiet for a moment, staring across the room. I don't have anything to say to that, both of us knowing damn well it won't, so I don't reply, instead aimlessly running my thumb over the side of the drink in front of me.

"I just—there are other things I should have told you that I couldn't bring myself to say either." He drops his head, pivoting in my direction, but I continue to avoid his gaze.

"Like what?" So help me god, if he's hiding something else, I will be out of this place so fast.

He grips my chin between his thumb and forefinger as he turns my head to face him, forcing me to meet his eyes. "I love you, Natalie."

My breath catches in my chest, the air sucked from my lungs, leaving me lightheaded and a little dazed. That is *not* what I thought he was about to say. "What?"

"I said I love you," he strokes his thumb across my chin. "And I have for a while now. I was just too scared to say it out loud. I wanted so badly to tell you that afternoon in the woods, that night. Every fucking moment since. But I didn't because I was worried it was too much. That this wasn't meant to be *that* kind of relationship. And then everything fell apart."

It's my turn to nod, appreciating the honesty, knowing where he stands, but—what good does the knowledge do when I don't know that I can trust him? When I can't even sort out my own feelings?

"I had a lot of time to think this past week, way too much time inside my head, but the one thought I kept coming back to repeatedly was how much I wish I had told you that. That I wish you knew. You don't have to say it back. I didn't come here expecting you to. I just needed you to know."

I take a shaky breath before turning away, shrugging off his grip on me. "I, um—I can't do this right now, Jake. I have a show to get through, and I just—I need some time."

"Yeah, of course."

I clear my mess, leaving Jake sitting on the edge of the table. Tossing my uneaten crackers into the trash, I take the drink with me.

I don't look back, rounding the corner and slipping into the women's restroom. It's only then that I crack open the can I'm holding, down half the energy drink and have a good cry.

All with time to spare before I hear Dex and Asher in the hallway, looking for me.

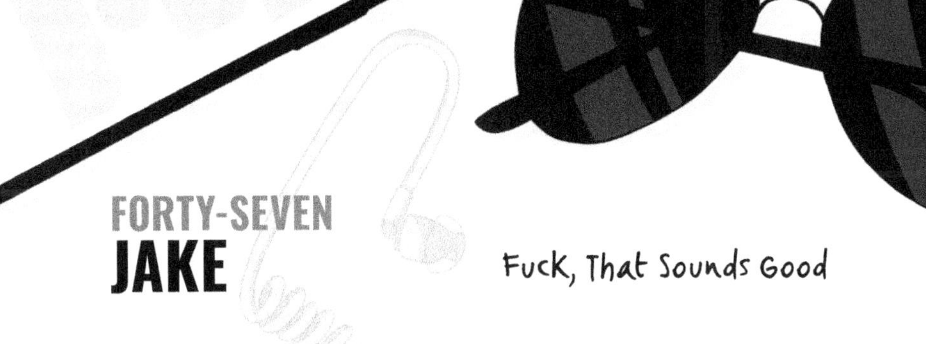

Fuck, That Sounds Good

After my conversation with Natalie went like shit, Dex took pity on me and snuck me into the VIP tent for the show. I kept hoping Natalie would make an appearance, but it seems she found a way to keep herself occupied for the night because I didn't catch a single glimpse of her. I don't really know what I expected to happen tonight, but *that* certainly wasn't it. The dismissal hurt, but the pain in her eyes hurt more.

When the show ended, I made my way back to the hotel, where I'm waiting in the downstairs bar for everyone to wrap up for the night. Unfortunately, I still have a lot of mess left to clean up. As much as I'd like to hole up and avoid any more confrontations, I know I can't.

I'm a full beer in when Knox makes his appearance. I'm honestly a little surprised he didn't brush me off when I texted him about meeting up, but I'm thankful because it means I might be able to make amends.

"Hey." His tone is clipped as he takes the stool next to me. The bartender doesn't miss a beat, grabbing Knox's order before I can even reply.

There's no point in hedging around this conversation, so instead I just rip the band-aid off. "I, uh—I owe you an apology. I obviously didn't think the implications of this through."

"No shit, you think?" He nods to the bartender as he slides a beer in front of him.

"I just—genuinely thought it wasn't worth bringing up and then the article released. I didn't know how I was supposed to explain it at that point, with everyone so on edge and furious. I mean, rightfully so." I pull at the label on the beer. "I should have just come clean. And I apologize for keeping that from you. You deserved the truth, and I own that."

"Well, good." He taps a sip of his own drink. "I'm not gonna say you're forgiven, but I'm willing to move on."

"Really?" I can't keep the hope from seeping into my voice.

"Said what I needed to when I hit you in the face." He smirks at that. "I don't think you're a bad person, Jake. I think you just made a really stupid decision."

"I'm not arguing that."

"None of us are." I look up as Dex's hand comes down on my shoulder, Asher standing behind him. "Mind if we join you?"

"Uh—nope." I watch as the two of them pull out the stools to my right, dropping onto them simultaneously.

"We're not interrupting anything, are we?" Dex directs the question at me.

"No, I just owed Knox an apology. Thought I should do it while I was in town."

"Ah, the great apology tour. When's my stop?" Asher leans forward on the bar as both Knox and Dex laugh.

"Rained out. Sorry, man." I take a drink of my beer as he laughs too.

"It's fine. I take my solace in knowing I'm smarter than you for once."

The grin on my face is genuine as I reply. "God, you're a smartass."

We fall into comfortable conversation. Things feel a little awkward, but it's the best I've felt in two weeks. The relief of knowing that if nothing else, these three are willing to move forward, still want to maintain a friendship, feels really fucking nice.

An hour later, I set my second empty beer onto the counter. "Alright, well I still need to find somewhere to crash, so I think I'm gonna call it a night."

I pull out my wallet, dropping a couple of twenties to cover my tab and the tip.

"You came to town with nowhere to stay?" Dex asks from beside me.

"Had other priorities." I huff a laugh, but the ease I've felt the last hour dwindles quickly, the reminder that Natalie still hasn't forgiven me sobering me.

"I still have your room here. Stay there."

"No, that's fine. I don't need to overstep more than I already have."

"Jake. It's one am, and the room is empty. Just take the damn thing." Dex throws his money on the counter with mine. "C'mon, the key's upstairs."

Reluctantly, I agree, saying a quick good night to Knox and Asher before following Dex to the elevator.

Several hours later, I roll over, shifting under the covers to stare at the wall, unable to find any semblance of sleep. My phone chimes from behind me, and I reach blindly across the bed, grabbing for the device.

Natalie's name lights up on the screen, and I sit up, my heart skipping a beat like a goddamn teenager. I fumble to unlock the phone, pulling open my messages.

RED

Did you stay in town?

ME

Yeah, Dex gave me one of the crew's rooms.

My pulse quickens as I wait for her reply.

RED

Which room?

ME

217

I'm immediately up and out of bed, throwing on a pair of sweats over my briefs, wishing I had anything nicer with me.

Ok, chill. The pants don't matter.

I fish a shirt out of my suitcase, smoothing out the wrinkles just as a knock comes at my door. Crossing the room, I throw the door open and find Natalie there, satin sleep shorts peeking out from underneath her oversized MBM crewneck.

A quick greeting is all I can manage, the lump in my throat making it difficult to speak.

"Can I come in?" Her voice is quiet, her eyes looking anywhere but at me.

I try not to let the dread creep in as I reply. "Yeah, of course."

I move off to the side as she enters the room, the sweet scent of her shampoo following in her wake.

The door falls closed as I make my way over to her, careful to give her space as I sit down at the desk, letting her have the bed. She drops onto the mattress; the comforter fluffing up around her.

"I'm sorry I'm here so late." She looks up, finally meeting my gaze. I can barely make out the red rim around her eyes, but it's there, and I know that's my fault.

"That's fine—honestly, wake me up at three am, anytime." I cringe at how desperate that sounds, but at this point, I'm not sure I care. I just want a chance to make this right.

She huffs a dry laugh.

"I don't know how to do this, Jake." She drops her head, scuffing her slipper along the carpet beneath her.

"Do what, Nat?"

"Put myself first." Her voice is so quiet, I can barely hear her over the hum of the air conditioner, but I understand her perfectly.

My stomach sinks, and I think I might be sick. I *knew* it was a long shot, getting her to give me a second chance, but until this moment, I don't think I actually *believed* there wasn't at least a small possibility.

That one sentence feels like a knife to the gut. She's right; she *needs* to put herself first, but the implication that she has to walk away from me to do it hurts.

"That... might not be want I meant." That one sentence has hope blooming in my chest. "Put what I *want* first? That's probably... more accurate."

"I'm not following."

"Yeah, sorry. I'm horrible at this." She takes a deep breath, pressing on. "What I'm trying to say is that I constantly do what's right. All the time. But the thing is, what's *right* isn't always *right for me*. And sometimes that isn't what I want. So, I'm trying to just ignore all the noise and do what *feels right*."

"Natalie—" I don't know how it's possible to feel like laughing and throwing up at once, but I do. "What are you trying to say right now?"

She scrubs her hands over her face. "God, sorry. I—I think the thing I'm supposed to say here is that I can't do this and I don't know how to trust you and it's probably best to just end this like we said we would. Keeping it casual. But what I want... is not that."

The air suddenly feels lighter. She drops her hands, looking right at me. "What I want, Jake, is you. And I don't know if that's a great decision because I think I might be setting myself up to be hurt again, but I want to try."

"Oh, it's a great decision." She laughs at that as I stand, climbing onto the bed next to her.

"I just—I'm scared, Jake. I've spent the entire week replaying every fucking moment, and I keep coming back to the same realization. When I broke up with Sean, I felt *nothing*."

I scrunch my nose up at the mention of her shitty ex.

"There's a point here, I promise. I left the man I thought I was supposed to *marry*, and all I had was anger. There was... nothing else. But every moment without you has felt like this persistent ache, this constant *pain*. And a weird emptiness. And for all the things I don't know and all the worries I still have, I know those feelings—that stark difference—tells me more than anything else will." She finally looks up, meeting my eye. "It doesn't feel right to think about a future without you."

She shifts so she's facing me, and I reach out, taking her hand in mine. "Listen, I can't promise I will never hurt you again, but I can promise I will do everything in my power not to. No more secrets, no more omissions. I meant it when I said I've never cared about someone else the way I care about you."

I brush a hand along her cheekbone, cupping her face. "I love you. So fucking much. And I hate that I made you feel like this. Please let me make it up to you. Prove to you I'm worthy of your trust."

A tear slips down her cheek, and I wipe it away.

Fuck, I need to stop being the reason she cries.

"Can we try again? Can we do this for real?" She nods this time, another tear streaking down her face. "Is that a yes? I need to hear you say it."

My thumb catches that tear, rubbing it away as well.

"Yes, Jake. Let's do this for real."

I drop the hand that I'm holding, cupping both sides of her face as I bring my lips to hers, the relief of a fresh chance feeling euphoric. I part her lips with mine, tilting her head back to deepen the kiss.

"I'm so glad I took this room." I can feel her smile against my lips.

"Convenient of you to stay close." She slides her hands over my shoulders, throwing a leg over my hips as she straddles me.

"I'm just really fucking glad you're here." I wrap my arms around her, feeling a profound sense of relief to be in this moment.

"Don't make me regret it." She threads her hands in my hair, tipping my head back now, the tilt of her lips a welcome sight. "Mel and Dex went to bat for you; it would be a shame to prove them wrong."

She drops her lips to mine, but I pull back. "Wait, they—what?"

She shifts, settling into my lap. "They both made good arguments for trying to understand where you're coming from. Not what you did—"

"Well, I'd hope not."

"But why you did it. I... didn't want to use logic, because it hurt, whatever the reason. But they were pretty persistent."

"I think I love them too." That makes her laugh. A new feeling of tenderness takes root inside me, knowing the two of them had my back, even though I probably didn't deserve it. I owe them. Fuck, Dex offered me a *job* despite everything.

Before I can get too lost in my own head, Natalie shifts in my lap, hips rolling against the thin fabric of my sweatpants.

The sudden urgency catches me off guard. "Fuck, Red. It's the middle of the night. Aren't you tired?"

She smirks deviously, a silent shake of her head the only response I get before she pushes me down on the mattress, her lips finding mine again as I hear her slippers fall to the carpet.

I snake my hands under her sweatshirt, gliding them up her sides. When they meet the bare skin of her breasts, I can't stop the moan that escapes from me.

"Jesus Christ, did you come here with nothing on under this shirt?" My thumbs trace over her pebbled nipples; the answer obvious.

"I might have been optimistic." She smiles through the kisses, her lips still fused to mine as she moves on top of me.

She sits up, out of my reach as she stretches and tosses her sweatshirt to the floor, naked from the waist up on top of me. I can feel my dick stiffen painfully between us as I take in the view, back arched like some ethereal goddess.

I sit up, holding her to me with one arm as I bring my mouth back to hers, my free hand finding the elastic in her bun as I gently remove it, her long hair falling down her back. I drop the hair tie, threading my fingers through the strands at the base of her neck.

"You have a thing for my hair being down, don't you?" She asks, her voice low and throaty.

"I love your hair," I say, combing my fingers through it. "The way you look with it down, carefree and unraveled."

Dropping a kiss on her temple, my lips skim along her jawline and down her neck to her collarbone. "Everyone else gets put together Natalie, and I like her too. Neat and orderly Natalie is hot as hell, but I like this version of you. The one that's relaxed and unbothered."

I slide my hands down her sides, grabbing her hips as I flip us, lowering her to the mattress before sliding off her shorts and underwear. My touch is light as I climb over her, covering her body with my own.

Trailing kisses over her exposed skin, I stop when I get to the crook of her neck. Leaning up, I whisper in her ear, "I fucking love that I'm the only one that gets this version of you. That has the privilege of worshipping you like this."

She whimpers as I trail my hand over her hips, sliding it between her legs, feeling the moisture already pooling there. I slide two fingers along her pussy, hearing a sharp intake of breath as I push inside her.

It occurs to me, as I take her in, laid out beneath me, that I will never get enough of this. Of seeing her this way. Of being the one who gets to undo her.

I work my hand in between her legs, moving my thumb over her clit as I rock my fingers. She arches her back when I draw her nipple into my mouth; the moans leaving her sounding fucking perfect.

Working my way down her body until my face is between her legs, I throw both her legs over my shoulders as I lay on my stomach. I hold her eyes as my tongue splits her open, the desire in her gaze so potent, I nearly come undone before she does.

It doesn't take long; the slide of my fingers and my tongue on her clit has her thighs tightening around me, hips writhing far too soon. I use my free arm to hold her to the mattress, controlling as much of her pleasure as I can.

"Jake, Jesus... fuck." She's incoherent, a string of curse words falling from her lips as I coax her orgasm out of her, maintaining a slow pace as I feel her clench around my fingers, the pulsing of her cunt around my hand utter perfection as I work her through each wave of her orgasm. When she's spent, I don't let up, encouraging a second on the heels of the first, as she shudders in front of me, the single hottest thing I have ever seen.

When she finally comes down, her breathing labored and limbs limp, I wipe my fingers on my shirt before I climb over her again, holding myself on my forearms as I meet her eye, her cheeks pink and hairline beaded with sweat.

I use my clean hand to wipe away a few rogue strands of hair, dropping a kiss to her forehead. Her fingers lace behind my neck, pulling me down to her as she pulls my tongue into her mouth. I meet her with equal enthusiasm, my skin on fire and dick throbbing.

She smirks as she slides her hand into the waistband of my pants, wrapping her hand around my cock. The smooth slide of her palm against me has me rocking my hips, desperate for more.

"Eager tonight." She whispers between kisses, and I can feel the last tether to my sanity slipping quickly away.

"Fucking feral, Red." I push up quickly, ditching my pants and briefs before I pull my shirt over my head, adding it to the pile.

I don't waste any time lining myself up with her entrance. Taking her hands in mine, I thread our fingers together and rest them above her head while I push in, sliding home in one deep thrust.

We heave matching sighs, our eyes locked as I move in her, the rocking of my hips slow and unhurried.

I drop my lips back to her forehead, her cheek, along her jawline, anywhere and everywhere I can reach. I feel her legs wrapping around, holding me to her as I snap my hips, my pace quickening, my movements becoming haphazard.

"Fuck, Natalie. I'm not gonna—"

"Come, Jake, please." It's the way her voice breaks as she begs that has me losing control, my balls drawing up as my orgasm rolls through me. I can feel her tightening around me as she arches into me, both of us coming simultaneously.

I slow my movements, careful to keep my weight off her as I roll off the bed. I quickly clean myself up before helping Natalie with a warm washcloth. When I finally crawl back under the covers, she's already half asleep on the pillow next to me.

I pull her into me, breathing in the scent of her shampoo as I wrap my arms around her waist, that incessant ache in my chest finally calm, instead replaced with a warmth of appreciation and contentment.

She brings her hands to mine as she snuggles into me, a soft sigh leaving her. Her hands slide up my wrists when she pulls back, holding my arm in her palm as she examines the leather bracelet I'm wearing.

"Jake, what is this!?" She turns over the cuff, the pressed penny from our trip to Nashville tucked inside the leather band I found while I was in town last week.

I can't stop the laugh that escapes me.

"Did you know books aren't the only things you can buy to store your pressed pennies?" I turn my arm over, showing her the leather wrap.

"I... can't say that I did. Where did you find a *bracelet* for a pressed penny?!"

"Same store we got the pennies from. I was downtown last week, and I saw it on the mannequin in the window." I smile at the memory, genuinely surprised something like this even exists. It was an impulse buy, but it was a good one.

She laughs this time, running her fingers over the bracelet and tracing the penny. "I love that."

She turns onto her back; her smile staying as her laughs fades out, her eyes holding mine. "I love you."

I can't stop the swell of emotion I feel at that confession, the words sounding sweeter than I ever imagined.

I lean into her, pressing my lips to hers as I tighten my hold on her waist. "Say that again."

"What?"

"You know what." I kiss her cheek and then her temple, my lips resting against her forehead.

"I love you, Jake."

"Fuck, that sounds good." She laughs, pulling me down toward her, and somehow, that sounds even better.

"Hey Caleb, how's it going?" He nods at me as I clap him on the shoulder and enter the VIP tent, making my way toward the front of the space as I zero in on a bobbing head of red hair, standing alongside Austin and Indy. Natalie's hair is down tonight, loose tendrils of curls flowing freely down her back as she moves to the music. It's a rare night where she's enjoying the concert from the comfort of the VIP tent, but she let her team take the lead on managing the media tonight and opted for a night off to enjoy her sister's show.

The VIP tent is calmer than it usually is, filled with just Melanie's closest friends and family. Dex and Asher are off to the side, both with eyes on Melanie up on stage as they talk about something together. Several of Natalie and Dex's team members are also here, but the usual chaos of the tent is absent with the smaller number of people in here.

I slide up behind Natalie, curling my fingers around her hip as I settle in behind her. She turns to look at me over her shoulder, a grin breaking out on her face as she does.

"Get everything taken care of backstage?" She yells at me, putting extra effort into being heard over the music on stage.

It's been several weeks since I accepted the job with Melanie's tour management team, working directly for Dex now. It was an easy transition, considering it was work I'd been taking on prior to being fired by Shield, but it's nice to have the time, and resources, to do it correctly now.

I took the time to put together formal procedures that we use at every stop now. Having a dedicated point of contact for security and venue communications has made everything easier on the team and is making the shows run much more smoothly on our end.

"Yep, all good." Tonight's delay was a minor emergency with the venue security. I swear all of my issues are with venue security not being trained, but at least this issue was an easy fix.

The best part of the new role is that Natalie and I no longer have to sneak around. Everyone knows, and no one cares. We no longer have to creep through the halls carrying empty folders when we want to see one another. In fact, everyone just knows that Natalie stays in my room at all the stops now, and everyone is happier for it.

It's near the end of the night, the show entering its final act. I watch as smoke billows from the stage, an unfamiliar set piece rising out of the floor.

"Is this the new part you've been talking about?" I lean in to Natalie's ear so she can hear me through all the noise.

She reaches back, wrapping her arm around me and threading her fingers into my hair, holding me close to her shoulder. "Yes! This is the new set Melanie swapped into the show." We both shift our attention forward as the stage props finish rising and Melanie appears from a trapdoor in the floor.

Melanie and the dancers have been doing extra rehearsals for several weeks now to work on a new set for the show. Mel said she wanted to celebrate the divorce officially being final by trading out some songs and bringing in a couple of new numbers. The general public doesn't know specifically why Mel switched it up, The Tracks shared it was just meant to be a fun surprise for a new song release. It was a lot of work to coordinate while already out on tour, but the Bennett girls have never been ones to slow down.

I keep my grip on Natalie as she watches the performance in front of us, letting my hands wander simply because I can and it feels so fucking nice.

Melanie moves through a crowd of half-dressed men, all shirtless as they swarm around her. She's singing her newest song, which is hilariously filled with double entendres. The guys are acting like she's praising them, but she's got her back to them as she makes a face at the crowd.

It's incredibly sassy and filled with vitriol, but it's one of my favorites of hers. It's also *very* clear who she wrote it about, but that thought just makes me laugh. What I would have given to see Gunner's face when he heard it for the first time.

As the song ends, I watch Natalie and Indy clapping and screaming, raw enthusiasm on display for Melanie's new performance. Over Indy's shoulder, I can see Austin, his eyes locked on Melanie as he remains motionless, arms crossed over his chest.

My eyes flick back to the stage where she stands, chest heaving from the exertion of the performance, a huge grin on her face, and with the men lined up on either side of her. A smile creeps over my face as I turn back to Austin, watching his jaw tick.

Interesting.

"If we hurry, we can beat the crowd out of here." Natalie's tug on my shirt redirects my attention.

She slips her hand in mine, leading me through the people exiting the VIP tent and heading toward the green room. The after-show ritual holds strong; the entire team meets up behind the scenes to celebrate the end of another show before we all disperse for the night. We make our way into the space; the familiar, dark velvets warm and welcoming.

We're early, one of the first few to show up tonight after the show, so we slink off to the side, Natalie still pulling me along by my hand. When we finally make it to the far side of the space, I drop onto one of the couches lining the wall and pull her down onto me.

She lets out a loud squeal, but she looks up, a wide smile spread across her face as her arms wrap around my shoulders. She situates herself, slapping my shoulder as she says, "A little warning next time."

I smirk at her as her brown eyes meet mine, shining in the low light of the green room. "My bad, Red."

The hum in the room grows louder as more of the cast and crew make their way inside, but I barely notice, my attention fully occupied by the girl in my lap.

My life looks completely different from what it did just a few short months ago, and some days, I'm still a little dumbfounded by it. I grew so used to keeping myself at arm's length from everyone and everything, it's strange to have someone I want to spend time with. Working side-by-side keeps Natalie and I together most of the time, but I know, even without those roles, I'd still find myself drawn to her.

Even now, sitting here after a long day of running around, I'm itching to get out of here. To get back to the hotel, just her and I. The late nights and early mornings in bed with her have become my favorite part of each day.

And to be honest, it's not just Natalie that has had an impact on me. Taking that original job with Shield brought so many people into my life. I spend our nights off with Austin, Dex, and Knox, occasionally dragging along a couple of the band members who have become buddies of mine as well. The circle of friends has grown so much I barely recognize the part of me that once thrived on isolation. I'm even keeping up with my brothers more often now, texts in our group chat becoming more and more frequent.

"Another one in the books!" Dex's voice breaks through the dull roar in the green room, everyone cutting off their conversations as they turn to face him. "Mel and crew absolutely killed the new sets!"

A loud chorus of cheers rumbles through the crowd, the excitement for the recent additions palpable. "But the numbers aren't the only thing that's new. Mel has one more surprise for everyone here..."

Melanie stands, taking the mic from Dex's hand. "I do! I'm so excited to share that once we close out the US leg of this tour, we are officially expanding the schedule and heading to Europe this winter!"

The cheers become so loud it's almost impossible to hear myself think. Clearly, the cast and crew are all in on the news.

Melanie and Dex wrap their speeches, and as quickly as the tent filled, it empties back out, everyone eager to wrap up their jobs and get back to the hotel for the night so we can do this again tomorrow.

"So, Austin, is The Tracks coming with us to Europe then?" Natalie directs her attention to Indy and Austin, who are now standing beside us.

Austin laughs, "I don't know, but I have a feeling management will be on board for just about anything you offer with the way ratings have been this year."

"If you're not careful, The Tracks might become a full-time road job. They're going to want you covering all major tours after this one." Natalie's smile broadens.

"God, I hope not." Indy chimes in. "I'm having a ton of fun, but I can't do this permanently. I miss my bed."

Natalie just laughs before turning to me. "Are you ready to go?"

"Ready when you are." We say a quick goodbye to Austin and Indy before she grabs my hand, leading me through the stadium and out to the waiting SUV.

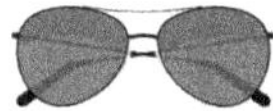

We're back in our hotel room not even twenty minutes later, the space littered with mine and Natalie's things. She's got her suitcases open on the bench to the right, her work papers stacked on the table across the room, two empty coffee cups from our breakfast this morning next to them. My laptop sits closed under the TV, Natalie's hairbrush on top of it. I kick off my shoes, which find a home right next to two pairs of Natalie's heels, and I can't help the smirk that crosses my face at the sight of our lives intertwined like this.

Natalie gasps, groaning an elongated, "noooo."

"What?" I make my way across the room, peeking over her shoulder to see a string of text messages open on her phone.

"Isla is leaving! I'm so sad." Isla is the tour's newest choreographer, one Melanie hired to work with them on the new songs. Natalie and Melanie have been spending a lot of time with her since she joined the crew.

"Well, that's a bummer. Where's she going?"

"She didn't say. She just said she got a new job. We're going to grab drinks tomorrow." She clicks her phone off and sets it down.

"How did you meet her? I know you hooked her and Melanie up, but I don't remember how you became friends?"

"Oh, it was when I was back in Nashville, I took a pole dancing class with her and she was so nice. We swapped phone numbers…"

She continues on, but my attention is completely lost. I cut her off. "Wait, back up. Did you say *pole dancing class?*"

She spins toward me, her cheeks turning pink. "I did say that, yes."

"Why is this the first time I'm hearing about it?" I reach down, threading my fingers through hers as I guide her back a step, then two, until she's up against the wall. "*That* feels like it should have been the big news. Not your friend getting a new job."

"Well, there's not really anything to share about it." She laughs, tipping her head up to meet my eyes. "I was horrible. It did not go well."

"I'd like to be the judge of that. How can we make that happen?" I drop her hands, moving mine to her waist.

"*We* will not be making that happen." She threads her arms around my neck, pulling me into her. "But I could make it up to you."

"I like the sound of that." My lips meet hers, and that familiar heat races through me at the contact. I can't help the smile that spreads across my face, the knowledge that I get *this,* with *her,* indefinitely.

"What?" She pulls back. "Why are you smiling like that?"

I shake my head, unable to stop the laugh that slips out of me. "No reason. I was just thinking… I'm really glad you threw coffee on me that morning in the café."

"I did not *throw* my coffee on you. As per usual, you were just all up in my space." She smiles, her eyes shining in the moonlight coming through the window. "Why would you be glad that happened?"

"Because it brought you into my life." Her eyes soften.

"One could argue that it was actually work that did that. Coffee or no coffee, you took the job with Shield."

"If we're arguing, maybe it was Gunner then who released the damn article, which made Knox switch the roles around."

She scrunches up her face. "We're not thanking Gunner for anything."

I drop my lips back to hers, whispering against them as I say, "Maybe I should just thank *you* for giving me a chance."

She pushes up, sealing her mouth to mine, and an unfamiliar feeling of contentment overwhelms me. I spent so long running from my past. I had no idea it was the very thing that would bring me to my future.

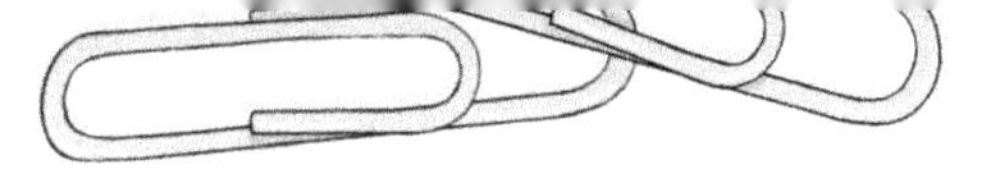

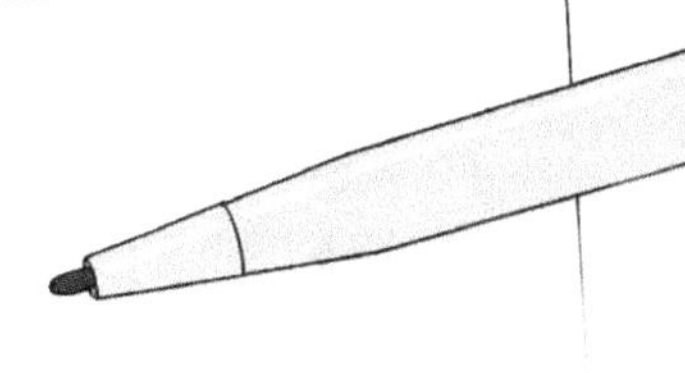

EPILOGUE
NATALIE

"You know what I haven't missed?" I lean into the mirror in front of me, sliding my earring in and closing the clasp.

Jake moves to stand beside me, fidgeting with the cufflinks on his sleeve as his eyes meet mine in our reflection. "What's that?"

"Hotel rooms." We both laugh as I reach for my other earring. "As nice as this one is, being home has been amazing."

"Mmm, yes, it has." He shifts, coming to stand behind me, his hands meeting my bare hips. "Is this what you're wearing tonight?"

His fingers trail up my sides, gripping my rib cage as he drops a kiss to my exposed shoulder.

"Yes, I was planning on just my bra and underwear for the party. What do you think?"

"I vote hell yes." He sweeps my hair off to the side as he runs his mouth along the side of my neck. "Might steal the spotlight though, and we wouldn't want that."

I grab for my bracelet, wrapping it around my wrist and securing the clasp. "No, that's probably in poor taste."

I tip my head into his as he whispers into my ear, goosebumps pebbling my skin. "How long do we have?"

"Not long enough." I sigh as I spin in his hold, turning to meet his heated gaze.

"You sure? Would anyone notice if we were a few minutes late?"

"I think they might, yeah." I smirk as I lace my fingers around the back of his neck, pulling his mouth down to meet mine. Pushing up into the kiss, I savor the way he still sets every nerve alight, even a year and a half later.

We finished the US leg of Melanie's Peripheral Vision Tour last August. After that, we had four months in Nashville before we left for Europe in January. Mel's tour was such a success, the worldwide schedule kept getting extended to add additional countries, and we ended up out on tour for another nine months this year."

We've been home for a month now and tonight is the wrap party. One last event before we officially close the books on this tour. As much as I really love being in my own bed, or rather, Jake's bed since I haven't used mine in the last month, I'm really excited to see everyone again tonight. I miss our tour crew.

I pull back, smoothing my hand over his shoulder, the tuxedo jacket a perfect fit. "I like the gray. That was a good choice."

Formal attire is not something I see him in very often, and damn, is that a shame. The fabric drapes over his body like it was made for him. I guess technically it was, since Antoni did the outfits for us for today.

"Tell your sister that, not me. I just put on what I was told." He steps back, running his hands down the lapels of his jacket.

"Well, remind me to thank her." I turn away, padding into the bathroom where my dress hangs on the door. The navy blue satin shimmers in the fluorescent lights, somehow looking regal even in this awful yellow glow.

Carefully removing the dress from the hanger, I shimmy into it, holding the sweetheart neckline to my chest as Jake walks through the door. Spinning, I gesture to the back of the dress. He steps toward me, his hands finding my bare skin again, sliding under the open zipper and around my waist.

"Jake! Just zip me up."

I feel his lips on my back before he pulls his hands out, tugging the zipper into place. "Sorry, I can't help it."

"Well, figure it out. You're going to have to hold yourself together for a few hours." I normally wouldn't complain, but it's a big night. I walk around him, patting his chest as I reach for my shoes in the box on the side table and slide them on.

"Are we ready then?" I look around the space, trying to decide if there's anything I've forgotten. "Do you have a room key?"

He nods to me as I snag my clutch from the desk by the hotel door and head for the hallway.

Jake follows me out of the hotel room, grabbing my hand as we step into the elevator.

"Matt texted earlier," He says as he pushes the button for the main floor. "He's gonna make it down for Thanksgiving."

"Oh, perfect! That means everyone will be coming down then, right?"

"Yep. I think Noah and Morgan plan to stay the full week."

"A whole week with the baby?" Jake's brother and his wife had a baby earlier this year. We haven't been able to see them since we got home from the tour, but we get near daily photos from them.

I haven't met Morgan in person, but at some point, Jake put me in a group chat with her, Noah, and Matt, and the two of us started talking on our own shortly after that. I already love her and Noah, so I'm looking forward to officially meeting them and the baby.

"I'm so excited! I'm glad they could make it work. You'll have to finish those guest rooms now." I tease, referring to his empty bedrooms that currently house random pieces of furniture.

"Or you could do it for me."

"I could, but it's not my house." I've made offhand decor suggestions to him a few times when I've been over, and he hasn't taken them. "I don't want to overstep."

"Yeah, but it could be your house." He squeezes my hand as he looks down at me.

"Sorry, what?" I say, taken aback. It's not that we haven't talked about a future together, because we have, but I've assumed we were talking in years, not months. We haven't had a lot of time together that wasn't out on the road.

"I mean, you've already moved half of your stuff over. Just bring the rest and make it official." He winks at me. "It's not like we didn't spend the last year living in hotel rooms together. I think we can handle a whole house."

I can't stop the smile that spreads over my face. "You want me to live with you? Permanently?"

Tugging on my hand, he pulls me into him as he wraps his arms around me. "I do, yeah."

He drops his lips to mine, and I'm too distracted to notice the ding of the elevator or the doors sliding open as we make it to the lobby. I do, however, hear the throat clearing from the other side of the threshold. I step back, spinning around to find myself face to face with my brother, his gray tux a perfect match to the one Jake has on.

"You two need to get a room." Dex cocks an eyebrow at us.

"We have one. Unfortunately, someone forced me to leave it." Jake's head tips toward me, but all I offer in response is a smirk.

"You know what? I walked right into that one, but I'm still gonna stop you right there." Dex turns on his heel, heading down the hall. We follow behind him, making our way to the towering wood doors that lead into the ballroom. He holds the door open for us as we cut by him, entering the space.

The room is opulent, decked out in florals as far as the eye can see. Melanie and I have been planning this event for months, sparing no expense to make sure every detail was perfect. I admire the centerpieces as I work my way across the room, making for my sister on the far side. The large white displays of flowers have shimmering gold and silver adornments tucked alongside the blooms, spilling over their gold vases onto the tablecloths, sleek gold place settings at each of the seats.

The two staff members chatting with Mel step away as we approach, a huge smile spreading across her face.

"Oh, you look good in that dress!" She reaches out to hug me, and I drop Jake's hand to lean into her. Stepping back, she takes in the guys behind us, standing side-by-side in their matching tuxes, hilariously posed the same way, each with a hand in their pocket.

They both throw us a look as we snicker, before turning to one another, realizing they are mirror images. Dex just laughs as I turn back to Melanie.

"The gold was a fabulous choice; wow, you look phenomenal." She does a little twirl, the shimmery fabric of the dress swirling around her.

"Thank you. Really glad I picked this one." She fluffs the skirt on the gown, the short train flowing elegantly behind her.

"Is anyone else here yet?" I take in the empty space, answering my own question.

She waves her hand in the air. "Austin was a minute ago, but he ran off to do… something. He didn't say."

Jake's hand snakes around my back as he leans in, whispering in my ear, "See, I told you we had time."

He drops a kiss on my temple before straightening. "I'm gonna grab us drinks."

"Oh, great idea." Dex slaps him on the shoulder as the two of them head toward the bar.

I can't help but laugh when I hear Jake and my brother antagonize one another as they walk off. "That wasn't an invitation, asshole."

"I wasn't aware I needed one."

The two of them have become close over the last year and a half. I'd love it if it weren't so annoying. They are constantly giving each other shit, which is entertaining, but also never ending.

"They're cute." Mel says as I turn my back on the guys.

"They're something." I roll my eyes, but we both know I love the friendship they've formed.

"He asked me to move in with him." I don't mean to just drop that on her, but I don't know if we'll get another moment alone tonight.

"Wait—what?" Melanie claps her hands, like a kid in a candy store. "About time."

"About time? Melanie, we've had like… four weeks of normalcy. Not even."

"So? What's normal got to do with anything? You've been together for over a year with shifting schedules, constant chaos, and a lot of stress. If you can handle that, I think you're good, girl. Take that key."

I can't help but laugh at her pure optimism. Despite everything life has thrown at her, she still finds the best in every situation and holds on with all she's got.

"You're right, I'm just… overthinking things. As usual."

"Well, stop it. Not this time." She winks at me. "Make sure I'm in town for the housewarming party."

We both laugh as Indy makes her way over to us. "Ooohhh, look at you two!"

We turn, finding her standing there with her usual wide smile firmly in place. She looks gorgeous in her own navy blue gown, with piles of curls perfectly styled on top of her head.

"So do you! The neckline on that dress is fabulous."

She runs her hands along the fabric draping off her shoulders. "Thank you, I do love this dress. Antoni is magic."

"That he is." Mel agrees.

"I'm going to need a few more excuses to wear gowns like these if you can make that happen, Mel." She smooths her hand down the front of her dress.

"Well, I don't know about that, but maybe we'll see if we can get you to an award show or two."

We chat for several minutes before Jake returns, handing me a glass of prosecco as he slides his hand around my hip, pulling me into him.

"Hey Indy. Sorry, I didn't know you were here, or I'd have brought something over for you." He tips his bottle in her direction before taking a sip.

She waves him off. "All good; the night is young. You can deliver the next one."

He smiles in her direction. "You got it."

"Did you lose Dex?" I twist in the direction of the bar, looking for my brother in the growing crowd of people in the ballroom.

"Ah, no. He got distracted." Jake points to the far end of the room, Dex holding a beer of his own as he wraps his arms around the waist of a tall blonde.

"Yep, that will do it. Good luck getting his attention for the rest of the night." I laugh as I take a sip of my drink.

"Damnit, he has one job today." Melanie glares at his back, her words laced with annoyance.

"I wouldn't worry, Mel." I turn back to my sister. "He's not going to let you down."

"I know, I know. I just—" she smooths her hands down her dress. "Nerves, I guess."

"It's going to be fine. You have nothing to worry about," Indy soothes her.

"Do you want me to go find Austin?" I haven't even finished asking Mel before the man in question appears by her side, a drink in each hand.

"I didn't know if you wanted wine or whiskey, so I brought both." He holds them up, and she snatches the lowball glass from his hand.

"Fuck, I love you," she murmurs as she takes a deep drink of the amber liquid. Austin just chuckles, grabbing her hand.

"If you'll excuse us, the DJ needed a word with the hosts." He tugs gently on Mel's hand as he pulls her toward the dance floor, stepping off to the side as they approach the DJ's booth.

"I'm going to get my own drink," Indy gestures toward the bar. "I'll catch up with you later."

"Sounds good." I offer her a grin as she wanders off.

We're alone for only a moment before Jake asks, "what time does this start officially?"

I look up at Jake. "Six-thirty, why?"

He checks his watch. "Because that gives us almost a half hour..."

He winks at me, taking my glass from my hand and setting both our drinks on the table behind him. Grabbing my hand, he tugs me along as he makes his way for the side door.

I pull on his arm, but he just keeps going. "Jake. We do not have time for this right now."

He ushers me through the ballroom door, whispering in my ear as he slides his hand along my back. "I don't even need fifteen minutes. I doubt they'll be done with the DJ before we get back."

I quirk an eyebrow. "Fifteen? Do you really think—"

I'm silenced as he slides into a nearby coatroom, the lock on the door clicking loudly in the dark space behind us.

"Did you know this was here?" He just smirks, hands sliding around the back of my dress and tugging on the zipper.

Turns out he only needed twelve.

I stumble back to my table from the dance floor several hours later, feet aching because once again, I've chosen brand new heels for a long ass event.

Some things never change.

We're at the tail end of the night and, to be honest, I'm not ready for it to end. This tour has been the most work I've ever taken on, but it's also been the most fun I've ever had. It's brought so many amazing people into my life, and from tomorrow on, that's going to look very different.

Sure, a lot of us will still show up at the MBM offices on Monday, but nothing will be like this last year on the road, and the idea of that makes me feel nostalgic for something I haven't even officially said goodbye to yet.

I ditch the gold slingbacks under the table, sighing at the immediate relief I feel.

"Where'd your other half go?" Indy drops into the chair next to me, feet equally bare, and I can't help but laugh at the two of us, dressed to the nines, without any shoes.

"Over there," I gesture toward Jake, Austin and Dex several feet away, standing with Knox and Asher. All five of them have a beer in hand, tuxedo jackets long gone.

This is what I'm going to miss the most, I think. This sense of community we have at all times. There's always a group of people to talk to, to laugh with. The guys are constantly bullshitting, but it's always in good spirits. There's a feeling of lightness being around so many *good* people all the time.

"Let's go for a walk!" Indy hops back up, gesturing for me to follow her.

"How do you have this much energy? It's like one in the morning." I sigh, using the table to push myself up.

"More alcohol than you? Or less maybe?" She laughs as we wind through the room, still full of cast and crew members, nearly as many people here at this late hour as there were when the party began hours ago. "Just the right amount of alcohol. That's the ticket."

I follow her through the patio doors, carefully making our way down the stone stairs toward the garden in the hotel's courtyard. I spot Melanie's gold dress, shimmering in the moonlight on the edge of the patio and instead change directions, heading in her direction.

"What are you doing out here?" I ask coming to stand beside her.

"Just… taking a minute. I felt a little overwhelmed; opted for fresh air." She shrugs, taking a sip of the wine in her hand.

"I think tonight feels a little bittersweet for all of us. It was a big day, and it's a long chapter of your life closing. I'd be overwhelmed too."

"Multiple chapters." Melanie laughs, leaning into me.

"Yes, multiple chapters. Never half ass anything, do you?"

"Neither of you two do." Dex slips an arm around each of our shoulders as he comes up behind us, situating himself in the middle. He pulls us into him. "I feel like the answer is obvious: if you write another album, we can just do this again."

"Yeah, let me just whip that up, Dex." Mel rolls her eyes.

I poke at his side. "Let the girl have a minute."

He dips his head, looking down at me. "She's about to go on vacation for two full weeks. Feels like plenty of minutes, if you ask me."

I give him a look, and he just chuckles. "I'm kidding, obviously. Just do enough work for me to keep my job, ok?"

He drops his arms, smiling over at Melanie.

Mel narrows her eyes at him. "You are insufferable."

"Ah, but you love me."

"Regrettably."

I chuckle at their banter as Jake's familiar scent wraps around me. He comes up behind me, sliding a hand over my collarbone as he tugs me into his chest, dropping a kiss on the top of my head. "Brought the party outside, did we?"

"Guess so." I look around at the growing crowd outside, watching as Austin cuts through the group, making his way past Indy. He gestures toward the building, "You were requested at the bar, Ind."

"Naturally. I've left them unattended for ten minutes." She just laughs before heading back toward the ballroom.

"Hey." Mel's soft smile widens as Austin wraps his arms around her, pulling Melanie into his body the same way Jake is holding on to me.

"Hi, sorry I didn't see you sneak out here." He drops a kiss on her cheek.

"Well, as much as I love being the third wheel..." Dex hikes his thumb toward the door. "I'm gonna see myself out."

"Oh, come on, we are not that bad," Mel argues as Austin's lips move over her shoulder.

"I beg to differ." He makes a dramatic face as he takes a step back.

"Oh, I don't want to hear shit from you, Warren Dexter. I saw you in the back hallway earlier." Both of the guys laugh as Melanie points her finger at him. He just flips her off, pivoting away from us without another word.

"Wait, Warren?" Jake looks down at me.

"Don't you dare. He's going to kill Melanie for that... hopefully not today." What a way to end the biggest day of your life, in a body bag.

Melanie just laughs. "He loathes his full name."

Jake looks over my head, meeting Austin's eyes.

"God, you two are trouble." It's barely audible, but on the empty patio, the other three have no trouble hearing me.

"I'll wait until he's earned it."

"Do not—" Austin points to Jake, "do it without me present."

"I make no promises." Jake smirks.

"Listen, I love that you guys are co-conspirators against Dex," I turn in Jake's hold, sliding my hands up around his neck. "But don't be making my life harder because of it."

"I would never." Jake meets my gaze with his.

Melanie talks over him. "Austin might."

The four of us laugh, and the sound echoes through the courtyard. It's interrupted when the DJ calls Melanie's name from inside the open doors.

"That's my cue, I guess," Melanie says, tapping Austin's wrist. "Come on, let's go wrap this up."

He unwinds his arms from around her, but keeps her hand as he follows her inside. They both pause on the stone steps as they turn back to us. "Are you coming?"

"Yeah, we'll be right there." I wave her off as I turn my attention back to Jake.

"You good?" He brushes a curl off my face.

"Yeah, I'm good. I'm just—a little sad. That it's all ending. So much has changed since this tour started. We're going back to the real world, but... everything's different."

"A good different though." It's a statement, not a question.

"The best kind, but it all happened so fast."

He chuckles, threading his hands into my hair as he tips my head back. "It did. But maybe that's because this is how it was always supposed to be. Look at Mel now. Dex. They have everything you always hoped they would."

"They do." I can feel his hands skating over my spine, gripping my waist. I pull him down to me, brushing my lips against his. "I do, too."

He leans into me, sealing his mouth over mine, tightening his arms as they wrap around me. I might have to go back to the real world, but he's right. Everything is exactly the way it's supposed to be.

ACKNOWLEDGEMENTS

Ok, wowww. How did we get here!? A couple of years, several hundred hours, more voice memos than I can count, and somehow, I'm supposed to put a bow on this journey?

It's still surreal that this book exists, and it's not lost on me that Love Blackout would never be the book it is without the help of so many people.

To Kayla — I honestly don't even know where to start. The fact that I can't message you and ask where the hell I'm supposed to be going with this is really telling of our relationship. Thank you for answering every question, dealing with every emotional spiral, and listening to eighty-one days of voice memos, just about this book. There is no creative endeavour that I do that doesn't have your fingerprints in it, and my work is all the better for the insight that you give and the encouragement that you provide. At this point in our friendship, I genuinely do not know what I would do without you.

To P — Thank you for sharing Kayla with me. I know I'm kind of needy.

To Leann — Work may have brought us together, but unfortunately, I fear you are now stuck with me. Thank you for the endless hours of conversation about this story and these characters. So much of who these people are would not have happened without your input. Hell, half these people wouldn't have names without you. I love and appreciate your enthusiasm for every creative whim that I have. And even when there are no more TS parties for us to celebrate together, please know I'm still going to be hounding you for our monthly coffee flight.

To Cassi — I'm sorry for deleting your favorite scene, but please know, the Below Deck shout out was just for you. Thank you for showing Love Blackout endless love and enthusiasm. Words seem inadequate for the work you put into this book, but here's a public promise that book two will have your most requested scene and I'll make it worth the wait.

To Britni — I'm forever grateful TS brought us together, but even more grateful for every late night listening party and our Writing Collab Hoes. I am so appreciative of all the support and input you've provided (and all the times you've listened to me whine and moan without complaint).

My TLBHs — Our eclectic little group of hoes could not make me happier. I love that the internet brought us together, but I love more who each of you are as people. You're always the first in line to support whatever new project I've cooked up, and you are continually my loudest cheerleaders. Thank you for all the love you have shown me, and Love Blackout, and more importantly, thank you for all the gifs of half-dressed men and hot bodyguards to keep me motivated.

My Betas — Thank you endlessly for your time and energy in making Love Blackout what it is. I appreciate every comment (and reaction) more than you know. Y'all know how to hype a girl up, and that means the world to me.

My ARC Team — Thank you for your excitement for my very first book. I am deeply appreciative of every single one of you helping to hype this release up and getting the word out there about Love Blackout.

To J — Thank you for two plus decades of unwavering support. None of my creative pursuits would be possible without you. <3

Last, but certainly not least, to you, Reader — If you made it this far that means you liked the story enough to finish it and that means the absolute world to me. Jake and Natalie have such a special place in my heart and I'm so grateful for the time and energy you've shared with them too.

READ ON FOR A SNEAK PEEK AT THE
NEXT BOOK IN THE TINTED TRUTHS
SERIES, LOST IN THE GRAY

PROLOGUE

"You are nothing without me behind you. You know that?"

Blinking slowly, I will the argument I'm currently having to be nothing more than a daydream. A nightmare. But as my eyes reopen, the gleaming white kitchen remains the same. The stoic expression on the man I've called my husband for the past three years hasn't changed.

"You were nothing before me, and you will be nothing without me. This industry won't support you if you walk out of here—if you leave me. I'll make damn sure of it." He smacks his hand on the counter to punctuate his sentence, but I don't so much as flinch.

On the precipice of the biggest tour of my career, sitting at the highest point I have ever reached… I feel completely empty.

And I'm looking at the cause.

"That's a lie and you know it, Gunner." My crossed arms feel like a weight pressing on my chest at a compounded rate. I drop them, but the iron bars tightening across my sternum don't loosen.

He's full of shit and you know it.

I've been mentally coaching myself for years, but at this point, I don't know if I believe it anymore. It used to help me navigate the minetraps, but lately it just feels like more lies.

He lies to me.

I lie to him.

And now, I lie to myself.

I've reached the point where I'm drowning in lies and I can't find the surface. I don't know if I even want to.

"Is it, Melanie?" He takes a step closer to me, and I instinctively retreat. He's never hit me, but his anger isn't anything I want to be near. Sometimes words are sharper than the pain of flesh on flesh. The bruises last longer, the cuts slice deeper.

I steel my spine, my stomach turning over as I realize it's now or never. We've been here before. Stood on opposite sides of this kitchen island and said ugly things to one another, but it's never felt quite like it does tonight.

Tonight it feels like the final straw.

"You know what? I'm not doing this. I'm not going back and forth with you for another six months just to end up where we are right now. I'm done." I pivot on my heel, but before I can take a step forward, he grabs my arm, yanking me toward him.

Stumbling, my shoulder collides with his chest as he glares at me.

"Let me go," I spin, pushing away from him with my free hand. The sharp bite of his watch grazes across my forearm as I yank it back.

The watch I bought him for our first wedding anniversary. The limited edition Rolex I spent far too much money on because I wanted to show him how much I loved him.

It's poetic, somehow, that the item I bought when I was so full of hope and optimism is now the weapon leaving a visible mark on my skin, an outward manifestation of the millions of tiny cuts this man has made to my heart over the years.

Red droplets slip out of the surface level scratch, not enough to go anywhere, but enough to draw my attention. I watch as more appear, the tiny spheres collecting on the surface of my skin, the surrounding area growing irritated and red.

"Melanie! Are you even listening to me?" My head snaps up, meeting the green gaze of my husband.

"No. I'm not." Without another glance, I take off, leaving the room. I keep my back to Gunner as he stands there, yelling at me.

His voice somehow grows louder as I make my way across our enormous house. I always thought eight-thousand square feet was ridiculous. It's enough space for several families to live here.

And yet, ours never will.

Glass shatters in the other room as I stomp up the stairs, and I know, without a doubt, there's no coming back from this.

Not this time.

Before I can think twice about it, there's a suitcase full of clothes packed on the bed in front of me. I'm blindly grabbing whatever is in my path, the urge to leave stronger than my will to care right now.

In record time, I'm hauling the luggage back through the house, careful to avoid the kitchen, and into the garage, loading it swiftly into the trunk of my BMW.

I climb behind the wheel, making my way out of our drive and through the gated community we live in. Finally reaching the main stretch of road, I take a long, drawn out breath.The jagged inhale fills my lungs with a broken sense of relief. My eyes burn, cheeks hot as I pull off to the side of the road, contemplating the repercussions of what I've just done.

I'm fresh out lies to tide me over, partial truths to get myself from one minute to the next. I grip the steering wheel as my mind races through the last hour, through the last several years playing out on a loop, a vice tightening around my heart.

Lights flash by outside my window, the golden glow of cars passing by, oblivious to the fact that my entire life has just imploded in a matter of minutes.

The tears start in earnest as I lean across the center console, struggling to reach my purse on the passenger floorboard. Hands shaky as I fish my phone out, I find the speed dial I need with two quick clicks.

The phone rings.

Once. Twice.

My sister's voice comes over the line. "Hello?"

"Natalie." I choke back a sob. "I need you."

CHAPTER ONE
MELANIE

"Shit." I hiss, tugging on the loose fabric as my wardrobe assistant taps on my ankle, signaling for me to shift feet so they can help me into the second shoe. "Can someone shine a flashlight over here? I fucked this up."

There's a fold of fabric under my left arm that doesn't feel right. I squint in the dim light. The dark and narrow space under the stage makes it hard to tell what's going on with this dress.

It's chaos beneath the stage as I try to swap costumes in the mere moments I'm allotted between sets. It's always a scramble when I'm down here for quick changes, but I am really struggling tonight.

The zipper slides home on my boot just as a bright light shines directly into my eyes.

"Sorry, sorry. I'm so sorry, Melanie." The apologetic voice of another assistant comes from my right as the light moves to my arm, but I wave her off.

"All good. I asked for a light. I got light." I try to keep my tone playful, but I sound frazzled even to myself.

"Ten seconds!" The deep voice of my stage manager comes through my ear piece as adrenaline zips through my veins. I'm going to have to go out on stage with my fucking dress on wrong.

Fantastic.

"Mel! Mic!" I snap my head to the left, taking the mic from the sound tech, the glittering black handle a perfect match to the black dress I'm trying to work myself into.

Why did we do black costumes knowing the outfit changes were in the dark?

"Mel! Quick!" Another loud call, by another team member, and I'm gently nudged two steps over, hitting my mark on the lift as my arm is tugged up and shoved through the draping fabric. My wardrobe assistant hikes the sleeve over my shoulder and ducks out of the way again.

"Oh, thank God." The relief at being dressed appropriately, just as the lift starts to move, is palpable, the smile on my face genuine for a moment.

I quickly shuffle my feet, moving into a low crouch as the lift rises. The deafening roar of the crowd greets me as I make my way to the stage floor and the band shifts from its transitional melody into the first song of the third act of the concert.

Plastering my showbiz smile onto my face and lifting the microphone, the crowd only sees the effervescent popstar they love. The first song of this set is one I'd written with my ex-husband, and while it's not explicitly a love song, every chorus still reminds me of him. It's all I can do to grin and bear it while belting out the lines everyone loves.

I wish now that I had put up more of a fight when management insisted it be included. It is one of my most popular songs, but the weight of performing it night-after-night, when it was written in such a different place in our relationship, is borderline nauseating.

What I once thought was love turned out to be an emotionally abusive relationship that drained the life from me. We're finally, finally at the tail end of nearly a year of divorce proceedings. Freedom is so close, I can taste it.

Getting back on this stage and performing every night was supposed to re-ignite the spark inside me that's been missing for so long. I love singing. I love performing. I love the glitz and the lights and the crowds... and yet, somehow, it's just... not enough anymore. This tour, the very thing that was supposed to bring me back to myself, has felt less like my savior and more like my captor.

The joy I once found under these lights has long since disappeared.

And I don't know how to get it back.

It seems I was, once again, wrong. And while it's been a whirlwind seven weeks, we have another sixteen left to go.

We're not even halfway.

The thought is exhausting, and I push it away as I focus all my effort on the choreography for this number. I keep my smile plastered in place as I move around the stage, hoping no one will notice how fake it is; how much effort it takes for me to maintain.

I fold myself into a bow at the end of the song. A single tear slips down my cheek, hidden behind the hair that has fallen around me as I bend forward. I'm careful to pivot as I bring the mic up and wipe at my cheek, making the movement look like a casual brush of hair instead of what it actually is: me erasing the evidence of anything less than utter perfection.

I'm an expert at false appearances, having spent years in the limelight. I know exactly when to smile, pose, and fake enthusiasm. I know what people want to see, and I know what the public doesn't tolerate.

Unfortunately, emotions fall under the latter. Between that and a husband whose image was more important to him than anything else in life, I've become a mirror ball: a reflection of everything that everyone else wants me to be.

I don't even know who I am anymore.

The lights dim briefly as the stage resets, and I hurry to my next mark, getting in line with the dancers around me as the beat picks up. I force myself to dial in, focus on the stage in front of me instead of what's going on in my head.

But even with the steady cadence of beats from my drummer, the vibrations of the music rolling through the stage, and the roar of the crowd surrounding me, nothing is louder than the noise in my head.

The green room is full when I head backstage after the show, one bodyguard two steps ahead of me, the other following right behind. My entire cast and crew are waiting for me when I enter, like they do every night. I love them and I love our tradition, but the thrill of the early shows has worn off and some nights I just want to slip out unnoticed, make my way back to my bed, and collapse in peace and quiet.

I scan the room as I enter to applause, looking for my sister, Natalie. She's across the room, talking to our brother, Dex and it takes me a while to cut a path to my siblings, familiar faces stopping me every few steps for a hug or a quick 'Congratulations.' I smile, maintaining my stage presence even down here, in a room full of people I know and love.

They're only supportive of you because you're a means to an end for them.

The voice in my head, which sounds a lot like my ex-husband, screams loudly these days. I didn't used to have such all-consuming negative thoughts, but in the last couple of years, they've been a constant companion. Even at my highest of highs, they slip through, reminding me I might be one of the most famous pop stars in the country, but I'm still not good enough.

I finally make it across the room, my sister rushing over to greet me. I give her a big hug, genuinely relieved she's here, before reaching over and offering my brother the same warm greeting.

Our parents died when I was just sixteen, leaving my oldest sibling, Natalie, in charge of the two of us, a role no eighteen-year-old should have thrust upon them. Her and our younger brother have dedicated their lives to making this dream of mine come true and though they both seem happy in their roles with Melanie Bennett Music, working as my publicist and tour manager, I feel an immense amount of guilt that their lives have been consumed by mine. Even when we're not on tour, they're still full-time employees of mine, still spending every day working for me.

"Do you have an extra hair tie?" I ask, turning toward Natalie as Dex breaks our hug. The two hours of singing and dancing have me feeling like I'm perpetually melting. Gathering up my hair, I wrap it quickly around my hand, the cool air hitting my neck providing a tiny amount of relief.

She glances down at her wrists before looking back up at me. "I don't. We could ask Indy if she has one on her."

I wave her off. "It's fine. I'll cool down, eventually."

I fan myself with my hand, feeling a bead of sweat run down my temple. My eyes scan the room, ice buckets of champagne sitting around, glasses being filled and passed between my crew members.

Did no one think to bring water?

I smack my lips as I realize how uncomfortable I am. The exertion of the last couple of hours and the insatiable heat rolling through me have my mouth feeling like a desert.

"Dex, can we get —" I turn around, intending to address my brother when a bottle of water is thrust in front of me, condensation rolling down the plastic, dripping onto the tan hand holding it out to me.

I lift my eyes to meet Austin's, a smirk plastered on his face.

"Fuck, I love you." I let my hair fall, enthusiastically grabbing for the bottle. Cracking the cap, I let out a sigh as I polish off half the contents in one go, the cold water immediately making me feel better.

Austin and Indy have been working with our crew for the duration of the tour, hired by my sister to follow us around, recording content documentary style for their podcast, The Tracks. It was Natalie's Hail Mary to save my reputation after my ex-husband dropped a less than savory article about our divorce right before this tour kicked off.

My lawyers have been working overtime handling his bullshit allegations, but my sister's idea to have The Tracks handle my reputation was genius. Their ratings have been through the roof, and the narrative Gunner had painted of me being the abusive one in our marriage has been all but silenced.

Originally, Austin and Indy were only supposed to be around for six weeks, but when both teams saw how well the show was doing, they reworked their plans and committed to the entire US leg of the tour. The two of them have folded themselves into our team seamlessly over the last couple of months, feeling much more like friends now than just co-collaborators.

I've let them get much closer to me than I normally would with the media, but they both have a very clear understanding of my boundaries and know exactly how much of our day-to-day I'm comfortable sharing. They're always conscientious of letting me approve their episode outlines and final cuts, and honestly, their attention to my preferences makes me like them that much more.

"Love you too." Austin winks playfully, but I can see his cheeks flush as he dips his head, shoving his hands into his pockets.

"Indy! Do you have a hair tie for Mel?" Natalie's voice startles me as we both turn to find Indy standing beside us.

"Shoot, I don't. The only one I have is in my hair." She gestures to the pile of curls on top of her head, her dark coils spilling artfully from a haphazard bun. "You can have it though if you need it."

"No, absolutely not." I laugh. "I'm just warm. I'll survive."

"Did you need something?" Dex appears beside me.

"Oh, no. I was going to ask if there was water, but," I shake the bottle in my hand. "Austin pulled off the surprise of the night."

"You had not one, but two Billboard Top Ten artists on stage with you tonight, and water was the MVP of the evening?" Natalie laughs from beside me.

"It absolutely was."

"Are you heading straight home?" It's Indy grabbing my attention now. I pivot back in her direction.

"Yeah, as soon as Knox gives me the all clear to escape the stadium." I catch my bodyguard out of the corner of my eye, standing just a couple of feet away with Natalie's bodyguard, Jake.

"I tried to talk Natalie into grabbing drinks, but she said she's turning in ASAP too." Indy sounds resigned.

I smirk at that. *I'm sure she is.*

It turns out my sister is also seeing her bodyguard, but no one is supposed to know that. It was a fun little surprise when I showed up at her apartment on our day off earlier this week and caught the two of them getting hot and heavy in her bedroom.

With this weekend's tour stop being in Nashville, we're lucky enough to skip the hotel stays and spend the week in our own beds. Except Knox, poor guy, who is staying with me for ease of convenience with our hectic schedule. That's not new to us, though. Ever since Knox started working for me around the clock when I left my ex-husband, he's now a constant presence in my life. I don't mind though because over the years he's worked for me, Knox has become a lot like a second brother to me and I like having him around.

"I'm sorry, Ind. Let's plan something next week? Book a lounge somewhere? Maybe Wednesday after the floral shop event? We can go out, all three of us." She perks up at that, the social butterfly loving nothing more than planning our group outings.

"Yes! I'm on it!" We chat for a while longer as we kill time, waiting for some of the crowd to disperse before we try to leave the stadium. When I finally get the all clear from Knox, it's nearly an hour later and I'm dead on my feet.

"Do you need anything before we head home?" Knox's voice cuts through the silence of the blacked out SUV that is currently idling at the exit to the stadium, waiting for traffic to clear.

"No, I just want my bed. And some sleep." I drop my head against the back of my seat, closing my eyes.

"You killed it tonight, as always."

I smirk, knowing damn well I did.

I might be falling apart on the inside, held together by nothing more than a few loose strands of fraying motivation and self-confidence, but if there's one thing I know how to do, it's put on a show.

ABOUT THE AUTHOR

Alexis Graham was born and raised in the Midwest, where she still resides with her husband, three kids, and four cats. She loves the opportunity to create in *any* form, her list of hobbies truly endless. In addition to being an Accountant, and a newly published author, she also co-owns Dark Midnight Design Co, where you can find her designing bookish merch.

@alexisgrahamauthor

alexisgraham.com

www.ingramcontent.com/pod-product-compliance
Lightning Source LLC
Chambersburg PA
CBHW071732110726
47908CB00006B/1574